A NIGHTINGALE'S LAST SONG

KATHLEEN HARRYMAN

A NIGHTINGALE'S LAST SONG
Copyright © 2023 Kathleen Harryman

ISBN 979-8-89145-235-0 (Paperback)
ISBN 979-8-89145-236-7 (Hardback)

Edited by Jess Lawrence (Freelance Fiction Copy-Editor)
http://www.jesslawrence.co.uk/

Books By Kathleen Harryman

HISTORICAL ROMANCE
THE PROMISE
A NIGHTINGALE'S LAST SONG

ROMANTIC SUSPENSE
THE OTHER SIDE OF THE LOOKING GLASS

PARANORMAL ROMANCE
HUNTED – A VAMPWTICH NOVEL

THRILLERS
WHEN DARKNESS FALLS
DARKNESS RISING
HIDDEN DANGER

POETRY
LIFE'S ECHOES

For Nightingales around the world
Thank you for your care and kindness

Between the light and dark,
I'll find you ...

1

LILIBETH

Seagull's Rest, Stonehaven, Scotland

From its lone vantage point overlooking the North Sea, the whitewashed exterior of Seagull's Rest blends like a ghost into the mist drifting up from the sea. The only sign of its presence is the density of mist, where the stone structure solidifies within its wispy shading. On clear days, you can see the seals as they accompany the fishing boats into the harbour with their catch. A short distance from the sand, buildings look out to sea.

This is the first time I have visited the cottage since the death of my grandmother, Lillian Elizabeth Lawrence, several months ago. Jane Anne, my great-grandmother, had a strong aversion to using traditional family titles, preferring to be called by her first name. Her commanding personality and my need for approval has left me wavering between the customary and the unconventional.

An air of coldness hangs over Seagull's Rest. The drop in temperature sends goosebumps crawling up my arms, nipping at my skin. My grandmother's passing leaves a vacuum. Death has sucked the life from this place. For once, the seagulls that give the cottage its name remain silent. Seagull's Rest is waiting for its heart to be returned—but Lillian Elizabeth Lawrence isn't returning.

With shaking fingers, I insert the large, old-fashioned, metal key into the lock. The latch drops and a cold tremor runs along my spine as I take the irrevocable step in accepting Lillian Elizabeth's death. Pulling at the cuffs of my hoodie, I slide the fabric over my hands, scrunching the material into my fists. The frosty morning dampness penetrates the layers of my clothing, and the cold eats into my flesh. To suppress the overwhelming sadness, I hug myself. Perhaps Seagull's Rest hasn't changed. The shift is mine. In a mix of loss, anguish, and heartache, I have projected my grief into this once-happy place.

Nostrils flaring, I reach for the handle and step inside. My grandmother's scent lingers, and the blade of loss slides deeper into my heart. Inside, everything remains the same, and yet different. These differences punctuate the area, signalling her absence. The clay vase, usually filled with white roses, sits empty on the small oval table. At the foot of the stairs, my grandmother's shopping basket waits to be filled with groceries.

From memory, Lillian Elizabeth descends the stairs, singing. Arthritis causes her face to wrinkle further, slowing her pace. Her bony hands grip the handrail as her ghostly form stops at the foot of the stairs. She smiles, her green eyes settling on me. "Goodness, Lilibeth, if these bones get any older, I swear they'll cease altogether. I'm not running too late, I hope."

My lips twitch at the apparition, and the cloak of grief I've been wearing since her death diminishes. It has taken Seagull's Rest, and the vivid memory of my grandmother, to strip away my sorrow. I'm not normally one to brood or allow negative emotions to dictate my actions, but the last few months have been difficult. On losing Lillian Elizabeth, I have allowed grief to consume me. It is time to let go.

I move the thermostat dial, and the boiler rumbles into action, sending the radiators clanking. With footwear unacceptable inside, I kick off my trainers, walking to the stairs and making my way to my old bedroom. Despite the long gaps between my visits, nothing has changed. Seagull's Rest remains my home.

With my mother, Pearl Alexandra, the global wanderer, never around, this became my childhood residence. My muscles tense in a natural reaction to my mother. With a deep inhalation, I let go of my angst. Today isn't about her shortcomings. Velvet curtains rest at the side of the large sash window in my room. Sunlight filters, bouncing off the pale blue walls. Jars of forgotten cosmetics, perfume, and body lotion sit on the dressing table. The Aran cardigan my grandmother knitted drapes from the peg on the door, and I toss my hoodie onto the bed, grabbing the woollen garment. Its thick cable knit warms my chilled skin, enveloping me in comfort—as it always has. Lillian Elizabeth's scent fills my senses, and I snuggle deeper into the woollen fibres. Tears falling, I walk further into the room as memories, long forgotten, surface. The warmth and love Lillian Elizabeth poured into Seagull's Rest ignites a bubble of belonging inside me. I am home. Her love soaks into my heart, comforting me.

In the middle of the bed, a small brown box sits. Curious, I stare at it. A handwritten envelope lies on top. Lillian Elizabeth's distinctive writing forms my name, Lilibeth. Time freezes. Transfixed, I gawk at the sealed envelope, a zillion questions whipping around my head. Blood gushes through my veins. My heart beats in rapid thumps, and adrenaline rushes through my system. Outside, my body remains stagnant, my eyelids frozen open, my hands resting at my sides. My breath catches in my throat, my lungs refusing to release it.

For months, this letter has sat waiting for me to come home. Lillian Elizabeth Lawrence had known for over a year she was dying—thirteen months and two weeks longer than the rest of us. Her bones, as she liked to refer to her coming demise, had stopped working. Still, her bones had found the strength to carry this box into my bedroom, waiting for my return. Visions flash, and her slow, laboured walk burns its way across my optics. Thud. Her walking stick hits the carpeted floor as she makes her painful journey into the room she knows only I will enter. On an exhausted sigh, her ghostly image places the box on the bed, laying the envelope on top. For several months, I sat at Lillian Elizabeth's bedside until her heart stopped beating. What secrets lay hidden inside the box that she could not reveal until her death?

A box carries more significance than I could ever imagine.

"Ogling it won't make it go away." My grandmother's voice fills my head. She is, of course, even in death, right.

My bottom perching on the edge of the bed, I pick up the envelope, running my fingers along the inside, pulling back the lip. Each swirl of the pen stabs at my heart. Tears blur my vision. The long breath I expel sends my fringe flying. Time ticks, and seconds turn to minutes before I can focus long enough to read her words.

Dearest Lilibeth,

I know you are hurting, trying, without success, to adjust to life without me. Remember what Christina Rossetti taught us within her solemn poem. "When I am dead, my dearest, sing no sad songs for me …" My passing from one plane to the next reunites me with those I have lost. I am delighted to see them again. So, please, no tears. Remember me with a smile in your heart, not the stab of grief's blunt blade. Turn up those lips and let this old woman see your beautiful smile.

Seagull's Rest is your home, and I have ensured it will remain that way, but it comes with an old woman's selfish request. Secrets are, for the most, harmless. Half-truths that allow us to carry on and maintain our sanity. To safeguard another's feelings, as well as our own. Such secrets flutter away like cherry blossom. But some secrets are too big to be silenced. They must be told. Rather cowardly, I have waited until now to expose mine. A promise made to your grandfather, and the passing of time, have left it too late.

Without the strength to disclose my secret in person, I am asking you to do what I couldn't. Only your Aunt Morag and your grandfather, Joseph Lawrence, my head now resting at his side, knows the truth.

The need to give my secret a voice has never dampened. Like an irritable imp, it has plagued me all my life. Find him, Lilibeth, find Alick. Let him know the truth, and may he forgive me for what I have done. This burden I place on you gives me no pleasure. I wish I'd been stronger. Your grandfather's death released me from my promise, but I no longer had the courage to exercise the freedom I gained.

Take care of this Nightingale, Lilibeth. Don't let her song be one of unfulfilled longing.

Love you forever and beyond,

Lillian Elizabeth Lawrence

The letter falls to my lap. My reflection in the dressing table mirror blurs as incoherent thoughts and questions run through my head at high speed. Who is Alick? What secret is so grave it robbed Lillian Elizabeth of her inner strength? Do I want to find out? The box next to me is no longer just a box. It is a message to deliver.

What secrets lay inside?

Where will it take me?

If Lillian Elizabeth didn't have the strength to reveal her secret, will I?

My stomach churns, and I wonder, on revealing my grandmother's secrets, will I still feel the same unconditional love I hold for her? This thought prevents me from opening the box, its dimensions growing in metaphorical size. It silently waits for me to find the backbone to remove its lid. Like a band-aid, I can peel off the lid in slow tortuous motion. I could hide the box under my bed and spend the next few days ignoring its presence. Or I can rip off the lid, now, and uncover the truth. Find out what was so important to my grandmother she left me Seagull's Rest, providing a place of comfort and safety, to learn her secret.

The latter of my options wins, and I whip the lid off the box. Once opened, there is no going back. Inside is a worn, black leather diary. In gold lettering, the name Lillian Elizabeth Nutman stares back at me. Nutman was my grandmother's maiden name. It appears her secret started long before she met and married my grandfather. On a deep exhale, I prepare to unearth her secret and the message I am to deliver. A secret she was determined never to be forgotten.

And so, this is it, *a Nightingale's last song ...*

THE DIARY OF
LILLIAN ELIZABETH NUTMAN

1939 ~ 1945

Born on March 24th, 1915, at the start of the Great War, I am the only daughter in a house of five sons. Unlike my brothers, my mother, Jane Anne, did not celebrate my birth. It no longer matters why, too much water has flowed under the bridge and my years provide me with a better insight into the complexities of human emotions. Clarity, as they say, comes with age, and a fruitful life. There is no reworking the past. To change one thing alters another, until I'm no longer the person I am now. That person isn't so bad. Yes, she's made mistakes. But she has always done what she felt is right.

Before war swept towards us like a tornado, I never thought to keep a diary. Any diary before 1939 and after 1945 wouldn't count. This journal is the one that matters. A life where such loss exists, it contains the true effect of war.

War isn't cheap. It takes, destroys, and leaves some barren. Devoid of emotion, invisible walls block out the pain, leaving no room for love. War is a hostile environment, and like a chameleon it wears many faces. Horror. Despair. Hope. Love. Most of all, war has given me strength, and reflection, and taught me forgiveness.

I have stood at the mouth of a great pit, looking at the dead as earth covers their faces. Next to me, the Chaplin reads from his bible—words of peace and resurrection that carry little solace when faced with such torment. With my hands, I have dug the grave of my dearest friend and shed more tears than the rivers that flow. My pain is immeasurable, yet my heart remains open to love.

War has shown me the darker and lighter side of human nature. Some instances I wish to forget, but never will. Others I cherish. I recall the face of each soldier who has died in my arms. Each letter, though the contents are fuzzy, I have written to their family, informing them of their son's bravery and death.

Some soldiers hold a special place in my heart. While I held you until your breath no longer flowed, we comforted each other. It is an honour to have known you. As death came, your trust in me never wavered. I was once told there is safety when a nurse is present. It is humbling to know that these brave men, during their worst experiences, remained steadfast in their belief in me and my Sisters. We gave everything we had to treat the wounded, no matter the danger; we remained committed until the last. For many seeking medical care, a nurse is a sign of hope.

Most of all, war has provided me with the greatest of friendships. It has brought me love, and a resting place for my soul.

For this, I am truly blessed.

2

 November 1939, London, England

*T*here is no softening the blow. Jane Anne will see my actions as abandonment. A complete disregard for her feelings. Since my brothers' departure in August, joining the fight against Hitler, and with Dad dead, the responsibility of caring for Jane Anne sits on my shoulders. If she knew I'd referred to Trevor Henry as Dad, her tongue would lash out. But these are my thoughts, and I am safe to call him Dad, if I choose. Jane Anne has a thing about names; "A name defines us, don't you forget it, Lillian Elizabeth. Never let someone strip it from you." She will hate the fact that when I open my diary tonight, I'm going to write 'Mum' next to her name. None of my friends call their mothers by their Christian name. As I am prone to overthinking, I believe Jane Anne Ellis Nutman never wanted to be a mother. Her naturally volatile disposition, and children's inherent habit to create chaos, have not made her the best of mothers.

While Trevor Henry Nutman allowed his wife to double-barrel her surname, he was forceful on the subject around ours. "Children should adopt their father's name; it provides them with roots. A double-barrelled surname suggests conflict. A child requires unity in the home." Matter closed. Or rather, it was for Trevor Henry. Forty years later, and after giving birth to six children—of which I am the only female—Jane Anne will not allow the subject to rest. Out of her husband's hearing, she curses us with our full name, adding Ellis before Nutman. When caught in the act of devilment, chastisement is a long, drawn-out affair. So much so, we stop listening as the first of our names is called; "Lillian Elizabeth Ellis Nutman …"

Grandma Ellis did not share her daughter's staunch requirement towards the use of her full Christian name—much to my mother's annoyance. This is as well, given Grandma Ellis' parents named her Rebeca Sarah Mary Jane Anne. Names are big business in the Ellis family. Perhaps it is a defect in our genes. Some kids inherit freckles, we inherit the need for abnormally long names.

The front door clicks behind me as I wander into the back room. My feet are sore and long for a good soaking. If fortune is on my side, Jane Anne will be in the backyard talking to Mrs Arnold over the wall, or out grocery shopping. Either scenario works. After completing the night shift at Cheyne Children's Hospital, I'm ready to sit, relax, and relish in the quiet, allowing the strain that evening shift has wrought to dissolve. The thought of my hands circling a cuppa, and my feet submerged in a bowl of warm soapy water, makes me sigh with longing—ah, paradise. Before I can untie my shoelaces and remove my cape, the back door squeaks, and my mother walks into the room from the kitchen, broom in hand. My lips twist with disappointment, and I turn my face, hiding my displeasure.

"Good, you're home. The coalman has just finished unloading the bags. Get yourself changed. Clean out the fire and fill the coal buckets ready for tonight."

In my head, I groan, and my feet throb out their displeasure. Not wanting to sour the morning, I suppress my tiredness. After all, this isn't unexpected. Life has changed drastically since Neville Chamberlain declared war against Germany. The papers may refer to it as the Phony War, but its effects are far-reaching. A lifetime has passed, and much has changed. The proclaimed Phony War has removed my brothers from their home and killed my father, who died during an army training exercise. The Army Council are—*were*—profusely sorry. Sorry doesn't change the fact Trevor Henry is dead. On his death, the dominoes fell, placing responsibility firmly on my shoulders. One by one, burden upon burden, obligation with Hitler at the helm, imprisoned me, chaining me to Jane Anne's demands.

My mother is accustomed to being looked after. Not that we are rich. Trevor Henry worked hard, so his wife didn't have to. His only requirement was for her to be a wonderful mother. Jane Anne's understanding of the arrangement was different. With hours spent priming herself in stylish clothes, and having her hair set every Thursday, motherhood didn't stand a chance. Until the war came, life for Jane Anne was simple. Not that bringing up six children is easy, but we are all now above the age of eighteen and have undertaken chores since we could walk—or so it seems.

Jane Anne stares, her hand gripping the broom handle. Mirth leaks from her at my lack of action. "Well, don't just stand there. The buckets won't fill themselves. And I've still to visit the butcher and get something for tea."

Exhaustion licks at my mind and body. "Can't I sit down for two minutes first?"

A snort punctuates the space between us. "I've been on my feet since I got up this morning at six, and you don't see me sitting down."

The privilege she has of waking at six and being on her feet for three hours makes my back stiffen. Night shift started at 8 p.m. and finished twelve hours later. Other than half an hour's break, when I ate my sandwich, my feet have not rested. It would be pointless to remind her of this. I like my head where it is. There is also the matter of delivering my news.

Her red lips compress, and her eyes narrow with suspicion. The skin on her hand whitens as her fingers tighten on the broom. She tilts her head, and her styled auburn hair meets her left shoulder. "Out with it, you've obviously got something rattling around that head of yours. Maybe once it's out, you can start your chores. It's not a boy, is it?"

A boy would be easier news to deliver. "No, it's not a boy."

Her fingers loosen on the wood. "Good. There's enough going on without you courting."

"I've handed in my Territorial Army form," I blurt.

She stumbles for dramatic effect, and the broom clatters to the floor as she clings to the frame of Trevor Henry's chair. For a second, I wonder if someone other than me is in the room, exaggerating her reaction to my news. "You've done what? Why would you do such a thing? How could you do this to me?" She sobs into her handkerchief. "Trevor Henry isn't cold in his grave and your … your … brothers … are goodness knows where, and only God knows if they are still alive."

As the French troops are invading Germany's Saar district, the government have only one military land operation on the Western Front. Given this, it is possible my brothers are still on UK soil. My nails bite into my palm as I quell my rising annoyance, remaining resolute in my decision.

"I know it's not what you want, but it's something I need to do." Her expression remains stony. Perhaps a different tack is required. "Matron says I might not be called up. Look when we evacuated the children from the hospital over the Munich Crisis. Despite Nazi Germany's demand for seizure of the Sudetenland, the children were back in the hospital within ten days."

"Then why complete the form?"

My nails dig further into my soft flesh. I could kick myself for underplaying the significance of joining the Territorial Army Nursing Services (TANS). "You know why. The Phony War will end, and this war will intensify. I want to be there, helping treat the wounded, that's why I became a nurse. Look what Hitler did to the Poles, despite Chamberlain's efforts for peace. Hitler won't stop. Not until we have forced him to. The training college is now transformed into a casualty reception, dressing, treatment, and restroom. With the First Aid Post complete, I can concentrate my efforts where they're needed."

Jane Anne thrusts out her chin. With a hard glint, she looks over her shoulder towards the mantle. "It's clear you think I haven't suffered enough. I am heartbroken … *broken*, you hear me, Lillian Elizabeth Ellis Nutman …"

It's Lillian Elizabeth Nutman, I correct in my head. Unspoken thoughts are necessary when in a room with Jane Anne. They protect me from her sharp tongue.

Her hand spreads at her side. "Here I am doing my best to keep this house together, and you're talking about deserting me, just like your brothers and Trevor Henry have done. How do you expect me to feel? Happy for you? Well, I'm not. Your betrayal is too much. You don't know what it's like. The loneliness—the sadness of seeing life drip through my fingers. Look at me …" Her hand wafts the length of her body. "My nails are a mess, and my Thursday visits to the hairdresser are over. It's once a fortnight—if I'm lucky. But you're not satisfied, are you, *no* … War has reduced my life to nothing, and now … *now* you want to abandon me. And I'm supposed to smile regardless and wish you well. Well, I won't."

Tight-lipped, I wait for her rant to finish.

With her handkerchief pressed against her chest, she regards me. "Why get so close to the war? Nurses are better suited here, in our hospitals. It surprises me that men don't understand this. Are we not the fairer sex? Our purpose is to carry babies. Not trudging across fields while some German shoots at us."

Indignation takes root, and my cheeks redden. "According to Sir Fredrick, nurses have a cheering effect on injured men, which is why we are being placed nearer the frontline."

Her jaw drops. "That's absurd."

"No, it's the truth."

"It is obvious the man doesn't know what he is talking about."

Stubbornness is not always a negative attitude. It coats my mind in its invisible armour. I will not give in to her emotional blackmail. Her brow furrows and I can almost hear her brain whirring as she plans her next assault. Like rain, her tears fall, and she pats her handkerchief against her cheeks. "You can never understand how I feel … no one can … Trevor Henry lived through the Great War only for the Germans to shoot him stone dead in this new, godforsaken war. It's cruel, that's what it is … cruel. This house is empty. There is no male laughter … *no* … My babies, your brothers, are fighting. And for what? So they can end up like Trevor Henry."

My father's death was an accident. There was no German involvement. Reminding Jane Anne of this will prolong the encounter and I remain silent.

She lets out a ragged breath as more tears slide down her cheeks. "When the Great War came and took Trevor Henry from me to fight, I prayed for God to look after him. Each morning, I would write him a poem so he would know how much I loved him. Now there are no prayers to be answered, no poems waiting for him to read, because he's dead."

She blows her nose. Though I've never heard a fog-horn, I'm betting it has serious competition. Aware I appear uncompassionate, I stand my ground. Florence Nightingale is my inspiration, and the reason I became a nurse. My dolls all wore bandages, suffering some ailment or injury which required constant supervision. Notes made on each toy's condition, and medication listed. Honey and lemon for colds, a warm blanket to ward off pneumonia. Trevor Henry would come home each night and ask how my patients were doing. Jane Anne has never hidden her disdain over my dream of becoming a nurse. When I left for Leeds Infirmary to start my nursing training, she refused to wave goodbye at the train station. Duty-bound, the youngest daughter—in my case, only daughter—carries the responsibility of caring for their parents in their old age.

Unlike my best friend, Daisy, who attended Leeds Infirmary with me, there was no celebrating my return and qualified status. My mother refused to acknowledge my achievement. There was no, "I'm proud of you," falling from her lips. Just the resentment that I had taken my father's attention away from his not-so-suffering wife for a few minutes. My mother does not behave this way towards my brothers. I think she views me as competition for Trevor Henry's attention. If I have one wish, I pray I will never become my mother.

Her tirade building momentum, I wait for the drama to end. Like the silent movie star Effie Atherton, without the silence—which is a pity—Jane Anne acts with exaggerated movement. As I won't withdraw my form, there is no stopping my application. I am a cruel, unfeeling person, I tell myself. Mum—see, I've used that word again—brings out the worst in me. Before my brothers left to do their duty, I had wrapped the illusion of freedom around me. Time would change Jane Anne; one day, she would be proud of me, and I would have a life outside of hers.

Trevor Henry's death has added to her woes. Widowed at forty-five, her plight suits her. In widowhood, she has gained leverage, and using it, she snips away at my attempt of freedom. Not more than a child herself, Jane Anne married Trevor Henry at seventeen. At eighteen, she became a mother. Under my father's love and protection, she never grew up, and remains a spoilt child. The allowances I make for her behaviour, I do out of habit. Though, on a wicked note, it is her fault she remains immature. Her attitude towards her children and women's accomplishments remains stilted.

The front door clicks, and the tapping of heels against the Victorian tiles echo into the back living room. My mother's sobs increase as her sister, Sarah Rebeca, walks into the room. Her soft humming comes to an abrupt stop as her eyes swing from niece to sister, and her delicate brows pinch. "What on earth is going on?"

Her question has an adverse effect on her sister.

My mother crumbles, her body draping over the back of the chair. I cringe. With a finger of accusation, she pulls herself together. "She's going into the Territorial Army Nursing Services. People here need her nursing skills. Not that she's bothered—*no*—their lives matter little to Lillian Elizabeth Ellis Nutman."

Like a beast held captive, Jane Anne paces the wooden floor. "London is to be bombed. And Hitler will send his army here. It's all anyone is talking about." Her damp handkerchief flaps at me. "You've said it yourself. The training college at Cheyne Children's Hospital is now a First Aid Post in readiness for the attacks. What more proof do you need?" Her feet halt. "My ... *my* heart skips a beat every time I think about those Nazi planes hovering over London, releasing their bombs. Every loud noise causes me to jump. With frayed nerves I wonder, is today the day God sends me to stand at Trevor Henry's side? Not that *she* cares."

Aunt Sarah Rebeca slides an arm across her sister's shoulders. "Our soldiers need nurses. You can't blame Lilly for wanting to do her bit in this war."

"Lillian Elizabeth," she corrects her sister.

Aunt Sarah Rebeca moved into the front room when her husband died. Anthony Kevin Broadman suffered a heart attack while on his way to sign up. The last four months have been hard for her. Unable to conceive, her husband was her life. 'Soulmates' is how she describes their love. My mother is not one to dwell on another's misery. Absorbed in her own selfishness, she has little time for anyone else.

Like a mountain, I stand my ground. How will I cope as an army nurse if I cannot stand up to Jane Anne? "It's not that I don't care about the people here, I do. Since the government set up the Central Emergency Committee for the Nursing Profession in 1938, the Civil Nursing Reserve have seen an influx of nurses. It's still not enough, not in a time of war. With my three years of experience, I'm sure my services are of value on the frontline."

"Let the government tend to the wounded. They make these stupid rules, with their fancy titles. They should live by their own words, rather than tearing families apart," Jane Anne says with a snort. Her powder-blue tea dress and yellow knitted cardigan is a happy contrast to its wearer. No one cries on demand like my mother. "Do as I say, not as I do. That's the government's problem."

To remain sane, I ignore her comments and continue with my defence. "I know we have a shortage of nurses here, but there is also a shortage on the frontline. Trevor Henry would want me to help our boys. I know he would."

"Don't you *dare* bring Trevor Henry into this. God rest his soul," she snarls as her fingers fly across her body, making the sign of the cross.

Heat rushes to my cheeks at her words, and I want to stamp my foot in frustration. "You're the one who brought him into the conversation."

"I did no such thing." Her cheeks puff with outrage. "Let's pray Trevor Henry can't hear you. He would spin in his grave listening to the way you're speaking to me."

My lips press together. I can't get through to her when she's like this.

"Leaving me here to fend for myself. Who will bring in the coal? Help with the laundry? There are bills to pay. I would work myself, but my fingers are already curling with arthritis."

There is nothing wrong with her fingers. She is as capable as the next person of working for a living.

"I can help," Aunt Sarah Rebeca says. "It's not like you're on your own, not with me here."

With eyes that could curdle milk, Jane Anne glances at her younger sister.

Aunt Sarah Rebeca steps away from her sister's heated glare. "I-I was just trying t-to help."

"Well don't," Jane Anne snaps.

"Don't take it out on Aunt Sarah Rebeca. I'm sorry for mentioning Trevor Henry if it helps." I don't mean a word of it, other than the bit about Aunt Sarah Rebeca. Why should I be sorry?

"Come on, I think you should sit down." She guides her sister to Trevor Henry's vacant chair.

Of all the chairs, why that one? Jane Anne grips the wooden armrest. Snot rolls as she blows her nose. From behind a black veil, Trevor Henry's photograph peers from the mantlepiece. Her eyes latch onto the veil, and her sobs intensify. Aunt Sarah Rebeca winces, and over her sister's bent head she mouths, 'Sorry'.

I shrug. It's hard to believe they are sisters. Mum— I'm calling her that on purpose; the silent slight makes me feel better—has always been one for theatrics. If a crowd gathers, Jane Anne will hold centre stage. At the flip of a coin, she can fill a room with emotional demand, draining others of life. In contrast, her sister is a quiet soul. Despite losing her husband, she doesn't buckle under the weight of grief. Sadness leaks from her but doesn't dominate. Unlike Jane Anne, my aunt holds the capacity to laugh. They are opposites, not only in personality, but looks. Jane Anne has auburn hair, pale skin, and sharp green eyes, that don't miss a thing. Aunt Sarah Rebeca's hair is mousey brown, and her soft hazel eyes hold the warmth her sister's lack.

With a loud sigh, my mother's gaze leaves her husband's photo. "I'll tell you what you're going to do, young lady. You're going back and telling them you've changed your mind. Explain that with Trevor Henry dead, you need to stay here, to support me. We'll put this nonsense behind us and move on."

"No," I say, shaking my head in case her rolling snot is blocking her ears.

"Can't or won't, Lillian Elizabeth? It makes no difference. This is what Trevor Henry would want, and that is what will happen."

"No, he wouldn't. It's what *you* want, and *I* won't do it."

She launches from the chair. Her shoes grind into the wooden floor and a mask of outrage falls over her features. "You will do as I tell you, young lady."

Engulfed in her perfume, my insides turn to jelly. I tilt my head in defiance, scrunching the apron of my uniform to stem my shaking hands. "No, I won't. This is my life, and I will live it as I see fit."

There is a sudden movement and before I can register what is happening, my mother's hand connects with my left cheek. Face stinging with shock, my eyes water as my skin pulsates. Heat radiates from my cheek beneath my hand.

Aunt Sarah Rebeca gasps. "Stop it, Jane Anne, think what you're doing."

Shock mingles with self-doubt, clouding my mother's face. Her hands ball at her side, and she looks unsure of what to do next. She has crossed a line, and she knows it. My mother has taught me many things. The fundamental lesson is never to judge a person on looks and how they act in a crowd. Underneath the most beautiful creatures, a monster can live. Perhaps I am being judgemental, but as mothers go, Jane Anne is lacking in the maternal love children require. There is no time to absorb her actions; Jane Anne's fight isn't over. If she can force me to withdraw my application from TANS, she will take it.

"Your life. *Fine,* go on. Go live it. But mark my words, young lady, you walk out that front door without rescinding your application, that's it. There's no going back … I-I'll disown you."

Without a word, I turn, picking up my handbag, and walk out the front door, leaving it hanging open. This is one fight my mother will never win. Duty is duty. I am proud to say there is no banging of wood against the frame as I leave. My departure is a dignified exit. Tears threaten to fall, stinging my eyes, but I won't let them. The fabric of my uniform blows in the wind, and I rub my arms, trying to keep myself warm as my cape flaps around me.

3

 November 1939, London, England

*T*houghts tumble around my head as I walk towards the station, back to Chelsea. Joining the few travellers waiting for the train to arrive, in a state of numbness, I stare down at the concrete platform. Once the train hisses to a stop, I climb onboard, finding a seat near the window. The rocking motion of the carriage soothes my overactive brain as I work through the emotions filtering round it. Anger. Sadness. Confusion. Where did it all go wrong? Jane Anne was never going to take the news of my application into TANS well, but her reaction, even for her, was irrational.

With my head resting against the fabric seat, I watch the scenery blur through the window. Time speeds up and before I've found any answers to my tumbling question, the train shudders to a stop. Passengers stand, reaching for bags and coats, and folding away their newspapers. On the platform, feet move with impatience as passengers step from the train. With my head down, I make my way to Cheyne Children's Hospital.

Founded in 1875, for sick and incurable children, the hospital has undergone many transitions. 1938 signalled yet another of those changes when the Germans invaded Czechoslovakia. With the possibility of war looming, the hospital prepared to evacuate its patients, should it be required. I have worked here for three years, under Matron Elsie Thompson's supervision. Unlike the matrons I worked under during my training, she is a kind woman. It was Matron Thompson who recruited me into TANS. When she asked if I would be prepared to drop tools and join the army on the declaration of a national emergency, my answer was simple—yes. On silent feet, I walk down the corridor of the hospital, nodding to the nurses on reception as I pass.

Daisy turns, seeing me, and she saunters over, her brows shooting up in question. "Ya look awful, what's 'appened?"

Her soft cockney drawl washes over me, lessening my tension. My mother does not approve of regional dialects. "The King sets the standard of speech. One does not stray from that standard." For my brothers and I, being a Londoner does not extend to local speech.

"Can I stay with you at your aunt and uncle's house until I've received my orders?"

Daisy moved in with her Aunt Mavis and Uncle Bill when she started working at the hospital. Early mornings have never suited her. Add travelling into the mix and Daisy's normal sunny personality dissolves into a monster of discontent. With her aunt and uncle's children called up to fight, and her uncle's health declining, they welcomed Daisy into their home. The high air pollution in London does not suit her Uncle Bill's asthma. Despite the doctor's advice to move to the country, he refuses to listen.

"I take it yer mother didn't take the news well."

"No, she didn't."

She looks at her watch. "I've anovver thirty minutes until me shift ends. Are ya alright ter wait?"

Given I'm now homeless, I don't have a choice. "Don't worry, I'll wait."

"What aren't ya tellin' me?"

"She wants me to rescind my application and tell them I've changed my mind. As I won't do it, she's disowned me." Tears sit on my lashes.

"Crikey." Daisy gasps.

"I know."

"What about yer stuff? Ya can't be living in yer uniform forever."

Horror falls over Daisy's face as she contemplates living without her vast wardrobe. The first item to move into the small bedroom at her aunt and uncle's was her Singer sewing machine. Daisy's wardrobe bulges with clothes, and fabric spews over the dresser onto the bedroom floor.

"Would you mind grabbing them for me, or coming with me? Jane Anne plays bridge at eight tonight. We could go then."

"Alright, that's fine, ya can change into summit of mine until then." She shoots me a broad smile. "It's not like I don't 'ave enough clothes."

"I'll pay towards rent. I don't want your aunt and uncle out of pocket."

She wafts off my offer. "We'll sort that out la'er. The way things are going, ya could receive ya orders sooner than ya think. I'd be'er get back to me post afore someone notices I've gone. I'll catch ya la'er."

With time to kill, I wander outside to be consumed by dark clouds promising rain. Tucked away behind the hospital is Amanda's café. The bell jingles as I enter.

Amanda smiles. "Be wi' ya in a mo."

I pull out a chair, waiting for Daisy's shift to end. It's been a long night. At 11 a.m., the day is proving to be even longer.

4

 December 1939, London, England

*C*hristmas without family is a desolate affair. In the week building up to it, I meet Aunt Sarah Rebeca at Amanda's. Her update confirms that Jane Anne's angst at my abandonment hasn't waned. My mother is having a miserable Christmas, thanks to my selfishness. With my brothers gone, there is no seasonal cheer at the Nutman residence. Jane Anne is taking my brothers' absence hard. "Are soldiers not given leave?" They are, but perhaps they choose to stay away. Who can blame them.

War fills the pages of the newspapers, creating a valid reason for their absence. *The Evening Telegraph* reports:

RAF MAINTAIN SECURITY PATROLS — GERMAN WIRE-
LESS STATIONS FADE OUT ... FINNISH PLANES BOMB
RUSSIAN RAILWAY
— 11 MILES OF LINE.

With so much unrest, my mother's continued anger is disheartening.

Her worries over the cost of living and the removal of my income are unfounded. Unlike my mother, the average family of five in these current times struggle to live on three pounds and thirteen shillings a week. Christmas for some will be harder than usual. Despite my brothers' absence, and the death of her husband, Jane Anne is fortunate. Her concerns for a miserable Christmas are her own making.

"I'm sorry, Lilly." Aunt Sarah Rebeca's tears fall over the rim of her teacup, and guilt presses down on me. "It's all so bleak, what with your mother remaining cross. I wish you would come home."

Jane Anne's uncompromising mood provides no opening for me to re-enter her life. "Me too."

Outside, the wind whips along the pavement, howling against the glass where we sit. Ice glistens on the windowsill, and fog reduces visibility. The unusual drop in temperature is because of an anticyclone, which is establishing the coldest winter on record for forty-five years. A shiver runs down my spine and my hands tighten against my warm cup. With my mother unrepentant and my determination not to cave to her pressure, we have reached a stalemate.

"We'd best make a move; Jane Anne will wonder what's keeping you," I say, reaching over and grabbing my handbag. The bell above the door rings as we leave, and I shiver into my cape. "Take care of yourself," I say, hugging my aunt.

With my head down against the wind, I make my way to my temporary home.

"Lilly," my aunt shouts, and I turn. "Merry Christmas."

Though there is nothing to be merry about, I smile. "Merry Christmas."

With Daisy home for Christmas, and her Uncle Bill and Aunt Mavis staying with family in Buxton, the house sits in darkness. Not bothering to turn on the light, I hang my cape on the vacant peg, slipping out of my shoes. Upstairs, I ready myself for bed. Staring at the ceiling, I wait for my body heat to warm the cotton sheets. Loneliness as my companion, I drift off to sleep.

Work keeps me busy, stopping me from dwelling on things I can't change. At the end of my shift on Christmas Eve, I leave work determined to make the most of Christmas. "Tis the season to be jolly. Fa la la la la, la la la la ..." as the song goes. Careful not to slip on the ice, I make my way over Cheyne Walk to Chelsea Old Church and light a candle in memory of Trevor Henry. The church is empty, and I sit, absorbing the peace as I watch the flames flicker.

As confrontation makes my stomach churn, it's something I avoid; I am a peacekeeper. In my capacity as an appeaser, my mother probably thought I would withdraw my application. I am renowned for placing others' feelings above my own. What my mother cannot understand is the level of commitment I place on being a nurse. Soldiers need nurses, and if we are to win this war, we need our soldiers.

With my hands clasped together, I pray for peace. For Germany to stop its unfairness, and that one day, Jane Anne and I will find the strength to mend our relationship. Sunlight enters the church, beaming through the stained-glass window. If I had wanted a sign that God was listening, this is it. And yet, I'm not altogether sure what it means. A stop to the war, or that my mother and I will one day be back on speaking terms? That's the problem with signs, they're open to interpretation.

January 1940 arrives, and so do my orders, along with the snow, which slows everything down. Buses run late, and trains run with irregularity. My wellington boots shuffle as I enter Amanda's. The gold tinsel framing the counter dips with exhaustion as the brightness of the festive season ends. Aunt Sarah Rebeca sits at the table near the counter.

"It doesn't get any warmer," I say, pulling out a chair, shaking the snow from my coat.

Behind the counter, Amanda sings along to the wireless, her brown hair swinging about her shoulders. She turns, placing the steaming teapot next to the cups on her tray before bringing them over. "There ya go."

"Thanks, Amanda," Aunt Sarah Rebeca and I say in unison.

"How are things at home?" I ask.

"Miserable."

I wince. "Sorry."

"You're not to blame, Lilly."

"That's not true but thank you."

She nods, accepting my apology. "The newspapers are saying Hitler is attempting to spread the war, seeking a coalition with the 'Young States', asking Italy, Russia, and Japan to join him. It's likely Italy will, though I'm not sure about Russia, their actions so far are hard to read. As for Japan, well, all we can do is wait and see."

My cup hits the saucer as I glance at my aunt. "I've received my orders."

"Oh," she says, her teacup hovering near her lips.

"I'm sorry."

"When do you leave?"

"Soon."

"Right. Do you want me to tell your mother?"

"I'll leave that up to you. It makes no difference to me. I'm not sure she's interested."

She lays a hand on my arm. "I know she has a funny way of showing it, but she cares about you."

"Maybe, but her rejection still hurts. I keep asking myself how it came to this. Why couldn't my mother support my decision to join the Territorial Army Nursing Services, like she supported my brothers when they signed up?"

"Your mother didn't have a choice with your brothers. It was their legal duty. With you, it's complicated. There is no legal obligation, and your mother cannot comprehend your need. She's scared of losing you and your brothers, Lilly."

I snort into my cup. "Perhaps, but she didn't have to disown me. I feel like an orphan. Isn't that what they call people with no parents, an orphan?" My fingers drum on the table. "When did life get so muddy?"

She shakes her head. "I don't know, Lilly."

5

 January 1940, Beckett's Park, Leeds

*T*he 6th of January finds me standing on the crowded platform at the train station. Around me, joyous shouts clash with tears of sadness and fear as parents hug their sons taking up their duty to fight. My stomach is doing cartwheels as I prepare to board the train, bound for Leeds. I'm to report to the 18th British General Hospital (BGH), mobilising at Beckett's Park, Leeds. Next to me, Daisy cries into her handkerchief.

"It's not that I'm not 'appy for ya. I just can't believe this is it. Will ya come back ter London?" she asks, wiping away her tears.

"I've got to survive this war first."

She blanches. "Don't say that, it's just ter awful."

"Sorry, I didn't mean it like it sounded."

As the last passenger dismounts, we move forward. I slip my hand into my pocket, pulling out a crumpled envelope. "Would you give this to Aunt Sarah Rebeca for me?"

Daisy stares at the envelope. "I thought ya were going ter tell yer aunt ya were leaving today."

I shrug. "I couldn't find the courage. Jane Anne is still mad at me, and I didn't want to raise her hackles by telling my aunt. My mother won't be happy that her sister chose my side over hers."

"And yer going ter work on the frontline, blimey. Lack of courage and fighting don't go together, Lilly."

A strand of hair falls into my eyes, and I wipe it away. Courage takes many forms. My lack of bravery in my home life differs from the horrors I will encounter as a nurse on the frontline. Emotions are messy. On the frontline, it is a matter of business, tending to the wounded, patching them up. Blood I can cope with. Emotional discord I can't. Besides, I'm still processing my mother's rejection. I can't deal with my aunt's sad face too; she is still grieving her husband, without me adding to that pain. Alright, I am adding to it, but at least I'm not there to witness it. A groan rings round my head. I'm such a coward. "Don't put it through the letterbox, Jane Anne might get to it first and knowing her, she won't tell my aunt. My mother opens everyone's mail."

"I don't know why yer aunt stays wit' 'er."

"After my uncle died, Jane Anne is all she has."

We reach the train and it's time to say goodbye. A look of panic falls over Daisy's face. "Stay safe out there, won't ya? Don't be 'eroic, leave that up ter the doctors and soldiers."

Before I get pulled along by the boarding passengers, I turn, hugging Daisy. "You be careful too, you hear.

London isn't that safe, if the predictions about Hitler's intentions are right, and he sends his planes to bomb us."

I muster a smile so Daisy can't see how scared I am. She raises her hand, saluting me. "Orders understood loud and crystal clear, Nurse Lillian Elizabeth Nutman," she says, mimicking my mother.

Hand covering my mouth, I laugh. "Stop it, you silly bat. You're not funny."

"Am so, ya just don't appreciate me kind of 'umour."

"Yes, well, if you're going to mimic my mother, it's Nurse Lillian Elizabeth Ellis Nutman, if you don't mind."

Daisy frowns. "When did the Ellis appear?"

"When Trevor Henry died."

She nods. "That makes sense."

I step away from Daisy and board the train, finding a seat by the window. The glass panel squeaks as I slide it down, leaning out. "I'll try to write or something, I promise."

"Nah, ya won't. Yer terrible at keeping in touch."

The whistle blows, the carriage sways, and the train lurches forward. I watch Daisy as she waves, patting at her wet face with her handkerchief. Tears trailing down my face, I close the window and sit down. Opposite me, a man reads the newspaper. The only thing I can see are his chubby fingers and black trousers, which wave above his ankles, showing off red striped socks. His polished shoes are like tiny mirrors.

Next to him, a woman knits. The needles click together as the woollen ball spins inside her open bag. A sense of loneliness slips over me. At twenty-four, and living in a house with five brothers, I've never experienced this type of solitariness until recent events. I wonder how my brothers, John Edward, Arthur James, Brian Wayne, George Peter, and Charles Jason are doing. And if Jane Anne has received any word of their whereabouts. If she has, she hasn't seen fit to pass this information onto her sister. No surprise. My eyes close and I let the swaying motion of the train lull me to sleep.

With my nerves warding off the cold, I turn off St. Chads Drive into Beckett's Park. A sizeable crowd gathers, and the forging of friendships has started. It's like I've arrived at the party too late. My spirits flagging, I lick at my drying lips. There is still the possibility that I might bump into someone I know, having undertaken my nurse's training at Leeds Infirmary with Daisy. This raises my bravado, and I scan the crowd for a familiar face. It's too late to wish I had stayed in touch with the trainee doctors and nurses I'd met while we were in Leeds. As Daisy said, I'm a terrible penfriend. Things have been hectic since returning to London and taking up my post at Cheyne Children's Hospital, and time marched too quickly. The excuse floats into my head. No, I'd not been too busy to pick up pen and paper. Truth is, it hadn't crossed my mind.

The wind picks up as I make my way to the nurses congregating on the grass. Their voices drift my way, and their excited screams give way to self-criticism. Sometimes I could kick myself for my lack of foresight. A sick feeling is stirring in the pit of my stomach; making new friends is an uphill struggle for me, one I try to avoid. Unlike my mother, I'm quiet, and large groups send butterflies fluttering through my insides. Where is Daisy when I need her? Knowing someone from birth makes becoming friends easy. My distress over large groups and strangers started at primary school and refuses to abate. Daisy finds my lack of confidence funny, but then she never had to grow up being the daughter of Jane Anne.

"Lilly! Lilly!"

The sound of my name has me spinning around. Relief hums through me, and the building tension evaporates. Morag McAdams throws her arms around me. Given our height and size difference, I find myself pressed against her ample bosom.

"Ah cannae believe ye're 'ere. Ye should have kept in touch. But never mind that noo, ye're 'ere 'n' that's what's important," Morag says, her Scottish twang making me laugh.

The McAdams family moved from Inverness, Scotland, to Horsforth, Leeds, ten years ago when Morag's mum took up a matron position at Leeds Infirmary. Morag's father died at the end of the Great War, and her mum never remarried. Words shoot from Morag's mouth a mile a minute, her accent thickening as her excitement grows. Her red curls fly about her face, her cheeks flushed as her arms fly around her. She's always been an animated talker.

"Ye nae goin' tae believe it, but all the old gang's 'ere. Is that nae wonderful?" she says, grabbing my arms, her green eyes assessing me. "Ye've lost weight. Nae that ye kin afford tae do that. Never mind, Morag's 'ere. C'mon, na time tae lose."

She drags me along the grass, pushing her way through the crowd. Her head swivels back my way, her smile broadening. "Och, 'n' ye'll never guess who else is 'ere. Well, ye will 'cause the entire gang is 'ere."

I stumble, missing my footing. Morag giggles, looping her arm through mine. "Oops, cannae have ye injurin' yerself. That said, ye're in the right place."

Like a spitfire, we travel through the throng of people, my breath coming out my mouth like a jet stream.

"O'course, Joe is all serious still. But don't let that hold ye back, he's always had a soft spot for ye. Ye make a bonnie couple. Och, this is goin' tae be such fun."

"Lilly!" Pearl shouts, waving at me.

"I wondered if we'd find you here." Joe's deep voice cuts through the escalating chatter.

Joseph Lawrence is one of the most handsome men I have ever met. His raven-black hair hangs about his ears and his deep brown eyes just about eat me up. At six-feet-something, he towers over my five-four frame. As much as I like Joe, I can't see us courting. Joe is a friend. Besides, despite Morag's comment to the contrary, he might not like me that way. A look doesn't say I'm interested, does it?

Morag giggles at my side, cupping her hand over my right ear. "He's even dreamier in his white doctor's jacket."

Heat spreads over my cheeks, and I open my mouth to find I'm incapable of speech.

Pearl pushes at Morag. "Stop your fussing, Morag, you're like a Scottish wildcat. Can't you see you're embarrassing her."

The wind sends Pearl's blonde, finger-curled hair swinging. Her lips stretch into a smile as she places her hands on her slender hips. She bears a striking resemblance to actress Sally Gray. "It's good to see you, Lilly. Of course, it would have been nicer if you'd kept in touch."

My teeth nibble at my lips. "Sorry, I'm the worse friend ever."

Pearl nods. "Yes, you are, but don't worry, I'll let you make it up to me."

Joe's deep voice cuts in before I can respond, "Where's Daisy?"

The statement has Morag's head spinning, her hand covering her mouth. "Och, the poor thin', ah'd best find her."

Before Morag can take off, I grab her arm. "I'm on my own. Daisy's remaining in London."

"Morag! Will you stop panicking and prick up those ears of yours," Pearl says, shaking her head. "I blame the hair. It creates a barrier."

"Dinnae start on mah locks. Tis taken me ages tae pin 'em back."

It's like I've walked back in time. Pearl and Morag have always bickered like sisters. "Your hair is beautiful, don't listen to her," I say, moving Morag's hands away from her head.

"Lilly's right, Pearl's being her normal, unkind self."

Pearl throws her hands up, trying to hide her smile. "That's it, Joe, side with Lilly, like always."

We look at each other and laugh. How I've missed them.

"Right, c'mon, ye 'orrible lot, let's get movin' … right, left, right, left," Morag says, deepening her voice, sounding every bit like a commanding officer.

It's good to be back with the old gang after such a bleak Christmas. "Never change, Morag," I say, hugging her.

Pearl runs for her bag. "Hold your horses."

The wind no longer feels like a hurricane, and the temperature lifts.

Surrounded by my friends, my confidence blossoms and I know that whatever uncertainty lays ahead, I'll be alright.

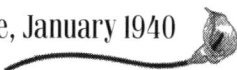

Dear Jane Anne,

I'm not sure why I'm writing to you. The chance of sending this letter is slim. However, indecision, and recrimination, all factor into my need to write. I fear this letter may stay hidden within the pages of my diary, though I hope to summon the courage to send it. Christmas was awful. Family is important. Absorbed within our clash of wills, we have forgotten that. My joining the Territorial Army Nursing Services was not rejection, but crucial. Our fight against the Nazis is just that, *our* fight. And that is what I am doing, joining the fight. In making hard choices and doing what is right, you felt I deserted you. You've lost so much, I understand, Trevor Henry, my brothers, and now me; my leaving shouldn't bring such conflict.

Life in the Territorial Army Nursing Services has shown me a resourcefulness I didn't know I possessed. Despite my fears and awkwardness toward large gatherings, and the dread of the unknown, I arrived at Leeds to find myself amongst friends. You won't remember Morag McAdams and Pearl Jones, who Daisy and I undertook our nursing training with at Leeds General Infirmary. Or Joseph Lawrence, who, as a doctor, is a major. But rest assured, I am amongst friends, and they are a decent lot.

A NIGHTINGALE'S LAST SONG

Equipped, and with our orders received in April, we embark the troop ships to France. Though overcrowded, excitement blots out the cold and our stomach's need to rid itself of its contents. The Channel is not on our side and the waves knock us about, but we remain in good cheer. With the Nazis advancing, Matron has informed us to expect air raids and the sound of gunfire and bombs when we reach France. What do gunfire and bombs sound like? They tell us this expecting us to understand. Most of us have never seen a gun to know the sounds it makes when fired. Several nurses onboard the troop ship served in the Great War, though much has changed since. With avid ears, we listen to the older nurses, preparing ourselves for what is coming. I shall store what I learn from them. After all, experience helps in war, does it not?

It's not the loud noises that bother me, though you may find that strange. Noise is just noise. Over the years, my brothers thrived on creating mischief, watching me jump at their loud bangs and shouts. Thanks to them I am accustomed to such chaos. As for air raids, we have our gas masks and tin hats at the ready. For everything else, I shall rely on my training and my faith. I'm sure both will prepare me for what lies ahead.

We sit with the few soldiers onboard. Most left England for France weeks earlier. I keep thinking, we can stitch a person back together, but the mind and soul is a separate matter. What about the devastation on the human mind? How do we reconcile it with the horrors it has seen? Comfort and understanding I can offer, but will this be

54

enough? There is no panicking about the place when a soldier needs us. Matron is strict. She will not allow her nurses to quake in fear, despite the bombs that fall. We must carry on, regardless. Perhaps I can give the soldiers more understanding than I could provide you. I've let you down, and I'm sorry. If I had been stronger and found the courage to make things right between us, there would be no melancholy forcing me to write to you. You wouldn't make it easy, but I should have tried.

Please look after yourself, and Aunt Sarah Rebeca. Remember, like you, she is mourning the loss of her husband. Right now, you need each other. Don't take advantage of her willingness to help. Strength comes from others, and I am sure that together you will find the courage to survive whatever Hitler throws at you and London. I hope John Edward, Arthur James, Brian Wayne, George Peter, and Charles Jason, make it to see you while they are on leave, if they remain in the United Kingdom. They are too much like me to write.

Lillian Elizabeth

6

 April 1940, 18th BGH, France

*O*n mounting bravado and eagerness, we make it to the shores of France. Vehicles wait, providing little time to stretch and regain our land legs before we climb onboard.

"What do ye think it will be like at the 18th?" Morag asks, her gaze glued on the passing scenery.

Apprehension gnaws along my flesh, and I try not to overthink things like normal. "I don't know. With most of the officers and soldiers arriving ahead, I guess it's going to be busy."

My brothers call my overthinking a girl thing, but it isn't. It's a Lillian Elizabeth thing. As a nurse, I understand my overthinking relates to general anxiety, but how does one stop worrying? Give me something to fret over and my brain grasps it.

"All the stories Ma told me 'n' mah brothers aboot the Great War keep goin' round mah head. Did ah tell ye that Ma read Florence Nightingale's paper she wrote for the

Leeds Conference o' Women Workers on Rural Health 'n' Rural Health Missioners?"

Pearl groans. "Who cares, Morag, I'm snoozing at the thought. How is rural health going to help us in France? We're in the middle of a war, not on a farm counting sheep."

"Hoo kin ye say that aboot Florence Nightingale? Ye a nurse."

"I was criticising your mum for reading a paper that isn't helpful."

"Ye bein' nasty," Morag says, throwing her glove at Pearl.

It lands on her head. Her arms fly as she shakes her head, dislodging the glove, protecting her styled hair. "Ahhh …"

A smug smile sits on Morag's lips. "That's for groanin' at mah ma."

"Watch the hair, Morag! It took me ages to style it and it's already been through enough, what with the wind and salt from the sea water. Despite what you think, hair doesn't style itself."

The glove falls to the floor, and I pick it up, passing it to Morag. Pearl grits her teeth, smoothing down her hair.

A bewildered expression on his face, Joe looks across at Pearl. "Tell me you didn't pack your rollers."

Pearl's features darken and her eyes narrow. "Don't be daft, Joe."

"That's because she couldn't fit them in her kit bag," Morag says.

"That's not true. I'm not at all bothered about my lack of waves. We have a job to do. That's far more important than styled hair."

Morag snorts. "Och, aye, that's why a bird could nest on ye bottom lip, is it?"

Pearl sticks out her tongue. "Ha-ha, you're hilarious. I'm going to let my personality shine instead. It may surprise you, but my hair can still be gorgeous without rollers. Besides, I'm going to rag it instead." Pearl pats her shoulder-length hair. "It's my duty to give those poor soldiers something good to look at."

"So long as lookin' is all they do. Ye ken yer nae allowed tae get involved with the soldiers. Matron scares me tae death," Morag says, shivering "Ah'm nae coverin' for ye, so don't expect me tae lie tae Matron. If ye get it taegether with a soldier, yer on yer own."

Pearl huffs. "Spoken like a genuine friend, Morag McAdams. Honest, I don't see the harm. Soldiers love a girl in a nurse's uniform."

Morag leans forward so Pearl can see her disapproval. "The noun nurse comes from the Latin word 'nurture', which means tae nourish. A nurse is a person whose trainin' is tae tend the sick. Nae gallivantin' around lookin' for a husband."

"And who carries out their duties under the instruction of the physician."

I lay a hand on Joe's arm. "Not now, Joe."

"For the record, Morag, I'm not looking for a husband, just fun. There's nothing wrong with looking after yourself. Not everyone likes the wild, abandoned look."

Morag pats down her red curls. "What's wrong with mah locks?"

"Nothing's wrong with your hair, it's lovely," I say, sending Pearl a sharp stare.

She shrugs.

Pearl Jones has a habit of concentrating too much on her appearance, not manners. With her sultry looks and fashionable blonde hair, she can appear shallow. Underneath, she's a softie with a big heart, and a loyal friend. It's why we love her.

Morag grabs my arm, pointing. "We've arrived! Och, ah think ah'm goin' tae be sick. Mah nerves are chewin' on mah stomach. Skippin' lunch was a bad idea."

Pearl shuffles left, pressing her shoulder into Joe's side.

"Ouch, be careful, Pearl."

"She's not vomiting over my shoes. Switch places, Joe," Pearl says, pushing him.

His black brows drop in annoyance as Pearl continues to muscle her way across. "Ouch, will you stop doing that."

"No, now move."

"Don't worry, she won't be sick," I say as Joe exchanges places with Pearl, sitting next to Morag.

"Why couldn't she stay where she was? We're stopping now."

"Because it's Pearl, and despite her faults, we love her," I remind him.

"If you say so, though it's more about tolerating her than love. I should have travelled with the other doctors," Joe grumbles.

"You don't mean that. They're old and stuffy, and not as entertaining as us."

Joe removes Pearl's elbow from his ribs. "How much room do you want?"

"Men …" She sighs, as if that explains everything.

The vehicle shudders to a stop, and before Pearl can elaborate further, we step out. Our mouths drop and we stare at a sea of tents and Nissen huts scattered across the field. Made from sheet metal, the huts offer temporary shelter.

Morag throws her kit bag over her shoulder. "Wow, there's a lot o' tents."

"Where do you suppose the 18th is?" I ask, my voice sounding hesitant.

"There." Joe points at the 18th BGH.

Pearl's kit bag falls to the ground. "You've got to be kidding."

Joe smirks. "Nope, that's the hospital."

"Well … I … hm … I'm not relishing the idea of nursing under canvas."

Morag threads her arm through Pearl's. "Dinnae worry, pet, we'll soon have it feelin' like haime."

"Pet?"

"Ye liked it when that Jordy called ye it durin' our trainin'."

A wicked smile flashes across Pearl's face. "I liked a lot of things that Jordy lad did and said, but he didn't have wild hair and boobs, so let's stick to Pearl."

With her left hand, Morag pats her breast. "Aye, the poor laddie."

"Poor laddie? Morag, if men had breasts, they'd get nothing done."

"Chop, chop, ladies, we'd best get moving," Joe says, stepping forward to join the other medical officers.

Behind his back, Pearl pulls a face, tutting. "Doctors!"

I wonder if she knows her one-word statement explains nothing.

We find our accommodation at the end of the larger wards of the 18th BGH. Pearl's nose wrinkles at the cosiness of the room, and the thin width of the beds.

"Remember, as officers they assign us servants," Morag says, in an attempt to brighten the mood.

Pearl smiles, placing her kit bag on an unassigned bed. "Servants, I like that."

I frown as the word rolls off Pearl's tongue. "They aren't servants, Pearl, for all that they're being called that. We'll be working long hours, and they're here to help us do our job. Not so we can sit around drinking tea and eating scones while someone does our laundry."

"Dinnae get all hooty 'n' above yer station, Pearl," Morag says. "Like Lilly says, they're 'ere tae wake us, clean our room, cook meals, 'n' bring hot water for washin'. Dinnae ye listen to Matron? They aren't here tae to take advantage of. Ye're a nurse, nae a lassie o' the manor."

The servants, as Matron classes them, are from the British Voluntary Aid Detachments (VADs), and civilians from France and Belgium.

"Sometimes, Morag, I fear you don't like me," Pearl says.

Hand on hips, Morag sighs. "Why ever would ye say that?"

"Oh, maybe because you're such a meanie to me."

"Me! Mean?"

I step between them, trying to focus their attention on what is important. "There's no time for bickering. We need to pull our socks up and get sorted. If we're quick, we can get to the Sisters' Mess and eat before Matron summons us. Didn't you say you were hungry, Morag?"

She nods. "Count me in. Why, ah could eat a scabby wildcat."

"Yuk … please remove that image from my mind," Pearl says, her hands covering her face.

The Sisters' Mess is the primary hub of activity when we aren't sleeping and on duty; it is where we eat, socialise, and relax. With few possessions, it doesn't take long to sort them, and we're soon on our way there. Though we have little in the way of expectations, the Sisters' Mess disappoints. The lighting in the single-lined marquee is inadequate and it has insufficient heating, offering little in the way of comfort. Tables and chairs take up most of the floor space and in the corner is a wireless.

Morag rubs her arms. "Ah'm nae sure aboot the relaxin' bit. Ah'd freeze tae death first."

Pearl's chest puffs out as she catches us up. "I don't believe it. Have you seen the Medical Officers' Mess? They've got huts. Huts! And a kitchen, scullery, anteroom, with big open brick grates."

"Ye don't waste yer time, do ye," Morag says, lifting a red eyebrow.

Pearl smirks. "I was getting to know my surroundings."

"In the Medical Officers' Mess?" I ask.

"I'm not sure I understand what you're implying. I was checking on Joe, seeing how he was settling in."

Morag's lips twist to the side. "O'course ye were."

"And how was Joe?" I ask.

"Hm … oh, I couldn't find him."

Morag winks at me. "Ye dinnae say."

"And what's that supposed to mean?"

There's little point in continuing this discussion. Time is ticking and we still haven't eaten. "Never mind, Pearl, I'm sure Morag meant nothing. Let's go eat."

7

 April 1940, 18ᵗʰ BGH, France

*T*he first few weeks at the 18th BGH are quiet, allowing time to make the place homier. There are eighty sisters in attendance at the twelve-hundred-bed hospital. With the war yet to pick up pace, we tend to the odd casualty or ailment, but nothing serious. On the 10th of May, the quietness ends and for the first time we see the destruction war wields. The casualties flood in, filling the hospital's waiting area. Groans of pain flow with the blood of the injured, and civilians blend with soldiers as they wait medical assessment. This sudden influx has us working around the clock, reducing sleeping time to five hours. Along with this gruelling schedule, the Germans begin their aerial attacks, and we wake to the sound of the air raid siren. Pearl groans, throwing an arm over her face and pressing her pillow around her ears. My legs swing over the bed, and I look across at Morag as she throws back her bedsheets, striding over to Pearl.

"C'mon, oot ye get."

With her pillow hiding her face, Pearl's legs kick against the mattress. "I just want to sleep. Can't I have an hour? I've only just got off shift."

"Ye think Hitler cares? C'mon, the trench awaits yer presence."

Pearl groans, climbing out of bed. "You're all heart …"

We dress, leaving our sleeping quarters, and run to the woods, slipping into the trenches as directed. When we hit the ground, Joe is already there with several medical officers. The whirring noise of aircraft drifts over, followed by the whizzing sound of bombs. Time drags and speeds up in a single action. Tin hats on our heads, we sit waiting for the air raid to end. The sun creeps higher and our legs cramp. With no sign of the aerial attack ending, I stretch out my arms, releasing the pressure between my shoulder blades.

Joe scurries over, crouching in front of us. "We can't sit here. We need to get to the hospital and help treat the casualties."

Incapable of speech, we nod, making our precarious way to the hospital. Our gas masks swing at our side as we follow Joe and some of the other medical officers, leaving the security of the trench. Dirt shoots up in the distance and the sound of a plane's engine rumbles over our heads, blending with our rapid heartbeats. There is no time to think, to give in to the thin trail of fear that slides down my back. As soon as we enter the 18th, we face a sea of soldiers requiring medical attention. Ambulances line up outside, coming from the Casualty Clearing Station (CCS).

Joe walks over to the medical officer in charge, offering his services.

"Blimey," Pearl breathes as we take in the scene, making mental notes of the injuries.

"There's Matron," Morag says, striding over.

Transfixed, I stare at the destruction in front of me. Never did I imagine such a scene. I've grown up listening to stories about the Great War, but to see it with my own eyes strips away my innocence. War is such a bloody, unfeeling monster.

"Lilly!" Matron shouts, waving me over. Morag and Pearl stand next to her, along with three other sisters.

"As you six are the senior nurses, you're to take it in turns to be Night Superintendent. Annie, you'll take up the first night duty, Jane you're next, then it's Morag, Pearl, Doreen, and Lilly."

Annie nods. "Yes, Matron."

"You're to go round the hospital and see to each patient, three times each night. Once you've done that, you will complete a report. I want you to include the soldier's name, rank, unit number, injuries, and treatment. You will then outline his condition, understand?"

"Yes, Matron," we say.

As Matron walks away, Morag sighs. "Och, that's an awful lot o' writin'."

Pearl folds her arms. "It's a lot of needless repetition."

"Incomplete medical records during the Great War badly affected a lot of veterans," Annie says, her voice subdued, "delaying their disability pensions. The paperwork might appear repetitive, but at least our men will get what is due to them."

"Noo ah feel awful aboot complainin'." Morag throws her arms in the air.

Pearl looks over at Annie. "You'd best go back to the trench and wait for the all-clear. It won't be long before night shift starts."

Annie nods, leaving the 18th. With the casualties arriving, there isn't time to stand around. Shrapnel wounds, I'm learning, are one of the worse. Metal tears at skin, burying clothing and dirt deep within the wounds. The damage it causes is immense, eating its way into muscle. Everywhere I look the hospital is a mass of blood, gore, cries of pain and moans of fear.

With the hospital waiting area filling, we sort through the patients, readying them for theatre. Lieutenant Colonel Cunningham is operating today, with Major Billingham anaesthetising. In the pre-operative room, each nurse has two stretchers assigned to them. On my right, Morag makes a patient comfortable. A bullet has entered his popliteal vein, which is the principal route for the venous return on the lower leg. His foot is gangrenous and requires amputating. Next to Morag, Pearl treats a patient with a fractured jaw, picking out his loose teeth and fragments of bone. Once this is done, she stitches his tongue to a button on his jacket, sending him down the line for theatre. This is what we do, repair and prepare the wounded for surgery, moving from stretcher to stretcher. Self-discipline is important. It is what Matron expects of her nurses. It is also what keeps us going. Adrenaline is a wonderful chemical, stopping me from drinking in the surrounding mortality, allowing me to function.

Joe's hand touches my shoulder, the contact brief, as I wrap a bandage around a passed-out soldier's head. "You're doing great," he says.

With a wobbly smile, I watch him walk over to a waiting soldier that has just arrived. His right leg is missing. Like me, Morag, and Pearl, Joe isn't supposed to be on duty today, but the vast number of casualties makes him stay.

The soldier's eyes flutter open as I secure the bandage. "Hosp-it-al ...?" he says, his voice breaking up the single word, as his disorientated gaze skims the ward.

I place a hand on his shoulder, preventing him from sitting up and becoming dizzy. "You're at the 18th British General Hospital."

The soldier blinks, absorbing the information. "How long was I out?"

"About an hour," I say, guessing. He was already unconscious when they stretchered him in.

He reaches across his body, his hands moving along his arm, trailing over his watch. With shaking limbs, he touches the bandage covering his head. This action allows his brain to categorise what has happened to him. I remove his hands from the bandage, taking them in mine, before placing them at his sides. "You're all patched up."

"Thank you," he says, his eyelids closing, losing consciousness.

Snared in a loop, the soldier will repeat this until his mind and body can remain focused.

At the front of the 18th, nurses admit the new casualties before sending them onto the ward. Soldiers pile up, each one requiring our attention. Around us, bombs explode. The noise of the ack-ack guns, shooting up at the bombers, next to the hospital, is deafening. A memory triggers and I recall Jane Anne and her jumping nerves at being bombed. For the first time, I agree with her, and her worries.

The air attacks are relentless, subjecting our nerves to a beating. Some soldiers suffer flashbacks during the raids, and we try to block out the noise the best we can, placing pillows around their heads and over their ears. For some, the noise is too much. Their screams filter over the drumming of passing aircraft. We lay next to them on the bed, holding them to us, pressing the pillow against their ears. No matter how we try, our eyes will never let our minds forget the devastation war has on the flesh and the life it takes.

Sentiments swirl and tiredness sets in as I near the end of my shift. The hours I worked at Cheyne Children's Hospital are nothing compared to those I now do. As night draws in, the casualties stop, and the ward drifts into a brief and blessed silence. The Night Sister takes up her post, signalling my time to leave. Each Night Sister handles the two hundred beds that make up four wards. The orderlies help to keep the ward tidy, lifting and turning patients, and assisting with the patients' personal care.

As I leave the hospital, I bump into Annie as she prepares to carry out Matron's orders. Too tired to talk, I nod. Outside, a nightingale sings. Its sweet song causes tears to fall, slipping down my cheeks. Not that I think the song is mournful; crying releases the pressure. Not ready to enter the Sisters' Mess, I make my way behind one of the

Nissen huts. Wrapped in the evening darkness, my tears fall until the nightingale stops singing. My lips move without voice as I thank the tiny bird, unaware until I heard its song how much emotional pressure I'd been carrying.

Why so many poets, like Sir Philip Sidney, find the nightingale's song plaintive, I don't know. Maybe it's because the nightingale sings when daytime ends. To me, the small bird's voice is beautiful, lifting my spirits. My lungs inflate, and I hum, replacing the bird's song with my own. Singing helps me relax, and as the first line of *Amazing Grace* pours from my lips, the quietness of the night brings peace.

Since walking out of my family home, doubt has festered, making me question if I have done the right thing. Not as a nurse, but as a person, and a daughter. My nerves may take a hammering, and sleep might be elusive, but I will never regret the decision to care for those fighting in this terrible war. As a daughter, I wonder, if I'd stayed in London, would the gap between daughter and mother have repaired itself? In leaving, did I do the right thing for me and Jane Anne? And that is the question doubt sows until all I have left is uncertainty.

Letter Home, May 1940

Dear Jane Anne,

Here, on paper, I can speak with candour, unlike when we are together. You are different here. Perhaps it's because you can't answer back, or that your face remains pleasant, no matter what I say. Whatever my reasons, I enjoy talking to you on paper, so, although you will never see these letters, I will continue to write. As time passes, I am hoping to find a resolution to our conflict. Sometimes, my thoughts about you become tainted with the past, interfering with the rational part of my brain. In these moments I am quick to judge you. There is such distance between us. One day, maybe, we can reduce the gap. A bond, like it or not, lives within our very essence. We are bound by threads of emotions, not just genetics, which aren't easy to negotiate. I am sure that time, and war, should we survive, will provide the answers.

It will not surprise you to learn I was wrong about the noise war brings. It's far worse than my brothers could have prepared me for. The first air raid happened at 4 a.m. within a few weeks of our arrival at the 18th, interrupting our sleep. With the siren ringing in our ears, and the ack-ack guns firing, we run to the trenches. Overhead, four light planes and three bombers gather like angry clouds ready to release their rain. The ack-ack guns sound like thunder, and anti-aircraft soon consumes the quietness of the morning. At 5:30 a.m. with no sign of the air raid ending, black coffee and rum is served. Though the rum does little to calm our nerves and stop our hands shaking, its sting warms our throats. Even as we sit in the dug-out, I know that soon my shift will start, and I will leave its safety.

Since arriving at the 18th, I've made some new friends; Adah and Effie Paxton are Queen Alexandra Nurses, like me, Morag, and Pearl. After serving in the Great War, and with so much happening here, Adah's medical knowledge is invaluable. She keeps us calm as the planes drop their bombs. Adah is an inspiration. By the time the Great War ended, it had taken her siblings, apart from Effie, and her parents. The fact Adah can serve in another world war is remarkable.

Do you remember when you baked those jam tarts? No sooner were they on the airing tray to cool than they were gone. Each time you took a batch out of the oven, half disappeared. It is similar here, but the opposite. No sooner have we seen to the new arrivals than more casualties arrive. This time, we cannot blame the sticky fingers of George Peter and Brian Wayne. Though, I suspect, John Edward had been the one to come up with the ingenious plan of using your best tea towel to transport their hot stolen goods. I also blame Arthur James and Charles Jason for the theft of the sweet treats, as they never shared them with me. This memory of my brothers is making me smile. What simple times they were.

It is a desolate sight each day when the ambulances arrive. The large numbers force the surgeons to operate through the night. As the soldiers are unloaded from the ambulances and admitted, we tend their wounds, preparing them for surgery. Some of the wounded have entire areas blown away. Even with all my training, I confess, some of their injuries make me queasy, not that I would ever let it show. They have endured enough. No one is safe from Hitler and his allies. Men and women from surrounding towns enter seeking medical attention. Their injuries shed new light on our disagreement and how important family is. One day, if I am given the opportunity, I hope we can mend our relationship, and arrive at a mutual understanding and respect.

I pray God is doing all he can to keep my brothers safe. God has many people to watch over, I know, but the Nazis have already taken Trevor Henry and Uncle Anthony Kevin. It doesn't seem fair to take more from us. Would Trevor Henry be alive if not for Hitler? Can anyone outrun a bullet once released from its chamber? Accident or not. The soldier pressed the trigger, and the bullet raced toward Trevor Henry. Perhaps you are right to blame the war for his death. Trevor Henry died because of this war.

Lillian Elizabeth

8

 May 1940, 18th BGH France

*O*rganised mayhem greets me when I start my shift as Night Superintendent. Casualties wait on the ward for dressings to be changed, while others wait for admission. There is no easy shift at the 18th. Without catching my breath, I take up my duties. As nurses leave, a fresh wave enters. Tiredness leaks from the day nurses, and I know by the end of my shift at 8 a.m., my knees will buckle with exhaustion, just like theirs. Despite the long hours, I will find the strength to keep pressing on.

The first staggered break comes at 3:30 a.m., with bully sandwiches made from corned beef, and hot sweet tea. Break time is the same—we eat without enjoyment or leisure. Our tastebuds don't have time to tingle in delight. The food is a means to an end, replacing dwindling energy levels. Our bodies may flag, but our spirits stay strong.

When I enter the ward, I see her in the far corner. She lies on the thin hospital bed, her arm slung over her face.

Underneath her blouse, a bandage wraps around her chest, protecting the burns she suffered during the bombing. The soiled dressing needs changing, and I grab a basin of saline solution, Vaseline, and fresh bandages.

"Good evening," I say, keeping my voice low as I set the items on the nightstand and grab the privacy screen. The wheels let out a muffled squeak as I pull it round the woman's bed. "I need to change your dressing."

Her eyes lock on the canvas roof of the hospital. Without changing her gaze, she drops her arm onto the bed. The gold band on her wedding finger tings against the metal bedframe. Unsure if she's heard me, I touch her shoulder before unfastening the buttons on her blouse. Her head turns and she stares at me. Pain shimmers within a pool of blue, and my heart tightens. She blinks, turning her head, fastening her gaze back on the canvas. Sadness leaks off her. It's hard to know what torment holds her mind prisoner. Lost within her chamber of sorrow, and not willing to sound superficial, I offer no words of comfort over her sorrows. Words won't remove her pain.

"Can you sit up for me, please?" I ask, unable to change her dressing while she's lying on the bed.

Without speaking, the woman moves to a sitting position, dragging her legs over the bedframe. She flinches as I help her, the damaged skin beneath the dressing stretching and inflicting pain. Her short brown hair kisses her jaw and freckles cover her face, providing the only colour to her pale skin. Her body is malnourished, her cheeks sinking into the crevice of her face. War and heartache are sucking the life from her. The medical notes don't provide her age, name, or where she came from. There is no next of kin, just a list of her injuries and treatment. Her silence leaves us no choice but to refer to her as Jane Doe.

Jane was admitted by the day shift with her husband. He never made it to theatre; his injuries were too severe, and his body, in a state of shock, shutdown. Unable to communicate, he passed away as the nurses treated his wife. Since learning of her husband's death, Jane has withdrawn deeper into herself. In her trance-like state, she looks calm — almost tranquil. Inside, I am aware of the avalanche of emotions building.

With gentle fingers, I remove the bandage. Rachmaninoff's *Rhapsody on a Theme of Paganini variation 18* vibrates from my lips. The music soothes as I work, blocking out the hum of activity on the ward. Many of the civilians entering the 18th suffer burns from the fires created by the bombs. Limbs crushed by falling masonry. The Germans and their allies have little care over the destruction they leave. As they attempt to stamp down their dominance, civilians become snared within the crossfire. Innocent people, left without homes, family, and friends.

A gentle hand on my arm pulls my attention to the owner. "Matron has summoned us to the Sisters' Mess," Adah Paxon says in a low voice.

Even for someone like me, who finds it difficult to forge friendships, Adah's warmth draws me to her, expanding my circle of close friends. Loose strands of peppercorn hair curl around her white cap. Her grey tippet, issued as standard to all Queen Alexandra (QA) nursing staff, covers her shoulders, warding off the evening chill. A rose band runs around the edges of the cape, the silver

'T' on the front point identifying Adah as part of TANS. The white apron that protects the grey dress has been removed. A nurse's uniform isn't just about identifying her as a QA, it is also practical. In warmer weather, the long sleeves unbutton at the elbow, halving their length. Adah's sister, Effie, works in the Queen Alexandra's Imperial Military Nursing Services (QAIMNS). It has never mattered to me if we are QAIMNS or TANS. What is important are our nursing roots. Chamberlain's declaration of war on Germany in 1939 saw the Reserves and TANS merged into the QAIMNS.

We are answerable to Matron, who answers to the army's Matron-in-Chief. Both are formidable women. When Matron summons her nurses to the Sisters' Mess, they are there—pronto. My eyebrows arch and I'm aware of the magnitude of breaking Matron's command, but there is no leaving the ward without a nurse present. I finish wrapping the dressing around Jane's chest, nodding at Adah. "Send the nurses to the Sisters' Mess. I'll stay here and admit the few remaining casualties."

"Are you sure? Matron won't be happy."

"Yes, you know how it is, Adah. A nurse never leaves her ward unattended."

Concern shining in her hazel eyes, Adah nods. I move the privacy screen back, watching Adah as she passes Matron's command to the other nurses. Their heads bob their acknowledgement as they finish what they are doing. On measured footsteps, so as not to upset the patients, they turn and leave.

I place a hand on Jane's shoulder as she lies on the bed. "Try and get some rest."

A tear runs down her face as her gaze fixes once more on the canvas roof. Grief is a hard emotion—one we all deal with differently. As controlled as the woman is on the outside, her pain festers inside, searching for release. That release will come. It's just a matter of when and how it will manifest itself. Until then, Jane's pain is unrelenting. The nurses' departure from the ward leaves behind barrenness. Like a field waiting for the farmer to turn the earth and sow the seed. To compensate, I hum as though there is nothing out of the ordinary occurring.

Pearl's head is bent, examining a new admission. I stop at her side. "I've got this," I say. "Matron is expecting you at the Sisters' Mess."

She moves away, allowing me to take over. With most of the two hundred casualties that arrived during the day admitted, it doesn't take long to finish the few remaining soldiers. The noise of war rattles round the canvas structure of the hospital. Bombs fall, followed by the rat-a-tat-tat of retaliating gunfire. There is a thunderous roar and a bomb lands close by.

In the bed at the end of the canvas wall, Richard Jefferson, a basic British soldier (Tommie) jumps. Nerves on edge, he screams, flashing back to the battlefield. His arms fly about him, and he knocks over the glass of water on the nightstand. It crashes to the floor, splintering into pieces. For Richard, the sound is as deafening as a bomb.

"Get down!" he screams, his hands waving in erratic motion. "Down, Pat ... down!"

Since arriving at the hospital, Richard has filled us with stories about his friend, Patrick. His need to talk helps to push him through his grief.

Patrick Noah Chapman, a fellow Tommie, died on the battlefield, his fingers gripping his rifle. The force of the explosion sent him flying backwards, into Richard. Acting as a shield, shrapnel tore into Pat's flesh, carving its way into his heart.

Within a few steps, I arrive at Richard's bedside. "Richard … Richard, it's alright you're in the hospital."

Despite Pat's body shielding him, shrapnel has ravaged Richard's face, leaving him blind. His fingers pull at the bandage, the flashback holding him captive. While he's unaware of where he is, I try to bring him back to the present, away from the horror that brought him here. "Shhh … shhh …" I whisper, taking his hands in mine, preventing them from disturbing the bandage.

He sits up, his body shuddering as the shrapnel, plucked from his memory, hits him. "Pat … Pat …"

With my back against the pillows, I pull him to me, my arms wrapping around his waist, my lips pressing against his ear. "You're safe, Richard, you're safe."

His body goes limp, his voice growing hoarse. "Pat …"

I hold him close, our bodies swaying in a gentle motion as I place my hand on his back. With a soft beat, I tap his back … lub dub … dub lub … the slow, even, rhythm mimicking the heartbeat from within the womb, helping to calm him. Together we rock, and I sing *Pennies From Heaven*.

Music is a powerful resource. Like the sun, it offers a brief interlude, releasing the mind from torment. There is little I can offer Richard, but I can give him a momentary reprieve from his fear. His body relaxes as I sing, and I lie him down on the bed. Without missing a beat, I continue singing as I plump up his pillow, covering his ears and reducing the sound of artillery. While I'm becoming accustomed to the sound of battle, my brain still triggers the natural fight-or-flight response. With no noticeable command, my body prioritises, placing what it doesn't need to survive on the back burner, while it prepares for the worse.

My senses heightening, I glance to where Jane lies. Her body trembles, her hands pressing against her ears as her eyelids close, and her lips move in silent, rapid motion. Much like Richard, Jane's brain takes her to a different place in time. With Richard quiet, I move towards her, placing my hand on her arm; she doesn't respond. Her shivers worsen, and I lie next to her, my arm draping over her stomach. With a soft hum, I try to calm her down. She moves her head to the side and blinks at me as the shaking subsides. It is the first time she has acknowledged anyone's presence. Unlike Jane, come the morning Richard will begin his journey home to the United Kingdom. His fighting days are over.

The sound of gunfire wanes and I long for the quiet days we experienced when we first arrived. Self-discipline is a QA's strength. Matron expects us to exercise control over our feelings, no matter the circumstances. When the close proximity of a bomb sent a young, trainee nurse crumbling into hysterics while on duty, Matron inflicted us with a stern speech. "If a bomb lands close by, we do not crumble. If the windows in the hospital blow in—if the hospital is fortunate to have glass windows—we continue to tend to our patients, without flinching. We carry on no matter what. No matter the emotional anguish raging inside us. Only later, when we are alone, are our hands allowed to shake and our legs to give out. We address these matters with a tight smile and a what-a-bore attitude. Even when our insides turn to mush, we present an unaffected exterior. Is. That. Clear!" In the end, Matron had the young nurse sent home.

With guarded expressions, nurses pour back onto the ward, and I leave Jane. Matron walks behind Pearl, signalling me to her. "New orders have arrived. Transport will arrive at five a.m. to collect fifty of our younger sisters. They are to return to the United Kingdom. The rest of you will leave as transport becomes available."

Dumfounded, I stare at her. Of late, the wireless in the Sisters' Mess has become background noise. News changes nothing. The casualties still pour into the hospital, and now fifty Sisters will return home. Rumours float in whispers, and we are under strict instructions from Matron to ignore them. She won't have her nurses engaging in tittle-tattle. Each day we've watched the refugees travel past the end of the hospital compound, their numbers increasing daily. Now I understand why. The Nazis are advancing, heading towards us. There is no other reason for the fifty nurses to leave with the rest of us to follow, vacating the 18th—it's bad out there.

Matron walks away and I turn to see Morag, Pearl and Adah huddled together, whispering while they sort through the supplies. Morag glances over her shoulder as I walk to them. "Tis like we're runnin' away," she whispers, not wanting to draw attention, but needing to say something.

"Just think what the fifty being sent home are going through. I'd feel rotten if it was me. We came here to care for our wounded, not run like frightened hares," I say, hugging myself.

From my right, Pearl snorts. "At least they'll still be alive."

"Ye say that like ye want tae be one o' those bein' sent haime?" Morag's cheeks inflate. "'N' we both ken ye'd be spittin' feathers if ye were."

"No, I'm not. At least there'll be nurses around to help if something happens to us, that's all I'm saying."

Morag's cheeks return to their normal size. "Aye, ye're right, sorry. Though ah came 'ere tae help tend the casualties, nae run away when thin's get tough."

"No one's running away, Morag. They are following orders," Adah says, her eyes scanning the ward for Effie.

Fifteen years separate Effie and Adah. Effie was the last born of eight children and three miscarriages. Her mother, left devastated, died in 1920. If I were Adah, I know I would feel the same. Time is often called a healer. I've never believed such nonsense—time never heals; it dims emotions but doesn't repair them. My quarrel with Jane Anne seems petty since arriving in France. Rather than moving back in with Daisy and her uncle and aunt, I shall try building a bridge over our differences.

"What's Joe doing?" Pearl asks, nudging my arm.

I turn. "Oh …"

Joe strides onto the ward, his large hands holding the hand of a small boy. The boy's right arm is in a sling. His matted hair sticks to his face, and dirt covers his skin. Track marks run down his cheeks where his tears have cleaned away the grime. Mud and blood line his ill-fitting clothes.

"Does anyone know who this belongs to?" Joe's voice fills the hospital. As everyone turns, he rests his hand on the boy's shoulders.

A lump forms in my throat as I glance at the dirty child. Broken glass and bodies I can cope with; a young boy being separated from his parents, perhaps facing a future as an orphan, breaks my heart. It's hard losing a parent to war—this boy is too young to experience such loss.

Pearl's lips press close to my ear. "Don't cry, Lilly, Matron won't like it."

On a deep inhale, I push through the gloom.

His fists pumping at his side, the boy looks lost and small. Never have I seen myself as the maternal type, but this boy triggers every mothering instinct I have.

"Félix!" a man shouts, his French accent echoing across the ward.

The boy turns, his mouth falling open. He hesitates, then like a stone from a catapult, he takes off across the room, bumping into beds. Matron will not like such a lack of respect for the sick in her hospital. But a little boy doesn't care about protocol. He cares only that he has found his daddy. Tears and snot running down his cheeks, he races over to where the man lies. "Papa! Papa!"

Nurses watch from the veil of eyelashes as they continue their work. Later, when off duty, there won't be a dry eye amongst us as we gather in the Sisters' Mess, recalling the little boy being reunited with his father. Joe nods in satisfaction, a shadow of a smile touching his lips.

He turns, making his way to check on a patient. My gaze lingers on his back. If Morag catches me, she'll be relentless in her teasing. Still, it's strange how one act of kindness can change how you see a person. Seeing Joe with the little boy has created a shift in my attitude towards him. I'm not sure what that means, but something inside me is different.

"I'd best go clean up the glass before someone stands on it," I say, remembering the events before Matron's news. It also gives me an excuse to ponder this new awareness I have for Joe without scrutiny.

Morag frowns. "What glass?"

"Richard knocked his water off the nightstand when a bomb landed nearby."

Not giving her chance to say anything, I walk over to the Tommie, picking up the shards of glass. This mundane task allows me to cogitate my rolling emotions for Joe. The more time I spend with him, the more I find I like him. Is it the beginning of love or are my emotions pulling me in that direction given our circumstances? I don't know. Though Joe doesn't make my heart skip, he touches the softer edges inside me—and I like how that feels.

Careful not to cut myself on the broken glass, I gather up the larger pieces. The rest I'll sweep up with a brush and dustpan.

"Here, put the glass in here," Adah says, handing me a small bucket.

"Thanks."

The glass clinks as they drop.

"Stay there and I'll get you a dustpan."

I nod.

The bucket swings as Adah walks towards the exit. Row upon row of metal beds fill the hospital ward, each one occupied. Bombs, landmines, flamethrowers, tanks, and machine guns, all designed to damage the flesh and end life. Weaponry isn't the only progression in this war. Adah, making it her mission to prepare us the best she can, has been recounting her experiences as a wartime nurse. Two days ago, as we sat huddled in the Sisters' Mess, she regaled us with stories.

"Never underestimate the Germans' desire to win this war. Why, back in April 1915, a special unit of the German Army undertook the first large-scale chemical attack. They used one hundred and fifty tons of chlorine gas against the French. It devastated the Allied line. That was the Germans' third attempt at introducing chemical weapons into war. Their first was back in October 1914, when they placed small amounts of tear gas into shells, firing them at the French."

We gasp, our eyes wide in horror.

"I know." She nods. "And in January 1915, they made their second effort. This time using xylyl bromide, which is a more lethal gas, within their shells, firing them at Russian troops. The chilly atmosphere froze the gas, putting a stop to their evil plan. Always look out for symptoms that aren't explained by their injuries. It pays to be vigilant."

While we know war has used toxic smoke since the ancient times, the knowledge that it can wipe out an entire brigade stuns me. It's hard to justify their use, even in war.

"Remember," —Adah wiggles her finger at us— "as well as the natural injuries of war, such as trench foot, trench fever, frostbite, and shellshock, we are treating the effects of poisonous gases."

Her words rattle around my head as I sweep up the glass.

9

May 1940, 18th BGH France

*A*s I finish the last report, I hum the tune to *Blessed Assurance*. It's a hymn of inspiration, exuding confidence. Blind author Fanny Crosby did not allow her impairment to limit her work and I shall not let tiredness impair mine. At some point, though I'm not sure when, I stopped humming and started singing.

When I get up from my desk, Richard turns his head. "Don't stop, please."

Day shift arrives and though I'm tired, and my bones are heavy, it doesn't feel like five minutes since I took up my duties. I stifle a yawn, hoping no one catches me. The sun is high in the sky when I leave the hospital, and a chill hangs in the air. Beneath my cape, I rub my arms, warming them as I stroll without direction, lost in my musings. Losing fifty nurses will have huge consequences.

"Where are ye goin'?" Morag asks as she falls into step at my side.

"I'm not sure, somewhere quiet. My head is going round."

"Ah'm nae sure that's a good idea. Thinkin' is dangerous."

"You're right," I say with a tight smile. "But I can't sleep, so I thought I'd find a quiet spot and sit for a while."

In the distance, a bomb goes off, and the sound of gunfire erupts. "Ye're nae in the right place tae find any type o' peace 'n' quiet."

"No, but if I go back, I'll toss and turn, so I might as well find the quietest spot I can."

Morag yawns, showing off her tonsils. "Do ye want me tae come with ye?"

"No. Go get something to eat and sleep. Pearl's waiting at the Sisters' Mess, with Adah and Effie."

Her hand covers her mouth, and she yawns again. "Ye ken, if ye'd grown up with brothers as noisy 'n' frustratin' as mine, then ye'd be able tae kip thro' anythin'."

"You make my brothers sound perfect, Morag, and they're not. Go on, I'll catch you up."

"Make sure ye do," she says, walking off to find food and her bed.

An icy breeze tickles my face as I walk. Morag is right, finding a quiet spot for contemplation isn't easy. Near the Nissen huts is a line of trees and I make my way over. Finding my make-do patch, I sit, tucking my legs into my chest and resting my head on my knees. When I'm nervous, upset, or melancholy, I sing—hm, scrap that, I sing no matter how I'm feeling. A song has the power to transport me to another place. Music is emotional, playing at the heartstrings and mind, that's why I enjoy it. The lyrics from I'll fly Away melt tension from my shoulders, and my mind finds a new, peaceful focus.

"Now then, Songbird, shouldn't you be getting some sleep?"

Joe smiles down at me, casting a shadow. Tiny lines appear at the corners of his eyes as he squints against the sun's glare. The wind tickles the ends of his hair, sending it falling over his face. With my hand covering my eyes, I smile up at him.

"Is there room for two down there?"

You could fit a small army where I'm sitting. "It's a tight squeeze, but I'm sure I can make room."

He chuckles, lowering his lanky frame; our knees touch as he gets comfortable. Even sitting, Joe's frame dwarfs mine. When I first met him, I remember thinking he looked like someone had put him on a rack, stretching out his limbs. Joe has no girth, just height.

"So, what's keeping you awake?"

The question sets my head spinning again. Absently, I tuck a loose strand of auburn hair behind my ear, letting out a long sigh. "They're sending fifty of the younger sisters back to the United Kingdom."

"And …" he prompts.

"Somewhere out there, my brothers are fighting. I've no clue where they are, or if they're alive. Being busy normally prevents me from overthinking, but now, with fifty nurses going home and the enemy advancing, I can't stop worrying about them. Then there's Jane Anne and Aunt Sarah Rebeca back in London."

Joe sits in silence, giving me space to make sense of my jumbled thoughts. Fidgety, I turn, gazing over at him. "Do you think I did the right thing coming here and leaving my mother and aunt?"

While I've made the right decision as a nurse, I need reassurance it was the right decision as a daughter.

Joe shrugs. "Remember when we got here and saw the tents? When the first soldiers arrived, along with the air raids, I kept reminding myself, despite my fear, this was why I'd offered my services. To help heal the injured. What we do, it makes a difference. That's what makes any conflict we've left behind worthwhile."

My head falls onto his shoulder, absorbing the comfort his presence offers. "You always make sense."

He twists a blade of grass between his fingers. "Life is fragile, but it is also supple. It allows us to make vast changes, and unpopular decisions, benefiting the many, rather than the one."

"I hope you're right. With Germany's threat increasing, there's no certainty. That's what worries me. What if I'm too late to make things up with Jane Anne?"

"That's war. And life. There is no guarantee in either. You've never regretted becoming a nurse, have you?"

I shake my head.

"Even though you knew your mother didn't approve?"

"No, never."

"Then you need to accept your decision to join the TANS and stop giving yourself a hard time."

In the distance Pearl giggles, and an answering male laugh follows. My lips twist, forming a smile, and I lift my head off Joe's shoulder, gazing in her direction. "Pearl sounds happy. I envy that."

The grass falls from Joe's fingers. "We all blow off steam in different ways, I suppose. That said, she'll get herself in trouble one day. Matron will have her head on a platter if she finds out what she's up to."

I shrug. "Jim is Pearl's way of coping. I envy her determination to live in the moment."

"Hm …" Joe stands up, brushing off his trousers. "I'd best get back to the 18th. Go get something to eat, then sleep." He reaches down, and I grab his hands, letting him pull me up. With his hands on my shoulders, he steers me toward the Sisters' Mess. "Go on, go get yourself some breakfast, doctor's orders."

I smile at him, raising the skirt of my uniform and curtsying. "Yes, doctor."

He laughs, shaking his head as he walks back to the 18th.

Morag appears at my side as I walk towards the Sisters' Mess, making me jump.

She rubs her stomach. "Mah stomach is keepin' me awake."

"Didn't you eat before you went to bed?"

"Ah just had a snack. Turns out ah was tae tired tae eat. Imagine that, eh."

I thread my arm through Morag's. "We can't have that."

"Ye 'n' Joe look cosy."

"Oh, Morag, do you ever miss anything?"

"Nae with these eyes 'n' ears. Ma says ah should have been born a bloodhound."

"As you're aware, I'm not one to argue, not with your mum, anyway."

She frowns, before pulling on my arm, grinning. "Hm … nice try, but ah'm nae that easy tae distract. C'mon, spit it oot, is love blossomin' with Joe?"

I shake my head. "You're relentless."

Morag flashes me an eager smile.

"Sorry to disappoint, but we were just talking."

"Yer made for each other. Even though ah've said it a thousand times, ye've still tae listen. Ah blame the cloth between yer ears 'n' the fact ye love listenin' tae mah bonnie voice."

She cups her hands around her mouth, pinning my arm to her side. "Joe likes ye, Lillian Elizabeth Nutman ... a lot."

My cheeks burn and I place my hand over Morag's mouth. "Shh ... Matron will have my guts for garters if she hears I'm courting. Not that I am."

"It dinnae bother Pearl."

"Not much bothers Pearl. Even if it does, she wouldn't let on. Part of me envies that about her."

Morag places a finger against her lips. "Shh ... she'll hear ye 'n' we'll never hear the end o' it."

We walk into the Sisters' Mess laughing. At the entrance, the fifty nurses selected to return to the United Kingdom congregate, waiting for transport. We wish them a safe journey as we pass. For those of us left, the future remains precarious. Still, I don't envy them. It's difficult going home when there is vital work to be done in France. But orders are orders and there is no disobeying them.

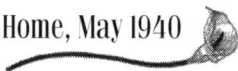

Dear Jane Anne,

I am exhausted. There is no other way to describe it. The last bit of news we receive is that the Germans have released the full might of their Luftwaffe on the towns and airfields. Across Belgium, Holland, and Northern France they drop their bombs. This information came from Pearl, who received it from Jim. How am I supposed to feel? Sad? Angry? Defeated? The answer is none of those. A patient needs a focused nurse. Not one flagging with fear.

The other day, when I started my shift, a soldier kept crying, "It's a red cape … a red cape … I'm safe … it's a red cape." I held him in my arms until his body stilled. Before that moment, I never realised how important our uniform is to a soldier. It is a symbol of hope and safety. A significance I have taken for granted and never shall again. Each day, we watch the refugees as they walk south. They are in such poor state of health and dress, with dirty skin and stained clothing. Children walk at their parents' sides, their feet dragging across the ground, while their younger siblings cry or sleep in their parents' arms. Whatever they own they carry with them. It is such a pitiful sight.

Where are they heading? And what will they do once they reach their destination? The refugee numbers swell as the

Germans increase their attack. In one form or another, we are all suffering the effect of the Luftwaffe.

Though I am stationed at the 18th British General Hospital, I hope I will travel closer to the battlefield. Under current rules, nurses may not venture further than the Casualty Clearing Stations, though as war progresses, this may change.

I appreciate we parted on a sour note, but I am contributing to the war efforts. Soldiers and civilians enter the hospital daily. Without nurses to assist the doctors, most would perish before medical help is available. It has taken time for me to make peace with my decision to leave London, abandoning you and Aunt Sarah Rebeca, but I have found it.

I hope you are remaining safe, and that my brothers visited while on leave (location permitting), or perhaps you've received a letter. London seems a safe place, for now, with no news of bombings. It also makes my being here better.

Oh, I almost forgot to say, I'm falling for Joe.

Lillian Elizabeth

10

 May 1940, 18th BGH, France

With the fifty nurses on their way home, we prepare the hospital for evacuation. If I thought the 18th was busy before, it's nothing compared to what we are now experiencing. Double shifts become the normal pattern. No sooner do we fall into our beds than we are back on duty. With four hours sleep, I walk into the 18th. The operating theatre is working through the night, to ready the three hundred casualties admitted during the day shift. On the doctor's release, those deemed in a fit state to travel leave the ward. Their beds fill with the next wave.

Pen in hand, I start my reports. Pearl stops at my desk. "Orders are in. We leave tomorrow."

I glance up, my pen hovering above the paper. "What about those still being operated on?"

She shrugs. "They've not said."

"I don't like it. We can't abandon them."

"The powers that be don't care if we like it," Pearl says, pointing at the canvas roof.

My lips press together.

Joe looks tired as he walks to a soldier Morag is treating. The patient is complaining of headaches. His left arm is in a sling and his right hand massages his temple. Shrapnel has ripped away half his face. While his injuries look terrifying, they aren't life-threatening. Unlike the patient next to him, who lost both his legs, he will walk out of here come tomorrow. Time and casualty numbers add to the stress. There is no easy way to evacuate a hospital. Those who can walk of their own accord will leave first. Immobile patients and those requiring help will follow the first wave. The orderlies and an officer are to assist any remaining patients. Outrage is rife amongst us— nurses don't up and leave their patients. It goes against all our training. We are abandoning our stations. But unlike last time, there is no disobeying this order.

My uniform sticks to my sweating skin and strands of hair hang down my face. I can't remember the last time I ate. My muscles scream for rest, but I plough on, helping patients from their beds. Groans of pain line the air as the patients move. Their feet drag on the ground. Bodies collide as they sway. It is a depressing sight. They should be resting, their bodies allowed to heal. Yet we have no choice but to ask them to endure more discomfort. As a place of hope, the 18th is falling short in its care.

Before I leave, I stop, turning to glance across the ward. Beds sit vacant, their sheets dishevelled. Cigarette smoke trails in wisps from ashtrays. Other than the patient Joe and Morag are treating, only two remain on the ward. These patients lay recuperating after surgery, their unconscious forms covered with a blanket. It is harrowing to think that there will be no nurse to comfort them when they wake. The 18th is a pitiful sight, offering nothing but desolation. Desertion looks and feels like this. My hands rub at my arms. I walk over to an empty bed, picking up a blanket from the floor. At the far end of the hospital, Morag nods as Joe leaves instructions for the patient. He smiles at me as he makes his way between the vacant cots.

"Don't stay too long, you still need to get some rest before we leave," he says.

"I won't, I promise."

He nods, leaving the hospital. It's hard to shake off the feeling of betrayal that hovers over the 18th. Our job isn't to question or stand as judge over our orders, but to obey. Despite the unsettling emotions gathering in my stomach, there is nothing I can do but accept the issued command. There is no song to brighten my flagging mood. No soft hum to restore order to my mind. Snared within its constant loop of doom, it's left to whir unsatiated. Morag falls into step next to me and we leave the hospital in the hands of the orderlies and the remaining officer.

Pearl waves us over as we exit. "Come on, we haven't got all day. Tomorrow is round the corner and transport is due early morning."

"It is tomorrow," I sigh.

"Never mind the semantics. If we're lucky we'll get a couple of hours sleep."

Morag's brow wrinkles in annoyance. "Ah dinnae like it."

"Neither do I, but what can we do? Orders are orders, and with transport due there's nothing else but to accept what's happening," I say.

"We do what we're told. That's all there is to it."

Morag sends Pearl a sharp stare. "Since when do ye follow orders tae the letter?"

"Since Jim said the Germans are winning the fight here."

The skin along my jaw pinches, and a cold thread of unease slides over my flesh, leaving goosebumps in its wake. "What else did Jim say?"

"Nothing."

Morag stops, hands on her hips. "What do ye mean nothin'? Hoo ken he say somethin' like that 'n' then … nothin'"

Pearl smiles. "We got busy with other things."

"One day, Pearl Jones, ye're goin' tae find yerself in trouble. Ah'm nae just talkin' aboot what Matron will do tae ye either." Morag wags a finger in Pearl's face.

Pearl waves off her concerns. "You sound like Lilly's mother."

"Jane Anne?" I frown, lost with how my mother became involved in this discussion.

"She means 'cause ah used her full name," Morag offers.

"In that case, Pearl, you should be grateful you've got no middle name, or names. It drags out the scolding."

Pearl huffs and we walk the rest of the way in silence.

Morag's feet stutter to a stop, pointing over at the refugees as they walk past the entrance of the field. "What the heck … Where do ye suppose they're goin'?"

Dirt stains their skin and clothes, and tiredness bows their spines as they carry their few belongings.

Pearl frowns. "Why are they heading back north? They've been heading south all this time."

We stand mesmerised as we try to work out what they're up to.

"Is it a sign?" Morag asks.

I grimace. "A sign?"

"You're not a parrot, Lilly."

"Well, I don't like it. Morag's right. Those refugees changing direction is a sign, and not a good one."

Pearl's face loses some of its colour. "You're all doom and gloom, Lilly. I'm sure the evacuation of the hospital has got to you."

"No, it's more than the evacuation. I'm telling you something is going on and they're proof of it," I say, shaking my head, my gaze glued on the refugees.

A shadow of frustration clouds Pearl's face. "Just stop it, Lilly, you know I don't like uncertainty. It plays havoc with my love life."

"Be thankful ye've got one," Morag says.

Pearl links her arms through mine and Morag's. "You could have a love life if you wanted one. Even with that wild hair of yours."

Morag digs her elbow into Pearl's side. "Leave mah locks oot o' it."

"Ouch!"

"Will you keep in touch with Jim?" I ask Pearl.

"I'm not the letter-writing type, and wishful longing isn't me either."

Morag yawns, her hand covering her mouth. "C'mon, there's packin' tae do. T'would be good tae have a kip afore we leave. Ah'm wiped oot."

11

 May 1940, 18th BGH, France

*M*orag is already stirring as I swing my legs over the bed. As I stretch my arms above my head, Pearl turns over, presenting us with her back.

Morag pokes her. "C'mon, sunshine, this is na time tae be lazy."

Pearl mutters something unintelligible.

Eyebrows raising, Morag looks across at me. "What did she say?"

A mischievous smile curves my lips, and I fold my arms. "I don't know, but I'm betting it wasn't polite."

Morag glances down at Pearl. "Do ah need tae wash her mouth oot with soapy water?"

Pearl peels the bedsheet back. "Try it and I'll bite you."

"Brave words comin' from an only child that dinnae ken hoo tae fight dirty. If ye think words are goin' tae scare me yer wrong. Ah've got brothers, remember," Morag says, a determined glint in her eyes.

Without concern, Pearl snuggles under the blanket. "Yeah, and I've learnt how to fight dirty, despite being an only child. Now bugger off and let me sleep."

Morag grins and I shake my head as she mouths out her plan in silent communication. It's too much to resist and I nod. Together we fall onto Pearl, pulling at the blanket. Our limbs, hair, and pillows fly as we grab her squirming body. Her legs kick out at us, and she clings to the bedding. We tumble to the floor in a fit of giggles as Adah walks in.

"Quick, Matron's on the warpath."

"Ahh!" Morag screams, rubbing her arm. "Pearl nipped me."

"And here I thought it was Matron's impending visit," I say.

"Ouch! Stop nippin' me!"

"Then get off me."

"Stop whingin', woman, ah'm movin'."

Adah walks out, shaking her head, a smile touching her lips. We leap into action, throwing on our uniforms. Within minutes, we exit our sleeping quarters as respectable QAs. Outside, our transport is nowhere to be seen.

Effie comes rushing up to us, her face flushed. "There's been a problem with our transport."

Pearl's kit bag hits the ground. Stony faced, she stares at me and Morag. "I can't believe you got me out of bed so I can stand looking at … nothing."

"Ye're nae lookin' at nothin', Pearl, see …" Morag sweeps her hand, taking in the Sisters' Mess and tents. "Over there are the Nissen huts 'n' …"

Pearl nudges Effie's arm as she giggles. "No, don't laugh at her, she's not funny."

The missing transport sends a sliver of panic creeping over my flesh. I try not to think about the refugees' change in direction. "What will happen if the transport doesn't arrive?" I ask. A heavy lump has taken up residence in my stomach and is causing it to cramp. Agitation does that to me.

"Let's go to the hospital and see if there's anything we can do," Adah says, coming up behind us. "There's no point in dallying here."

Not waiting for us to respond, she turns, making her way over to the 18th.

"I'd rather be in bed," Pearl grumbles as we follow.

When we enter, the orderlies are running around the place like blue-bottomed flies. A sense of panic fills the 18th. My unease over the missing transport melts as instinct takes over, and I stride across the ward, leaving my kit bag at the entrance.

"What the heck is going on?" Pearl asks, her mouth dropping open.

"Laird kens," Morag hisses.

Within a few minutes, we bring order back to the 18th as we see to the few remaining patients. The orderlies know more than us about what's going on, though they rarely say anything. Today is different.

"The Germans have us surrounded," Danny Robson says, in a low, harassed voice as I tend to one of the patients.

Danny's dark brown hair flops about his face, which has lost its normal bronzed colouring. Freckles line his nose, and his dimples have disappeared. At nineteen, Danny is facing mortality, and he's crumbling under its weight. Corporal Wayne Jetton glances up from beneath the bandage I've finished wrapping around his head. His body shakes. I send Danny a sharp stare as I lay a hand on Wayne's shoulder.

"That's enough of such talk, we will be just fine. Not even the Germans will want to face Matron; she's already annoyed because of delays in transportation. Goodness knows what she will do to them if they arrive before we leave. It's not looking good for them."

Wayne's chest rumbles as he laughs and the panic lacing the surrounding atmosphere ebbs. Despite my flippant words, my heart, for a fraction of a second, stops beating, and my mouth becomes dry. Suddenly, the refugees' change in direction makes sense. "Right, Wayne, you're all patched up, and this time leave the bandage alone," I say, picking up the spoiled dressing.

"Sorry, Sister, my forehead was itching."

"Next time it itches you think of what Matron will do to you and your fingers."

He pulls a face but doesn't argue.

By 11 a.m., all operations have ceased and the 18th is empty of patients. Beds stand as if waiting for new arrivals, reminding me of when we first arrived. Back in April, there had been a bubble of excitement and awe— adventure waiting in the wings. Now, the hospital sits still, its usefulness expiring, along with our own.

When I was six, we lived along the coast at Kings Lynn for a brief time. At the edges of the sand, near the dunes, were three wooden huts: abandoned holiday homes. The wooden structures had rotted away in places and the windows were broken. Despair hung about them. As much as I tried, I couldn't envision anyone living there but the devil himself. It's strange how the wooden structures affected me. Some of my foreboding was the by-product of my brother, John Edward, who, encouraged by Arthur James, liked to tell ghost stories. His stories were always gruesome and very bloody. Today, the 18th reminds me of those wooden buildings, that waited and waited for the sea to gather enough strength to wash them away, releasing them from their misery.

With nothing left for me to do at the hospital, I join Pearl and Morag as they stand at its entrance. In silence, we make our way to the Nissen huts. Eight sisters stand outside, their faces grim and their clothes dishevelled. Adah stands between two of the sisters, talking to them. The eight nurses are in their early-to-mid-twenties. Adah's head bobs as she listens. Her arms wrap around her chest, holding up her ample bosom, as her fingers tap her elbows. Effie walks alongside Danny, whose dimples are back on display. Adah's brows raise and Effie scurries over, joining in the conversation. Curiosity, or just plain nosiness, has me, Morag, and Pearl heading their way.

"Their Commanding Officer pushed them into an ambulance last night, instructing their driver not to stop, no matter what," Adah explains when we reach her. "When the ambulance containing their luggage stopped for the sentry, the Germans detained it. Fortunately, their driver didn't do the same. A brave soul: his actions saved their lives."

"Crikey …" Morag's voice trails off as we look at the nurses.

"Helen" — Effie points at the nurse on the far right, her black hair in disarray — "says they left at one a.m. and, warned not to go via Abbeville, they travelled along minor roads to Montreuil."

Pearl gasps. "It must have been awful for them."

Effie is more of a gossip than her sister, and we get all the details. "Annemarie said" — she points at the nurse standing on Adah's right — "that the roads were littered with the dead and wounded. Most of them were civilians. Their driver said he suspected the other ambulance stopped because he probably thought the tanks and guns were French surrenders. When they reached Montreuil, they met up with some officers escaping from the No 13 Casualty Clearing Station. That's when they came here."

Pearl looks down at her kit bag. "That's it, this bugger is staying with me. I'm not prepared to lose it to poor judgement and some Nazi."

With no warning, the alarm sounds, signalling an air raid. Adah and Effie grab the nurses and we run for the trenches to wait it out. Danny's words haunt me, "The Germans have us surrounded."

In the distance, great plumes of dirt stream into sky and the sound of battle echoes around us. Time slows down, grinding to a horrible halt as we wait for the attack to be over.

BANG …

BOOM …

RAT-A-TAT-TAT …

Air raids can last for hours, sometimes days, before the all-clear. It appears we won't be leaving here soon, even if our transport arrives. Morning gives way to the afternoon and the clouds darken, threatening rain. BOOM … Earth splatters between the trees.

"That's close," I whisper.

"Will you stop patting my arm, I'm not a dog, Morag," Pearl snaps, her nerves showing.

"Look …"

Colonel Bridgewater, refusing to take shelter, paces from trench to trench, using the trees as cover. Soon after he's visited the third trench, two orderlies run to the cook-house. Without a word, we watch them reappear with two large buckets. Like rabbits with a fox after their tails, they run over to our trench.

With shaking hands and erratic breathing, Danny sets his bucket down in front of us. "Here, Colonel, said to get this for you. Adrian!" Danny shouts above the sirens.

There is a scraping of boots as Adrian jumps into the trench, bringing another bucket. "I'm here, no need to shout."

We gape at them as they turn and run back over to the trench they'd vacated.

Her lips curving up, Adah looks inside the buckets. "I'm not sure how we're supposed to eat this. Anyone got a spoon?"

Inside one bucket is beef stew, and the other stewed rhubarb. "They're doin' this tae torture us, aren't they?" Morag's stomach lets out a groan as she rocks back against the trench.

"Colonel Bridgewater should have been clearer in his orders. Get the nurses something to eat and don't forget the cutlery," Pearl mimics Colonel, making us laugh.

"I don't think it's going to matter anyway," Effie says. "A dispatch rider is heading our way."

The dispatcher thunders towards us. "Your transport has arrived. You need to get in the ambulances immediately," he says, breath coming in huge huffs. "Colonel's orders. You're to take to the woods in small groups and make your way over to the ambulances at the Nissen huts."

Adah leans over. "Let's organise ourselves into groups of five. You take the first group, Lilly, with Morag, Pearl, Effie, and Annie. I'll go next with Isabel, Helen, Annemarie, and Jane once you hit the woods. Everyone alright with that?"

We nod our agreement.

"Lilly?' Adah places a hand on my arm as I ready myself to leave the safety of the trench. "Look after her."

"Don't worry, I'll make sure she makes it."

"Thank you."

Together we run for the trees, Pearl, Morag, and Annie in front, and Effie and me following behind. Dirt shoots up in front of us and I scream. Effie falls and I grab her hand, pulling her forward to the trees. My legs are shaking worse than jelly, but I don't stop, not until we reach the ambulances. With my hand against my chest, I take in a huge lungful of air. My hair pokes out from my tin hat and my kit bag falls to the ground as I steady my breathing. The sound of my heart fills my ears, above the drumming of the bombers. Effie is white as a sheet, and I grip her arm, following her gaze to the trees. A few minutes later, Adah and the others come racing towards us. Joe and a few of the other medical officers break through the clearing. My heart skips in relief as they make it to the waiting ambulances.

A smile on his lips, Joe catches his breath. "It seems our chariots await us."

"In that case, you'd best stop talking and get in," Pearl says.

A bomb lands and the ground trembles beneath our feet. Her brow creasing, Pearl glances towards the trenches.

"Don't worry, I'm sure Jim will make it," I say.

"I'll probably never see him again."

"Never say never, Pearl. You know what they say about men and buses."

Joe frowns. "What do they say about men and buses?"

Pearl sniffs, ignoring him.

His arms flap at his sides. "Why do nurses stick together?"

"Because we're sisters," I say, smiling at him.

He groans as we climb into the ambulance. "It's looking cramped in there. I'll get in the next one."

Before I get inside, I turn, reaching for his arm. "Take care, Joe."

"Don't worry, I'll be on the next bus," he says, smiling at me.

Pearl stabs a finger into my ribs. "This is the reason we don't tell them anything; they make fun of us."

Joe's laughter echoes as he steps away.

As soon as we're settled, the doors close and we leave for Boulogne. Refugees block the roads and the normal fifteen-minute journey takes forever. At 6 p.m. we enter Boulogne. The ambulance slows and the doors open. In relief, we grab our kit bags, glad that we've made it in one piece. With Colonel Timpson instructing Major Taylor-Bates to 'arrange' for our safe return to England, there is nothing we can do but wait. The noise of aircraft, bombs, and gunfire grate against our raw nerves. Boulogne has changed beyond recognition. Rubble replaces our headquarters and fires roar around us. French and Belgian refugees fill the town. A chill runs along my spine. Our gruelling schedule at the 18th has shielded us from what was happening elsewhere.

Pearl lowers her head onto my shoulder, and I snuggle deeper into Morag, keeping warm. I watch the ambulances as they arrive. Each time the doors open, I search for Joe. My heart skinks when he's not amongst them.

"See, ye kin stop worryin' aboot him noo," Morag says, patting my hand as Joe steps out from the arriving ambulance.

"Who said I was worrying?"

"Aye ..."

On seeing us, Joe walks over. Sadness leaks from him as he looks at the destruction.

"It's terrible, isn't it," I say.

He nods, unable to put into words what we are all feeling.

Pearl lifts her head from my shoulder, and Joe spins round. Colonel and Major Taylor-Bates run towards us.

"Come on! This way!" Colonel shouts as Major Taylor-Bates waves at us.

We jump to our feet, and with our legs moving like a racing horse, we follow Colonel and Major down the subway, onto the quay. Merchant ships wait and we run along the gangway onto the ships. As soon as we're onboard, the ship sets sail. My nerves rattle along with my bones. Above us, dive-bombers circle like vultures. With so many ships and small boats, crowding the water, the risk of the harbour becoming blocked increases with each new boat that arrives. A shudder goes through me, being trapped on the water becoming too real. With so many onboard, we huddle together. The constant drumming of aircraft overhead and the dropping of bombs eat away at our nerves. I've never felt so petrified. For the first time, I face the prospect of my death. Screams cut through the engine noise and water flies up. My fingers dig into Morag's arm as we steady ourselves on the rocking boat, holding onto our kit bags. The ship lurches, stealing my breath, and my stomach flips as it pulls away, negotiating our way through the fleet of bobbing boats.

"Look!" Morag screams, and I turn to see three of our RAF boys running for the gangway.

They're too late, they'll never make it onboard. Blood pumping through our veins, we watch them stumble to a stop, staring in disbelief. Dive-bombers swoop at them. With little to lose, they jump into the water. Behind them, a bomb explodes. Hands over our mouths, our breath catching in our throats, we wait for them to reappear. A head breaks the water's surface, then another, and another. Their arms reaching out, their legs kicking, they swim for our ship. Like spools, we bob on the waves, the ship's engine driving us on as the dive-bombers release their explosives. The RAF boys go unnoticed by the ship's captain as they fight against the current to reach us. I grab a life ring and throw it overboard, aiming it the best I can at the RAF boys. With the rope around my waist, I steady myself. Adah and Pearl follow my lead, and with Morag leaning over the ship, we await her command to pull.

Pearl nods at me, her hands shaking as she ties the rope around her waist. With it fastened, Adah signals to the waiting sisters. Their arms wrap around us, some grabbing the relaxed rope as we prepare ourselves. We're used to making split-second decisions, acting according to our training to preserve life. Joe and the other medical officers on board grab the rope, standing in front, shielding us from the waves as they hit the deck. Morag leans over the side of the ship, her fingers curling round the railing, water slapping her face. She doesn't move.

"Pull!" she screams, her right hand wafting behind her back. "Pull!"

We yank the rope, our hands moving along the cord. Morag reaches over the ship and in a beat she's joined by another four sisters. Working together, we pull the RAF boys on board. They land on deck and Joe pushes his way through, dropping to his knees, pumping water from their lungs.

"Do we have blankets?" Joe asks as the RAF coughs up water.

There's a scurrying and blankets arrive. A feeling of utter relief, joy, and pride washes over me as the men huddle into their blankets. A few nurses sit with them, lending their body heat. We saved them. Even the dive-bombers and sprays of water don't dampen our spirits. The three RAF are onboard, and we're heading home. Sometimes living in the moment is all that counts—this is one of those times.

There's a loud bang, and the ship in front of us explodes. In a plume of smoke, wood shoots into the air. Waves crash into us, soaking through our clothes, sending water like a tidal wave onto the deck. Pearl loses her balance, the water dragging her back to the sea. Her mouth opens in shock, her arms flying about her, her legs banging against the wooden floor. The noise of the bombs hides her screams as she slides towards the railings.

Morag dives for my feet as I throw myself at Pearl. My hand catches her ankle, and I pull her to me as Morag pins me to the deck. I squeeze Pearl against my chest as she screams. My ears ring, and I hold her tighter. Morag's breath tickles my ear from where she sits behind me, her hands on my shoulders. Joe walks over, his face white. Pearl sobs, into my neck, her arms draping across my shoulders, her body shaking. I hug her until the ship settles and her body quietens.

"It's alright, we're fine," I mouth at Joe.

He stares at me, nods, and sits near Morag.

"I-I t-thought I was a goner."

"Never, Pearl." I kiss the top of her head. "The world would be dull without you."

She raises her head, sending me a wobbly smile.

Morag leans forward. "Odin's glory, Pearl, ye tryin' tae gimme a heart attack."

Joe sits, his gaze locking onto the water, his arms resting on his knees as his fingers tremble.

BOOM …

In the distance, another ship suffers a direct hit. When the water settles, there's nothing but pieces of wood and body parts. Loaded with munitions, there was only one outcome. As nurses, we are used to blood and destruction, but this is different. There is nothing left to save. A crackle sounds, and a voice cuts through the air from the bridge. "No one is to go below deck, or smoke. We're loaded with weapons."

Morag gasps, her eyes fastening onto the wreckage floating along the sea. Stunned, I twist, glancing at her as I hold Pearl. Words won't take the memory of the ship away. Lives lost just when they think they'll make it home to their families. Silently, I pray my brothers are safe, and that Jane Anne and Aunt Sarah Rebeca remain untouched by the horrors that war subjects us to. Dread holds me in place, the news of our cargo sucking at the remnants of my earlier joy and bravado. Even the normal threat of Matron seems of little value. Wet and cold, all we can do is huddle together and be grateful for our lives. Above us, the Luftwaffe continue to swoop, dropping their bombs at the rescue ships. We are nothing more than targets, floating on the surface of the water, waiting for the aptly named Luftwaffe (Air Weapon) to release its bombs.

Pearl shivers and I tighten my grip. "We've made it this far; we'll make it home."

"You think?"

"I do," I say, nodding.

Snot rattles round her nose as she blows into her handkerchief. "You're always nice, Lilly. No matter what I say and do, you never chastise me. I know what awful names the others call me. Maybe it's true, but you know, Lilly, I just don't care. Mum died when I was seven. After four miscarriages, she gave birth to my brother. He was stillborn."

She raises her head, and our gazes meet. "Mum died giving birth to a baby that never got to draw one breath. She left Dad broken and unable to look at me. Before Mum died, Dad would tell me how much I looked like her. There was so much pride and happiness in the way he'd gaze at me. After, he couldn't bear to be in the same room as me. I was a reminder of everything he'd lost. I made a promise to myself from that day, I was going to make sure I lived each day to the full. So yeah, I have male friends. I laugh with them and let them touch me. But you know what? At least when God calls, I'll know I put everything I had into living. I'm not cruel, and I never pick on anybody who can't take a joke.

"Do you know how my dad greets each day? With his lips wrapped around the neck of a bottle. Tears running down his face as he waits for oblivion to take him. He's never gotten over Mum's death. Love kills you, Lilly, just like grief. But only if you let it. I don't want to be like my dad, wishing that death would take me because it's easier than living."

Pearl lowers her head, resting it against my arm. I kiss her temple, stroking back her hair. She's not expecting me to answer, so I don't. Instead, I let her talk until there is nothing left to say.

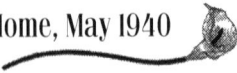

Dear Jane Anne,

Our time at the 18th British General Hospital has ended. We flee from France like rats whose tunnels fill with water. Forced into the light, where danger waits. I sit on a small boat, with the other nurses and medical officers. Weapons fill its belly and dive-bombers swirl overhead, like hungry seagulls, making a fearful cry as they swoop. The Luftwaffe have taken a neighbouring ship. There is no one left to save, just pieces of driftwood and red-tinted water. As we travel, the dive-bombers leave us, intent on destroying the ships still making their way from the harbour. Pearl has fallen asleep at my side. Her breathing is even. Dirt lines her face, and her arm drapes over my knees. Her head on my lap, I use her back to write to you.

When this war is over, I wonder what the aftermath will bring. Will its rage live on? After all, isn't that why we find ourselves at war again? Rage never dampens, it simmers, ready to strike. That's what has happened here. Germany never accepted its defeat in 1918. The first war tarnishes our lives, until the transformation is irreversible. This thought scares me, more than the dive-bombers.

Night is falling and I can no longer see what I am writing. The water is calmer. On deck, some sleep while others stare out at the sea, lost in thought. Joe sits near Morag. He hasn't moved since I stopped Pearl from sliding off the boat. If it wasn't for Morag, Pearl and I would have gone overboard to our watery graves. His hands have stopped trembling, and his breathing is even. I wonder, as he stares into the coming darkness, what he's thinking. So contained within himself, an invisible door has closed, protecting him, and imprisoning him inside.

England beckons us back to her bosom, and our next chapter will begin. I'm not sure what orders I will receive when I get back, but I am determined to fix our broken relationship. Am I welcome at home? A sickening feeling erupts, as I write that question. "Am I welcome at home?" I can't build a bridge if I don't try. Therefore, I shall trust in my faith, and family, and pray that when I arrive in London, we shall make more of an effort to be nicer and more considerate to each other. God, if you are listening, please help me, I'm going to need your strength and wisdom.

Lillian Elizabeth

12

 May 1940, Dover, England

*O*ur ship pulls into Dover at 9 p.m. Pearl stirs, stretching her arms above her head and yawning. Her jaws snap together as she looks over her shoulder at me. "I can't wait to brush my teeth; there's a nasty taste in my mouth and I bet my breath stinks."

Her fingers rake though her lifeless hair, and I take them in mine. "You're beautiful, and your breath smells no different from ours."

She snorts.

Morag lifts her head from my shoulder. "What's happenin'?"

"We've arrived in Dover," I say.

The space near Morag is empty. Joe left during the night. A quick survey provides no hint of his whereabouts. I don't remember falling asleep, but I must have. Our bodies are stiff from our journey. We move, stretching our limbs, preparing to leave the ship. Pearl looks beat, her movements sluggish. Mascara sits on top of the dark circles beneath her eyes. Her blonde hair sticks to her pale face, and dirt lines her cheeks and forehead. It's as well there isn't a mirror; she would scream if she saw herself. The thought makes me smile and I chuckle under my breath—I dread to think how I look.

Mud coats my skin, and my clothes are wrinkled and stained. Most of my hair has escaped its binding and hangs at my shoulders. The auburn strands are lifeless, and that's precisely how my feet and legs feel. We disembark, our kit bags over our shoulders, climbing into the waiting transport. As the vehicles fill, they leave, heading along the quayside. Too tired to talk, we shuffle forward until it's our turn to clamber on board. Adah and Effie make it in the same vehicle as me, Pearl, and Morag. Its engine revs and it moves forward a short distance before shuddering to a stop. The doors open and we're ushered like sheep inside a small shed.

Her eyebrows raising, Pearl's gaze sweeps the area as we queue to enter. "Why aren't we going to the Lord Warden Hotel?"

My teeth nibble at my bottom lip. "I don't know, they're not saying."

"Ah dinnae like this," Morag huffs, her head swivelling as her eyes scan the dark.

Inside, the shed is void of furniture. Those near a wall lean against it for support. Dread is an ugly word, but it falls over us, leaving us blinking into the semi-darkness. The door slams as the last nurse enters, and with a thud, a lock slides in place. Confined within the semi-lit wooden structure, we have no option but to wait. My muscles still ache from the cramped conditions of the ship, so I try to make myself comfortable. This journey doesn't want to end its torture. Relief dissolves before it has the chance to develop into joy. Confusion and doubt are too familiar. The door opens and more step inside.

Footsteps sound behind me, and I turn to see Joe. "Here," he says, dropping his kit bag to the floor, "we might as well make ourselves comfortable."

He tugs my arm and I place my kit bag next to his. Morag, Pearl, Effie, and Adah follow suit, using their bags as stools. Joe's breath tickles the side of my head, the warmth of his body seeping through my clothing. As time passes, I lower my head onto his knees, and his fingers move the stray hair from my face.

"What's going on?" Pearl asks from my right.

"I don't know," I mutter, too weary to lift my head.

The door opens and more enter; we shuffle, giving them room. There is a rustling of fabric as people move, and low voices converse. Some huff, groan, and swear under their breaths as we wait for the news to reach us.

Pearl nudges my arm. "Well?"

"We're to wait here until they can give us the all-clear," Adah says, her voice carrying a depressing tone.

I long for a bath, clean clothes, and a bed. My stomach can't stop growling and my eyelids want to close as my tear ducts release water, flooding my eyes.

Joe's hands still as they run through my hair. "All-clear?"

Pearl expels a long-laboured breath. "What do you mean 'the all-clear'?"

"There's an air raid."

Silence meets Adah's words as we tilt back our heads towards the roof. When we left the boat, the sky was overcast, darkness settling in. There was no sound of bombs or aircraft. No lights from fires caused by an aerial attack. With no visible signs of an air aid, it's hard to make sense of our situation.

Effie's brow wrinkles. "An air raid? But it's so quiet."

"Well, that's what they've said. We can disagree, but it won't change things," Adah says, her voice clipped.

On a whisper of a groan, Pearl snuggles into me. I close my eyes, lowering my head back onto Joe's knees. His fingers rake through my hair. The hands on the clock turn in slow motion and the hours drip away. At 1 a.m., the all-clear arrives on the creaking of hinges. Outside, our transport waits to take us to the Lord Warden Hotel. With my back bent like a willow branch, I try to straighten it. My bones click as I release the pressure. Our shoes drag over concrete, and like an army of sleep-deprived ghouls we tumble towards the vehicles.

Bedraggled, tired and hungry, we congregate in the large foyer at the Lord Warden Hotel. Samuel Beazley designed the hotel in 1851, to impress wealthy cross-Channel travellers. In 1896, Gordon Hotels took over the running of the Lord Warden, extending and refurbing it. The eighty sleeping apartments increased to one hundred and ten, offering plenty of room to house the battle-worn. Inside the hotel, the high ceiling causes an acoustic effect. Our voices echo around the room, bouncing from the ceiling and vibrating off the walls. With the military commandeering the hotel, the Lord Warden takes on a new role, housing weary troops, politicians, journalists, and medical staff.

"Did you know that Napoleon III and his wife, Empress Eugenie, reunited here during his exile to England in 1871? Don't you think it's romantic?" Effie gushes, her gaze gooey.

Pearl snorts. "Love's overrated. Romance is about the first rush of passion, not forever."

"There speaks the voice of experience," someone says, sniggering, Pearl's back stiffens in response.

"Don't pay them any attention," I say, touching her arm.

Pearl shrugs. "I never do. They're just uptight busybodies that haven't had a day's fun in their lives. Their only enjoyment is humiliating others. Petty minded, that's what they are."

From behind, someone snorts. "That told you, Miss Petty Minded."

There's a sharp "Humph" then nothing.

Morag's cheeks are pink with the same mushy expression as Effie's as she places her hand on her chest. "Well, ah think it's romantic."

Effie beams. "Thanks, Morag."

Adah shakes her head at her sister. In my young, idealistic heart, Adah spending her life as a spinster makes me sad—not that she needs a man to make her happy. The Great War was insightful in establishing how important resilient and strong women are. We are no longer content to be pushed back into the kitchen and told to raise children. Our social standing is progressing. Men need to pay attention.

"Stop being mushy, Morag, or Effie will drone on."

"Be nice, Pearl. Yer always grumpy aboot romance. Ye need tae lighten up. Who kens, ye might like it if ye try it." From behind her, Morag drops her chin on Pearl's shoulder.

Shock shadows Pearl's face and she shrugs off Morag's head. "I'm always nice."

"Aye, in a cuttin' sort o' way."

"Your wild hair is blocking your ears again. You can't hear the care and love I put into every word I speak."

Morag swipes at her, giggling. "Ye daft bat."

"Hey! Mind the hair," Pearl screams, shoving Morag away.

"That's the least o' yer worries. Wait till ye see yer reflection. Sister, ye are goin' tae scream."

Pearl turns to me, horrified. "Is it that bad?"

I sigh. "We all look that bad."

She tugs at her hair, gasping. "Great! Just great. Like things aren't bad enough."

The tension in my shoulders ease as we joke with one another.

"Food!" someone shouts, and our stomachs growl.

"Ah'm dribblin' already," Morag says, hand on her stomach.

Pearl tugs her arm out from Morag's. "Don't pull at me, there'll be plenty. You don't need to be first."

"I'm sensing desperation, I'd go with it, Pearl, it's for the best," I say, allowing Morag to steer us towards the open door.

13

May 1940, Dover, England

In the morning we're back on the road, travelling for London. Joe remains at the Lord Warden to wait for further orders. There isn't time to catch him before I leave, and I feel like I'm deserting him. If—it's such a terrible word—we're lucky, we'll meet again. The carriage rocks as the train travels along the tracks, its speed turning the countryside into a blur. Colours merge as we move. A few months after departing England for France, we are back. A few months can span a lifetime. How has London fared since I left it in January?

Winter has given way to spring. My favourite season. There is something about spring that renews my inner self. A freshness threads through the light breeze, and the promise of a better tomorrow whispers through the wind. Birds fill the day with song, and intoxicating fragrances fill the air—brighter days, and life, that's spring. The train comes to a stop on a cloud of steam, and we stand, grabbing our kit bags. Today I say goodbye to my friends and begin reducing the rift between me and Jane Anne. Bridges made from the overture of understanding, reuniting mother and daughter—or so I hope.

Principal Matron from the War Office waits for us as we arrive at Kings Cross Station. We congregate on the platform, away from the train and boarding passengers, as she dismisses us, sending us home to wait for further instructions. Morag hugs me, Pearl, and Effie before she picks up her kit bag and makes her way to her platform. With a gloved hand, she wipes away her tears. "Stay safe," she says, her voice sounding hollow.

Pearl sniffs. "I'm going to miss her."

"Me too," I say, watching Morag disappear into the crowd.

Effie's feet shuffle as she waits for Adah to say her goodbyes. "It's so strange, leaving everyone behind."

"Come on, come on … our train is due in ten minutes," Adah shouts as she walks over, waving at Effie.

She rolls her eyes. "I was waiting for you."

"Well, I'm here now. Take care, you two." Adah gives us a quick hug, turns and, grabbing Effie's free hand, runs across the platform to catch the train.

Pearl and I stare after them.

"So, I guess this is it, until the next time," Pearl says, her voice solemn.

Until next time … Tears run down our faces as we say goodbye. With Morag, Adah, and Effie already on their way home, and now Pearl, I'm soon left at the station on my own. Home—where exactly is that? Jane Anne's face appears in my head—bridges, I remind myself. The journey to central London is short. With no time to prepare myself, I'm standing looking at the blue-painted door of my childhood home. Nervous, I debate if I should knock or walk inside or go to Daisy's aunt and uncle's. Bridges, however much I'd like to delay the inevitable, don't build themselves.

Squaring my shoulders, I prepare for battle. Jane Anne has never been consistent in her approach. Yes, she's one for dramatics, but her unpredictable nature is the most unsettling quality about her. Big breath in … big breath out … and I'm as ready as I'm going to be to build those damn bridges.

The hinges creak and sunlight filters over the Victorian tiles. On a deep inhale, the familiar scent of home fills my senses. A clattering comes from the back of the house, and I close the door, walking to the back room. Jane Anne steps from the kitchen, a coal bucket in her right hand. Her wide-leg grey trousers swing about her ankles and a red scarf secures her styled hair. Though her painted face remains flawless, fatigue dims the light in her eyes. The coal bucket clatters to the wooden floor where she stands, and she wipes her brow with the sleeve of her shirt.

"So, you're back."

My words stick in my throat, and I nod.

"Good."

Unsure what 'good' means, I hover in the doorway between the hall and back room.

"Well, don't just stand there, put your things down and put the kettle on. I haven't had a drink since I got up this morning."

Jane Anne's words kick-start my brain, and leaning my bag against the wall, I stride to the kitchen. My mother stands by Trevor Henry's chair, the coal bucket at her feet, refusing to step out of my way.

"It's good to have you home."

She picks up the bucket and walks over to the fire. With my jaw hanging open in surprise, I stand motionless, staring at her. Is she pleased to see me? Or the person who cleaned out the fires and helped around the house?

"Well, don't stand there looking like a fly trap, that kettle won't boil itself."

I turn, entering the kitchen. Shovel in hand, she empties the ashes from the grate. She's always hated clearing out the fire. Soot gets under her nails and dries her skin, that's why the fire is my job. Maybe my mother misses me after all. The kitchen is neat, with pans stacked on a shelf by the larder. A white gas oven and hob stands to the side, and along the back wall, a small cupboard containing dinner plates and cups sits next to it. Above are several shelves. Flower curtains hide the contents, giving the room a tidy appearance. I turn on the tap, filling the kettle while looking out the window. The small concrete yard is spotless. Jane Anne may have her faults, but she likes everything ship-shape.

Outside, the wind is getting up, and dark clouds gather. The sun hides, casting a shadow over the yard. Since Chamberlain declared war on Germany, we stopped lighting the fires in the bedrooms and front room. Trevor Henry's death and the escalating price of coal reduced the time the main fire is lit. Jane Anne walks into the kitchen, soot staining her hands. The tin bucket used for collecting the ashes swings at her side as she makes her silent way past me, into the yard, tipping the ashes into the metal bin. Tension builds along my shoulders as I make the tea.

A small wooden table hugs the wall on my left in the back room, a flowery tablecloth covering its surface. The cups rattle against the saucers as I set down the tray, reaching for the teapot. In the kitchen, the tap screeches as Jane Anne washes her hands.

Her fingers tease her hair as she sits down. "How long are you home for?"

"I'm not sure. Principal Matron said we should receive further orders in a few days."

She clicks her fingers. "And just like that, I suppose everything returns to normal."

My teacup clatters onto the saucer.

She waves her right hand, warding off my response. "Don't bother. It seems the army cares little about how I'm to produce enough food to feed another mouth, given the rationing."

"I can stay at Daisy's aunt and uncle's if it's easier."

Her brow wrinkles. "Why? Is my house not good enough?"

Sometimes there is no winning. "No, of course not. I don't want to be a burden."

Her tongue makes a clicking noise. "Burden … indeed …"

Suddenly my tea tastes sour.

Bridges, I remind myself.

"I'm not in the habit of throwing my flesh and blood out on the street, no matter what you may think of me, Lillian Elizabeth. Besides, your Aunt Sarah Rebeca will be glad to see you."

It must be nice to have a pliable memory, editing events to comply with your wishes.

"And what about you? Are you happy to see me?"

Her lips twist. "You're sitting at my table, drinking tea, what do you think?"

Bridges …

"I think I'm fortunate, given our parting last year, that you've welcomed me back as you have."

"Yes, well, bygones must be bygones. That's what the bible teaches us. I am but a Good Samaritan, doing my bit for my family."

The tea slides down my throat the wrong way and I cough. She shoots me a stern look, her lips forming a thin line.

"Sorry," I say, my hand covering my mouth.

"If you didn't guzzle, it wouldn't happen."

The tea tastes sweeter and for the first time I question my opinion of my mother. She appears less selfish. Perhaps she is growing up.

Dear Jane Anne,

As I sit in my old room, you downstairs, I write to you. Isn't that peculiar? The Jane Anne here helps to calm my jumbled thoughts and emotions. She is a comfort I draw solace from. For that reason, I continue to write, hoping both my fictional and actual mother will, one day, become one.

There were no bluebirds flying over the white cliffs of Dover when our ship arrived. It was 9 p.m. and darkness was setting in, I suppose. Still, it would have been good to see those cliffs. My arrival back on England's shores came with mixed emotions—happiness, sadness, apprehension. With no orders waiting to ferry us off to war, we go home. Home, for me, is a scary word. I recall looking down at my gas mask, my tin hat on my head, wondering how much easier it would be to sit in a trench. At least I know what to expect. Isn't that shameful?

Train stations are lonesome places when friends have gone. One by one, they left, picking up their lives. With no excuses left to linger at the station, I made my way home. My brain whirling at the questions filtering through it. I don't remember consciously deciding to visit Daisy at Cheyne Children's Hospital, but that's where I ended up. A brief interlude before facing you and mending the holes in our relationship. Daisy still works the same shift pattern, and I was lucky to catch her on a break. We sit and talk, and I grow lonelier.

She's getting married. The news surprises me, and I try to look excited, covering up my rising anguish. Worst of all, I find I want to cry. My friend is moving on with her life, and those plans don't include me. I understand I did the same when I went to France, but still ... Aware of my selfish thoughts, I sound excited about her news, while inside, my loneliness consumes me. With aching cheek muscles from forcing a smile, I hug her, whispering my happiness into her ear. But I'm not happy, I'm miserable over her wedding plans. Now, I'm left hoping new orders arrive before her wedding. Scared, I wonder what happens if the next time Joe and I meet, he's found someone else. We aren't courting, and he is a free agent, but ... It's too awful to contemplate, but I do. There is no guarantee I will see him, or Morag, Pearl, Adah, and Effie again. War can take us in different directions, like Daisy. Then what?

When I enter the back room, there you are, immaculate, coal bucket in hand, I want to throw my arms around you. I've missed you. Missed my mother. My home. The normality of life in London. But I don't hug you. The barrier is too great, and it makes me sad. Will we be honest with one another? Allow ourselves the freedom to show we care. Like a mother and daughter should. I think of Pearl and how she works at maintaining her defences, so the pain won't leak through the gaps. I wonder, do you have cracks that require you to erect such fences? Ones that remain secreted away, like a beaver builds a dam to stop the water. Is that why we aren't close? If you let the light between the cracks, there might be space enough for me to slip through. As it is, we are beginning yet another dance of politeness. You are still the maestro and I your violin, longing for the strings to play a different tune.

There is so much I want to tell you, advice I wish to seek, about Daisy and Joe. Joe is such a beautiful person. Full of kindness, and I'm so, so, so scared to reach out. To love him, in case I extinguish the light that burns so bright within him. What happens, Jane Anne, if I become you?

Lillian Elizabeth

14

 August 1940, London, England

A few days of waiting for new orders turns into months, and I return to Cheyne Children's Hospital while I wait. The likelihood of meeting Joe, Adah, Effie, Morag, and Pearl dims as time passes. Life, on paper, as I write in my diary, returns to normal, even as everything changes. Daisy is marrying the baker's son in four weeks. Peter Carlton has asthma, and though he tried signing up, the army rejected his application on medical grounds. He's taken the disappointment well; I believe Daisy is the reason for this. The wedding keeps her busy, and she has little time for meeting up.

Today is my day off and I'm stomping the streets with Jane Anne as she leads the way to church. My mother informs my aunt and I of her plans during breakfast—along with her expectations. The command given, Jane Anne excuses herself from the table. An hour later, we exit the underground with my mother leading the way. My aunt and

I dodge past shoppers, workers, and children, opening our umbrellas as we follow. Ahead of us, my mother's shoes click against the pavement as we turn onto Fore Street towards St Giles-without-Cripplegate Church.

Dark clouds fill the sky and rain bounces off the pavement slabs. A typical English summer is upon us. The umbrella keeps my hair and shoulders dry while my shoes fill with water. My stockinged feet swim inside of my footwear, the fabric clinging to my skin, and a blister forms on my right heel. Jane Anne's back is a red flag flying in the bull's face and my nostrils flare in response.

Undeterred by the weather, people fill the street. My mother disappears, and the bull raging inside me stamps down its foot in readiness for the sea of people to part, and the matador to reappear. Next to me, Aunt Sarah Rebeca lengthens her steps, attempting to match her sister. There's no point in asking Jane Anne to slow down. She's on one of her missions, refusing to acknowledge her sister's struggle.

"Not much further," I say, as my aunt huffs at my side.

The clock from St Giles-without-Cripplegate Church strikes, the sound loud and reassuring. As the building comes into view, the rain slows to a fine drizzle. Jane Anne stops inside the doorway of the church, glancing down the street at us. Her eyebrows raise in frustration at our lack of progress. Without a care, she shakes the water from her umbrella. Droplets fly around her, wetting the legs of a woman as she exits the church. With a sharp glare at her, the woman continues onto the street, muttering her annoyance. Jane Anne doesn't respond. To-day, she is less aware of others' needs than normal.

Except for Daisy's continued social absence, life has returned to pre-France. Jane Anne's flinching at an unexpected knock at the door the exception. Telegrams bring bad news during wartime. There is no news from my brothers and their absence is causing the house to become claustrophobic. Like me, my brothers are lousy at keeping in touch—it must be a Nutman thing. To date, they have taken no leave afforded them in London. It could be my brothers being my brothers, rather than location. Though I can't blame them, we have never been a cheerful house. Still, as their absence lengthens, so does the potential of unwanted news. The phantom knocking at the door, bringing confirmation of their death, coming ever closer and more real.

Jane Anne's right foot taps as she waits, her umbrella now hooked over her arm. "Any slower and the pair of you will catch cold."

Aunt Sarah Rebeca's lungs deflate, and her feet move faster. "It's hardly my fault God gave me short legs."

I cover my mouth, pretending to cough, suppressing a giggle.

Unaware of her sister's annoyance, my mother enters the church. The dull sound of our heels against the wooden floor fills the empty room. We walk past the pews to the metal stand where rows of tiny candles burn. Their flickering light casts a shadow along the floor. Without speaking, Jane Anne and Aunt Sarah Rebeca take a candle, dropping a penny into the metal box, fixed at the front of the stand. As I don't have a penny, I drop four farthings in the box. I'm not being tight, four farthings is the same as one penny. With twenty shillings in the pound, and one shilling equalling twelve pennies, it pays to be savvy with your money. With bowed heads, we light our candles before making our way over to the front pew for reflection and prayer. Today is Trevor Henry's birthday. He would have been fifty-five. The black veil over his photograph, on the mantle at home, remains in place. Adopted into our daily lives, we've stopped seeing it. But today, his death leaves a new pain in our hearts, and we relive the news of his passing. This time around, it hurts more.

My aunt's gloved hands tremble. Her loss is greater than ours. She pats at the tears trailing down her cheeks, while beside her, my mother sits, her eyes closed and her hands raised in prayer. Churches can be such solemn places. Sunlight seeps through the stained-glass window at the altar, lighting the area in a kaleidoscope of colour. It is a bewitching and cheering sight; one I take comfort from. Signs, if we want to see them, are everywhere. Whispers of Trevor Henry's love drift through my head, lighting the room and vanquishing my gloom. This is how I want to remember him. Not the pain ripping at my heart, or the empty chair in the back room, but the man that loved his little girl with all his heart.

My hands rest on the wooden pew, my knees sinking into the green leather tuffet as I cast my eyes over the medieval church. The church's name is in recognition of St Giles in the Middle Ages. Cripplegate referring to a gate through the old City wall of London, built by the Romans to fortify and protect the city. How many people pass through these doors to pray for good health, or the safe return of loved ones? And how many more, like ourselves, come to mourn the loss of a family member or friend? Grief is part of war and life. It is harsh and uncompromising, stealing a person's splendour, replacing their warmth with sadness.

Above our heads the thunder of a plane rattles through the church; my head tilts as I listen. The noise is familiar, and I track the sound, assessing its closeness. My heart thumps as it gets nearer, and I grab Jane Anne and Aunt Sarah Rebeca, forcing them onto the floor. Our shoes collide with the wooden pews, our heads resting on the leather tuffet.

"What are you doing? Let go!" Jane Anne snaps, as she tries to remove my hand from her back.

"Get down!" I shout, refusing to move my hand.

"Lill—"

The distinct whizzing sound of a bomb passes over the rooftop, cutting off my mother's protest. She falls silent, colour draining from her face. BANG … Prayer books topple and the door of the church rattles as dust falls from the rafters. A candle tips on the altar, the flame extinguishing as it rolls off the surface, clanking onto the floor. Beneath our legs, the ground shakes at the bomb's impact. Jane Anne and Aunt Sarah Rebeca, faces concealed beneath the pew, scream. Their hands cover their heads and their bodies tremble beneath my palms. For a split second, the church is quiet. I hold Jane Anne and Aunt Sarah Rebeca tight, my hands pressing them down. Jane Anne's words from long ago sound in my ear. "People here need her …"

Within minutes of the first bomb landing, a second one hits. We stay like this for over an hour until the bomber's whirring disappears. When I'm sure it's over, I leap into action. "Stay here!" I shout, running out of the church.

The blister rubs against my shoe, sending out spikes of pain. My brain receptors aren't listening. When a nurse is on duty, there is no such thing as pain. Chaos greets me as I turn the corner onto Fore Street. The gates of hell have opened, and every imaginable horror has hit London. People wander in a daze, their clothing dishevelled, their faces white, and their skin tarnished with dirt. Some sit, some stand, frozen, screaming in a mixture of confusion, fear, disbelief, anger, and grief. Bricks tumble, and buildings fall, as fires rage. Plumes of smoke billow into the sky. Sightless eyes stare glued to the spot, transfixed in misery.

Across the road, a boy lies on the ground, blood pouring from his head. At his side, a woman lifts him, hugging him, her body rocking them. The contents of her shopping bag spills over the pavement. An apple rolls, stuttering to a stop, and milk pours between fragments of glass. Immune to the bedlam surrounding them, lost within her nightmare, she holds onto the boy. Sirens scream out a warning. Fore Street is a mass of hysteria.

War has come to London.

An air raid warden steps forward, trying to bring order. Without a semblance of panic, I walk to the woman. A calmness I don't feel settles over me as I sit within the rubble in front of the boy. France has taught me one thing;

panic breeds panic. I place a hand on the woman, keeping my voice low. "Let me have a look, I'm a nurse."

Tears well in her eyes, intensifying their colour. She looks down at the boy. He grips her raincoat, his cries like tiny weapons, stabbing at my heart. Mortar matts the woman's hair, and small pieces of brick have sliced at her flesh. With no awareness of her injuries, she comforts the wailing child in her arms. Uncertainty clouds her face as she glances down at her son. Her head bobs and her grip loosens, allowing me access. Blood pours from the boy's head, dripping over his face. Head wounds often appear worse than they are—I'm hoping this is one of those times. Gently, I tilt his head, a smile forming as I look down at him. Liquid brown eyes stare back at me, his fingers grabbing at the fabric of his mother's coat.

"Goodness, wait until your friends see you. Why, I bet they are going to be jealous. The first bomb to hit us and look at you right in the thick of it," I say, diverting his attention while I assess his injuries.

A thread of excitement lights his face.

"Watch my finger," I say, looking for any signs of concussion.

The wound, though deep, is a flesh wound, scaring him and his mother more than anything else. There is no sign of concussion. "Nothing but a scratch, but don't go telling your friends that. You tell them how brave you were when Hitler's army came to visit."

The boy's tears stop, his mouth gaping, and the beginning of a smile forms. His mind busy with what he is going to tell his friends, he becomes fidgety. "Stand still, soldier, I'll need to put a temporary bandage on."

I tear off a length of my underskirt, wrapping the strip of cloth around the boy's head, using my handkerchief as padding to absorb the blood. As I work, the boy becomes animated, forcing me to hurry. The young are impatient.

"Mummy, can I go see Tommy?"

His mother tuts at him, shaking her head. Fear has left her face and her lips twitch as she looks down at her son. Her hand caresses his face; love pours from her into him.

"He's a little battered, but there's no sign of concussion. Monitor him, but he should be alright to see his friend. Go to the First Aid Station and get his dressing changed first."

The woman nods. "Thank you."

"Does that mean I can see Tommy?"

"First Aid Station, home and cleaned up first," his mum says, reaching for her handbag, dusting off the rubble. I help gather her shopping, handing her the wayward apple. There isn't anything I can do about the milk.

Horrified, the boy's face falls. "But Tommy won't be able to see the blood on my bandage if it gets changed."

"True, but you can tell Tommy all about the First Aid Station and getting patched up. Just like a soldier," I say, ruffling his hair, before leaving them to their discussion.

There are others with more serious wounds needing my attention. As the ambulances arrive, I help with the casualties. The Nazis have taken London by surprise, but we are prepared for such eventualities. Within minutes of the bombs landing, fire engines and ambulances fill Fore Street. We deal with the minor injuries on the street, while the seriously wounded are taken to the nearest hospital. The dead follow once the firefighters have finished.

In my peripheral vision, I see my mother and aunt walk over to those waiting to be tended to. Jane Anne's arm circles the shoulders of a woman as she sits on the curb crying. Trapped within the rubble, a bloody hand emerges. The fingers don't move, and legs stick out at odd angles. Her hand covering the woman's, Jane Anne draws her away from the body. The woman turns, throwing her arms around my mother as her body convulses.

August 23rd will live in our memories. It is the day the Nazis sent their planes to destroy London. This is what we've been preparing for at Cheyne Children's Hospital. As I glance over Fore Street, I know nothing will ever be the same. A fresh memory forms; London is no longer a place of sanctuary. Instead, it is a place of sadness, where people lost their lives, businesses, and homes. We will rise from this, but we shall never, ever forget. For some, a wound has opened and though it will knit together, a scar replaces the purity.

The walk home is quiet. Jane Anne's stride is short, matching her sister's. We are dirty and our bodies ache. Dust, mortar, and the smell of smoke cling to our hair, clothes, and skin. I long for a hot drink and slice of bread and butter.

Light bleeds into the hall as Jane Anne hits the switch by the door. "I'll get the fire going," she says, weariness hanging from her words.

"Should we wash first?" Aunt Sarah Rebeca asks, with a sideways glance at her sister.

My mother's lips stretch in disapproval. "We may not have two ha'pennies to rub together, but we aren't barbarians."

Her voice carries down the hall as I close the front door. It kills any hope my stomach has of easing its imminent discomfort.

The sigh I'm longing to release doesn't fall. "Of course," I say, not feeling a word of it.

A lifespan later, I sit at the table with Jane Anne, waiting for Aunt Sarah Rebeca to finish washing and changing. My wet hair drips down my back, soaking into the thick cotton dressing gown. Jane Anne raises a thin brow at my attire but doesn't comment further. A first for her. The grumble in my stomach becomes louder, and my cheeks warm. My mouth salivates, and I try to peel my eyes off the plate of bread and butter in the centre of the table. Lost in thought, Jane Anne sits in silence, her mind so far away that she shakes to rouse herself.

"You did a good job today, on Fore Street."

Stunned, my gaze leaves the food. "T-t-thanks."

Respect shines in her eyes. I've never seen it directed my way, and it makes my heart skip and my blood race, gushing through my veins—I believe I've made my mother proud.

"I know I haven't been the best of mothers, but I've done my best. Today, when I saw you taking care of those poor people, I understood why you wanted to become a nurse and join the army. You're needed out there, I see that now. If the Germans come back, we'll be ready." Her hands smooth the tablecloth, and determination falls over her features. "I'm going to offer my services. It's time I took part in this dreadful war and did my bit."

With a shrug, her normal expression returns. She reaches over, passing me a small plate and laying one down in my aunt's vacant place. Footsteps sound on the hall tiles and my aunt walks in from the front room. She hesitates on the threshold, glancing from Jane Anne to me. Her eyebrows pinch. "Am I interrupting?"

"Other than Lillian Elizabeth's stomach serenading me for these last fifteen minutes, no."

As if on cue, my stomach lets out a long, agonising rumble. Aunt Sarah Rebeca laughs, pulling out a chair next to her sister. "We have missed lunch."

"Yet Lillian Elizabeth's stomach is the only one making its displeasure known."

"Sorry," I say, wishing my stomach would cease its complaining.

"Tuck in. There is no point in apologising over something you can't control."

With eagerness, I grab a slice of bread, a small groan of ecstasy falling from my lips as my teeth sink into the fluffy texture. The slices are thicker than normal, and a liberal spread of butter coats them. Given the rationing in place, we will have to go steadier over the next few days. Weekly rationing allows us two ounces of butter a week per adult. Preserves rationed to one pound every two months. Tonight, we eat like kings. Well, maybe not kings, but we are indulging ourselves.

When Britain declared war on Germany, the government set up a department to help people make the most of their rations. Pamphlets issued by the Ministry of Food contain recipes to prevent the wasting of food and provide ideas for more interesting mealtimes. While bread and butter aren't innovative, it is quick to prepare, and just what we need. I reach for the strawberry jam, aware that tonight will see the last. I'm so hungry, I could eat seconds, thirds and sevenths; hang rationing and its fair distribution of food and supplies—for tonight. But there is no cheating the rationing system. The local shop has registered our ration book, and the shopkeeper marks it in the book against every item sold. We shall have to wait another week before the sticky red preserve can adorn our meals and be more conservative when cutting bread.

Letter Home, August 1940

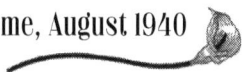

Dear Jane Anne,

The newspapers fill with stories about Dunkirk. Thousands of ships save 335,000 soldiers and medical staff. And yet, today, the 23rd of August 1940, people lay dying or injured on the streets of London. In the shadow of what has happened, I find it hard to celebrate this victory. When we woke this morning, it was with purpose; to light a candle and remember Trevor Henry on his birthday. The only enemy we had was the rain that filled our shoes. I worry at the innocence Londoners have lost and how the bombing of Fore Street, and what is to come, will scar us.

When the whirring engines of the bomber filtered over the church, my only thought was yours and my aunt's safety. While France has tuned my ears to the noise of enemy aircraft, it doesn't make the waiting and fear any easier to bear. Huddled between the pews, praying for the plane to pass, is all we can do.

But out of destruction, great things happen. Today, I believe I witnessed this, for, Jane Anne, you looked at me with pride. I wonder why so many needed to die before you could understand me.

It is a welcoming sight, seeing you comfort others. Your arms holding the broken. You were a child when you married Trevor Henry, and with no chance to grow into a woman, you gave birth to your children. For all your eccentric ways and your polished exterior, a child remains. Selfish and stunted, and we never let you grow. When Trevor Henry left along with my brothers to take their places in this war, I stepped in, taking my father's place. However, you have shown me my error. You are finding your independence. What that means for you, and me, I'm unsure. But it holds such significance that I must mention it here, as I write to you.

When we returned home, we feasted, but you didn't care. Your generosity shows how war is changing you, shaping you into someone new. I hope, by the end of this war, it creates better people. That we learn from our failure of the Great War. Anger breeds discontentment, it separates and alienates, clouding our minds, and stops us from seeing the damage.

If I try to evaluate our relationship, I wonder, is this what we have become? A mother and daughter who don't care enough to love each other, so we wage our own unspoken war. My brothers say I am an overthinker; perhaps they are right. These rambling letters help me work out my issues where you are concerned. Will you look at me again with such pride? And will I be able to accept you for the mother you are, not the mother I wish you were? They teach us preconception at a young age. A mother is loving, placing her children above her needs. She is there to wipe away our tears, hold us tight, and keep the night-mares away. As a child, when I woke, crying from a night terror, Trevor Henry wiped away my tears, sitting with me, reading *Winnie The Pooh* until I fell back to sleep. You were never there, and a little girl grew up bereft of her mother. A lifetime of being disappointed in you has made me bitter. I wonder if those preconceptions have stilted my growth.

This is a hard letter to write. When I read it back, I will cry. Am I the selfish one? Not fitting into the mother image, my discontentment has grown into distrust. I've always felt we were in direct competition for Trevor Henry's affections. When I was young, and night fell, we would sit, you in your chair beside Trevor Henry's, me at his feet, listening to the wireless. Some nights I would crawl onto his lap and snuggle in deep, falling asleep. I enjoyed waking in the morning, in my bed, knowing he had carried me there. His little girl. Never yours.

I can hear you downstairs, turning off the lights. It's time for me to stop writing. Turn off my light and sleep. I don't want you to find me writing to you. The image of my Writing Mother differs from the one you are. Until the day we both grow to speak with candour, I shall continue to write to you.

Lillian Elizabeth

15

With lousy timing, two days after the bombing on Fore Street, my orders arrive. London is reeling from the attack, and with anxious faces, Londoners glance skyward in fear. For the last two days, the sun has been glorious, but no one cares. Over walls and on doorsteps, conversation holds one subject—war. Jane Anne stands in the doorway of my bedroom, her arms folded at her waist, her lips set in a hard line as she watches me pack. I'm to report to the National Orthopaedic Hospital at Stanmore, in preparation to admit the Dunkirk casualties. Though the Dunkirk evacuation occurred between May 26th and 4th of June, it has taken the army until now to assign hospitals to the injured. When I left France in May, I never realised how close the Nazis were.

For five minutes, Jane Anne's bottom jaw has opened, shut, and opened, before setting her lips into an impenetrable line. For a woman with no comprehension of tact, her actions are out of character, and my nerves are fraying. My unease festers under her scrutiny, and I prolong my packing. Procrastination isn't healthy, but it prevents the uncomfortable moment when my departure needs confronting. Unsure how to say goodbye, ten minutes of packing turns into twenty. At the back of my mind, I recall our last parting. The foundations I came home to build are there—how stable they prove to be is up to me, Jane Anne, and time.

"That's everything," I say, standing at the foot of the bed.

Jane Anne nods. "Right."

"I'd best go …"

She remains in the doorway, her head bent, staring at her hands. "I've applied to become an air raid warden."

Surprise hits and my jaw falls. When I think of my mother, I don't see helpful, compassionate, or friendly. I see organised, bossy, opinionated, and stubborn. When the need to restore control and calm arrives, Jane Anne's skills are an asset. The role will suit her. "T-that's great."

Her delicate eyebrow arches. Rather than dig a larger hole, I force a strained smile. She stares, waiting—for what? "They can do with your organisational skills. People panic and lose efficiency," I say, offering support.

Her head tips back, her fingers pulling at the hem of her cardigan as her eyes pin me to the spot. "Yes, they will."

The bombing on Fore Street, and the senseless loss of life, has affected us. Rubble stands in place of buildings, and the homeless move into shelters, or with family. It serves as a constant reminder; we aren't safe from the Nazis.

"You'll make a great air raid warden."

"Yes, I will, I'm very good at bossing people about."

Her comment makes me laugh.

Long before we declared war, in December 1937, Britain was busy preparing itself for an attack. Fearful of heavy aerial bombing in civilian areas, the Government passed the Air Raid Precautions Act (ARP). Under this act, local authorities ready themselves. ARP bodies include firefighters, rescue, and first aid facilities—ambulance crew and medics. The recent bombing is bound to swell the ARP numbers. People will come to realise war is a breath away from their front door, intensifying their need to assist in the fight. It is our nature to rally the troops, banding together in one common goal. To defeat Hitler.

"I'm proud of you …" I say, coughing as the word Mum forms.

Jane Anne nods. "So am I."

The Germans have shown her what they are capable of. She didn't buckle under their attack. When the Nazis hit London, it must have been a frightening experience for her. Unlike me, Jane Anne didn't recognise the drumming of the plane's engine, or the whizzing of the bombs as they fell. To stay safe is to recognise when danger is close. My mother is adapting. The hysterical, sobbing person who tried manipulating me to stay has been replaced. When I see Hitler's face in a newspaper, I will thank him. "Thank you for showing us how courageous we are. And by the way, this country is not yours to take. Good day, Hitler."

"You will need to wear a tin hat."

With her yellow cotton Dorothy dress and styled hair, she resembles a model. Pristine in every way. My lips twitch at the thought of her in a tin hat.

She shrugs. "I don't know what's so funny. My hair spends more time tied back these days than under a dryer. It's frightful how war ravages a woman's style."

It would have been nice to inherit my mother's sense of style. She can make a tablecloth look fashionable. Out of all her children, John Edward is the only one of us to possess our mother's genetic code of elegance. It is why my eldest sibling is never without female attention.

"This war will never dent your style. You make anything look good, even heavy cotton overalls."

She smiles. "Blue has always looked good on me."

My head bobs in agreement as I swing my kit bag over my shoulder.

She catches my upper arm as I walk through the doorway. "Take care, Lillian Elizabeth. Not being the best of mothers doesn't mean I don't care—I do. I just find it difficult to express myself."

I place my hand on top of hers. "I know."

At the bottom of the steps, Aunt Sarah Rebeca waits. My shoes thumping on the thin carpet runner, I fall into her arms. Beneath my fingers, her bones protrude. Weight falls from her slender form as she mourns the loss of her husband. I lay a kiss on her cheek as I open the front door.

"Be careful," she says, her fingers lingering on my arm.

"Don't mourn forever. Uncle Anthony Kevin wouldn't be happy to see you so sad."

"I know, dear."

My mother stands at her sister's side on the pavement, their gaze following me as I walk down the street. My time at home has been interesting. While these new feelings I have for Jane Anne won't develop into those a child should possess for their mother, I am content to acknowledge they are daughterly.

Bird song fills the streets as I make my way to the train station. Life has changed since I left for France. Friendships I once thought strong are gone, and family ties are strengthening. Now it is time to face this next chapter, one I hope to embrace with friends at my side. If I am fortunate Pearl, Morag, Adah, and Effie will have received the same orders and we shall all meet again soon.

Letter Home, September 1940

Dear Jane Anne,

On my journey to Stanmore, I have chastised myself many times. The natural warmth I have for my aunt is missing with you. It is unfair of me to throw my arms around her, and not to show you, my mother, the same affection. You exhibit no sign that this bothers you, though I often wonder if it does, deep inside. When I was thirteen, Mrs Daniels down the road dragged up her children. Sally, (Mrs Daniels' eldest child) lived with her grandmother until she was ten. For a decade, Mrs Daniels had nothing to do with Sally. Then one day she grabs her daughter, demanding Sally break all ties with her grandmother. Kowtowing to her mother's jealousy, Sally complies to her demand. What I find stranger is that Sally defended her mother. Mothers hold a lot of sway over their children. Perhaps that's why I try so hard to please you.

The journey to the National Orthopaedic Hospital at Stanmore is tedious, and my nerves cramp my stomach. All I can think about is Pearl, Morag, Adah, and Effie. Will they be there when I arrive? It will be interesting to find out how the hospital has fared since I visited as a child. Trevor Henry took me there, back when it was called the Mary Wardell Convalescent Home. It was a simple building. With my interest in Florence Nightingale, Trevor

Henry would often take me to different hospitals. We'd stand gazing at them, as the nurses came and went. My tiny hand in his, Trevor Henry would crouch next to me and say, "One day, that will be you." He believed for my dream to keep momentum and attach itself to the dreamer, reality also needed to play its part. My father was a man beyond his time, even though he was a traditionalist at heart. His wife's purpose was to raise their children.

I recall, aged seven, sitting on the bottom step, hugging my knees as I listened to your conversation with your sister. You told her how you dreamed of being on the front of the Picturegoer Magazine. With my mind spinning, I saw you, graceful and poised, wearing the latest style. Even though the Picturegoer is about screen stars, then fashioned, to me you belonged on the cover. It is a shame you never got to live your dream.

We will soon reach Brockley Hill. The National Orthopaedic Hospital is looming closer and I'm terrified. I hope Pearl, Morag, Adah, and Effie are there. Oh, and Joe. Wouldn't that be wonderful? The entire team reunited. My nerves are showing in my writing and my heart is hammering ten-to-the-dozen. Unfortunately, my nerves play havoc with my bladder and I need the toilet. I'm squirming in my seat, and people are staring. Wish me luck, though I'm sure once I get there I will be fine. Still, it doesn't hurt to have a bit of luck on your side.

Maybe my brothers will make it home. Though it will only take a pretty girl for them to forget about London. You brought them up to appreciate the finer, more glamorous people in life.

Lillian Elizabeth

16

August 1940, National Orthopaedic Hospital,
Stanmore, England

With wide eyes, I swallow down my negative
thoughts as I stare at the National Orthopaedic Hospital. Its humble beginning is
gone. Mr T. H Openshaw has wasted no time in convert-
ing the Mary Wardell Convalescent Home into a modern
hospital. Thanks to the Country Branch, and Committee
of Management, who issued the green light, they have
obliterated my childhood memories. With their thirst un-
quenched, they fixed their sights on the neighbouring
twenty-three acres of fields and garden. Without care,
they have gobbled up the four-acre plot, with its grass-
land and wildlife, transforming it into a humungous concrete beast. The simplistic beauty of the Wardell Convalescent Home has mutated into a crisp, unsympathetic
monster. In 1922, this grand monster opened its doors and
the first patients entered. I appreciate that the advancement was necessary. As a nurse, I should welcome the

new hospital. Instead, I mourn the loss of my childish memory.

Thanks to an anonymous donor, the new frontage of the hospital causes my nose to wrinkle. Four massive pillars loom, demanding attention. Iron gates hang on the inner two pillars, providing a dominating presence. The grotesque grandeur returns my stare, and I turn my head, lifting my gaze as I did as a small child, staring at my father. In my mind, Trevor Henry shakes his head. *"That's modernisation for you, Lilly,"* he says, sadness clouding his features.

"I don't like it."

"No, but you'll like what it can do."

Trevor Henry's vision is right; I will like what it can do and so I shall accept it. After all, everyone has a price. Mine is within the treatment block added in 1939—it is breathtaking. Not the building, but the treasures it holds. The upper floor house the central linen store with over three hundred cupboards. On the ground floor is a large, fully equipped gymnasium and treatment room, for massage, artificial light therapy, and dental care. It also has a heated swimming pool. Awe cascades over me as my mind feasts once more on the treatment pool, used for infantile paralysis (polio). The nurse in me drools. At around the same time that the treatment block opened, they erected ten prefabricated huts, named The Slope Wards. A covered walkway, nicknamed The Slope, connects the huts.

"What do ye think?" Morag asks.

My gaze sweeps the red brickwork and large windows. "It's not a tent, which is nice, but it's rather gloomy."

"I think you'll find the gloom is coming from the grey clouds. It's a brick building, with glass windows and heating. We'll be warm," Pearl says, rubbing the chill from her arms.

"Though it pains me tae say it, on this occasion ah'm with Pearl, sorry, Lilly."

"It's good to see your low opinion of me hasn't changed over the last few months, Morag. I can't believe I got stuck with you again." Pearl flaps her arms at her sides. "What are the chances?"

"Ah wasnae aware ah wis supposed tae change. Why do ah need tae change? Ah've a very sunny disposition, ah'll have ye ken."

Pearl sniggers. "When it suits."

"You two get more like siblings every day," I say, looping my arms through theirs, steering them forward.

Pearl removes her arm, placing her hands on her hips. "Lilly, that is a terrible thing to say. You take it back."

"Why? Is bein' mah sister so terrible?" Morag asks, her frown lines deepening.

"The sheer thought of us being blood-related is too hideous for me to consider. Why, one day I might wake up and find someone has replaced my luscious blonde hair with that of a bird's nest."

"Ye're mean, Pearl."

"Am not."

Morag sticks out her tongue. "Are so."

I let out a heavy sigh. "And there." I wave at the pair of them. "I rest my case."

Adah steps forward. "I'd leave them to it, Lilly, they're never going to change."

"You're right," I say with a dramatic shake of my head, a sad look clouding my features, making Effie laugh.

The tour of the hospital accustoms us to its size and layout; now it's time to familiarise ourselves with the wards. As one, we move up the steps into the building. Our numbers dwindle as we make our way onto our assigned wards. Rows of neatly made beds wait for the casualties to arrive. Between each bed is a locker, containing a temperature chart, case notes holder, and sputum mug. The sputum mug catches the mucus coughed up from the lower airways for examination. An ashtray, denture bowl, soap, and towel sit on top of the lockers. Belgian soldiers and those unfit for active services occupy one hundred and thirty of the beds.

The Third British Troops from Valery, France, are amongst the first wave of evacuees due at the hospital. We have a few days to prepare and organise ourselves and get to work knitting theatre stockings. Our experience in France provides an insight into the chaos due to hit Stanmore, and we try to prepare the trainee nurses for the coming typhoon.

A week after being told of the Third British Troops' imminent arrival, the first wave of casualties is to arrive late morning. In the staffroom, I sit with Adah and Effie, along with two trainee nurses, Beatrice Atwater and Jessica James, knitting theatre stockings. Sunlight floods the room as our balls of yarn dance at our feet. In the middle of our circled chairs is a basket, containing the finished stockings. As our knitting needles clack together, we monitor the time. The hands on the wall clock move past midday and the minute hand slows until an hour feels like several. One of Grandma Ellis' favourite sayings was, "A watched clock never moves." Nor does it seem the military know how to tell the time.

To allow time for us to process the patients, they are to arrive in groups of ten. The patients are to be organised in relation to the seriousness of their injuries. Those deemed 'minor' are to be washed, changed, and provided with a cup of tea. 'Urgent' cases are to be readied for theatre. The severity of the injuries will depend on the treatment received since they embarked on their journey home.

"You're looking at the clock again, Beatrice," Adah says, her needles clicking.

Beatrice's lips twist and she nibbles at the corner of her mouth, pulling her bottom lip between her teeth. "Sorry, I can't help it."

The woollen ball at Adah's feet stops spinning. "The clock only shows the time, it won't tell you when the casualties are arriving. Go stretch your legs, I'm sure they won't be much longer."

Jessica puts down her knitting needles. "Come on, Beatrice, I'll come with you."

"If you're sure."

Adah waves them off. "It will do you good."

"Have you heard from Joe?" Effie asks me, lowering her knitting as Beatrice and Jessica leave the staffroom.

"No, but then I'm not the best person at keeping in touch. I'd hoped to see him here, but …" I shrug.

"Do you like him?"

Effie's question catches me off guard and I drop a stitch.

Hand over her mouth, worry covers Effie's face. "Sorry, am I being nosey?"

"More like you've been listening to Morag," Adah says.

My cheeks turn pink, and I pick up the dropped stitch. "Joe's the nicest man I've ever met, of course I miss him."

Effie sighs at my ambiguous answer, her needles sitting dormant in her lap. "Before the war hit, I was courting Jake Tranby. He kept asking me to marry him, and I kept saying not yet. I'd give anything to say yes. But back then I thought I'd all the time in the world. Now I'm not sure how much time I have, or if he'll be coming home."

Adah looks up from her knitting. "All we can do is hope Jake makes it home. Maybe then you'll both get that second chance."

"I hope so."

There's a wistfulness to Effie's voice, making me wonder about Joe and me. While he has never asked me to step out with him, I know he would, if I encouraged it. So why hadn't I? A million reasons bubble inside my head, but they're just excuses hiding my fear. I am petrified that I will be like Jane Anne. Who knows what kind of mother or wife I will be. Those inherited genes I've received from my mother are part of my molecular structure of deoxyribonucleic acid—DNA. There's no running from them.

"Until then, keep knitting," Adah says, nodding at Effie's still needles.

We fall into silence, our knitting needles clacking. To break the silence, I sing Josephine Baker's *Blue Skies*. Effie joins in, with Adah humming the tune.

Morag's head pokes around the door frame as we finish our song. "They're here!"

Pearl's head appears above Morag's. "And it seems no one can count. There's about a hundred of them."

Within three hours, soldiers clutter the once tidy ward. Dirty boots and soiled uniforms, packs, respirators, and rifles scatter over the floor. With little time at our disposal, we push the items under the soldier's beds to attend to later. Next to me, Pearl finishes stripping a soldier. Once stripped, he falls asleep, causing her to huff in frustration. This is the tenth soldier in a row to fall into unconsciousness once their toes wiggle free.

"Well, that's another one out cold." Effie stares down at him.

Pearl lifts her head, gazing over at the soldier as she picks up his soiled boots. "The administration of anaesthetic before his operation is pointless, if you ask me."

"It's not personal," I say, my voice low.

Morag chuckles as she walks past. She winks. "Yer losin' ye touch, Pearl."

Face turning thunderous, Pearl grabs the soldier's boots, glaring over at me.

With my hands in front of me, I ward off her dirty look, pointing at the boots. "You're not throwing them at me, are you?"

"Of course I won't throw the bloody boots at you. I'm going to throw them at Morag later," Pearl says, dropping the boots under the bed and walking off to a waiting soldier.

The soldiers inside are the worse of the casualties. Outside, across the opulent lawns, the walking wounded fall asleep until we can admit them. With more arriving as we work, we categorise them into their treatment groups. Those spread across the lawns are 'minor cases' and are liable to wait several hours before we can tend to them.

Adah grabs hold of a soldier's boot, pulling it off. He turns his head away from her, wincing. "Sorry, nurse." He coughs before continuing, "I haven't had my boots off for weeks."

"And why would that be a problem? Seems that your feet are overdue a bit of freedom."

Surprised, his lips twitch into a smile. "Thank you, nurse."

Adah nods. "Don't thank me. You're the one putting up with them."

There's a throaty laugh, and his chest gurgles. In all the confusion and rush to rescue, many soldiers didn't receive medical treatment. With their injuries left to fester, some have become infected and gangrenous. This leaves the surgeon no choice but to amputate. Those who have received medical treatment arrive with their injuries enveloped in plaster. While these injuries will fare much better, the likelihood of infection remains high. It's not uncommon for flies to get under the plaster, laying their eggs. When we remove the plaster, we'll know how bad the infection is. Or if the maggots have done their job, leaving the wound clean and granulating. While maggots are loathsome creatures, they have their uses; it's why they have been used to clean wounds since the Spanish Civil War.

In the days that follow, the casualties keep coming. Their numbers are overwhelming. Most are in a poor state of health. These are the lucky ones. For the troops remaining on the beaches of Dunkirk and La Panne, time is running out.

Morag wipes her brow as she moves from one soldier to the next, stripping them and storing away their belongings. On a loud snore, the soldier falls back onto the bed. "Tis like a production line in 'ere."

We gaze over at the sea of soldiers waiting to be sent to theatre.

"I'll be asking for name and rank in my sleep," Pearl mutters.

Morag nods. "Aye."

"It's the soldiers suffering from flashbacks I feel sorry for. Theatre is a traumatic place with its bright lights and clattering instruments," I say.

"With theatre runnin' through the night, there's nae time tae accustom them tae their surroundin's before, whoosh ... they're whisked onto the operating table." Morag sighs. "Tis awful. They've endured so much 'n' we're askin' them tae suffer more."

In the far corner, a patient cries out in pain, and I rush over.

"It's my leg, nurse," the soldier says, pointing at his missing leg.

The psychological impact of losing a limb is immense. Many of the soldiers are experiencing 'phantom limbs', feeling pain coming from their missing limb. I place a hand on his shoulder. He winces, crying over a leg he no longer has. "Come on, let's get you more comfortable, release some of that tension and pain."

"Thank you, nurse."

Sometimes movement helps to dim the phantom pain, moving the mind on from the loop it's caught up in.

17

 September 1940, National Orthopaedic Hospital,
Stanmore, England

With little time for rest, we continue to be reassigned from ward to theatre. Work in theatre fascinates me. It's not for every nurse; Morag groans, out of Matron's earshot, when assigned. Me, I love it. A thirst gathers inside me, and I find I want to learn more, to be a better nurse. This morning, Nurse Catherine Holloway is attending theatre with me, and orderly George Taylor. It's Catherine's and my job to move from the top, middle, and bottom of the table, handing the surgeons the instruments. The prospect of being part of something as revolutionary as plastic surgery is thrilling, and I can't stop smiling—it's as well a mask covers my lower face.

Sergeant Cooper's injuries comprise a shattered lower jaw and lower left leg. Despite his discomfort, he remains strong, with no display of nerves. His courage has kept him alive, now the surgeons will put him back together. The plastic surgeon, Brigadier Jacob Halt, undertakes a Pedicle graft. The tube of flesh cut from the patient's abdomen is to form his new chin. Once complete, the orthopaedic surgeon, Brigadier Oliver Baker-Davies, chisels off a fragment of bone from the patient's hip. On removal, he hands the bone to the faciomaxillary surgeon, Brigadier Edward Simmons. Brigadier Simmons specialises in facial reconstruction. He uses the bone to replace Sergeant Cooper's missing lower jaw.

I follow Brigadier Baker-Davies as he begins work on the patient's lower leg. The surgeons remind me of dancers, each working in seamless union with the other. A sense of amazement embraces me as I work with these gifted surgeons. It's like watching a miracle unfold, and I can't wait to tell Pearl, Adah, Morag, and Effie all about it. For those fighting on the frontline, disfigurement is a natural part of war. The advancement in medicine is allowing us to present these soldiers with a healthier image. War doesn't care about the horrific memories it generates, or the reminder a soldier faces each day in the mirror. Even though plastic surgery is in its embryonic stage, it is providing soldiers with a sense of self.

With surgery finished, they wheel Sergeant Cooper to the ward. The sanitising of the theatre allows for a few minutes break. Surgery was lengthy and my neck and shoulders are feeling the strain. I stand outside, sipping my sweetened tea as the cool breeze teases the fine hair on my skin. Being busy curbs my worries over Joe's silence. Hitler has his eye on Britain, and I can't shake the feeling that trouble is heading our way.

On the 12th of September, new reports come in confirming a German air attack on Dover. The attack was a coverup for twelve Nazi ships sneaking along the coast to Boulogne's border. My stomach flips, my thoughts turning to Joe and the place I last saw him. Wherever he is, I pray God is looking after him. While I understand God is at breaking point, what with so many of us making the same request, if he's listening, I'd be appreciative if he would move Joe up his list of priorities. After all, not that this is emotional blackmail, God did take Trevor Henry and Uncle Anthony Kevin from me. And while I'm being greedy, I'd also appreciate him checking up on my brothers. With a silent thank you, I make my way back towards the theatre.

Discarded plaster splints and dressings saturate the air in the back lobby and the most gruesome odour hits me as I open the door. Grateful for the small barrier the face mask affords my nasal passage, I walk past the redundant dressings. Blood and plaster stick to the swing doors of the theatre as I push my way through. With more pressing matters stopping the clearing of the dressings, we live with the stink and mess.

When surgery and my shift is over, I wheel the stretcher carrying Tommie Donald Gilbank from the theatre. Donald is nineteen and has been suffering from flashbacks since he arrived at the hospital. Shrapnel has destroyed the left side of his face, and extensive surgery is rebuilding what weaponry has taken from him. The anaesthetic will provide him with some much-needed rest, away from the nightmares that hound him. When he wakes, a nurse will be there to help ease his tormented mind. An orderly takes Donald as I enter the ward. Despite my shift ending, I walk over to the group of soldiers waiting administration. Several nurses join me, and we each take a soldier, guiding them to a vacant cot.

His cheeks reddening beneath the dirt, the soldier grimaces as I remove his boots. The aroma is worse than John Edwards' farts. Pickled eggs don't agree with him; not that it stops him eating the blighters. I grab the second boot and concentrate on smiling and stopping my nose from wrinkling. "Don't worry. Compared to my brother's feet, these are like daisies."

The soldier nods, his eyelids falling as he lays back in relief. A hand touches my shoulder, and I turn. Morag stands behind me and I raise a questioning brow.

Pearl brushes past, tending to the soldier. "I've got this, Lilly, you go with Morag."

Like a vice, her fingers close round my arm, and I allow Morag to pull me away from the patient. Stone faced, she refuses to speak, and my heart hammers in my chest. We exit the hospital and stride towards the soldiers lying over the grass and asphalt, waiting to be administered into the hospital. Fear curdles within my belly, producing a sour taste in my mouth. There is no reason for Pearl to take over my duties, or for me to be outside, unless something is wrong. I try to keep my panic from surfacing. "What's going on?"

"Over 'ere," Morag says, avoiding my question.

As we reach the grass, a head of auburn hair glistens in the early morning sun. My breath catches in my throat for the briefest of seconds, and I doubt what my eyes are telling me. It can't be … I should have been clearer when

I asked God to check on my brothers. What I meant was to keep them safe, out of trouble, and in one piece. Not deposit them in a hospital. That said, Charles Jason is better off here than stranded on the beaches of France.

Outside, soldiers are being categorised and coded according to their injuries. Stretchers wait to carry those requiring immediate attention into the hospital. With feet that want to run, I maintain an unhurried walk. Morag remains at my side her fingers never letting go of my arm. My youngest brother, Charles Jason, is at Stanmore. I dread to think of all that he's seen and experienced. His deep brown eyes light up when he sees me, and I kneel on the grass at his side, looking him over. "Well, it looks like you've got yourself into a fine mess this time, Charlie."

He scratches at his right leg, his features contorting in pain as he shuffles.

"We'll cover for ye, take yer time," Morag says, returning to her duties.

That is what I should be doing. What I am trained to do. Relative, friend, or stranger, we shouldn't treat them differently. But this is my brother, and I can't leave him until I've carried out a full assessment.

I smooth away the matted hair from his face, kissing the top of his head.

"You're fussing," Charles Jason complains.

"No, I'm just making sure you're real."

"Of course I'm bloody real. Now stop fussing."

I ruffle his hair. "True, dreams don't smell as bad as you."

The soldiers near us laugh.

"Bugger off."

"Not until I've looked you over."

He sighs but doesn't argue. From where we sit, I start my examination. Charles Jason winces, squirming like a toddler. Dried blood cakes the tear in his trousers, and I pull the fabric apart to reveal a large blister. The skin tone is paler than usual and the bluish, purple, and black staining of gangrene stares back at me. Charlie's fighting days are over. "Well, you've certainly made a mess."

"It wasn't me; it was that Jerry bugger."

"In that case, we'd best be grateful the Jerry bugger couldn't shoot straight."

Sweat bleeds along his forehead, and his skin is hot beneath my fingers, confirming infection. With glazed eyes, he attempts to smile. In a short time, my brother has aged many years. The look of innocence he carried is gone. Perhaps our generation is one of people growing up too fast. A product of the horrors we have seen and will never forget.

"It's not good, is it?"

"I've seen worse," I say.

His hand touches mine. "I'm losing the leg, aren't I?"

"No," I correct him, "you're keeping your life."

He shrugs. "It doesn't matter, I've known for some time something wasn't right. If it wasn't for Alick, I'd be dead, I've got to be grateful for that."

There's a sadness about him I don't like. "What happened, Charlie?"

"That's twice you've called me that. If Jane Anne hears you, she'll have you strung up."

"Not even Jane Anne's hearing is that good."

His gaze loses awareness as his mind travels to a different time and place. I squeeze his hand, bringing him back to the present. "It's alright, you don't have to tell me."

"No, I want to. Then if you meet Alick, you can thank him for me. It'll be like finding a blue tiddly wink in a bag of red counters, but never say never, eh."

His eyelashes flutter. He's having difficulty staying awake. I kiss his cheek. "It's ok, Charlie, tell me later. Get some rest and I'll come and see you after they've operated."

On instruction from the doctor, two orderlies move forward, placing the stretcher on the ground near my brother. I step back and they lift him onto the litter. There is nothing I can do but wait for him to come out of surgery, and I make my way back inside. Morag and Pearl are waiting for me.

Pearl's brows crease in concern. "Try not to worry, Lilly, he'll be on the ward soon enough."

Morag threads her arm through mine. "At least ye ken where he is."

"You're both right, but …"

"It's harder when it's your flesh and blood, I get that, but you need to look after yourself, too. You're exhausted, you've done a double shift today, you need to rest," Pearl says as we walk down the corridor.

My uniform is stained with blood and dirt, and I'm dead on my feet. "I don't think I'm going to sleep."

Morag pulls away, her footsteps slowing. "If ye won't kip, then at least eat somethin'."

"Let's freshen up and go for something to eat, so Morag won't spend the night whinging in my ear about you not eating," Pearl says.

I look down at my uniform. "Alright, I don't want to frighten Charlie when he comes round."

My brother looks so young as he sleeps. His infected leg is gone, and it is time for his body to heal.

A white chair appears at my side. "Here, you'll be more comfortable sitting on this."

"Thanks, Adah."

I stroke my brother's hair as I softly sing to him. Charlie is a big fan of Sam Browne, who sings with Jack Hylton and His Orchestra. *Hang On To Me* has a nice upbeat rhythm; it's also his favourite. His eyes flutter open, and there is a moment of confusion as his brain makes sense of recent events.

"How long have you been sitting there?"

I smile down at him, removing my hand. "A while."

"You'll have been on shift all day; you need to rest."

"No, I need to be right here."

With my hand in his, I revel in the fact he made it from France. Not in one piece, but alive. Tears appear, sliding down his cheek. Charles Jason Nutman looks more vulnerable than I have ever seen him, and I brush away his tears. "It's alright, Charlie, you're safe."

"I wanted to thank him, Lilly … Alick … I wanted him to understand … he saved my life … and I never got the chance to say thank you …"

"He'll know, Charlie. Sometimes you don't need to say the words, you just know."

"But …"

"Please don't worry."

He becomes agitated.

"Alright, Charlie, you can tell me, if it will help."

"W-when …" He coughs, and I hand him a glass of water. He sips, regaining his composure. "When we made it to the beaches, we sat. There was no food or water. Nowhere to hide. Nowhere to go. And nothing to defend ourselves with. For forty-eight hours we sat on that beach waiting for the order to be given. It was Alick's birthday, he was twenty-seven. I remember thinking, it's no way to spend a birthday, but thank God he was there … He gave me the courage to keep fighting when all I wanted was to die. For the pain in my leg to stop and my mind to cease its torture, to stop reliving the last several days."

He grows quiet. His mouth opens and closes. With my hand in his, I wait for him to speak.

"A day earlier, while making our way to the beaches, a Jerry came charging at us, firing. Perhaps he thought we were out of bullets, maybe that's why he came at us like he did. Courage is easy when your enemy can't defend themselves. That's when my leg got shot up. Alick used his last bullet to save my life. When that Jerry went down, it was the most satisfying thing I've felt. Alick smiled at me. 'That will teach him,' he said.

"The bullet in my leg slowed us down. With snipers operating in the area, I kept telling him to leave me and get the hell out while he had a chance. Alick wouldn't listen. He all but dragged me to that beach. And when we arrived, there was nothing to do but sit on the sand and watch them bomb the rescue ships. We were useless against them. The only ammunition we had were prayers. I kept saying to myself, 'What good are prayers?' They're not bulletproof. Even if we made it off the beach, there was a bomber waiting for us. Bulletproof or not, I prayed … I prayed so hard to survive.

"Our company was a-hundred-and-seven strong. When we got to the beach, there were thirty of us left. Shrapnel was flying everywhere. Colin got hit. He died instantly … I remember crying … seeing him like that, torn to pieces, metal-eating at flesh like jelly … i-it was horrible. H-he was nineteen, Lilly. Nineteen … H-he shouldn't of died, his body ripped apart like that."

He takes a deep, steadying breath. "Alick held me to him. 'Dinnae worry,' he said, in that Scottish accent of his that always makes me smile, even when I don't want to. 'Ah've nae saved ye just so ye kin die noo. Ye goin' haime.' I was so frightened, Lilly, really frightened. I'm twenty-three. Like Colin, that's no age to die. Yet Colin died, so what did age have to do with it?

"When they gave the signal for us to board the waiting ships, Alick dragged me off the beach, wading into the water. My teeth were clattering so bad I feared I'd bite my tongue clean off. As we got closer, they hung ropes down the side of the ships for us. Alick hooked his arm around me, swimming the last few yards. Grabbing onto the rope, he tied it around my chest, and they hauled me up. As I hit the deck, I passed out. I-I never saw Alick after that. He made it on the ship, but I'm not sure what happened to him." His fingers comb his hair and a smile flutters. "You can't miss Alick, he's built like an oversized bulldog."

Tears sting my eyes as he talks. Pain hangs in his voice and his gaze fills with sadness.

His hand grips mine. "If you ever get the chance, Lilly, his name is Sergeant Alick McNavis. Tell him I said thank you, and I'm grateful he saved my life."

"I promise, Charlie, I'll tell him."

"He was so fearless, Lilly. Just a few years older than me … and he was fearless. I wish I could have been more like him."

"Don't talk like that, Charlie, you're brave, just as brave as Alick. You've just stopped seeing it."

His eyelids flutter and he falls back against the pillows, unconscious. "I'll find Sergeant Alick McNavis, Charlie. If not now, when this war is over, and I'll tell him you said thank you."

Pearl's hand rests on my shoulder as I cry. My hand covers hers, and I absorb the strength she offers. Charlie's bed is near the window and together, Pearl and I watch the most beautiful sunrise emerge. It lights up the sky, turning the clouds red, setting the sky on fire.

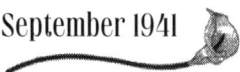

Dear Jane Anne,

You've always been an enigma, a glamourous, distant, and impenetrable mystery. Charisma oozes from you like an intoxicating perfume. It is one of your many attributes. They say an onion has many layers; don't we all. We aren't vegetables to be sliced, diced, and served at dinner; neither are our emotions. It's peculiar how we compare ourselves to food—mutton dressed as lamb, toffee-nosed, good egg ...

Charles Jason is amongst the survivors entering the National Orthopaedic Hospital. Many soldiers tell their stories to us. It is a way of unburdening their soul or remembering that one special person who provided light in their darkest of days. A fellow soldier who became a hero that saved them. It is truly amazing and humbling to hear the soldiers talk. I feel a deep connection to the man who saved my brother's life. We owe a great debt to Sergeant Alick McNavis for getting him to the beach and aboard the ship. My dearest wish is to one day meet him and let him know how indebted we are.

Like so many, Charles Jason's injuries went unattended, and the surgeon had no option but to amputate his leg. He keeps telling me, "A carpenter doesn't require legs, just his hands." I wish I were as positive and unfazed as my brother. He doesn't see his bravery. His courage is as strong as any hero; not once has he complained. He is as cheery as ever. His smile lights the ward and has the other patients laughing into their teacups and nurses hiding their smiles. Even though my brother remains in such high spirits, please remember to be good to him. A boy still needs his mother, no matter what he has seen or how old he gets.

The other night I sat by his bed, watching him sleep. My fingers combing his hair, he became a little boy again. His cheeks flushed against his pale skin, a scattering of freckles along his nose. Love is precious, and so is family. It binds and defines us. It brings us happiness and sorrow. But it is always there, waiting for us to embrace it. I love you, Jane Anne, even though I'm not sure what that means. It's hard loving someone you don't know.

Lillian Elizabeth

18

*C*harles Jason is making excellent progress. The removal of his right leg brings down the infection, and he spends his time in physio. He's still a little wobbly on his crutches, and when tired, he will drop where he is. And on anyone. Life at the hospital remains busy with the new admissions, but their numbers are dwindling, much to our relief. The transition from autumn to winter brings the cooler, more unpredictable weather. We can't have casualties strewn over the lawns in the rain or snow, waiting to be processed. They'll end up with pneumonia. The change in weather also brings news to prepare to leave. Aware my time with my brother is ending, I spend as much time with him as work allows.

Cigarette smoke filters over Charlie from the neighbouring patient. His head is bent, and his pencil taps against his chin as he stares at the newspaper.

He looks up as I approach. "What's a dunkable delight?"

"How many letters?" I ask, leaning over at the crossword puzzle.

"Seven."

"Try biscuit."

Charles Jason smiles. "Go on, as you're offering."

The patient next to Charlie stubs out his cigarette, chuckling. "You fell for that one, nurse."

I shake my head. "It's not the first time, either. You'd think where my brother is concerned, I would know better."

The newspaper resting on his lap, Charles Jason sniggers. "I can't help it if you're a slow learner."

I grab his crutches, ignoring his comment on my lack of intelligence. "Come on, it's time for physio."

"Is that code for, 'let's raid the biscuit barrel'?"

"No, it's code for, 'grab your crutches before you're late and have to explain why to Matron'."

"I liked the biscuit barrel option best."

My brows arch. "You can always discuss the biscuit barrel option with Matron."

He grabs the crutches. "You're such a spoilsport, Lilly."

"Hmm ... It's shameful," I say, grinning at him.

In late February 1941, new orders have Morag, Pearl, Adah, Effie, and I, along with five other sisters, packing in readiness to go to Carlton Towers, Yorkshire. London continues to take a battering from enemy aircraft. The air raids last around six to ten hours, during which troops, police and Home Guard are called to hunt for parachutists. Germany is stepping up its campaign. The 10th of September 1940 sees the longest air raid yet (8 p.m. Sunday until 5:40 a.m. the next day). Relays of German raiders drop high explosives and incendiary bombs. The following day, the newspapers estimate that one hundred and fifty planes took part in the raid. London is no longer a safe place to live.

Each day the newspapers fill their pages with the number of dead and wounded as the London Blitz continues. They make for ghastly yet addictive reading. The more information I get, the more I want.

I hug Charles Jason as we prepare to leave. "Let me know when they release you and you're back in London."

"What's the point, you'll only worry."

"I'll worry regardless. Even if it's a couple of lines, please write."

"What about you?"

"Carlton Towers is a far cry from the bombings, so no need to worry about me, I'll be fine."

"It's what comes after Carlton Towers that troubles me. I understand what it's like out there. What it's like to be helpless. I don't want that for you."

"Don't, Charlie, you need to think about keeping yourself, Aunt Sarah Rebecca, and Jane Anne safe."

Morag comes into the ward. "Tis time tae go."

"Promise you'll write, Charlie."

He nods. "It won't be anything fancy."

I get up, placing a hand on his shoulder. "Thanks."

He grabs my arm as I walk away. "Not everyone has a Sergeant McNavis getting them out of a jam, Lilly. You remember that. Wherever they send you next, look after yourself. Don't think I've not noticed how you put others first. It's time to put yourself first."

Morag pulls on my arm. "Sorry …"

I kiss the top of his head and leave the ward with Morag. Outside, Pearl, Adah and Effie wait, along with the other nurses. Pearl throws her arm over my shoulder. I feel so small and lost. Charlie is leaving the frontline, but this war isn't over.

"No brooding, it creates lines," Pearl says, and my lips tremble into a small smile.

After four hours on the road, we get our first glimpse of Carlton Towers. Our vehicle enters through a stone gateway with ornate pillars and wrought-iron gates. The manor house is the perfect setting for a fairy tale, and the romancers in us gasp and squeal in delight.

Pearl's face darkens at our reaction. "Pull yourselves together."

"C'mon, even ye have tae feel somethin'," Morag says in exasperation.

"Other than cramp in my calf, not a thing."

Tires crunch to a stop, and the driver pulls on the handbrake. We stand together by the vehicle, stretching our legs. With my hands on my hips, I take a deep breath of country air. Two hundred and fifty acres of rolling lawns and pretty flowerbeds great us. Carlton Towers is the grandest auxiliary military hospital I have ever seen, and I feast my eyes on its splendour. The building has a Victorian appearance, though its origins date back to around the 14th century, or so we are told. Age and beauty don't allow for a modern operating theatre or fully working hospital. Much like us, the manor house is adapting to its new role and purpose.

One day, people will forget about the role this stately home played as we care for the soldiers fighting in this horrid war. Carlton Towers will once again be a place for people to enjoy. A place to sit in extravagant gardens, drinking tea and enjoying the sun. There is nothing wrong with idealism during conflict. We will win this war, and life will return to some normality. Changed, but stronger, we will sit in the sun, and drink tea, and eat scones. Belief in a peaceful future is paramount in facing each day.

Pearl's elbow sinks into my ribs. "At least there's nothing gloomy about this place."

My lips twitch. "No, nothing glum about it at all."

"Ah hope they've locked up their sons."

Her features clouding with indignation, Pearl faces Morag. "Why would they lock up their sons?"

"Look!" I say, pointing.

A deer hides between the trees, and it diverts their attention, saving our ears from another outpouring of non-sibling sniping.

"Och, wow, did ye see that?"

Pearl huffs. "Of course I saw it, Morag, I have eyes."

"A deer, Adah. Quick, before you miss it," Effie shouts, pulling on her sister's arm.

Adah turns, her kit bag banging against her legs. The deer bolts, running deeper into the woods. "At least I got a glimpse of its rear end."

"Oh, poor Adah," I say, laughing at her.

We enter the makeshift hospital, and serenity falls on us. It's a far cry from our time at the National Orthopaedic Hospital. With ten nurses doing the job of two, lazy days become part of our time here. Guilt with razor-sharp claws rake at my insides. The slow pace of Carlton Towers fills me with a lack of satisfaction. After three months, we're sent to Norton Hall, near Lincolnshire. Though we are busier, it's nothing like we experienced at Stanmore. With time on our hands, we teach the orderlies—something we lacked in France. When I have too much time on my hands, I overthink things. Therefore, I spend my spare time worrying about my mother, aunt, brothers, and Joe.

On the 10th of October, I receive a letter from Charles Jason.

Dear Lilly,

I've left Stanmore. Jane Anne is busy doing ARP things. Her job leaves her no time to weep over my lost leg, leaving me grateful to ARP. There are times I catch her staring, her lips drawing in a thin line like she does when she's unhappy over something. That's when I get the impression she misses my leg more than I do. With so many lads called to duty, Old Gary Mattison has offered me my carpentry job back. He's under a lot of pressure—too much work and little in the way of resources. My luck.

I bumped into Daisy; she's expecting her first baby and thought you might want to know.

Given my lack of mobility, Aunt Sarah Rebeca has moved upstairs into our old room. I'm not sure what John Edward, Arthur James, Brian Wayne, or George Peter will make of the new sleeping arrangements when they come home. George Peter has had his eye on the front room for years, though he'll never admit it.

Anyway, keep up the good work.

Charles Jason

19

December 1941, Norton Hall, Near Lincolnshire, England

*O*ur time at Norton Hall drags. We celebrate Christmas and New Year, welcoming in 1942. In mid-January, uncertainty strikes. For months we receive orders to equip for colder climates, only for them to change to tropical climates. On the day of embarkation, with our kit bags ready for colder climates, we are called to see Matron. Our hackles are up as we wait for the pantomime to begin. This is the trillionth time this scenario has occurred. We pack and the army cancels their order.

"There's a change of plans, ladies. Unpack while we wait for further instruction."

I want to groan so much it becomes an ache. Matron leaves the room, and we drop our kit bags to the floor. "Why do they always leave it until the last minute to let us know?"

Pearl's blood pressure soars, deteriorating her vocabulary, which is getting more colourful. "Bloody hell …"

"Pearl." Adah sends her a scathing stare.

"What? I only said blood …"

"My ears have taken enough of a battering."

Morag paces in front of us, muttering something un-fathomable in Gaelic. Over the last few months, we've all gained some bad habits. I've learnt to smile until my jaw aches. Adah tuts a lot, and Effie's eyes fix on the sky. Away from the earshot of the patients, Morag and Pearl's bickering becomes less friendly as our frustration builds.

In May 1942, new orders arrive, and we pack for warmer weather, ready for embarkation. When we leave Norton Hall, it's heaven to my suffering ears. With up-heaval affecting Pearl's requirement for structure and consistency, the last few weeks have not been easy. Morag and I interpret her requirement for more 'structure and consistency' to a lack of able-bodied men. Of course, Pearl is less than polite with our interpretation—even if it's true. Much to everyone's relief, on the 14th of June we find ourselves at Norton Station waiting for our train to arrive. Unfortunately, trains never run on time.

This knowledge doesn't stop Pearl from complaining. "How much longer? The cold is nibbling at my feet. And this cap is making my head itch."

We look down at Pearl's brown leather shoes. The starched shirt, heavy cotton trousers, and jacket of our battledress uniform is more practical for travelling. With the military not used to designing women's clothing, they've adapted the men's battledress (trouser, jacket, shirt, tie, and cap). The battledress is a recent addition to our wardrobe. While it is now standard issue, the provi-sion of the uniform depends on availability. Queen

Alexandra is probably weeping in her grave seeing her nurses in trousers.

Before Pearl can grumble further, the train pulls into the station, and I look at my watch, using humour to lighten our mood. "Eight forty-five a.m. They need Matron running things, she'd have them running to schedule."

Pearl side arms me. "Humph ... how hard can it be to drive a train over some tracks."

"There are always holdups somewhere, Pearl. Leaves on the track, breakdowns," I say, accepting the train's tardiness.

"Enough, Lilly. If I wanted optimism, I would have asked for it."

Morag slaps Pearl on the back. "There's na pleasin' ye."

The train hisses to a stop and we board. Storing our kit bags, we sit down, getting comfortable.

"Come on, Morag, get a riddle on, the train will move soon."

"Alright, alright, ah'm goin' as quick as ah can. Move along, Effie, 'n' ah'll sit next tae ye."

Effie slides along the seat closer to Adah, and Pearl sits down next to me. With a shudder, the train rocks into motion.

"I don't suppose you fancy swapping places? I travel better next to the window."

Morag lets out a loud, disgruntled sigh. "For Lairds' sake, Pearl, the window's blacked oot, ye cannae see anythin'. Stay where ye are."

"It's alright, I don't mind moving," I say, standing up.

Pearl shuffles over, placing her head against the window, her cap trapped between the glass and her head. "Thanks, Lilly."

We change trains several times before reaching Liverpool at 2:40 p.m. At the station, we're herded into the waiting transportation. There is just time for a quick visit to the bathroom before we're off.

"Ah feel like a highland cow," Morag says above the vehicle's engine.

Pearl laughs. "Then mooo-ve up and give me some room."

Adah and Effie groan, their heads shaking at Pearl's grim joke.

Hand over my mouth, I laugh. "I see your humour is coming back."

Pearl shrugs. "It never left."

"Ye could have fooled us," Morag grumbles, shifting to give Pearl more room.

We arrive at Liverpool docks at 3:15 p.m. A cool breeze whips over us as we stand gawking at the *Duchess of Richmond*, which is to be our new home. A crowd gathers, waiting for the signal to board, and we move towards them. It's hard to say how many of us wait on the docks, but there are at least six or seven thousand of us.

Jaws hitting our chests, Pearl smiles up at the *Duchess of Richmond*. "It's grander than the last troopship we were on."

I stare at the cruise liner. "I'll say."

"My grandfather worked on the *Sobraon*. In April 1901, while sailing from Shanghai to London, the *Sobraon* became shipwrecked. It was her third voyage. My grandfather loved the liners. This ..."—Adah waves a hand at the ship—"is a Canadian Pacific liner. The *Duchess of Richmond* is the sister ship to the *SS Duchess of York*, *SS Duchess of Bedford*, and *SS Duchess of Atholl*. Together they're known as the *Drunken Duchesses*.'"

Morag frowns. "Why name them the *Drunken Duchesses*? Tis nae like the ships kin drink. Or ah hope nae, given ah cannae swim."

Adah laughs. "The name isn't due to them drinking in water, but their lively performance on heavy seas."

Morag wrinkles her nose. "It dinnae seem much o' a party ship."

Pearl taps Morag's shoulder. "I wouldn't worry about partying, but the performance on heavy seas. It's making my stomach churn."

The signal given, we move, tiny steps at a time, boarding the liner. Excitement sings through my veins—I've never been on something so posh as a cruise liner before. A vision of being whisked away to exotic places, eating, drinking, and partying my days and evenings away makes me smile.

Morag looks over her shoulder at the line of waiting passengers. "How many does this thin' hold?"

"Around one-thousand-five-hundred," Adah says with a shrug.

Nervous, Morag nibbles at her bottom lip. "But there's thousands of us boardin'. It won't sink, will it? Ye ken, if there's tae many on board?"

Pearl loses her footing and trips. "Don't you dare start with such nonsense."

"Twas just a thought."

"Well keep it to yourself."

"Morag has a point."

"No, Lilly, don't encourage her."

"Tis alright for ye, ah cannae swim."

"You won't have to swim, Morag," Adah says. "The liner isn't about to sink."

"Cross ye heart."

Adah sends Morag a stony glare.

By the time we board, many of the servicewomen are already there. The khaki uniform of the Auxiliary Territorial Service (ATS) blends with the uniform of the Women's Royal Naval Service (WRNS). To their left, a cluster of Women's Auxiliary Air Force (WAAF) gather with the First Aid Nursing Yeomanry (FANY) and Voluntary Aid Detachments (VADs).

Inside the *Duchess of Richmond*, a new and fascinating world opens. In its capacity as a luxury liner, it is accustomed to providing a top-class, comfortable service. The first-class cabins are on the upper deck, and as QAs, we hold an officer's rank, therefore we're allocated those cabins. They are small, though comfortable, our accommodation gaining extra beds to allow further sleeping capacity. I share with Morag and Pearl in one of the smaller cabins. A feeling of being part of a society I could only have viewed from afar washes over me, and I can't stop smiling.

Pearl and I kneel on one of the three beds, looking through the small port window, our shoulders touching as we point at the smaller ships. On the floor, near our cots, our kit bags wait to be unpacked. Morag's Scottish accent echoes along the corridor as she chats with the other QAs, and we turn as she enters, our smiles so big they take over our facial features.

Morag's bag hits the floor, and she plops down on one of the empty beds, sinking into the mattress, her arms spread in front of her. "Och, have ye heard? We get tae dine at the captain's table 'n' drink cocktails … cocktails … Hoo posh is that."

"I predict we are going to be in high demand. Have you seen how many men are boarding or have boarded? There aren't enough women to go round. Why, I've died and gone to heaven," Pearl breathes, falling back against the mattress, her left arm draping over the side of the bed as she pretends to faint.

Giddy, I flop down, my back hitting the side of the ship as I nudge Pearl's legs. "Never change, Pearl."

Morag's brows wrinkle in concern. "Noo remember that talk from Matron aboot the dangers o' love affairs with married men. Dinnae get carried away with yerself. Yer 'ere tae work, nae break hearts."

Pearl sits up, waving off Morag's comment. "You're such a pooper. Well, you can be all prim and proper if you like, I'm going to enjoy myself while I can. Besides, I'm not about to get serious with anyone."

My mouth falls open in shock. "Good Lord, Pearl, don't let Matron hear you say that."

Pearl wiggles her eyebrows. "I'm always very discreet."

I giggle into my hand. "You're awful."

Morag jumps off the bed, her feet hitting the floor with a thump. "As we cannae change her, we'll ignore her."

She grabs my hands, pulling me off the bed. "C'mon, let's go get Effie 'n' Adah 'n' get back on deck."

Like the Cheshire cat in Lewis Carroll's *Alice's Adventures in Wonderland*, Pearl's grin grows huge. "You know, Morag, I couldn't have said that better."

We march down the corridor, giggling as we collect Adah and Effie. The numbers on deck have grown and I gulp, hoping Adah is right about the ship not sinking.

Scottish twang mixes with other accents, and Morag points at the distinctive stag badge on the soldiers' caps. "That's the badge o' the 51st Highlanders. Mah granddaddy was a Highlander when they formed the division in 1915."

"I thought your granddaddy didn't fight in the Great War because of his clubfoot?" Pearl asks.

"Aye, 'twas nae his fault his foot turned down 'n' inward."

"Then how did he join the 51st Highlanders?"

"Och, Pearl, do ye have tae be such a spoilsport. Mah granddaddy made it tae his medical. That's when they discovered his clubfoot 'n' sent him haime." She shrugs. "'Tis the same thin'."

Pearl shakes her head. "No, it's different."

"How come it took him until 1915 to try joining the war?" Effie asks, shouting to be heard above the noise of the embarking troops.

"He tried loads o' times, boot they kept rejectin' him. He was tryin' tae get away from grandma."

Pearl snorts. "If she was anything like you, I'm not surprised."

"What's that supposed tae mean?"

"Nothing, Morag, Pearl was just saying it was such a shame about your granddaddy, weren't you, Pearl?"

She sighs at me. "If that makes you happy, Lilly, that's what I said."

Effie nods at the troops. "There's a lot of them."

"There is," I say, staring at the sea of uniforms, stunned by the magnitude and the limited living accommodation on the ship. "Where are they going to sleep?"

Adah's lips almost disappear as she stretches them into a thin line. "They'll be in the bowels of the ship."

"What's that?" Morag asks.

Adah's face pinches in concern. "It's the smelly part of the ship."

We gaze at the troops with fresh eyes.

"No point in mulling that over now, let's go get jovial with the new arrivals. Welcome them onboard."

Morag rolls her eyes. "Yer all heart, Pearl."

"I know, it's shocking, isn't it?"

We follow Pearl onto the main deck. A jubilant atmosphere pours over us. It doesn't feel like we're setting sail to an unknown destination, to care for the sick and wounded.

Pearl taps my arm. "Listen to them, Lilly, don't their accents sound so yummy? My toes are curling in my shoes."

"But you don't like the Scottish twang."

"Oh no, I have nothing against it at all when it's deep and masculine. It's Morag's high-pitched accent that grates."

Though her face darkens and her eyes narrow, Morag remains silent.

The Scots bring the promise I made Charles Jason into focus, and I scan the troops, looking for Sergeant McNavis. As I don't know what he looks like, it's a silly thing to do, but I can't help myself. Is it even possible that Alick McNavis is on board? And what if he is? The chance of bumping into him is remote, unless he falls sick—not impossible, optimism reminds me.

Pearl pats her hair, rearranging her cap. "Well?"

"Ah assume ye mean yer hair 'n' nae the men."

"Sometimes, Morag, I think you're ghastly to me because you're jealous."

Morag scoffs. "Though ah'm goin' tae hate myself for askin' … Why am ah jealous o' ye?"

"Well, for one, I don't have wild red hair."

"Na, ye have limp blonde hair that takes an age tae style."

Adah and Effie stand behind us, and I turn to them, leaving Morag and Pearl to wage their war on each other. "They love each other really."

Effie giggles at me. "Their arguing is oddly comforting."

"I know what you mean," I say.

A hand presses down on my shoulder, and I jump.

"Whoa there," a masculine voice says. Joe stands behind me, his hand resting on my shoulder.

"Joe!" I scream, throwing my arms around his neck, hugging him tight.

Given that God sent Charles Jason back with only one leg, I hold Joe at arm's length, my gaze sweeping over him. All legs, hands, arms, eyes, ears, and fingers accounted for—I smile in satisfaction.

His arms wrap around my waist, pulling me to him, making me giggle. "Now that's a better greeting."

Morag claps. "This is brilliant, the gang's back taegether."

"So, what brings you to a place like this? Looking for adventure?" Pearl asks in sultry tones.

"Stop that, Joe's spoken for," Morag says, making my cheeks burn.

Adah rubs her hands together. "Come on, let's grab a cuppa, my hands are getting cold."

Pearl's head tilts up at the sky. "The sun's out."

"That means nothing when there's a northerly wind," Adah says, walking away, leaving Pearl looking puzzled.

"Huh?"

Effie leans into Pearl, cupping her hand over her ear. "She's trying to give Lilly and Joe some privacy."

Pearl bats Effie's hand away from her ear. "Then why didn't she say that?"

Morag stands transfixed next to me and Joe, soaking up the Scottish accent, bathing in its familiarity. A faraway look clouds her face as she gazes at the mass of soldiers.

"Ah've nae been back tae Scotland since ah was a wee lassie. Ah never realised hoo much ah missed it 'til noo."

With his hand still on my waist, Joe looks over at the troops. "You'll get the chance to go back to Scotland when this war is over."

Morag sighs. "Aye, mibbie."

I place a hand on her shoulder. "I'm sure you will."

She looks over at Adah, Effie, and Pearl. "Where the heck are they goin'?"

"There's a northerly wind so they've gone for a cuppa," Joe says, hiding his smile.

Morag grabs my hand. "C'mon, Lilly, looks like we're on the move."

A group of soldiers step forward, blocking Morag's view, and she scowls at them.

"It's good tae see ye, Joe," she says, pulling me forward.

His eyebrows meet in a quizzical expression as he waves at me. "But … I'll catch up with you later …"

I turn, grinning at him. "That'll be nice."

We become lost in the crowd as Morag continues to pull me along. My shoulder connects with a soldier, and I turn, shouting, "Sorry," as I try to keep my footing.

Pearl waves at Morag as we break through the throng. "What do you think you're doing with Lilly? We were giving her and Joe some privacy, dummy."

"Och, ye mean there is na northerly wind?"

Effie shakes her head.

Morag lets go of my arm, placing her hands on her hips. "Adah needs tae be clearer."

"Honestly, have you never heard of tact?"

"Like ye ken what the word 'tact' means."

"Joe and Lilly make the cutest couple," Effie says, wistfulness hanging in her voice, sending heat to my cheeks.

Pearl pulls a face, her lips rolling in distaste. "Ugh, Effie, stop with all the mush. As for you, Lilly, you need to snap Joe up before someone else does."

"Aye, she's got a point. What ye waitin' for?"

"I know, I just don't know if I like Joe like that or even how much."

"Then ye'd best make yer mind up quick."

There is little I can say in my defence; Morag and Pearl are right. Does it matter that my heart doesn't flutter when I see him?

Our earlier experiences have widened our tolerance towards long waiting times. Which is as well, given that the ship remains docked until Friday the 19th of June. With so many available men on board, Pearl's earlier disdain for waiting vanishes. As the morning mist lifts, we move in readiness for our escort. Sirens shrieking, the boats still in harbour hoot a farewell. People shout, wishing us a happy and safe journey. A thrill washes over us as we begin our voyage to the unknown. Morag and Pearl laugh, waving at the boats still in the harbour. Joe has disappeared. Like a mirage, it's as if he was never here. With the *Duchess of Richmond* over its intended occupancy, it's hard to keep track of everyone onboard. We'll meet up at some point, on the ward or deck, I'm sure.

Doubt is a torturous emotion; it stops me from embracing a deeper, more personal relationship with Joe. When I'm not with him, my thoughts stray, and I wonder where he is, and what he's doing. His face keeps popping up in my head, along with the expectation of bumping into him. Pearl and Morag are right; if I'm not careful someone will snap him up. Joe is a good man. Choices aren't always easy, add uncertainty and war and they become an unbearable adversary.

"Oh, Lilly, isn't it exciting," Effie says, leaning over the railing at my side, the breeze carrying her laughter away.

Her enthusiasm is infectious, and I join in, cheering as the docked boats become smaller and their waving hands get harder to see.

20

*L*ife on board the *Duchess of Richmond* starts at 7:30 a.m. with an hour of PE on deck, followed by lectures. These lectures hold a variety of topics, from medicine to culture. With duty on a rota of two days on, two days off, and little to do and our wandering limited, we become bored. Matron comes up with a plan to prevent our boredom from escalating, tasking us with organising daily activities. As nurses we are excellent organisers, and we form an Entertainment Committee to provide a mix of events to suit all onboard. Morag, Adah, Effie, Pearl, and I, in our new role, sit on deck, enjoying the mild weather.

The task at hand is to publish a list of activities and timings on posters and scatter them around the corridors of the ship. The weather is forever changing, which causes more problems than it does solutions in our planning. With Pearl's focus taken up by a Tommie, her lack of concentration is frustrating. At twenty-six, and with a face filled with freckles, Patrick Thompson is the son of a doctor, whom he had no wish to take after. There is, I feel, a story there, but Pearl's interest relates to Patrick's physical attributes, more than learning his life history. He has a stocky build and muscles, which Pearl says would put David Cecil to shame. This would be shocking news to the three-gold medal athlete, I'm sure, given his rigorous training. Pearl may not have a romantic bone in her body, but she is a dreamer. David George Brownlow Cecil, 6th Marquess of Exeter, and athlete, is a striking man. By comparison, he makes Patrick appear ordinary. Though I'm no expert in this field, if asked, I'd say that David Cecil is more muscular and striking in appearance.

From the look Morag sends Pearl, it's clear her patience is wearing thin. "Ye need tae stop thinkin' aboot the Tommie 'n' start contributin' tae the plannin'. Get control o' yerself."

"You heard Matron, we need to keep the men active. That's all I'm doing. You're such a fuddy-duddy."

"Ah'm nae a fuddy-duddy. Matron dinnae mean active the way ye've taken it. Entertainment is supposed tae keep us all occupied. Nae a one-on-one thin'."

Pearl raises an eyebrow. "More than a twosome, Morag, that has a whole different meaning."

"Keep it clean, Pearl," I warn her.

Adah leans across, handing me the pad and pen. "Here, Lilly, you'd best take this. At this rate, I'm liable to do something improper with the pen."

Morag gives a satisfied sniff. "If it shuts Pearl up, ah'm all for doin' somethin' improper, pen or na pen, count me in."

"Me! What have I got to do with Adah and where she wants to stick her pen?"

With a laboured sigh, I pick up the notebook and pen. "Adah was referring to both of you." My hand flies up. "No, you're not allowed to comment. Your sniping is getting us nowhere. The entertainment programme is our chance to show our commitment and rally the troops. Organising entertainment is a world away from the humdrum of nursing; let's enjoy it and remember the events must be inclusive."

Effie slaps her hands on her lap. "Lilly's right, it's nice to do something fun for a change."

Pearl opens her mouth.

"The troops," Adah grinds out and Pearl huffs.

"What about a dance night?" Effie asks.

Pearl pushes her hair behind her right ear. "I like that idea. We'll need some music."

"Lilly kin sing 'n' the Highlanders have their bagpipes. We kin do some Ceilidh dancing. Ah'm a very skilled dancer." Morag taps her feet in demonstration.

Pearl smiles, getting into the spirit. "Patrick can play the trombone …"

"Humph … 'n' we're back tae Patrick."

"It's not my fault he's a musician."

"Aye …"

"Did Patrick bring his trombone with him?" I ask, as this will be the deciding factor.

Pearl shakes her head, and Morag snorts.

Effie pats her sister's hand. "We can play the piano. There's one in the lounge, we can have a dance and music there one night, when the weather is ghastly."

My pen hovers over the notebook. "They don't allow Tommies in the lounge, so we'll need a bad weather plan for them, too. Let's stick to bagpipes as the Highlanders have them. They can play them on and below deck."

"What do you think about adding your name to the list of singers, Lilly? I can always see if there is anyone else to join you."

"Thanks, Effie, I'm happy to add my name. You have a pretty voice, Pearl, why don't you sing with me?"

"If you like to hear a magpie warble. No, organising the music so we don't duplicate is more my thing."

I take notes, scribbling a list of activities for the evening's entertainment. "If you get me a list of those willing to sing, Effie. And, Pearl, would you check if anyone has a mouth organ, too?"

Effie nods. "I'll have a list for you by tomorrow."

"Great. What about you, Pearl, can you start a list of music? Also, what about a music request night?"

"No problem, circulating is my thing, I'll find out what music everyone wants and compile a list, as well as a mouth organist."

"Ah'll get a list o' the soldiers tae play the bagpipes 'n' dance."

I smile. "Great, thanks, Morag."

Adah stretches her arms high above her head. "This is going well."

"We make a fabulous Entertainment Committee," I say as my pen glides across the page.

"What about an arm wrestling match? Ye kin referee, announcin' the winners, Pearl."

Pearl smiles at Morag. "I like that idea. What other physical activities do you think we should arrange?"

"How about a magic show?" Effie asks. "I've always loved magic."

Pearl wrinkles her nose. "I'm not keen, I think we need to keep it sporty. How about a three-legged race?"

"A magic show is different," I say. "We can't make everything about sport. What about asking Joe to do some sketches, to make the posters stand out? He's good at caricatures."

Pearl's head tips back in thought. "I didn't know Joe could draw."

"Remember his notebook when we were doin' our trainin'? 'Twas covered in wee sketches," Morag says.

Pearl nods. "You're right, I'd forgotten about that."

I make a mental note to find Joe and ask him. "Brilliant. Right, all in favour of a magic show and Joe doing the sketches put your hands up."

I raise my hand, followed by Adah, Effie, and a reluctant Pearl.

"Morag?"

"Sorry, Lilly, ah'm in. Ah was thinkin' aboot a strongman contest."

"I'm liking Morag's idea. It sounds fun. We can see how many nurses they can lift at once."

"Pearl!" Effie hisses, her hand against her mouth.

"The strongman competition is good. I'm liking it, but they can't use anything live as weights …"

"You're such a stick-in-the-mud, Lilly," Pearl cuts in, grumbling.

I grin at her as I consult my list. "Let's vote on the sports activities. We've arm wrestling, a three-legged race, and a strongman contest. Everyone agree to this?"

"I'm in," Adah says.

"Me too," Effie and Morag say together.

Pearl nods and I scribble. "That's settled. So what about a sack, ball and spoon race, as we don't want to break any eggs?"

Morag laughs. "Ah like that. We kin use pillowcases rather than sacks."

"Going back to evening entertainment, what about a play?"

Morag glances at Pearl, a dreamy expression on her face. "That's a brilliant idea, ah've always loved the theatre. When ah was a wee lassie, Ma took me tae watch *Babes in the Wood*. 'Twas brilliant."

"What about *Macbeth*?" Effie asks.

Pearl shakes her head. "Too heavy."

"*A Midsummer Night's Dream* is one of Shakespeare's more fun plays," Adah suggests.

"Can anyone think of another play?" Pearl asks.

"What about *Romeo and Juliet*?"

"Excellent suggestion, Effie."

Pearl groans. "You would agree to a romance, Morag. But there must be something more upbeat."

Pen tapping against my lips I look up from the notebook. "As we can't agree, let's leave the play. We've got a lot here already, it's a good start for now."

"Right," Effie and Adah say.

Pearl shrugs and Morag nods.

I snap the notebook closed with my pen inside, keeping my page. "I'd best start getting ready, I'm on shift soon."

"You going to catch up with Joe about the drawings?" Pearl asks.

"Can do, though if either of you spy him first, it would be worth mentioning it."

My legs have gone stiff, and I stretch them before making my way below deck. A bubble of excitement snips at my heels; it feels good to be doing something fun and constructive.

Letter Home, June 1942

Dear Jane Anne,

Before I left England, I noticed, from the newspapers, that London is taking a battering, and so are the Nazis. *The Daily Herald* claims our RAF shot down one hundred and seventy-five Nazi planes, in what they're calling "The biggest air battle of the war so far." What also catches my eye is that the Nazis have bombed Buckingham Palace again. That's three times so far. Is Germany trying to rid us of our monarchy and, in doing so, our history, to break us? It's as well we're made of sterner stuff. Still, it's worrying.

We sail on a cruise liner, commandeered by the military as a rather posh troopship. The *Duchess of Richmond* is huge, and it's taken a while to accustom myself to the floor plan. I can't tell you how many times I've taken a wrong turn. Instead of finding myself at the captain's table to dine, I've ended up in a broom closet. Well, not quite, but very close. All I can see is miles upon miles of water, and our convoy. Where we travel, I don't know; the military enjoys making life mysterious.

We've been at sea for days and the weather is up and down, though the *Duchess of Richmond* is coping well, and our journey is smooth. Many of us can't swim and with the ship overcrowded, it's worrying when a storm hits.

It's hard being here, knowing somewhere out there, in many countries, people are dying. I am on a cruise liner, with lavish meals that would steal your breath. Rationing doesn't exist on the *Duchess of Richmond*, not that I'm trying to make you jealous. With food being restricted back home, it wouldn't be right. You would fit in here amongst the finery and extravagance; I'm far too clumsy for such fanciness. Life on the *Duchess of Richmond* is like "the calm before the storm." Whatever happens, we will face it with the poise and dignity our uniform commands.

Joe is here, though he seems elusive. I see him in the hospital while working, though socially he remains absent. When we were in France, I was used to him being around. While he spent time with the other officers, he always had time for me. I keep wondering if he feels different towards me. It makes me queasy. Isn't that an odd thing to write, given I'm on water? All my old insecurities about our relationship are plaguing me, and I fear Joe is avoiding me. To think I was afraid I'd turn out like you and mess things up, when in fact I haven't even considered that Joe wouldn't remain interested. Gosh, don't I sound egotistical? I wish I was confident. Instead, I'm all churned up inside like a batch of butter. Are all relationships like this, or am I overcomplicating things? I wish that this piece of paper could talk. Any advice would be welcome.

Despite the ship's size, there aren't that many places a doctor can hide—not that I'm saying Joe is hiding from me. I'm going to have to grow a backbone as I've heard Brian Wayne tell George Peter when he's snivelling over something. Or I'll drive myself insane, or something similar. Well, I'd best go, I'm singing on deck tonight.

Lillian Elizabeth

21

June 1942, The Duchess of Richmond

*A*t 11 a.m. on the 20th of June, we reach the coast off the Isle of Man. The sun, which has been in hiding, breaks out, and a thousand tiny water diamonds scatter across the surface of the ocean. It is a magical sight. Sometimes we wake to the ocean spreading out before us, other times, the coastline of the United Kingdom. Rumours of our destination are rife, and by the second week it's like I am Jules Verne's Phileas Fogg, proceeding forward on an epic journey.

Morag is the first of us to find Joe and ask him about the sketches. I'm being oversensitive and I can't shake the notion he's avoiding me. His behaviour is out of character. There are plenty of women onboard the *Duchess of Richmond* to snap him up, and I fear I'm getting desperate. Unsure how to proceed, I bury my head in the sand, hoping everything works out.

Any probing by Morag, concerning Joe, needs handling delicately. Our Scottish wildcat is sensing discord and is determined to find its root cause. I dismiss her concerns; Joe is busy with lectures. That sounds suspicious. The sketches on the corridor walls suggest he isn't that busy. What is it Jane Anne says about keeping people keen? "Treat them mean, to keep them keen." Hmm … Joe doesn't play games, so now I'm back to being sensitive.

Entertainment onboard the ship is in full swing and well received. We've even added a card night—no gambling though, that's strictly against the rules. Pride might be a sin, but it's justified. The atmosphere is giddy and everyone is wearing a smile. A warm, radiant feeling explodes inside me. The captain and crew are complimentary, and even Matron has commented.

Pearl dances along the corridor as we make our way to our cabin, snagging Morag's hand and twirling her round as I clap out a beat. Morag breaks into a Highland jig, her arms above her head as she reaches the door.

"Hey, Pearl, have ye seen this from Joe?" Morag says, giggling and puffing as she regains her breath.

Removing a piece of paper from the door, Morag holds it out in front of her so Pearl and I can see it. Spread across the paper is a caricature drawing of me while I was singing on stage. Perhaps I've been judgemental about Joe's absence. The drawing gives me a funny side I wasn't aware of having. My features are exaggerated, and my eyes resemble saucers, while my lips create a perch big enough for a bird to nest on.

Pearl's hand covers her mouth in shock. "Crikey, love a duck. What's Joe on? If you have the chance to enhance a woman's body part, why the lips and eyes and not the breasts?"

Morag takes the sketch from Pearl, handing it to me. "Joe is a gentleman, nae like the Tommies ye hang around with. He wouldnae do somethin' so vulgar tae Lilly."

Pearl shrugs. "He's still a man."

"Aye, well this is Joe."

"I like my picture, I think it makes me look fun," I say, hugging the sketch to my chest. Every molecule in my body is doing a happy dance, and I refuse to become critical about the overzealous proportioning of my eyes and lips, and lack of breasts.

Pearl taps the edge of the paper. "Girls aren't different to boys; we want a bit of fun the same as they do. If your heart isn't pounding, it's boring. That picture of Lilly might say respect, but what it doesn't say is desire."

I stare at Pearl, then back at the picture. Oh dear, is that why Joe's been avoiding me? He's put me in the undesirable friend category.

"Big breasts dinnae say desire, it says this girl nae a keeper. Lilly's a woman a man settles down 'n' marries. She's nae the kind a man uses until the lust burns oot."

"Humph … What would you know about lust?"

Her face reddens, and I walk between them. "Morag, don't answer that. Pearl, play nice. I like my picture, tiny breasts don't matter. Though"—I place a protective hand over the paper—"for the record, there is nothing wrong with my breasts. My head is double its size, making them appear small, is all. Besides, the sketch proves I've been on Joe's mind."

Pearl laughs. "Oh, Lilly, you are a hoot. You've got it bad."

Joe hasn't been avoiding me, he's been busy, the drawing is proof. Isn't self-doubt terrible?

"Yer cheeks are goin' red," Morag says, laughing at me.

I cup my face, hiding my cheeks. "Are they? It's the nice weather, I'm not used to it after the cold spell."

Pearl folds her arms over her chest with a smug expression. "Of course it is."

"We kin warm our hands on yer cheeks." Morag stretches her hands towards me, rubbing them together.

I laugh, batting her off. "Stop it."

Pearl dances. "Lilly and Joe, sitting in a tree, K-I-S-S-I-N-G. First comes love, then comes marriage. Then comes Lilly with a baby carriage."

We sail up the coast of Scotland, and on the 21st of June, we wake to the Mull of Kintyre, passing Ailsa Craig and Spoon Island, in the Scottish Hebrides, and the Isle of Islay. Rain batters our faces, playing havoc with our hair. Pearl remains under cover, suffering through our playful banter. The high winds and rolling sea soon wipe the smiles from our faces as our stomachs churn.

When the sea is at its worse, life onboard as a QA is demanding. Seasickness is one of the major contributors to our increased shift patterns and patients. Unfortunately, we are not immune to the rolling ship. When not on duty, we confine ourselves to our cabins, where we allow ourselves to indulge in the most unspeakable illness. The lavish meals served at the captain's table turn our stomachs, and we stay away. Our only source of comfort is our beds, where we lay waiting for the sea to calm, the ship to stop rolling, and the sickness to end.

Before boarding the *Duchess of Richmond*, I never realised how demanding work on a ship can be. Its constant rocking is frustrating and raises further issues. It's not just the sickness that challenges us. Things have a habit of falling and breaking, and moving from where we've placed them. If it's not nailed down, within seconds the item has vanished. Bottles in locked dispensary cupboards clatter and fall, and privacy screens never remain standing. It is of little comfort that the gallery, staffed by regular sailors, is suffering breakages. We are at the sea's mercy. Some days it has the notion it is the master.

When waves bash at the ship, I flashback to France and I see again the small boat being blown up. The bomb throws wood and bodies into the air, tossing them about like dandelion seeds. War does not confine itself to land—a lesson I understand too well. Rank may dictate the luxury of our cabins and where we dine, but the danger we face from the sea, Nazis, and their allies, is the same for us all. Our cabin doors remain open in case a torpedo hits us, causing the doors to twist and trapping us inside on a sinking or burning vessel. It's not a pleasant thought. At the start of every day, we practice a boat drill, no matter the weather. The summons depends on the type of attack: U-boat, or aerial. One summons is a bell, the other a klaxon. On hearing the alarm, we make our way to the allocated station point. In the middle of the ocean, with no land in sight, even if we could swim, our bodies would tire long before we encountered land.

Effie stands on deck as the sea calms. With our stomachs stopping their churning, we gather to watch the new ships as they join our escort. The drier weather brings Pearl out and we sit, huddled together, watching the waves as they gently move. We cup our mugs, drawing heat back into our flesh.

"It doesn't look like a tyrant, does it?" Pearl says, her mug hovering at her lips.

Morag and I glance at the sea, and I sigh. "It looks beautiful, and not bullish at all."

"So do mah brothers, n' they're horrible. Jamie has this lock o' red hair that likes tae sit in the middle o' his forehead. With his freckles 'n' curly locks, 'n' baby face, he resembles a cherub. Nae that he is, he's the devil. Ah've three brothers 'n' Jamie's the worse o' the lot."

I nudge her shoulder. "But you miss and love them."

"Someone's got tae, might as well be me."

Effie walks over, tucking the skirt of her dress under her. "You never talk about your brothers, what are they like?"

"Like Lilly's, a pain the bottom, always fussin' 'n' makin' hell."

"I never met my brothers, they died in the Great War."

Pearl stares out to sea. "I'm an only child."

"Aye, well, nae havin' brothers means there's less tae worry ye."

With pleading eyes, Effie gazes at Morag. "Tell me about them."

"Dinnae look at me like that."

"Please …"

"Och, alright, alright, cut it oot … Robbie's a farm-worker, so he's still at haime. He's Ma's favourite, 'n' never does a thin' wrong, even when he does somethin' wrong. Fergus is mah twin brother, nae that ye'd ken it; we're as different as kin be. Ah havenae heard from him since he signed up. He's like Lilly at keepin' in touch. Then there's Jamie, who suffers from asthma 'n' is still at haime with Ma. She wraps him in cotton wool. Ah keep tellin' them asthma 'tis nae a disability, boot they dinnae listen. The sod gets away with murder. Ah'm the only sensible one. Well, other than Robbie, but he's mean 'n' always biggin' himself up. Like, 'Ah'm the eldest 'n' Ma's favourite, so ye've got tae do as ah say.' Despite all that, ah love the miserable lot."

"Hang on … you're a twin?" I say.

"Aye well, there's nae much tae say. Fergus was born first, so he says technically that makes him older. Cannae argue with that. Boot ah hope he goes grey first. 'Twill serve him right. That's aboot all there is. We've never been close. He's a laddie 'n' enjoys hangin' round with Robbie 'n' Jamie more than me."

I nod. "My brothers are the same. I think it's a gender thing."

"Aye."

Effie rests her chin on her hand, a faraway expression on her face. "I'd still have liked to have known my brothers, but at least I've got Adah."

On June 23rd, a Sunderland flying boat circles as the cruiser leaves. They're used for maritime patrols, submarine hunting, and transporting passengers. In the extreme tail of the large four-engine flying boat are browning machine guns and pair of manually operated .303 bolt action, magazine-fed rifles, known as a Lee–Enfield rifle. The .303 are on either side of the fuselage. This detailed information comes from Pearl; Patrick wanted to be in the RAF, but the Army had other ideas. When you sign up, your placement in the military is made for you.

"Why is it their presence makes me uncomfortable?" I ask.

Effie sits next to me, her eyes glued to the Sunderland flying boat. "I think it's because it means they're expecting trouble."

"Hmm … probably."

Morag leans over my shoulder. "Ah for one feel safer with them 'ere."

"Me too," Pearl says, her head resting on my shoulder.

"It's going to be all right, isn't it?" Effie asks. "We'll make it to wherever we're going, won't we? I've always had a fear of water. It's irrational, I know, but it's just so vast."

"Don't start making me nervous. I'm supposed to be judging the arm wrestling tonight. I need to focus on biceps and the smell of testosterone wafting in the air."

I drop a kiss on Pearl's head. "If it wasn't for you, I would have led a sheltered life."

"Me tae. Even with mah brothers, ah'd nae ken so much aboot men."

"You'd best include me in that too," Effie says.

"Ye kin include most o' the women 'ere in that statement."

Pearl lifts her head. "Hey, I'm not that bad."

The wind carries our laughter away as we gaze over the sea at the Sunderland flying boat.

Letter Home, June 1942

Dear Jane Anne,

We've been aboard the *Duchess of Richmond* for several weeks and the sea has thrown its lot in with Hitler. Seasickness is a dreadful condition that affects most onboard. Even the ship's crew, used to such ailments, are victims to it. I swear, I will never eat another bite again. I can no longer walk in a straight line, and my stomach flips and churns. How the crew go about their jobs with a smile on their faces, vomiting one minute and carrying on the next, is beyond understanding. But they do. When not on duty, I stay in my cabin, sprawled on my bed, wishing I was on land. Who knew seasickness could make you feel this wretched? Throughout all our joviality when we set sail, never did I envisage my head in a bucket and dreaming of land. I hate buckets. Your eyes stare at the bottom, with nothing to look at but your own sick.

The constant rocking of the ship means that if it's not tied down, it's gone. Everything has a habit of growing legs. Do you remember how you used to say that about your lipstick? You blamed me for their disappearance, but I never touched them. It was Arthur James who came up with the novel idea of forming their very own secret society. Of course, because they're boys, and thought I didn't have ears, they maintained no secrecy around me. Arthur

James came up with the clever plan of using your lipstick to place stripes on the inside of their arms, to identify members. I wonder where he got his inspiration from; I suspect it was from Grandad Nutman's stories about the Great War. What a source of stimulation they were. I loved listening to them with my brothers. It seems so long ago when we would gather on the wooden floor in Grandma and Grandad Nutman's front room, drinking up his tales with an insatiable appetite.

Secret societies are not for girls, or so Arthur James said. It was his idea and therefore his rules. I was allowed entry into the society on special occasions, mainly when I had sweets. Yes, I'd learnt to bribe my way in. I was used to dealing with my brother's oddness towards girls, or rather, me. As the only girl, I am an anomaly they can't fathom.

Childhood memories are keeping me going. My brother's faces float in and out of my dreams and mind. I never realised until now how lucky I am to have them. The world is becoming a different place. You are becoming a different person as I explore the past. I've always thought our home life was often unhappy, but that's not the case. Does it matter that you aren't some fictional mother who cleaned our wounds and read us stories? There hasn't been a dull moment, not with my brothers around. I guess what I'm trying to say is, thank you.

Lillian Elizabeth

22

June 1942, The Duchess of Richmond

The brief interlude of calm weather ceases, and waves batter the ship. While we're confined to our cabins when not on duty, water spills onto the deck and waves hit the small window of our room. Within twenty-four hours, we're back to throwing up, wrapping arms round our stomachs and being miserable. Joe is impervious to the erratic seesawing of the ship. While he is sympathetic, a spark of amusement lights his features. I want to stick my fingers in his eyes even though I know the eye, including the optic nerve and retina, have no pain receptors. It's the satisfaction of watching the smile slip from his face I crave.

With my fingers twitching at my sides, I watch Joe's lips curve at the corners. The billy goat inside me stamps its feet, snorting, pushing air through its nostrils, ready to butt him to the back of beyond. He doesn't see the goat; he sees my ashen face as I clamp my lips together to keep down my meal of dry bread. I've lost a stone since leaving

Liverpool, and my uniform hangs from my shoulders. Joe smiles down at me, like he understands my plight, and those suffering from the sea's onslaught. How can he? The sea has yet to make his stomach the slightest bit queasy.

The ward is busy, most of our patients suffering from dehydration. If the weather doesn't calm soon, we'll be out of capacity at the hospital—and nurses. I walk away from Joe, ignoring his empathetic stare, collecting spent bedpans. Unaware of him standing behind me, I nearly bump into him as I turn. It's a shame I didn't; the bedpan I'm holding is full of vomit. Any doubt about Joe's lack of interest in me has disintegrated, replaced with resentment. His cheeks are flushed, and his skin holds a healthy glow. How boorish of him.

"You should have been born a fish," I say, my voice low as I walk past him.

The soldier looks at me apologetically as I hand him a clean bedpan. He leans forward and throws up. I'm out of pans until the stack waiting for cleaning is done.

Compassion falls over Joe's face. "I take it you're still suffering."

I snort my reply and grip the filled bedpan until my knuckles turn white. Seasick or not, when on duty I have no choice but to hold it at bay, sneaking off to empty the contents of my stomach unseen.

Joe falls into step at my side as I make my way from the ward. "I'm going to be blunt, Joe. It's not like me, but it needs saying. I find it offensive that you're a picture of good health."

His shoulders lift and his lips tremble as he tries to hold in his laughter. Amusement contained, Joe places a hand on my shoulder. It takes tremendous effort not to shrug it off and drop the bedpan on his clean shoes.

"Would you want me any other way?"

"Right now, yes. I want your head in a bucket, your skin holding a green tinge, and misery shining in your eyes."

He looks surprised as he follows me down the corridor. "Oh."

"I'm being rather selfish and unreasonable, so yes, what I'd like is to see you throw up at least once. Then you wouldn't be so perky. Cheerful isn't acceptable round here, given the circumstances."

"Oh."

"Stop saying that."

The ship lurches and I have time to nod at the bucket by the washroom door. Joe holds the bucket under my chin while my stomach heaves. I lift my head out without a flicker of embarrassment.

"Better?" Joe asks.

"No."

"You don't make a good patient."

Why would he think I would?

"Hmm …" I sigh. "I make an even worse friend."

He puts the bucket down, pushes the door open into the wash area and reaches for a cloth, running it under the tap. The cool fabric feels good against my flushed skin.

"Here," I say, handing him the filled bedpan, and I take a glass from the shelf, filling it with water and swilling out my mouth. Joe places the bedpan on the floor at my feet. My hand grips the sink and tears sting my eyes. "Do you have to be nice, Joe?"

He turns me round, taking the glass and putting it in the sink. As his arms slide around me, stupid tears of self-pity tumble down my cheeks. I cling to his white coat as he holds me. Snot sticks to the lapels of his jacket, and embarrassment makes itself known.

"Sorry, I've messed up your coat," I say, wiping a hand over the lapel, dragging the snot further down it, making me cringe.

Joe laughs, laying a light kiss against my forehead. "Think nothing of it."

My lips tremble, and tears hang onto my eyelashes—strangely, I'm feeling a lot better. Thank goodness I didn't give into Pearl's demands to try her mascara. She keeps telling me it emphasises the eyes, making them appear sexier—not that Matron would approve. Nurses aren't allowed to wear makeup. At least I don't have pools of black running down my face. Tears are easier to wipe away than mascara.

"Go wash up. I'll see to the bedpans and bucket. We can't have Matron discovering you like this."

My eyes widen at his suggestion, not because of Matron; a doctor doesn't undertake menial duties, such as cleaning out bedpans and buckets of vomit.

"Don't look shocked. Splash some cold water on your face and return to the ward. It will be our little secret."

I kiss his cheek, closing the door.

Over the next few days, the dark clouds disappear, and the high winds lose their intensity. Today, the sky peeks from behind grey clouds and the wind is nothing more than a gentle caress. We are in for a calmer day.

Morag lies on the bed in our cabin, reading Agatha Christie's *The Adventure of the Egyptian Tomb*, a Poirot Investigates novel. Her gaze swings in Pearl's direction as she snaps the book closed, throwing it on the bed. "Ah dinnae ken why ye read this stuff."

"Says the girl reading her second Agatha Christie novel," Pearl grumbles, raising a delicate eyebrow.

"Ah'm nae sayin' tis nae good, boot where's the romance?" She places a hand on her chest. "'Ah murdered him for love' … It adds a wee bit o' spice tae thin's."

"No, Morag, it makes it mushy and loses the thrill of suspense. Not everything is about love, including murder."

Twirling a finger around my hair, I turn away from the window, placing my back to the ocean. "I agree with Pearl, romance will take the edge off Agatha Christie's novels. John Edward has most of Christie's books, and I've pretty much read his entire collection."

Morag sits up, horror falling over her face. "Poor Joe. Where's the romance, the love, the heart beatin' ten-tae-the-dozen, as ye gaze in tae each other's eyes …"

Pearl holds up her hand. "Stop it, I'm nauseous enough, and the sea's just settled down."

With my teeth grazing my lip, I turn over her comment, playing it round my head. "Am I that bad?"

Before Morag can answer, the summon sounds for an air attack.

Morag leaps off the bed. "Bloody hell!"

Like mice caught napping in the sun, we scurry around our small cabin, grabbing our tin hats and gas masks. My heart beats against my ribs as I follow Morag and Pearl into the crowded corridor. Adah's grey head bobs in front of us. Effie glances behind and gives us a small wave as we're swept forward. Despite the urgency of the matter, we don't run around hysterically. Instead, we walk with purpose as our training dictates. A QA does not run like a deer afraid of the hunter, she remains calm and ready for action, hoping the hunter doesn't shoot her in the arse. Nor does she listen to the thumping of her panicking heart, or the inner voice telling her to run like a crazy person down the corridor.

Pearl's breath tickles my neck as she leans into me. "Did someone extend the corridor while we were in our cabins?"

"Not that I know of."

"Ouch! Lilly!" Morag complains as I bump into her, my foot scraping her heel. "Eyes forward. Eyes forward …"

"Sorry, I was talking to Pearl."

From over her shoulder, Morag glares at her.

"How'd I get the blame for Lilly not paying attention?"

"It's a Scottish thing. Don't take it personally, but anyone called Pearl always gets the blame … for *everything*," I say, with a dramatic sigh.

"Humph …"

My head bobs in understanding, and I try not to smile. "I know, it's terrible."

The deck is congested, and it takes longer than our practice sessions to make it to the Action Station. Vulnerability replaces fear. Exposed on the deck of the *Duchess of Richmond,* we are at the mercy of Hitler's air forces. We cling to each other as the whirring sound of an engine echoes overhead. I squeeze my eyelids together, so I won't look up. When I open them, colour bleeds from Morag's face, and her hair becomes a mass of flames as the sun hits it.

"Where's your hat?" Pearl asks.

Morag blinks. "It came off."

"Well, put the bloody thing back on. Your hair is like a beacon."

I unravel my hand from Pearl and Morag's. "Here, let me help you."

Morag touches my arm as I place the hat on her head, tightening the strap. "Ah cannae swim."

"Don't worry, you're in good company, neither can I."

"That's not reassuring," Pearl mutters.

"Don't listen to her, they've got rubber rings to keep us afloat ..."

"Yeah, and a lot of water to drown us in."

"Pearl! Not now. You listen to me, Morag. No one is going to drown, not today," I say, my voice firm.

Morag's hands quiver as they rest on mine. "Ah have this fear o' drownin', ever since I watched them pull Callum Jackson oot o' the swimmin' pool when ah was a bairn. Tis hoo come ah never learnt tae swim like mah brothers."

Colour fades from Pearl's face. "Did he drown?"

"Na, he got a tellin' off for jumpin' in 'n' nae waitin' for the instructor tae get in the pool. The silly sod."

There's a loud whirring and we tilt our heads, turning our gaze up at the cloud-littered sky. Even though we've been preparing for such an attack since we boarded, when the bomb hits the water, air flies from our lungs.

"You'd best be right, about us not drowning, Lilly, or I'm holding you responsible if anything happens."

Incapable of speech, I squeeze Pearl's hand.

There's a whistling noise as another bomb sails towards us. It misses the ship by a whisker. Our stomachs churn, and the skin on our faces pinch as our hearts thump. Knuckles turning white, our knees knocking, we hold on to each other.

A sickening feeling sits in the pit of my stomach. "Where's Joe? Did any of you see him?"

Morag and Pearl shake their heads. The crowded Action Station makes finding him impossible. Adah and Effie huddle together in front of us, and I can see some of the other officers, but not Joe. Where is he?

"Joe's so tall, I should be able to see him."

"Dinnae worry, he'll be safe," Morag says, her teeth chattering.

Pearl looks over her shoulder. "Joe is like a cat, Lilly."

"You're right, of course, I'm being silly."

Not wanting to show doubt, I send up a silent prayer that the *Duchess of Richmond* won't suffer a direct hit. That we will all remain safe, especially Joe, Morag, Pearl, Adah, and Effie—oh, and me—with all our limbs intact, just to be clear. The bomb sends the ship lurching violently to the left. Morag's grip tightens on mine and sweat lines our palms. People are still making their way to the Action Station; some lose their footing as the ship hurtles sideways, trying to right itself. Our screams rise above the crashing waves and the drum of the plane's engine.

Above, the aircraft circles like a buzzard, readying itself for another attack. Legs going in all directions, arms thrashing around them, those making their way to the Action Station fall, sliding along the ship's floor. As the captain gains control of the vessel, they stand, running to us before the next bomb hits. With outstretched arms, we welcome them into our group as the whizzing noise of another bomb sounds.

BOOM …

In front of us, a smaller boat splinters. Wood flies into the sky, followed by body parts. Screams ricochet as the living grapple in the sea. Morag gasps, burying her head into my shoulder, and Pearl huddles closer. It's hard to say where one of our bodies ends and another begins. Those that aren't killed from the bomb battle against the waves, their arms flying about them, splashing against the water's surface. Some grab onto the boat's debris to keep afloat. Within a blink, waves roll over them and they disappear.

There's no time to react or save those in the water as we had the RAF men, as another bomb hits the sea. Our ship pitches the other way and dread shines in Pearl's eyes as she looks at me. A crewman stands up, shouting and signalling to one of the QAs. Scanning the deck, we see her, spread on the floor like a starfish. Her right hand grips at her tin hat, in her other is her gas mask. With waving arms, the crewman tries to get the nurse moving, his voice bouncing off our tin hats, and I know I will forever hear him shouting at her. Panic rising, we watch one of our own struggle to make it to safety.

The crewman points in our direction. "Get up! You need to move! Get to the Action Station."

"Oh, God," Effie whispers, her hand pressing against her lips.

With our breaths catching in our throats and the plane holding us prisoner, we watch her get up. On legs that have no coordination or balance, she trips and falls.

"If you can't run, crawl!" the crewman barks.

And that is what she does. Her hand holding onto her tin hat, and her wet clothing sticking to her skin, she inches her way to us. As she gets closer, the crewman jumps down, running over to her. Grabbing her arm, he hauls her to her feet and launches her at us. With no hint of annoyance over his lack of respect, the nurse nods in quiet gratitude.

SPLASH …

Another bomb hits the water, wiping out any chance of survivors from the smaller boat. Saltwater hits our faces, blending with our tears as we grieve for those lost and the safe return of our sister. Like a corkscrew, the *Duchess of Richmond* ducks and dives on the waves.

Morag raises her ashen face from my shoulder. "Ah've been secretly prayin' since the ship started rockin' for the engines tae halt 'n' give mah tummy a wee bit o' peace … noo that seems like a bad idea."

In disbelief, Pearl's mouth falls open. "Why would you want the engines to stop? The waves would still have the ship moving regardless, and you'd still be suffering from seasickness. That's a stupid idea."

"Ah dinnae ken. It seemed like a good idea when ah was throwin' up."

I lay a kiss on Morag's cheek. "You're a crazy woman, but we wouldn't be without you."

Thin strands of red hair tickle my face.

Pearl tightens her grip on mine and Morag's arms. "You speak for yourself."

A whirring of an engine has our jaws locking as another bomb hits. The ship stutters and for a second Pearl and I stare at Morag as the engine stops, then restarts. Bile rises in my mouth and every muscle in my body tenses. Before us is nothing but ocean—we've lost our convoy and there's no land to be seen. The term 'sitting duck' comes to mind and I pray the aircraft doesn't come back to drop more bombs. It's hard to know the number of planes undertaking the attack—one, three, it doesn't matter, the intention to destroy is there. Our breath captive, our hearts racing, and our blood gushing in our ears, we listen for the sound of a plane. Every muscle in my body is tense, preparing for my brain's command for flight—not that there is anywhere to run. It's hard to quantify the time spent waiting for the captain to announce the end of this nightmare. Somewhere our convoy continues without us—we need to re-join them and continue to who-knows-where.

There is a crackling noise over the tannoy and the calm voice of the captain hisses over the speaker. "Two planes have dropped five bombs. We've suffered minor damage, but everyone remains in good health. The dining room is out of bounds while we clean up. Remain on deck and I'll send sandwiches up—and well done."

I swallow back my guilt, aware that during the attack I never once thought about the men keeping the engines running—steering the ship from danger. As the captain confirms no loss of life or injuries, I give silent thanks to the brave men commanding the ship, keeping us afloat.

"Sandwiches!" Morag looks green at the thought. "'N' ye say ah'm crazy."

The muscles in my arms and legs scream as we move and I shake the tension from my limbs, straightening my back. Above our heads, the clouds give way to a pale blue sky. The surface of the sea sparkles bright against the deep blue of the water below.

"You should marry the captain, Morag. Two crazy people together, it sounds like the perfect romance story," Pearl says, removing her tin hat and patting her hair.

Aghast, Morag's green tinge contains a pink glow. "Have ye seen hoo auld he is? He's mah da's age if he were alive."

"Pearl was just teasing, weren't you, Pearl?"

She shrugs. "If you say so, Lilly."

Adah taps my shoulder. "Thank God that's over."

"We should have a wee service tae pray for the souls o' those lost," Morag says, turning my way. "Lilly, would ye sing *Amazing Grace* if ah organise the rest?"

"I can do a reading." Adah reaches into her pocket, producing a small worn bible. "I always keep it on me, just in case."

Morag nods. "That would be nice."

Hands grab me from behind and I'm suddenly pressed against Joe's chest. "Thank God, I was so worried."

"Joe!"

He pulls me back and we smile at each other like idiots.

"Lilly," —Pearl touches my arm—"sorry to break things up, but Morag is already gathering the troops. You'd better start lubricating your vocal cords."

"We're having a service for the souls from the boat that got bombed," I explain to Joe.

"Is there anything you want me to do?"

"Thanks, Morag has most of it covered, but it would help if you could gather everyone."

Joe kisses my cheek. "Consider it done."

Within ten minutes, we gather on the main deck facing the sea. Adah walks forward and I follow as she opens her bible. Quietness falls, and even the wind seems to still. "Revelation 21:4. God shall wipe away all tears from their eyes; and there shall be no more death, neither sorrow, nor crying, neither shall there be any more pain …"

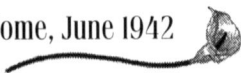

Dear Jane Anne,

When the sea stops its battering, the Nazis bomb us. The air attack warning goes off, just as we are viewing food more favourably. On a ship, in the middle of an ocean, there is nowhere to hide. Our days in France, sitting in a trench, seem much safer. The bombs came close to hitting us, and thrown off course, we lose our convoy. But we survive.

I hope that things in London are bearable for you. The aerial attack brings you closer. This war will forever change many lives. It's difficult to imagine where we'll be tomorrow. Never mind a year from now. But whatever, or wherever, we go, I hope we survive to experience tomorrow. Did you ever hear from my brothers, I wonder. If not, I suppose no news is good news under such circumstances.

Do you recall the poor state of George Peter's clothes? His garments never seemed up for the job, did they? It makes me laugh to think of him with his scuffed knees and holes in his trousers. He should have been born a moth. No one gains holes like George Peter. Of course now, as a soldier, the army expect him to mend his own holes. What is it you would say to him? Ah, yes; "You should have been born a priest, your clothing is holy enough." That always had me giggling. It's funny when I think how George Peter would come slithering over, like a snake pretending friendship when really it wanted to eat you. Garment in hand, he would ask me to patch his trousers before you noticed. For every patch I sewed, I charged him one sweetie. He'd huff and complain, saying, "It's a woman's job to sew up men's garments." I'd tell him that might be so in the old days, but not now. Nowadays, if he wants something sewing, there is a price to pay, and my price is one sweetie. If he became too quarrelsome, I would direct him your way. That always shut him up and put a sweetie in my hand.

These memories keep the connection of home alive, reminding me, no matter what happens, I have my family. Strange, isn't it, how I appreciate my brothers more when they aren't around?

Lillian Elizabeth

23

June 1942, The Duchess of Richmond

*I*n late June, we reach warmer climates. Flying fish leap out of the water, and the sun shines down on us. The fish are bewitching, and I spend my free time sitting on deck watching them in the warm, light breeze. Despite their name, flying fish don't fly. They skim the water's surface, dancing on their tails, their large, wing-like fins spread out at their sides. When the wind hits them, they glide, skimming the sea. It's something I never get bored of.

Warmer weather brings the deck to life and there is dancing and singing most days. In the early days, with the sickness and dreadful weather, it was hard to see a time when a new chapter in our voyage would arrive. But when it does, it exceeds both expectations and experiences of sea travel. The Entertainment Committee is in full swing once again, and we are busy planning new events for the ship's calendar. For now, we choose to overlook the fact we're moving closer to the war and enjoy ourselves.

With our tropical uniforms replacing our heavier winter ones, there is a sense of shedding our skins. Our watches move forward and back as we enter different time zones. If time travelling were possible, that's what we are doing. Sometimes we get to relive hours. Much to Pearl's amusement, our watches go back when I'm on shift and forward when it's her shift. She is the only one amused by this.

The warmer climate brings our shift patterns back to normal—two days on, two days off. Today's shift starts slow, with general housekeeping, stocktaking, and treating the few patients on the ward. At 1 p.m. I'm summoned to help Joe, who is assisting in an appendectomy on Sergeant Travis, of the Queen's Own Cameron Highlands Regiment, 51st Highland Division. It's exciting to be back in theatre. Sergeant Donald Travis is a good-humoured Scotsman, in his late thirties, with ruddy cheeks and leathery skin. While I'm used to Morag's soft Scottish drawl, Sergeant Travis' thick accent makes his words unfathomable. I'm forever apologising and asking him to repeat his sentences.

"Aye, lass, I tell ya, I dinnae ken it was mah appendix thing-is causin' mah pain. Kin ye believe it? Thought it was Roberts goin' on aboot his lassie at haime causin' the ache."

How Roberts talking about his girlfriend could make Sergeant Travis double over in pain and his belly swell likes he's swallowed a rugby ball, is a mystery.

Subsequently, Travis is vomiting and has a fever of one hundred and two Fahrenheit. "At least you'll get a break from Roberts and his girlfriend while we take out your appendix," I say, trying not to shake my head in despair.

Tabaco-stained teeth on display, he grins. "Aye, nurse, that ah will.'

The operation is a simple procedure, and Sergeant Travis is soon recovering on the ward.

"Had Sergeant Travis delayed any longer, his appendix would have burst, causing peritonitis in his stomach. He'd be fighting for his life," I say, following Joe from theatre.

The ship glides over still water, the warm air caressing our skin as we sit on deck. Further along, soldiers dance with the women not on duty, and music envelopes us, along with their laughter and cheers.

Joe grins. "As we haven't heard Roberts talk about his girl, we don't know how painful it can be on the ears."

"Well, it's sweet that Roberts has a girl he likes to talk about."

"Hmmm … you do, do you?"

Playful, I punch Joe's arm. "Are you making fun of me, Joseph Lawrence?"

"No, never, I just didn't peg you for the romantic type."

"Is that a bad thing?" I say, biting my bottom lip.

Joe's arm snakes over my shoulders, pulling me to him. "Not at all."

There is a sense of tranquillity; the tropical sun beams down, and the marine life puts on a dazzling performance. Inside, I recognise the ease with which Joe and I sit together, sharing this wonderful moment. A feeling of belonging washes over me. It has nothing to do with the wonderful weather or aquarian life. For the first time, I don't allow my doubts to surface; instead, I enjoy the peace of sitting next to him, basking in the rightness of us. "Isn't it beautiful, Joe?"

A Sunderland flying boat speeds out to join the convoy, disrupting the calm surface of the sea.

Joe smiles. "If I overlook the other ships and Sunderland flying boats, I'd say it was serene."

"That's an awful lot to discard."

"Then it's as well I've got the imagination."

"They're like a reality check. A reminder that war still exists."

Joe nods in agreement.

"Sometimes, I want to believe in the lyrics of *There'll be Bluebirds Over the White Cliffs of Dover*. It's such a powerful song. Wouldn't it be nice to have such peace."

Joe kisses the top of my head and I snuggle deeper into the crook of his arm. "Sing it for me, Lilly."

With my head resting against Joe's side, I sing. Far from home, the song is more poignant than back in 1941, when I first heard it.

Peace ever after—it sounds delightful. When I fall asleep out on deck tonight, with the soft wind tickling my skin, I'm hoping those words will seep through into my dreams.

June gives way to July, and on the second day, the African coast comes into view. A few days later, we enter Freetown Harbour. Sierra Leone is part of the British Colony, with Freetown housing the naval base. There isn't the opportunity to disembark, so I drink in the tropical scenery. The views of the harbour and the reassuring presence of the naval battleships *HMS Rodney* and *HMS Nelson*. The air is dry and hot, and tiny beads of sweat sit on the surface of my skin. Unlike Morag, mine and Pearl's hair is faring well in the sticky, moist heat—poor Morag, no matter how many pins she sticks in her hair it frizzes about her face.

Pearl opens her mouth and Morag's face darkens as she tries to smooth the unruly curls. "Dinnae say a word, Pearl."

"I was only going to say it's a lost cause."

Effie's face appears between them, pointing at a group of officers. "We've visitors boarding."

Pearl's gaze trails over the men as they embark the ship. "They're rather stuffy looking."

Morag shakes her head. "They nae sweets linin' up tae see which one ye'll pick, ye ken. Besides, what aboot Patrick?"

"Hmm … Patrick who? We went our separate ways. He was getting serious, and you know I don't do serious," Pearl says, nodding at the men disembarking. "It's as well they're not sweets, they don't seem edible from here, and I'm betting they won't taste nice. Far too chewy."

"You're being vulgar," Effie says, nudging Pearl.

"No, that was Morag, she was the one who referred to them as sweeties."

"Don't bother responding, you'll never win," I say, glancing at Effie.

Several Hurricanes fly overhead, and we cover our ears to block out the noise.

Once they pass, Pearl gets up. "Well, I need to eat before I go on duty." She bends, slapping at Morag's hands. "Will you leave that bush of yours alone, you're making it worse."

Morag groans. "Ah cannae help it."

"What, your wild hair or fussing over it?"

"Both."

Pearl sighs. "I'm stuck with you and your hair for the next several hours, it's going to be a long shift."

"Never mind, Adah's on shift too, and her hair is impeccable."

"Not comforting, Effie." Pearl points at Morag. "It will make her hair appear fifty times worse."

"Sorry."

"Don't be sorry," I say, sliding my arm through Effie's. "Pearl just enjoys whinging."

"I heard that, Lilly."

I cup my hand over Effie's ear. "She's also got big ears."

Pearl pulls at her earlobes. "All the better to hear you with, my dear."

"'N' my, what a big mouth ye've got," Morag says.

Pearl grins, twisting round to face us, a wicked gleam in her eyes. "All the better to shout at you with, my dear."

Morag frowns. "That's nae right."

"Well, I'm not eating you, I'd be throwing up hairballs for the next five years."

Morag swipes at Pearl's arm. "Nae funny! 'Tis all right for ye, ye'll be bonnie tonight at the captain's table, while ah will resemble an electric shock victim."

Pearl flings her arm over Morag's shoulders. "We all have our crosses to bear."

Hands shaped like claws, Morag grabs Pearl. "Bear … huh … Grr …"

Pearl screams as Morag chases her about the deck, making me and Effie laugh until we have stitch.

24

 July 1942, The Duchess of Richmond

W hat do you think? Why am I asking you? Your hair is a mess."

Pearl runs about the small cabin as best she can, her arms flying. Her hair falls about her shoulders in soft waves and rouge stains her cheeks. With the use of makeup forbidden, she ensures the application is light, so Matron won't notice.

"Ah dinnae ken hoo come ye're flappin'," Morag grumbles. "Will ye stand still. Ah'm gettin' headache."

"Were you not listening when they said party? Honestly, Morag, a party! One we haven't arranged. Dinner at the captain's table has turned into more than dinner. Fresh blood is out there, I can sense it. I could meet the officer of my dreams. For me, that's romance with a big fat R."

"With a hooter like yers ah'm surprised fresh blood is all ye can smell."

Pearl glares at Morag. "I'm too excited to even care about arguing with you."

I lean against the doorway, folding my arms. "What changed your mind? The officers we saw weren't for you. 'Too old and stuffy,' you said. Besides, given their age, we don't want you giving them a heart attack. What would Matron say, especially after Edith."

Pearl rolls her eyes. "I'm not like that nutty girl, would-be nurse who entered nursing to have lots of sex. For the record, I don't offer myself up like meat. Yes, I like to have fun, even exchange a few heated kisses, but I never make myself available to every soldier I come across. And for the record, Effie said younger officers have arrived."

"Does that mean ye're still a virgin?"

"Don't be daft, Morag, but it doesn't mean I'm a prostitute either."

"Aye, if yer say so."

Pearl's lips draw into a thin line, and she stops her pacing. "You're crossing waters you don't want to step in. I'm not stupid, I've heard what some of those self-righteous women onboard say about me, and I don't give a stuff. If you'd lived the life I have, you'd understand the importance of living."

Before Morag can respond, Effie rushes in, stumbling to a stop. "Aren't you ready yet?"

I wave a hand at Pearl. "She's flapping."

Effie looks at her. "Goodness, what's taking so long? Didn't you hear what I said about the wave of officers who boarded? Not the first lot, they were old, but the second lot. I thought you'd want first pickings, Pearl."

"That's why she's pruning her hair within an inch of its life," I say.

"Come on, Pearl, you're perfect." Effie's words flutter away like confetti.

"You're all judging me. Yet Lilly is spending time with Joe, and no one is saying anything about them."

My fingers twist around a lock of hair, and I bite nervously at my lip, aware that Pearl is intentionally shifting Morag's attention onto me. "I'm not sure what you mean."

Like a wildcat, Morag turns on me. "Aye, noo ah come tae think of it, ye've been spendin' a lot o' time with Joe lately."

Pearl smiles in triumph and I dig my elbow into her side as she walks past—she sends me a lethal glare.

"We're spending time together because our shifts match."

Effie grabs Morag's arm. "Come on, we're already running late. We can't keep the captain waiting," she pleads. "Leave Lilly's interrogation for another time."

Morag flounces past, throwing her hair over her shoulder. "Alright, Effie, boot this conversation is nae over. Ye 'ear that, Lilly? Ah'm goin' tae have mah gossip, 'n' ah want all the juicy facts."

I nod in surrender. Pearl's giggle follows me down the corridor to the lounge. When we reach the party, Adah is already there, talking with the captain and sipping on sherry.

A waiter carries a tray of tiny, amber-filled glasses, and we each take a glass.

"I hate sherry," Pearl whispers in my ear, "it plays havoc with my digestion."

"Aren't you young for poor digestion?"

She shrugs. "Cocktails are better for me. They have a smoother approach on my tender stomach."

"Of course," I say, unconvinced.

Lavishly set, the dining table spreads out before us. Polished silverware sits on a white jacquard tablecloth, and long-stemmed crystal glasses wait to be filled with wine. No matter how many times we've dined at the captain's table, this glimpse into a world so different from mine leaves me breathless. In the United Kingdom, where rationing is in place, the extravagant three-course meal placed in front of us comes laced in guilt. We dine on succulent steaks, fish, thick-cut bread, and mouth-watering desserts. With Pearl sitting on my right, and Morag on my left, we tuck into our food. Sometimes I want to pinch myself, just so I know this is real. I reach across, taking a thick slice of bread, lathering it with butter.

When we were at Norton Hall, there was a time we felt we'd never leave, and here we are dining with the captain, sipping sherry, and tucking into a banquet a king would be proud of. It's too bizarre to be real. When dinner is over, we move to the lounge where the party is underway. Bagpipes play, officers chatter, and people dance. As Pearl often says, "We need to enjoy the moment." For tonight, we shall dance, sing, drink, and revel in the celebrations. Too soon, we'll be back in the thick of it.

Joe walks forward, cupping my elbow, guiding me further into the room. "You're gorgeous."

"I'm not sure I look any different from normal. It's not like I packed a party dress in my kit bag."

His deep, throaty laugh trickles down my spine. I'm falling for Joseph Lawrence. On the dance floor, Morag joins the soldiers, her feet moving in time with the bagpipes as she leaps into dannsa Gàidhealach—Highland dance. She grabs Effie and Pearl, forcing them onto the floor, and they laugh as they try to keep up with her. At a small table behind the dance floor, Adah sits, speaking with an unknown officer, playing with a half-empty sherry glass.

"Fancy getting some fresh air?" Joe asks, dragging my attention his way.

"Sure."

We hit the deck and Joe wraps his arm around my waist, grabbing my right hand, and we dance to *I've Got a Feeling I'm Falling*. He spins us over the floor, our bodies swaying in time to the beat.

As the music turns slower, I rest my head against his chest, letting the moment carry me away, focusing on the way our bodies move. Somewhere deep inside, contentment settles over me. The question of 'Could Joe be The One' disappears. I've never been one for fanciful romance books, where a person's heart beats uncontrollably at the sight of 'The One'. Love is an emotion that grows. When the heart is safe, it opens itself up. There's no sweeping me off my feet, or flashes of intense desire. Like a flame dowsed in water, passion burns out fast. Genuine love is about two hearts fusing—it is an epiphany. A single moment in time so profound it lasts forever—like now with Joe.

Our bodies sway together and a bubble of happiness ignites in my chest. There is no hiding the person I am from him, afraid of rejection when he discovers his fantasy isn't real. Joe is someone who will hold my heart without crushing it or demanding too much. He will always respect the person I am. So why am I dithering? Perhaps it's the insecurity of war more than Joe. Or my fear of becoming my mother. Do we become our parents? There are small traits, but am I not my person, too? Right now, this person is enjoying being with Joe, our body's moving as one.

Joe's lips touch my forehead. "You're far away."

"Sorry, I was cogitating."

"Anything you care to share?"

"Just how perfect dancing with you is."

His feet stop, and his arms fall away. Surprised, I glance up at him. His smile widens and he drapes his arm over my shoulders, pulling me against his side. We walk from the makeshift dance floor to the railings. The ocean glistens in the moonlight, and he drops a soft kiss on the top of my head, cocooning me in his arms. My back presses against his chest, and we stare out at the rippling water.

Joe's voice vibrates against my back, "I like you, Lilly, I've never hidden that. The question I'm asking is whether I take the risk in the two of us. What's holding you back? Not that I want to sound overconfident, but I get the impression you like me."

"Oh, Joe, I don't know what to say."

"When I saw you in Leeds, I took it as a sign, but then after France things drifted again. Life doesn't give us many chances, yet here we are playing the same game. Chance isn't coming round a third time, Lilly."

My insides are flipping so bad, my heart hammers, thump, thump, thump. I can't think straight. Jane Anne's face appears, her nostrils flaring, her lips pressed tight. Not the Jane Anne I left in August 1940, but the person she was in November 1939.

"There is no rush, we're on the ship for a while. Let's enjoy getting to know each other and see where chance takes us."

Does true love or soulmates exist? People say 'I do' at the church altar, but it doesn't mean they stay together. It took Henry VIII three wives before he found 'The One.' But did he find 'The One', or did Jane Seymour's premature death stop him from divorcing her or chopping off her head? Would he still have gone on to marry Anne of Cleves, Kathryn Howard, and Catherine Parr, becoming Henry VIII and his six wives, had Jane lived?

"I like you … It's … I'm scared … of myself more than you … of us."

His arms tighten at my waist, and I hold on to him, tears shimmering, threatening to spill over my cheeks.

"If you could see yourself as I do, Lilly, you'd see there's nothing to fear."

"You make it sound easy, but I've seen my potential within my mother. What happens if I turn out like her? Would you still want me?"

"I've never met Jane Anne, but I could never imagine you treating someone that way."

"Perhaps, but people change."

"We all change, that's life."

Joe's right, but those changes aren't always for the better. When we change, there's no going back, the damage is done. We are all a product of our parents and environment. Pearl wouldn't be the Pearl she is today if her mum had lived. Her dad wouldn't be an alcoholic. And Pearl could commit to a relationship, rather than running from herself and life.

In silence, we watch the water lap against the ship. The evening brings a gentle breeze, playing with the loose strands escaping from the bun at the nape of my neck. Joe's fingers brush against my face as he pushes back my hair, turning me to face him. A softness lights his eyes. It makes me vulnerable, and scared. I gaze down, my eyelashes creating a barrier; trying to rebuild my defences.

"Don't hide," Joe says, his voice a whisper. His lips touch mine, gentle and inquisitive. "There, that wasn't so bad."

"Joe …"

He places a finger against my lips. "Shh … let's give chance a go."

This isn't just me getting hurt, it's Joe. The fear I'm leading him on stirs. Am I acting like Pearl, but for different reasons? Worse, I could marry Joe and become my mother. There is no rational way to describe every emotion whipping around my insides, eating into my mind. Joe is right, perhaps it's time to stop the questions and let chance in. To enjoy each moment. I missed him so much when he went into hiding. His lips meet mine, and I allow myself to return his kiss.

Letter Home, July 1942

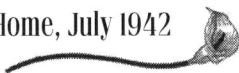

Dear Jane Anne,

Just when I have it all worked out, I hesitate. Old habits are hard to break. Last night, Joe was honest about his feelings towards me. I don't want to lose him, but doubt keeps niggling away at me. 'What if?' is such a cruel companion. My head is giving me claustrophobic vibes. Joe is a kind and honest man. Yet, what happens if I stop seeing the beautiful person he is, and become unsatisfied, wanting more, never knowing what more is?

Sometimes I'm standing on deck, and there are a million birds pecking at my head. Each one squawks out their doubt. Am I good enough for Joe? Will our love survive? War? Us? These doubts are so real, even if the birds pecking aren't. I'd like to say that war was creating these mumblings, but it's me. I've never felt good enough. As my relationship with Joe blossoms, it has me second guessing myself. I'm so scared of loving and losing that all I see is a dark hole with no bottom.

I can love Joe; I know I can. In some ways, I already do, but I'm too afraid to open my heart. He deserves better. Is loving someone enough? Or is there more to love? Do we love to our capacity, and sometimes that capacity falls short? Oh, I wish this paper and pen could provide some sound advice. Yesterday, Joe and I stood looking over the water. There was nowhere I wanted to be but on the *Duchess of Richmond*, his arms wrapped around me. Yet, uncertainty stopped me from taking things further.

How many people peek into someone else's life and observe the truth? I'm betting most see idealism. They want that vision, never understanding it's an illusion. When I was twelve, I recall looking in the mirror, and telling my reflection, "Wait until you're twenty, you'll know everything. And this self-doubt will be gone." Twenty came and went and I'm still the same. Well, I've tormented myself enough. There are no answers here. I shall trust in myself and Joe and be the person he sees. It would be helpful to know what she looks like.

Lillian Elizabeth

25

July 1942, The Duchess of Richmond

A cruiser arrives on the 17th of July, dividing our convoy, with eight ships leaving for Durban. By 10:45 a.m., the ships are out of sight. Twenty-four hours later, we reach Cape Town, to re-stock on oil, food, and water, providing us with the opportunity of shore leave.

On hearing this, Morag becomes a girl possessed. "It's eleven am., Pearl, c'mon, get a shift on."

Pearl unpins her hair and starts restyling it, ignoring Morag.

With patience running thin, Morag grabs her arm. "Stop fussin'."

Pearl wrenches her arm from her grasp, and Morag flops on the bed. "Pack it in, Morag, I'm doing my best."

"Aye, 'course ye are." On a loud sigh, Morag slides off the bed. "Ah've had enough."

"I'm sorry, Pearl, but Morag's right, we need to be making tracks. I said I'd meet Joe later. At this rate, there won't be time for sightseeing, never mind meeting him."

"Your exaggerating, like always." Pearl stares at us, her eyes like daggers.

"But not with Joe, on shore … in Cape Town …"

She huffs. "Well, I'm glad things are going well with you and Joe. But don't you worry about me, looking all drab, so long as you and Joe explore Cape Town."

"I didn't mean it like that, you're being mean."

She sticks out her tongue.

"You look incredible, Pearl."

Suspicion shines in her eyes, though her features relax. "You're just saying that because you want to be off this ship."

"True, to a point. We all want to be off this ship, but it doesn't make what I said any less genuine."

Pearl looks in the mirror. "Don't make me smudge my mascara. I'm welling up at your kind words."

Morag groans, flopping back on the bed, almost bumping her head. "Na need tae be sarcastic."

Effie rushes in. "Aren't you ready yet? Come on, we're going ashore, solid ground beneath our feet and walking on something that doesn't rock or make you lose your dinner."

Morag runs out of patience, and her hands slap her thighs. "That's it, ah'm nae waitin' na longer." She grabs my hand, pulling me out. I stop in the doorway, my palm against the open door. Pearl's mouth falls open in disbelief as Morag disappears.

"Are you deserting me too, Lilly?"

My face pinches with guilt. "You look pretty good to me."

"Humph… so it's like that." She slams down the hair-brush. "Alright, you and Morag win. Now I'm as un-stylish as you two."

Without another word, she picks up her bag and steps past, a thunderous expression marring her features. Insides groaning, I roll my eyes.

"I may not have seen you make that face, but it doesn't mean I'm not aware of it."

I place a soft kiss on her cheek. "Despite you noticing, I still love you."

Pearl wipes her face with the back of her hand. "Ugh … stop being mushy."

Morag points an accusing finger at her "See, that's why ah'm never nice tae her. She makes it difficult 'n' is unappreciative. Ah dinnae ken hoo come ye bother, Lilly."

"You don't even know what nice is, Morag."

"Like ye do."

"I have my moments."

It's like being in the middle of a ping-pong match. "Now, now, let's play nice."

"Bugger off, Lilly," Pearl and Morag say simultaneously.

Effie sends me a wink. "At least they agree on something."

I sigh in defeat. "Hmm …"

The clock slowly turns its hands to mid-afternoon as we wait our turn to disembark. Joe waves as he leaves with a group of officers. Pearl grumbles in my ear about how unfair and typical it is the male officers get to disembark first. At 5 p.m., it's our turn and excitement has us smiling like ninnies. Any comment Pearl might have about being rushed for no reason dries up as our feet touch earth. We stamp at the ground, laughing. Our arms linked, we walk along the harbour.

South Africa welcomes us ashore. Everywhere we go the people of Cape Town open their homes. Music, the swaying of dancing bodies, singing and the hum of parties echoes down the streets. Picnics filled with African delights are available for purchase. Local wives provide a canteen service for a shilling, with meals of sausages, bacon, eggs, and tomatoes. There are all kinds of exotic fruit salads and cups of tea. With huge smiles, we feast on the celebratory atmosphere, losing ourselves to the wonder of the experience. Tommies stagger past us, shouting, singing, arguing, dancing, and jostling each other. The smell of alcohol rolls off them and we zigzag out their way.

Pearl wrinkles her nose. "Honestly, don't they know how potent South African brandy is?"

Morag grins. "Ye jealous?"

"Please, what is there to be jealous of? A hangover as big as South Africa itself? I'll give it a miss, thanks." Pearl watches the men stumble across the street, where a bar and local women welcome them. "Those soldiers are in no condition to show a lady a good time."

A loud whoop has us spinning towards the commotion. In the open doorway of a house, a group of soldiers stand. One of them leans into a South African woman, his mouth devouring hers. His hands grip her bottom, moulding her against him.

"It's been ages since anyone kissed me like that." Pearl sighs.

"Ye think that's bad; na one's ever kissed me like that."

"Jake kissed me like that before he signed up," Effie says.

Morag gasps. "N' ye let him go withoot a backward glance?"

"I didn't let him go. But I wish I'd told him I loved him."

"It's absence," Pearl says.

Effie frowns. "What?"

A sigh bursts from Pearl's lips. "Do I have to explain everything?"

"I think Pearl means absence makes the heart grow fonder. Or as the Roman Poet Sextus Propertius once said, 'Always toward absent lovers, love's tide stronger flows,'" I say.

Morag throws her hands up, scowling at me. "Then how come she dinnae say that."

Effie nods. "Pearl didn't like it when Adah wasn't clear about giving Joe and Lilly some private time, with her 'northerly wind' comment."

Pearl ignores them. "Speaking of Adah, where is she tonight?"

"She wanted to spend time with John."

Like vultures, Morag and Pearl turn on Effie.

At the scent of gossip, Pearl's nostrils flare. "Who the heck is John? I thought Adah was spending a lot of time at the captain's table during the dance."

"Aye, who's John 'n' hoo come we're just findin' oot aboot him noo?"

"I think he's an officer, I saw Adah speaking to one at the dance with the new arrivals," I say, as Effie fidgets under Pearl and Morag's scrutiny.

"And you didn't think to say anything? Who is he? How old is he? What are his intentions?" Pearl's questions are coming at me like machinegun fire.

My hands warding her off, I step back. "I … Sorry … I …"

"His name is John Benson. Adah and John were courting before Mum died. She stopped seeing him because of her duty to me. I've only ever seen a photo of him, and though Adah says it was her decision and I'm not to blame myself for her being a spinster, it's hard not to. She didn't realise John was onboard the *Duchess of Richmond*, with the Highlanders, until she saw him at the party. Back home, before he moved away, after Adah ended things with him, and the war, he was a plumber. I'm hoping, as I'm older, Adah will start living her own life. Fall in love with John all over again and marry him. Wouldn't it be lovely?"

Lost in the romance of Adah and John finding each other after so many years, Morag grins. "Och, like a true *Romeo 'n' Juliet*."

"Hopefully not, we all know how that ended."

"Pearl!" Morag and I shout.

"What? I'm just saying."

Some of the colour leaves Effie's cheeks. "Don't say that. Adah deserves to be happy."

"I'm only saying that Shakespeare didn't give *Romeo and Juliet* a fairytale ending."

I rest my hand on Effie's shoulder. "Think of it more like Charlotte Brontë's *Jane Eyre*, and how love conquers all."

"*Jane Eyre*? Lilly, that's no better than *Romeo and Juliet*. Let's hope John doesn't have a crazy wife locked up somewhere so she can burn the house down, along with herself, and make him blind."

Morag snorts. "Ye're all heart 'n' flowers aren't ye, Pearl?"

"Let's shop and leave grumpy, old Miss Havisham to her sourness. I want to get something for Jane Anne and Aunt Sarah Rebeca."

Morag laughs. "Miss Havisham, ah like that. Noo ye mention it ah kin see the resemblance."

Pearl strides ahead, turning and sticking out her tongue. "Meanie Morag, with her untameable hair and och aye na noos. So jealous of pretty Pearl."

"Scottish people dinnae say och aye na noo," Morag shouts.

"Pearl's one of a kind isn't she," Effie says.

"Aye, 'n' she's all ours."

Pearl waves at us. "Come on, slow coaches, otherwise the shops will shut, and Lilly won't be buying anything for anyone."

The next day at 11 a.m. we set sail, leaving Cape Town behind. A woman in white takes up position singing a song of farewell as we leave. Her voice is hauntingly beautiful, a melody I wish never to forget. Joe stands next to me as we watch her disappear; a cooling breeze tickles my skin and the hair on my arms stand to attention. Our interlude at Cape Town is over, but I'll never forget their kind generosity and hospitality. "Look, Joe, isn't it beautiful," I say, pointing at the albatross flying in the distance as it soars just above the surface of the water. "Don't you sometimes wish you were as free as a bird?"

Joe puts his arm over my shoulders. "You're quite the romantic, Lilly."

"I'm not sure about that. It's the illusion of freedom I love more than the romance."

His lips graze the top of my head, and I lean into him. Joe never makes me feel silly or laughs at my whimsical ways. He accepts me. Maybe that's what loving someone is like. Not being in love before, it's difficult to say.

Letter Home, July 1942

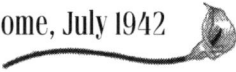

Dear Jane Anne,

Excitement is in the air! After so long at sea, we arrive in Cape Town. For the first time in months, we leave the ship. We disembark to a chorus of welcoming smiles and cries of "Howzit", the traditional greeting South Africans use, which translates as "Hello" or "How are you." Traders line the waterfront and mouth-watering aromas hang in the air. Spices lace the food; some make me sweat, they're that hot on the palette. I'm told, by one of the African Officers, that the spiciness of the food is because of the warm climate, which causes them to become more potent. The most common spices are chilli peppers, ginger, garlic, and cumin. They appear harmless and smell heavenly, but pack quite the punch. Traditional English food is available, but I want to experience this wonderful, colourful place in all its glory, so I am determined to stick to local cuisine.

Our stop in Cape Town is brief, allowing the ship to refuel, so we are on a mission to sample as much of South Africa as we can. So far, I have tried Chakalaka and pap, which is a vegetable dish containing onions, tomatoes, peppers, carrots, beans, and spices. Pap means porridge, though it looks and tastes nothing like the porridge back home. With things so uncertain in London, I'm hoping to send you and Aunt Sarah Rebeca a gift to cheer you both up. The headscarves here are nothing like at home. The colours are magnificent, and some are a complete work of art in the way they're worn. Your scarves are called a "long belt." They tie around your head like an Alice band; you will look divine in them.

When I approached the trader to buy the scarves, he kept saying "Shap … shap." Unsure what he was saying, I kept smiling and he'd smile back, nodding his head, so I took it to be something pleasant. I later learnt that "shap … shap" means good. He is right, the scarves are most definitely good. I will be sad to leave this vibrant, gracious place behind. It has been such a beautiful interlude, placing a spring back in our steps, ready for what lies before us. Rumours over our destination are rife. I keep wondering if it matters where they send us. Danger lies, and our troops need our medical services. So long as we all remain together, Joe, Morag, Pearl, Adah, Effie, and me, I don't mind where they send us.

Joe and I are taking things slow. I'm still nervous over our relationship, but I'm determined to hang onto him. We spend as much free time together as we can, watching the fish and birds, singing, and dancing. I don't know what love is, but if it is what Joe and I have, it's amazing.

Lillian Elizabeth

26

July 1942, The Duchess of Richmond

*L*ance-Corporal James Andrews stumbles onto the ward, sweat trickling down his face. His once-tanned skin contains a yellow tinge. "Ah dinnae feel so well." His rattling jaw thickens his Scottish accent.

He raises his arm, wiping away beads of sweat. I run to his side, signalling Pearl to help.

"Mah head aches like ah've been on the whisky all night 'n' ah've got the runs. Nae that ah've got anythin' left tae run."

His symptoms relayed, Lance-Corporal James Andrews loses consciousness, and we drag him over to the nearest cot. Pearl whips the privacy screen around him as I pull off his boots.

"You finish up undressing him, and I'll get the ice packs," Pearl says.

I nod, unbuttoning his shirt. The fabric sticks to his sweaty skin, making it difficult to remove his arms. Pearl arrives with the ice packs as I'm removing his trousers. A photograph falls out of his pocket. In the picture, Andrews stands next to a young woman, his arm round her waist. In the woman's arms is a baby. On the back someone has written, 'James, Bryony, and Kenny Andrews 1940'. I place the photo on the bedside table. Once undressed, we place ice packs beneath his groin and armpits to bring down his temperature, covering him with a thin sheet. At 8 a.m., the doctor confirms Andrews is suffering from Malaria. It's our first case since arriving in the tropics. He is twenty-four years old.

On the 24th of July, life on the *Duchess of Richmond* changes. It happens at an alarming rate. Africa not only brings the warmer climate and beauty, but also the mosquitoes; and she has a sting in her tail, or perhaps I should say jaws. By 10 a.m., despite treatment, Andrews' condition worsens. Pearl's brows pinch as she looks at the medical chart. The news isn't good. Out of medical options, we make him as comfortable as possible, with fresh ice packs and a cool towel against his forehead. The doctor's assessment places Andrews in the Seriously Ill category. What this means is modern medicine has failed him. He's dying. Nurses leave, replaced by night shift, and I'm made aware that at some point today, time has quickened its pace. It is one of those shifts where my muscles and shoulders are tight with fatigue, yet it's like I've just arrived. Time displacement is common on the ward.

Morag appears behind the privacy screen, and I gaze up from where I sit, wiping at the beads of sweat on Andrews' brow. His body trembles beneath the towel.

"Pearl said ye'd be 'ere. Ah thought ye might need this."

"Thanks," I say, taking the cup.

She leans over and I take a sip of tea as she glances at Lance-Corporal Andrews' medical file. It is full of bad news. In the last hour, his temperature has risen and is still climbing.

Morag touches my shoulder. "Ah'll get some mare ice."

"Do your rounds first, there's no rush, the ice packs can last."

"Aye, suppose they will."

She kisses the top of my head and walks from behind the screen.

I smooth away the wrinkles from his bedsheet. The action giving me an air of usefulness. His hand catches mine.

"Ah'm goin' tae die, aren't ah?"

A religious person might say, "No, you're going to a better place." Perhaps it is a failing in my faith that I can't utter that kind of reassurance. Yes, Lance-Corporal James Andrews is dying, and even if I were to acknowledge this out loud, it wouldn't make either of us feel better. Before I can think of how to respond without appearing blunt, a soldier walks around the privacy screen. Dressed in the 51st Highland Division Gordon Highlanders uniform, his bulk fills the material. His brown hair is short, and his skin holds a light golden tan. Concern shines in his blue eyes, which melts as he gets closer, replaced by a smile.

"Noo then, Andrews, ah see ye got yerself a crackin' spot, full o' bonnie nurses." His hands on his hips, the Scot surveys the area as if drinking in a beauty spot. "Ah would nae mind a bonnie view like this mahself."

I'm not sure Andrews' spot is as nice as the non-commissioned officer is making out. Or that Andrews has much choice about it. As for being a pretty nurse, I have no comment to make.

A ghost of a smile stretches across Andrews' lips. "Aye, Alick, tis a bonnie spot alright."

Alick. The name catches me off guard and I take a second glance at the man hovering at my side. Alick is a common name. I've met several while onboard the *Duchess of Richmond*. But not all are Scottish and wearing a sergeant's uniform. Or built like an 'oversized bulldog' like the man at my side. As much as I try, I can't remember how old Charles Jason said Sergeant Alick McNavis was. This soldier looks to be in his late twenties, maybe early thirties. Is it possible that this soldier is him? If so, I have a very important message to deliver.

Morag appears, carrying another chair.

"'Twill save ye standin'."

Alick lowers his bulky frame, his legs spreading, his right knee bumping mine. "Thank ye, nurse."

Even though I've worked myself into a frenzy, now is not the time to ask if he is Charlie's Alick.

"Noo then, Andrews, ye're stuck with me, 'cause ah cannae trust the lads tae be around the pretty nurses. Ah've told them ah'm 'ere tae see ye, nae go gettin' in the nurse's way."

Lance-Corporal Andrews laughs. Though it's more of a wheeze. Morag appears with the new ice packs, and we quickly change them, working under the sheet to preserve his dignity. The exchange complete, Morag leaves.

I wipe away the sweat as Lance-Corporal James Andrews slips into a fever-induced sleep.

Alick taps my arm as I straighten the sheet. He nods at Andrews. "Hoo's he doin'?"

I sit, my hand lingering on the sheet. "It's not good."

"Aye."

In silence, we watch Andrews struggle to fight the fever. A sense of hopelessness falls over me. Even with so many advancements in medicine, it won't save this young soldier's life.

Andrews turns his head. His eyelids half open, he gazes across at me. "Sin' for me, nurse, like ye do when entertainin' on deck. Dinnae leave me tae die in silence."

It is such a small request, yet I struggle to respond, other than to nod. Alick reaches over, squeezing my hand, offering support, and my fingers wrap around his as I absorb the strength he offers. With a smile on my lips, I meet Andrews' request. "Of course, what would you like me to sing?"

"Ye choose."

Lance-Corporal James Andrews is a religious man. Scottish hymns aren't something I'm familiar with but being onboard a ship full of Scots I've learnt a few.

"What aboot *There is a Happy Land*?" Alick suggests. "'Twas written by a Scottish schoolmaster called Andrew Young. They dinnae get mare Scottish than that noo, do they?

I nod. "Then that is what I will sing."

Towards the end of the hymn, Alick joins in.

At 10 p.m., Lance-Corporal James Andrews' fight against malaria ends.

27

 July 1942, The Duchess of Richmond

*O*n deck, people dance. Music mingles with laughter as their feet hit the floor in time with the beat. It's strange how life carries on as one ends. As a nurse, I'm trained to deal with death. To comfort the grieving and never question medicine's shortcomings. Today I can neither accept Lance-Corporal James Andrews' death or medicine's inadequacy. Sadness builds inside, weighing me down. I tell myself we can't save everyone, but acceptance won't come.

Pearl's feet tap along the floor as a soldier spins her round. His kilt sways about his legs as he loops his arm through hers, and they twirl, their arms hooking and unhooking. Her head tilts back and she laughs. She looks so free and happy. Behind her, Adah sits, talking with Officer John Benson, cuddling into him. Never have I felt like I don't belong. Tonight, the thought of dancing and shaking off today's events sends a shiver down my spine. I don't fit in here, with this merry scene. It all feels so wrong. Someone must grieve for Lance-Corporal Andrews, paying tribute to the man and soldier.

Further along the ship, I find a quieter spot. The wind grows, reducing the humidity levels as night falls. I wrap my arms around my chest, my hands rubbing my arms, fending off the chill. With my head resting against the ship, I watch the waves roll as I say a silent prayer, bidding farewell to Lance-Corporal James Andrews. The most powerful prayer for protection and healing is Psalm 91, and that is the one I use. "He will cover you with his feathers, and under his wings, you will find refuge."

The thump of footsteps pulls me from my thoughts. Alick's wide frame casts a shadow as he stops in front of me. "Ye left afore ah had a chance tae thank ye for takin' care o' Andrews."

His thick Scottish accent fades into the wind, and without invitation, he sits next to me. The closeness of his body makes me aware of his muscular frame pressing against mine. His biceps bulge as he moves his arms. Alick is different to Joe; Joe is tall and all limbs, like someone put him on a stretching rack at birth and forgot to take him off. Alick resembles a Highland bull. Scooting further into the ship's side, I try to give him room. If he notices, he doesn't comment.

My arms around my legs, I draw them into my chest. Normally the cool evening breeze, when it comes, is a welcome relief from the hot days—today, it chills me to my core. Alick's 'thank you' doesn't reach my brain receptors. There are no feelings of warmth to be gained from his words. Andrews is dead. Medicine has failed him. And so have I. Wordless, I nod at Alick, before turning my attention back to the water.

We are strangers, and yet there is no awkwardness as silence falls. Part of me acknowledges the oddness of that, but I leave it there, happy to accept the comfort his presence brings. We watch the water ripple in the moonlight. There is no dead of night here, stars light the blackened sky, twinkling above our heads. I single out a star; it shimmers more than the rest, and I lay claim to it—this star is Andrews.

While it would be nice to sit and lose myself to the stars, there is the matter of fulfilling Charles Jason's request. If Alick is Sergeant McNavis, I will have successfully granted two wishes today. One for Andrews when I sang to him, the other for my brother. That's good going for someone onboard a ship heading somewhere.

Alick catches me looking at him and I divert my gaze back to the water.

"Ye seem tae have somethin' on yer mind."

My teeth worry at my bottom lip. I don't want to fail Charles Jason. But there is only one way to be certain. "Are you Sergeant Alick McNavis?"

Tiny lines appear at the corner of his eyes. "This Alick McNavis, is he in some kind o' trouble?"

"Goodness, no. Nothing like that," I say, my cheeks warming.

He laughs, the sound deep, rumbling from his stomach into his chest. "In that case, aye, ah'm Sergeant Alick McNavis, 'n' whoo wants tae ken?"

If I thought my cheeks couldn't get hotter, I was wrong. "Sorry, how rude of me. I'm Lillian Elizabeth

Nutman. You saved my brother, Charles Jason's life in France. He said if I was to meet you, to say thank you."

"Ah … young Charlie. Hoo's he doin'?"

"He's minus a leg, but he's doing well."

"Sorry tae hear aboot the leg."

"Don't be sorry. Better his leg than his life."

Alick nods. "Aye."

My arms loosen and I drop my hands to my ankles, cocking my head. "Charlie wanted to thank you when he made it onto the boat, but he couldn't find you. What you did, for Charlie, it's not forgotten. We owe you."

"Ye owe me nothin', ah couldnae let the Jerry kill him, 'n' ah wasnae aboot tae leave him on the beach. That's the way it is. With na time tae think, ye act 'n' hope ye make the right decision."

"I suppose. Still, it was brave of you, and like it or not we're in your debt."

"Brave." Alick tuts. "Stupid mare like. Ah only had one bullet left."

"Yes, that too." That has him laughing again. "But I'm glad you did."

A shadow flitters across his face. "Charlie's a good laddie, 'twas nae his time tae die."

"No, it wasn't. But it wasn't Lance-Corporal Andrews' time either, though God took him anyway." I wipe my hand over my face, trying to remove the anger from my voice. "It's easier when a soldier dies in battle. I'm sure that sounds strange. As a nurse, we must accept we can't save everyone, but Lance-Corporal Andrews' death is senseless. A life taken by an infected bug. It's not right."

"Ah kin see that. Boot a life lost is still a life lost, bug or bullet. Tis all unnecessary."

"You're right," I say with a shrug. "Still, his death is needless. Medicine let him down. I should have been able to save him. Not that I believe in miracle cures, that's silly."

"Ye're takin' it personally. Ye should nae. The bug saw a meal 'n' took advantage."

With my chin on my knees, I fix my gaze on the blurring water. "Why am I so sad about it?"

"Tis good that ye are. That war hasnae taken that from ye."

Perhaps Alick is right. Or are the cracks war has made inside me showing?

"He reminded me of Charlie … Lance-Corporal Andrews. Young, with so much life still to live. You saved my brother, but I couldn't save Andrews. Maybe that's why his death hurts so much. Life goes on, there's no stopping that, but what about those that die? Who remembers them?"

"We do."

I close my eyes, resting my forehead on my knees. Tears threaten and I take a moment, breathing deep, composing myself, before placing my chin back on my knees. "Yes, I suppose we do. It's a shame it's not enough. There's a hole inside that needs filling, and I don't know how to fill it or close it."

"Ye might nae see it, boot what ye did for Andrews taenight, stayin' with him 'n' grantin' his wish, 'twas as brave as when ah saved yer brother."

The comparison makes me snort. All I had done was sing a song for a dying soldier and tended to his medical needs.

Alick's hand rests on my back. "Ye did a good thing taenight, Nightingale."

Nightingale. The endearment crashes into me, sending a jolt through my blood, touching something deep inside me, something I wasn't aware existed. I've experienced nothing like it before and it scares me, without knowing why. When the notion comes, it's too bizarre to make sense of. Home, that is what this sentiment is. An invisible door opens in me and the person standing in the doorway knows Alick. He is her home. The girl on the outside ignores the girl on the inside. Alick is a stranger no matter what the inside girl says. One does not fall instantly for a stranger.

Good heavens, Pearl would laugh until her sides split if I told her—and with good reason. No, much better to ignore it and put this familiarity down to the fact Alick saved Charles Jason. That's it. I cling to my reasoning, calming my swirling emotions. Alick is familiar because he saved my brother's life, how silly of me not to see it.

The next day, we admit more patients with malaria. By the following day, the ward is rapidly filling. With Lance-Corporal Andrews' death still so raw, the fresh cases affect me more than they should. While on the outside my facade remains unaltered, inside is different. I am a nurse.

Seasoned in the art of concealing her emotions and carrying out her duties without fuss. Like Lance-Corporal James Andrews, some will never return to their families. Life is harsh, that's what I tell myself as we divide the treatment of malaria patients between those who will live, the maybes, and those who will die. Those patients unresponsive to treatment we make comfortable.

At the end of my shift, I leave the ward, making my way to the spot I found when Andrews died. There I sit staring at the water, watching the ripples dance, allowing the unfairness of it all to soothe away. Men dying in battle is one thing, dying from a bug that used them to snack on is quite another. Despite what Alick said, I can't seem to stop thinking I've somehow let my patients down, nor can I stop the bloody infected bugs from sinking their jaws into us.

A small piece of paper flaps on the railings. I watch it move in the breeze before curiosity has me investigating. It's a note. A strange place to leave one, unless you are expecting someone to be here. Perhaps my newly-found spot for cogitation is also a lovers' rendezvous. It's addressed to Nightingale, and I stare at the thick scrawl. Alick? Curious, I pull the note off the railings, reading the first lines of a poem by Emily Dickinson.

> Hope is the thing with feathers,
> That perches in the soul,
> And sings the tune without the words,
> And never stops—at all.

Alick's note makes me smile. Hope is endless, living in the soul forever, empowering us to go on, even when we are unworthy. Or, as in my case, discouraged by medicine's failure to preserve life. I tuck the paper into my pocket and sit down. The words resonate. The girl on the inside connects with the one on the outside, and together we bask in Emily Dickinson's poem and Alick's thoughtfulness. Medicine may have its limitations, but it is saving more lives than it is allowing to die. And that is hope. With each fresh case, we hope to make a difference. Live or die, we offer our patients something, letting them know we care. That they are never alone. The darkness that I've been carrying lifts and I hum to the music playing on deck, joining the sound of bagpipes filtering through the air.

"Noo then, Nightingale, tis good tae see ye smilin'."

I scoot over and Alick sits next to me. "Have I been that glum?"

"Mah ma would say a lassie is nae glum, just thoughtful."

His comment makes me laugh. "I like your mum's reasoning."

"O' course, mah da would say if ye were bein' so thoughtful, ye might have thought to smile."

I nudge Alick's arm, shaking my head. "I bet your dad said that out of your mum's earshot."

"Aye, mibbie. O' course, that was 'cause he liked his head where it was, ye ken."

"I'm sure your mum is a very reasonable woman." I place a hand near my mouth as if to tell him a secret. He leans close, frowning. "It's the men, they don't understand female logic. The poor dears."

Alick throws back his head and laughs. "Ah, Nightingale …"

"It's true, you know. Men don't understand us, so they don't listen properly. Where would men be without us? As Virginia Woolf once said, 'For most of history, Anonymous was a woman.'"

"Aye, it would be a sad world withoot lassies."

I smile in satisfaction.

"O' course, if there were no lassies, laddies would nae have somethin' bonnie tae look at."

"You're incorrigible, Alick."

I nudge him, laughing as he scratches his head.

"Mah ma says that—incorrigible. Is that nae a good thin'? She made it sound like ah was doin' somethin' right."

28

 July 1942, The Duchess of Richmond

*T*wo days after Lance-Corporal Andrews' death, the *Duchess of Richmond* moors off Durban, picking up the rest of our convoy. The battleship that joined us before Cape Town leaves, replaced with a battle cruiser and destroyer.

Malaria also forces us to adjust the entertainment schedule.

"Sport isn't the same anymore." Pearl sighs as we sit on deck watching Durban become a dot on the horizon.

"You've still got the dancing to look forward to," I remind her.

"True, but there's less testosterone with dancing. Men always like to prove themselves in sports. It brings out their competitive nature."

"It could be worse."

"You're a regular Job's comforter, Lilly."

I smile at her.

Morag comes over, wiping her brow. "The bugs are workin' with Hitler."

"What has a mosquito got to do with Hitler?" Pearl asks.

Lips compressing, I shake my head. "Hitler doesn't have that kind of power, Morag."

"Ye kin say that all ye like, boot ah'm tellin' ye, tis awful on the ward. We've had another five cases since mah shift started."

With my hand shielding my eyes, I glance up at her. "At least most are responding well to treatment."

"She's Job's comforter today," Pearl says, pointing in my direction.

Morag huffs as she sits down next to Pearl. "Aye, well, if the bugs dinnae stop bitin' soon, there'll be na soldiers left tae fight."

"I don't want to sound like Lilly, but things aren't that bad. Thankfully, we have more able-bodied soldiers than sick ones."

"Aye, yer probably right. 'Twas a depressin' shift."

Pearl nudges Morag. "We've all had those of late."

"Well, as in the words of Lewis Carroll, 'The time has come, the Walrus said …'" I say, getting to my feet.

An arm circles my waist from behind. "And what is it the Walrus said?"

I smile, leaning back against Joe. "It's time to make a move, I'm on shift in ten minutes."

"In that case, allow me to walk you to the ward." Joe offers me his arm.

"Tis more like time to rally the troops, if ye ask me. At least Effie is on shift with ye taenight. Ye're lucky, ah had tae listen tae Agnus moan aboot her wretched bunions, in-between dealin' with the recent malaria cases." Morag scratches her head. "Ye ken, the malaria cases weren't the depressin' part, that 'twas Agnus' bunions."

Pearl stretches like a cat. "As it's my day off, I get to be lazy."

"Nae that lazy, ah'm lookin' tae dance later, once mah feet have rested."

Pearl smiles. "On this occasion, Morag, I'm more than happy to oblige."

With my arm linked through Joe's, we walk below deck. Since the ward has been so busy, we haven't been able to spend much time together.

"And here is where I shall leave you," Joe says as we near the hospital.

He kisses my cheek and disappears down the corridor.

The sister on reception smiles up at me as I enter. "Oh here, Lilly, someone left this for you."

"Thanks."

I take the slip of paper. Alick's scrawl spells out 'Nightingale', and my heart thumps. He's been leaving notes the last few days. It's his way of cheering me up as my workload increases. Sometimes it's poetry, other times it's the odd quote from Lewis Carroll, Alan Alexander Milne or Oscar Wilde. My favourite quotes are from Alan Alexander Milne. Pooh Bear has been my childhood friend for many years. For a bear, he speaks a lot of sense with no flowery dialogue. Without thinking, I grab a piece of paper and a pen, and with five minutes to spare until my shift begins, I run to our meeting spot, sticking the note to the railings.

> You can't stay in your corner of the forest waiting
> For others to come to you.
> You have to go to them sometimes …
> Meet me here at noon,
> Nightingale.

When I walk back onto the ward, my cheeks are flushed.

My shift ends and I leave, making my way to the deck. The sun is high and my hair sticks to the back of my neck. The note is gone and there is no Alick. My heart sinks and doubt has me questioning why I asked him to meet me. Normally when I've finished a shift, I'm ready to drop. Today, serotonin pumps round my body, making sleep impossible. These small interludes with Alick calm my mind. We are friends, I tell myself, as my fingers play with his note within my pocket.

"You're aware it won't end well, aren't you?"

I jump, turning. Pearl stands behind me, her arms folded over her chest.

"You startled me," I say, my hand at my breast.

She inclines her head at my pocket. "I thought it was you I saw last night. Alick came just after you left, picked up the note and grinned just like you were doing a second ago. I told myself, this friend of mine is playing a dangerous game. The problem is, she's lacking in experience to realise what she's doing. What do you think is going on between you and Alick, Lilly?"

My cheeks warm. "Nothing, it's harmless fun. I'm not playing any games."

"If it was harmless fun, no one would get hurt. And someone's getting hurt, they always do with matters of the heart."

Air puffs between my lips and I push away from the railing, walking to the side of the ship and sitting down. Pearl sits next to me.

"Honest, Pearl, it's just a few silly notes to make us smile. The ward is so dreary nowadays with fresh malaria cases coming in daily. This"—I pat my pocket—"is a break from the gloom."

"I wish that was true. But all I see is a girl who's falling so deep she won't be able to climb out of the hole she's digging. What about Joe? How does he figure in all this?"

"Joe? What does he have to do with me and Alick leaving silly notes for each other?"

"Lilly, your naivety scares me. You're not just having a friendly time with Alick. What you're doing is experiencing the first rush of courting. When your heart gives little skips, and you smile for no reason, or when your head conjures his image, and all you want to do is giggle. That's what this is."

I shake my head, though somewhere in the pit of my stomach, what Pearl is saying makes sense. "It's not like that, honest it's not. Joe and me, we're together. It's not like that with Alick, we're just friends."

"I wish that was true. The heart is a strange thing, Lilly. You get it all worked out, then BOOM ..." She smacks her hands together and I jump. "A bomb explodes, and you find you're the one left crying because you never saw the end coming. They call courting a couple's game. Not a threesome. That's something entirely different."

My forehead wrinkles. "I'm not seeing Alick, not like that. Poor Joe, I wouldn't do such a ghastly thing to him. You know how hard it was for me, all the uncertainty I went through before I started courting him. I wouldn't do something so awful to him or Alick."

"I'm not saying you're doing it intentionally. How would you feel if Joe started leaving notes for another woman? Knowing that smile on his face isn't for you."

I close my eyes, but Pearl's words sink into my brain. "It's not like that, Pearl, honest it's not."

She looks sad. "Men can't be friends with a woman unless he's not into women. Nature gave us hormones for a reason."

The gentle breeze tickles my face, and a stone wedges itself in my stomach.

She stands up, smoothing down her dress. "I'd best get back to dancing. Just do me a favour, Lilly, be careful."

"I'm trying."

"Hmm ... if you say. Right now, your hearing is suffering from the same problem Morag has without the wild hair blocking your ears." She takes a step, then turns back. "Sometimes it all gets messed up and the brain gets foggy, and we stop seeing what's important. I'm not bothered about Joe or Alick, just you. I don't do the love thing, but you do. I don't want to see you playing piggy-in-the-middle and getting hurt."

She walks over and kisses the top of my head. "I might be outspoken, and like having fun, but I never lead them on. Or myself. If they're getting serious, I end it. There's no marriage or two-up-two-down house with kids in my future. Whatever you do, or how it ends, I'm here for you, remember that."

My earlier zing of happiness dissolves as Pearl walks away, and melancholy falls. Alick's note sits in my pocket, and all I can think is, *"If the person you are talking to doesn't appear to be listening, be patient. It may simply be that he has a small piece of fluff in his ear."* Oh, Pooh, how easy you make everything sound. While I understand what Pearl is saying, the fluff in my ears is stopping me from letting her words sink in too deep.

I hug my legs, resting my chin on my knees, my gaze locking on the flying fish as they skim the water's surface. My head is a mass of jumbled thoughts, making my palms sweat and my heart beat a sad tune. Realisation is horrible, and I want to cry, because it hits me; I don't want to give Alick up, but I don't want to give Joe up either. I care for them both. Birds swoop, twisting and turning in synchronised perfection. Sensing feathered predators, the fish return to the water. If only I could do that. Let the pressure of the water gurgle in my ears and hide me from the danger of my mind. Footsteps sound, and Alick appears.

"Ye seem pensive, Nightingale."

My heart summersaults, and I try to straighten out the creases on my forehead. With my hand protecting my eyes, I gaze at him. Alick smiles at me, lowering his body next to mine. A tiny bubble of happiness explodes in my chest; it feels so right to be together. While I've spent the last few minutes tormenting myself, there's one thing I know: Pearl's right—Alick is more than a friend. How did I let this happen?

"It was a long shift."

"Aye."

What am I doing with Alick? I love Joe. So, there it is; I love Joe, and Alick is nothing more than a friend. Who am I kidding? So what am I going to do? Give Alick up? Tell him I can't do this to Joe? To myself? To him? There is something comforting about Alick. It's hard to pin down what that something is, but it's there. If I tried, I'd say it's like arriving home from a long day at work, kicking off your shoes, knowing you are where you're meant to be. How do I give something like that up? I burst into tears.

Alick slides his arm over my shoulders, drawing me into his side. "There, there … it cannae be that bad."

But it is that bad.

"W-w-what am I doing, A-A-Alick?"

"Ye're nae doin' anythin'."

If only that was true. I lift my head, my eyes swimming with tears, and I hiccup. "Why do you feel like home?"

"Och, Nightingale, ah ken …" His hands cup my face. He looks so sad, and I see the same torment that rages inside me etched on his face. "Ah'm married, Nightingale."

"Oh, God … this is awful."

I lean forward, huddling into myself, my hands covering my face. Tears drip through the cracks between my fingers. That's what my life is. A crack that's getting so big I can't mend it.

His hand lays against my back. "Ah was nineteen when ah married Mary. Tae young tae ken hoo vicious people kin be. Ah had na understandin' o' hoo unstable she was, or hoo manipulative her kinfolk are. All ah could see was a lassie, wild, bonnie, 'n' fun. A free spirit. By the time ah realised hoo unbalanced she was, it was tae late. Her claws had sunk in tae mah flesh. When ah wanted tae end thin's, she tried tae commit suicide, throwin' herself in front o' a car. She broke her back in the accident 'n' will never walk again. That's when ah found oot Mary had mental problems.

"O' course, her kinfolk blamed me for everythin'. Nae the fact they kept her problems hidden. Suddenly, there ah was, trapped. Nae even a man 'n' responsible for a woman whoo was so disturbed, she'd attempted tae kill herself, just tae bind me tae her. Ah've never run from responsibility, nae even at nineteen. The McNavises are loyal. Mary's kinfolk ken this. They took advantage o' it. Ah'm nae tellin' ye this tae make excuses, ah ken what ah've been doin' is wrong 'n' unfair."

His tongue clicks, and he drops a gentle kiss on top of my head. "Ah'm sorry, Nightingale, ah should have kept mah distance."

"Alick ..."

His face clouds over and the muscle twitches in his cheek. "Ye want tae ken hoo come ah'm so reckless, savin' ye brother's life?" He doesn't wait for me to answer. "When ye have nothin' tae live for, life is meaningless."

My fingers grip his arm. "Oh, Alick …"

His hand caresses my cheek. "Ah've been selfish. Ye say ah make ye feel like haime. Ye are mah haime, Nightingale. In the short time ah've been talkin' tae ye ah've found a peace ah thought never tae have."

Tears roll down my cheeks. "Why is everything so complicated? You're not the one being selfish, it's me. I'm asking myself what I'm doing, leaving notes, sitting here waiting for you. There's Joe, and I love him, I do, but I don't want to let you go."

His thumb brushes away my tears. "Na, Nightingale. Ye're nae selfish. A heart kin love many folk at one time. Boot a soul kin only make a connection once. Ye're mah soulmate. The moment ah saw ye sittin' at Andrews' side … Ah also ken ah could nae have ye. Love Joe. Be with him. Ah'm nae free. Ye deserve tae be with someone that will be with ye, 'n' only ye. Nae shared."

"Alick?"

His lips touch mine and I drink him in as my tears continue to fall, coating our lips, entering our mouths. When our lips part, we're both breathless.

"Are you leaving me?"

He smiles. "Ah've nawhere tae go. As ah told ye, ah'm selfish, 'n' if ah get tae spend a bit mare time with ye, that's what ah will do. Ah ken ye're with Joe, 'n' ah'll nae ask ye tae forget that. So, we'll keep this thin' between us platonic. Let's enjoy this interlude. Ah dinnae want mare than tae sit 'n' talk with ye."

His fingers lace through mine and I lower my head onto his shoulder. Silence grows and there is a weight in my heart that wasn't there before. My head is still whirring. It's less confused than it was. I love Joe. But Alick will always be my home.

A yawn threatens, and I stifle it as lack of sleep catches up with me. Alick stands and my head loses its pillow. His hand dangles in front of me. "C'mon, tae bed with ye." His lips touch my forehead before he spins me toward the cabins. "Sleep."

On weary feet, I drag them across the floor to my cabin. Pearl's laugh echoes down the hall. I stop in the threshold, looking at her. Morag stands, her arms crossed, eyes following Pearl as she dances around the room. Unaware of my presence, Pearl stops in the middle of the floor, her hands on the scarf around her neck. Her cheeks are flushed and sweat sits on the surface of her skin.

"Someone's full o' joy. Ah take it ye've had a good night 'n'…"—Morag checks her watch—"mornin'."

Pearl stops spinning momentarily. "Wonderful, thank you."

"Will ye stop that, ye makin' me dizzy."

"Stop being a bore."

Her eyes widening, Morag points at Pearl. "Ah'm not a bore 'n' that's mah scarf!"

"No, this"—Pearl runs the silky fabric through her hands—"we decided was more my colour than yours."

"Na, ye decided that on yer own."

Pearl huffs. "It's red, Morag, why on earth would you want to wear something that clashes with your hair?"

"The scarf tis cherry red, mah locks are copper."

With a sad face, Pearl regards Morag. "That's even worse. Cherry red and copper together, you'll look like a tomato that can't decide if it's supposed to be orange or red."

Morag makes a grab for the scarf, and I walk between them, breaking them apart.

"Aw …" they grumble at me as I sit on the bed.

"Morning, sunshines," I say. "I see you're both in fine fettle this morning. Pearl, give Morag her scarf back, it's easier for everyone, including you."

"Spoilsport," Pearl hisses, handing the scarf back to Morag.

"Nae, ye kin keep it, ye might be right. Mibbie cherry red isnae mah colour."

Pearl sits next to me. "Sometimes there's no winning whatever I do."

Morag joins us. "Ye seem tired."

"I couldn't sleep and decided to grab some fresh air."

Pearl snorts and I grab Morag's arm, pulling her against the side of the ship, throwing a pillow behind our heads, avoiding confrontation. She continues to stare at me, and I give her a nudge with my foot. "You best start getting ready, you're on duty soon.'

"Ugh," Pearl complains.

Morag giggles as we watch her grab her uniform, straightening out her apron.

"It sounded like you've had a good night," I say.

Pearl's smile returns as she pins her hair up. Comb in hand, she turns round. "It was fabulous. Luke says I'm the best he's had the pleasure of dancing with."

"Who's Luke?"

Morag's elbow lodges in my side. "He's the engineer, remember."

"Oh right, sorry, I can't keep up."

With a scowl, Pearl taps her comb on my leg. "Don't be rude, Lilly, I've been seeing Luke since we left Cape Town."

I don't mention that we only left Cape Town a few weeks ago. "You're right, how silly of me, it's the long shifts."

"Yeah, course it is. It's not like your head's in the clouds, riding a Scottish storm or anything."

Morag's brows pinch together. "What is she goin' on aboot?"

"I don't have a clue. There's only one Scot in my life and she's right here," I say, hugging Morag.

Pearl rolls her eyes at me.

Outside, someone knocks on the wall near our open cabin door.

"What!" Morag calls.

Joe pokes his head around the doorframe, his hair falling into his eyes. "Adah's got malaria."

My heart gives a desolate thud.

"Hoo bad is it?" Morag asks.

"I'm not sure. I've not seen her. Effie caught me as I was leaving the ward."

I push off the bed. "Come on, troops, let's go support our women in crisis. There's not only Adah needing our support, but Effie, too. She must be beside herself with worry."

Morag shuffles off the bed and Pearl puts down her comb, securing her cap in place.

I kiss Joe's cheek as I reach him. "Thank you. Now get some rest."

His hand lingers on my arm. I'm still dressed in my uniform and worry lines appear on his face. "When did you last sleep?"

"Don't worry, I'll be fine."

He pulls me to him. "Promise me you'll get some sleep later."

"I promise."

30

 July 1942, The Duchess of Richmond

When we enter the hospital, Effie looks like a woman hit with unspeakable disaster. Adah lies on the small bed, her skin slick with sweat as the fever ravages her body.

Effie gazes up from the chair by her sister's bed with watery eyes, despair pinching at her features. "She's all I've got ... I can't lose her."

Together, we wrap our arms around her.

"You won't lose her," Pearl says.

What little composure Effie possesses disintegrates, and she bursts into tears.

"You've still got us. You're not on your own."

"Pearl's right, Effie," I say.

There is such confidence in Pearl's voice, and I wish I could be more like her. Andrews' death reminds me there are no guarantees.

The damp cloth on her head slides off. Effie grabs it, patting at her sister's face. "She isn't responding to treatment."

Morag's hand rests on Effie's shoulder. "Have faith. Tis tae early tae say if treatment is workin'. Adah's a fighter."

Her hand closing over Morag's, Effie nods. "You're right, I'm being silly."

Adah's peppercorn hair is damp with sweat, and she shows no awareness of our presence. Lance-Corporal Andrews' face replaces hers, and ice trickles down my spine—is it a sign? I hope not. I rouse from the vision, bending to smooth away the creases from the bed linen. "You need to grab some rest, Effie."

Morag slides an arm over her shoulders. "Aye, Lilly's right, ye're tired. Ye've been on shift all night, twill nae seem so bad once ye've had some kip."

"I don't think I can sleep, not with Adah here like she is."

Pearl takes the cloth from Effie, handing it to me. "You can and you will. Lilly will stay with Adah; you go with Morag and get some sleep. Once I've finished my shift, I'll get you and Lilly can get some rest."

"Ah'd do as she says. Pearl's such a bossy-boots, 'n' ye ken hoo abrupt she kin be when she dinnae get her own way."

Pearl playfully swipes Morag's arm. "I'll give you bossy if you don't shut up and get moving."

My tiredness from earlier slips away. "Go on, Effie, I swear I'll get you if Adah's condition changes."

Her gaze lingers on her sister, and she stands rooted to the spot. "I—"

Pearl takes her arm, cutting her off. "I'm officially on duty, so I get to boss everyone about, now clear off, the pair of you, you're cluttering up the place."

Morag pulls Effie to her. "C'mon, afore Bossy-Boots has us forcibly removed."

With a quivering smile, Effie hugs Pearl. "I don't know what I'd do without you all."

"It's as well you don't have to." Pearl places a hand on her back. "Now go with Morag. I promise we'll do everything we can for Adah."

Effie sniffs into her handkerchief, leaving with Morag. I can feel the sting of tears, but I won't cry, not here. Later, out of sight, Morag, Pearl, and I will hold each other, allowing our worries for Adah to fall with our tears. Until then, we won't let our concern show, not on the ward. If we cut ourselves, our blood wouldn't fall, not until we leave the hospital and our duty is done.

"I'll get you some fresh water," Pearl says, picking up the bowl.

"Thanks."

I sit on the vacant chair, nurses walk from bed to bed, tending to the sick, providing refreshments, checking temperatures. Patients groan, muttering in their sleep, others sit reading, passing the time while they wait for the on-duty doctor to release them. Despite the bustling atmosphere, hope floats around the ward. John Benson enters, his ears sticking out from between his dishevelled hair. His nose is red, his cheeks flushed. Tears glaze his eyes. He looks less like an officer and more like a man losing everything.

He strides over to Adah's bed with determination. It's outside of visiting times, and I shake my head at the approaching nurse. "He's with me."

John blinks, interested in nothing but the woman lying in the bed. His fingers rake through his hair. "How is she?"

His gaze fixes on Adah, drinking in her condition. The top of the ice packs under her shoulders are visible from beneath the single sheet that covers her naked body.

"Not good."

There is no point in lying to him; situations like these require the truth.

"Will she live?"

"It's hard to say, but we're doing everything we can for her."

Colour drains from his face as his features harden. "I won't lose her a second time."

I nod.

His fingers dance at his side as his body sways. His knees buckle, but before he hits the ground, his legs straighten, and his back stiffens. "I won't lose her. You hear that, Adah, I'm not walking away again."

"Here," I say, guiding him to the chair. "Sit with her for a while."

He shakes his head. "No, I'd best not. She'd tell me I was littering the place up."

The comment makes me smile. "We'd all be in trouble for fussing, but as Adah can't say anything, we're taking advantage." I place a finger on my lips. "Don't tell her."

Adah stirs, and the cloth on her forehead falls. John picks it up, placing it back, his hand lingering on the cloth. He bends, placing a soft kiss on her cheek. "Look after her."

"We will."

Without a word, he walks out. His presence leaves its mark and I stare at the vacant space next to Adah. "You've got yourself someone special there," I say, my voice low.

Tucking the skirt of my dress under me, I sit. A song floats through my head, and without consciousness, I sing.

The first time I heard Vera Lynn sing *Wishing Will Make It So* was in 1939. Within a month of it being recorded, we were at war. Right now, Adah is waging her own war against malaria. It doesn't feel like two minutes since I sat down and already day shift is ending. A hand on my shoulder makes me jump. Joe smiles down at me, and my fingers seek his. No words of reassurance pour from his lips; we both know better. All we can do is wait, hope, and pray.

"Here."

I take the offered cup, wrapping my hands round it, blowing at the hot liquid inside. "You should be asleep," I say, as the tea trickles down my throat.

"And so should you."

I shrug. It's not that simple.

Pearl walks over. "I'll get Morag and Effie, then you can go get some rest, Lilly." She picks up Adah's medical chart.

"There's no change," I tell her.

She puts the file back. "I disagree, that's a change right there. If she's no worse, then she's on the mend."

I wait in silence with Joe for Morag and Effie. When they arrive, Joe takes my hand, and we leave. The deck is littered with sleeping forms. Some lay their heads on pillows made from folded uniform jackets, and others use their arms. Some have brought their pillows from their cabins. With them are their tin hats and gas masks in case of an air attack. Joe and I sit together, absorbing the night sky. My head in his lap, his fingers stroke my hair. Stars light the sky, and I fall to sleep.

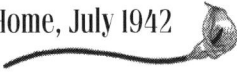

Dear Jane Anne,

So much is happening onboard the *Duchess of Richmond*. Malaria is strengthening its hold, and conflict is creating restless times, much of the conflict is my doing. First, I think it best to concentrate on the malaria outbreak. My hand is steadier and my heart, though filled with sadness, also carries hope, something that is missing with my inner conflict. Adah has malaria, and though the hospital is full of victims, her case brings home our susceptibility to this dreadful disease. Morag, Pearl, and I are working in shifts, alongside our normal duties, to sit with Adah and care for her sister. For the first time, I understand that terrible saying "A watched pot never boils." Effie is distraught. While our concerns and worries for Adah are consuming, they are nothing compared to what Effie is going through. Both need our support.

Joe has been marvellous, bringing us tea and making sure we rest. Never have I known a doctor of his standing to bring such comfort and care to us nurses. Not all in Joe's rank share his high opinion of us. This brings me to the subject of conflict. Would it not be easier if ignorance made such matters disappear? However, there is no magician to place this rabbit back in its hat.

I love Joe. Even though I know this, I am struggling with it. Guilt is loitering, whispering in my ear, carrying Alick's name, and threatening to swallow me whole. Is it possible to love two men at once in differing degrees? Joe and Alick are very different. Joe is my rock, the one who provides comfort, strength, and reassurance. While Alick truly understands me. It is like he has looked deep within my soul and there he has made his home. Why did God bring these men into my life, providing such joy and dread at the same time? Confusion, worry, and doubt builds inside like a rabid dog.

Alick is married. A fact I overlook, as nothing will happen between us, other than our stolen moments together, where we laugh, sing, and talk. I'm unsure what this says about me, but I don't care. Memories are for treasuring, and I am collecting mine with Alick. Trapped in a loveless marriage, I understand why he is brave. Perhaps, for Alick, war is not all bad; it allows him to taste freedom, away from his wife's control. To make friends and rediscover what life is about. I worry about him. Soon we disembark the *Duchess of Richmond*, and he will act like a man with nothing to lose. And what of my beautiful, kind-hearted Joe?

I sit with Adah, wiping the sweat from her skin, wishing to see the future. Just five years from now. To know God has a plan and everything will work out. A strategy that will bring me, Joe, and Alick peace and happiness. With Alick, I have no willpower. Just my faith. God is not cruel, he must have a reason for bringing Alick and Joe into my life. Perhaps I'm looking for a miracle, not a plan from God at all.

Lillian Elizabeth

30

 August 1942, The Duchess of Richmond

*E*ach night since Adah entered the ship's hospital as a patient, John hovers in the background, standing at her bedside. He says nothing. Worry deepens the lines across his forehead. Lost. Scared. That's how I describe this lonely figure at her side. Four days after being admitted, Adah's fever breaks, and so does her tolerance towards our fussing.

Pearl helps me plump the pillows behind Adah's head as a loud, ungrateful sigh escapes. "You're making this into a storm in a teacup, now stop your fussing. I might be old, but my keeper isn't calling my name. There are plenty of other patients to prod and poke. Shoo, the pair of you. Go on."

Pearl and I exchange smiles. The thud of boots echoes along the hall, stopping as they reach the ward. John Benson stands on the threshold. He visibly shakes himself, and on lighter feet enters the hospital, striding towards Adah. The lines at the corners of his eyes fold into each other as his frown lines disappear. His lips turn up, and the tension in his shoulders evaporates as he looks down at his sweetheart. Adah's colouring has returned, and she sits up in her cot, dressed in thick cotton pyjamas.

"I was in the neighbourhood and thought I'd call in. Sorry, no flowers, but I sure could do to rest my feet for a while," John says, pulling nervously at his shirt cuffs.

Whatever remark Adah is about to make dies, and she laughs. "You're a daft sod, John Benson."

Grins on our faces, Pearl and I leave them, going in search of Effie and Morag. Adah is on the mend.

Some shifts are worse than others. This shift is the worse I've known since malaria hit. An hour into my shift and with fresh cases arriving, beds are in short supply. The doctor on duty hasn't turned up to release the patients who are well, and we are experiencing a backlog, which is threatening to spill into the corridor.

Matron's forehead wrinkles in a permanent scowl, her lips pressing tight together. She's like a bear with a very sore behind. An hour later, the doctor arrives, without a word of apology, not that we expect one. Me, I'd be grovelling like a dog, crawling along the ship floor with my tin hat for protection. One does not mess with Matron. With an air of authority, Matron at his side, the doctor releases the patients deemed fit to leave. Matron's lips lessen their grip and her scowl eases.

In a flurry of activity, we ready patients for discharge. As they leave, we help the orderlies strip the beds, scrubbing down the area ready for the next patient. With my arms full of dirty bed linen, I make my way from the hospital, weaving round the beds, adding more to the pile.

"Noo then, Nightingale, fancy meetin' ye 'ere."

My footsteps falter, and my brows pinch as I turn. "Alick?"

His brow is slick with sweat. For a big man, he appears fragile. White sheets cover his body, fading the tan from his skin.

"Finally got mahself a bed with the prettiest o' views."

A lump lodges in my throat, and fear slides down my spine. Calmly, I walk over to him, setting the linen on the floor, reaching for his medical chart. It's not good reading, but this is Alick, he's made of sterner stuff. Well, he'd better be. Despite the panic clawing at my sides like a tiger snared in a net, I fake a smile. "It says here"—I tap the medical chart—"those with a pretty view can only stay a day or so."

A puzzled expression falls over his face. "It does?"

"Certainly, it's in the fine print. I'm surprised someone didn't mention it when they tucked you in."

"Ye ken nurses, Nightingale, when a man has muscles like mine, they forget aboot the fine print."

"Hmm … you don't say."

His lips wobble. "Aye."

"I see, well, you're lucky that such a display of male muscle doesn't sway this nurse."

"Och, tis a shame." Alick's lips struggle to turn down. "If the nurse is nae overcome by such maleness, what aboot the woman?"

"Right now, the woman's primary concern is getting you out from under her feet."

He laughs. I'm unsure if those are tears running down his cheeks or sweat.

A basin sits on the bedside cabinet, and I take the cloth, wringing out the excess water, wiping his face. "There are better views for you, Alick. Ones that don't require you to have malaria. Watching the sunrise as it turns the sea red is a view. This ward has no view to it unless you like battleship grey."

His lashes flutter as he fights to keep his focus. "Aye, boot a sunrise cannae sing like a bonnie Nightingale, kin it."

"I'm singing tonight, on deck."

"Boot 'ere ah get a chance o' mare than one song."

I shake my head. "Hmm ..."

"Ah'm nae arguin' with ye, statin' a fact is all."

"While you're stating your fact," I say, bending to collect the soiled linen, "I'll get rid of this lot and bring some fresh water and ice to cool that fevered head of yours."

Alick chuckles, his eyes closing. Worry creases my brow as I glance at him. He pulls the sheet to his chin, shivering despite the high temperature flooding his body.

When I return with the basin of water, his fever has worsened, and he is no longer conscious. Beneath the sheet, Alick is naked, and the ice packs need changing. As a nurse, I've seen my share of naked men, but this is Alick, and I'm not sure I can be clinical about it. Temptation couples with curiosity; this is my chance to see *all* of Alick. Put like that, well, what woman wouldn't give in to temptation? Remain professional, I tell myself, Alick is sick, he doesn't need a ninny tending to him. I lift the sheet.

He's right about the muscle. Makes me curious about the rest of him. His skin is firm beneath my fingers as I place the ice packs under his armpits. Now the groin. I think I'm blushing. Oh, wow, I stare for a fraction longer than I should. Well … I mean, I've seen a few … quite a lot … but … Conscious of where I am, I grab the ice packs and place them under Alick's groin, removing the old ones and returning the sheet. With a damp cloth, I wipe the sweat from his face, hoping no one caught me peeking.

Time, medicine, and Alick's immune system will be the deciding factor on who wins this battle.

I hate malaria.

Sometimes I feel so weary. Emotions build. My trigger point was Lance-Corporal Andrews. Why that soldier in particular? Honest, I don't know. Was it the residue of fear, seeing Charles Jason, his leg rotten with gangrene? Or mortality reminding me none of us are safe from death? Presently, I'm being plunged from one crisis to the next, with no time to fix my armour before the onslaught begins a fresh. Adah's fever has broken, and now here is Alick.

Alick …

I press the cool damp cloth on his brow. The foundation of my home trembles, along with Alick's body. Pearl glances over as she enters. There's a look on her face I can't read. Worry, sadness … At least she never judges me. With little choice, I go about my work, keeping a close eye on him. Admissions still pour in. It would be nice to treat a different ailment, other than malaria. A bruised foot, or even seasickness. That passes as the sea calms. Malaria doesn't have such a gentle hand.

As the clock hands move, signalling the end of my shift, Joe walks in. His face darkens as he reads Alick's chart. Under lashes, he searches for me. A slight nod lets him know I'm aware of the situation. Joe knows how important Alick is, what with saving my brother's life. There is no time to dwell on the triangle emerging between the three of us; I need to change and be ready to sing. Sing, blimey, how am I going to do that when all I want is to sit by Alick's bedside?

31

August 1942, The Duchess of Richmond

*P*earl folds her arms, leaning against the cabin door. "Your hands are shaking, Lilly. Aren't you and Alick on hold?"

The inside of my mouth has gone furry, and I'm finding it difficult to form words.

She raises a brow. It arches perfectly toward her hairline.

"Alick has malaria."

The brow arches further. "I was there when they brought him in, remember."

"I'm worried about him."

Sigh. "And …"

With my gaze fixed on my shoes, I tuck my hair behind my ear. I wonder how I'm going to explain about Alick and Joe. It's not that she won't understand, this is Pearl—the only one who *will* understand.

I flop on the bed. "Alick is home, Pearl. How do I turn my back on that?"

Her arms flap about her sides. "Home? What does that even mean?"

My teeth graze my bottom lip. "He is everything that fills my heart with joy. He's familiar, and I'm so comfortable with him, like I've known him since forever. He says I'm his soulmate, and … well … I guess … I know what he means … I feel that way, too."

She walks over, our knees touching as she sits down, angling her body towards mine. "And Joe?" she asks, her voice soft.

My throat has gone dry. I want to swallow but can't. My fingers are busy picking at the fabric of my uniform. Joe and Alick's faces dance behind my closed eyelids. Their smiles are different, but their eyes, they both hold such trust in them. I look at Pearl. "I love Joe."

She sends me a quizzical look. "So, Alick is home, but you love Joe." I nod. "It sounds complicated."

"You make it sound stupid. Before Alick, the only thing that bothered me was self-doubt and committing to a relationship with Joe. Now all I can think about is Alick and Joe. But I can't cut off my feelings like that." I click my fingers. "I don't want to lose either of them."

"But you love Joe?" Pearl asks, a neutral expression on her face.

"Joe's my safety net. He'll never hurt me. He eases my worries and makes me strong."

"And Alick? Just so I'm clear."

"He makes me whole."

Pearl rakes a hand through her hair. "What are you going to do?"

"I've tried ignoring it."

"Past tense, so I'm assuming ignoring the issue didn't work." Pearl pats my knee as she stands up, stripping out of her soiled uniform. "I'd say it will sort itself out in the wash, but it's not looking probable. Have you slept with Alick?"

Shocked, I stare at her, my cheeks on fire. "Alick and I … No … We've just spent time together, talking, shared a kiss, not …" I squirm.

"Is Joe going to say kissing Alick is nothing?"

I lean back against the ship, drawing my knees into my chest. "No."

"Neither do I. So, the question is, what are you going to do about it?"

She moves about the cabin as she re-dresses. With my head on my knees, I watch her.

"You're not like me, Lilly, you can't turn your back on the big stuff. There's a point when you've got to choose between them, and I'd say that time has come. Leave it too long and it will tear you apart."

Tears fall down my cheeks. I don't know when I started crying. "He's married, Pearl. Alick … he's married."

"Bloody hell." She sits next to me again.

"He told me a few days ago, after our conversation. Then Adah got sick, and I didn't have time to think about much else. Now Alick's got malaria. I recognise there's no future for us, he'd never leave his wife, not because he loves her or anything, but because … well … it's Alick."

"There's no point in stopping now. I'd say confession is good for the soul, though in your case, I'm not so sure."

"Oh, Pearl, Alick's wife gave him no choice but to marry her. She tried to kill herself when he ended things. Now she's stuck in a wheelchair, and he's stuck with her. I don't even know what I'd do if he was available. I love Joe. I'm aware I keep saying it, but I do."

She hugs me. "It's a mess, Lilly, but I'm sure you'll find a solution."

"I'm such a horrible person, aren't I?"

"No, just human, and humans make mistakes."

"What am I going to do?"

"Honest, I haven't got the answer. Maybe take it one step at a time and see what happens. You'll either end up with Joe, or not."

Fumbling with the fabric of my dress, I pull out my handkerchief, releasing the pressure from my nasal passages. "What should I do?"

"You need to work that one out on your own."

Pearl takes my hands, pulling me to my feet and kissing my cheek. "You can't go looking like that. You'll scare Alick and the other patients to death. Splash some cold water on your face and brush your hair."

I walk over to the small sink nestled in the corner. Avoiding the mirror, I run the tap. The cool water is good against my heated skin. I smooth out the wrinkles of my dress as I take an uneven breath. On my feet are a pair of soft tread pumps—my occupation doesn't lend itself to shoes that announce their arrival.

My hair brushed and secured at the nape of my neck, I'm ready to go back onto the ward.

Pearl gives me the once-over, nodding. "You'll do."

"Thanks for listening and not judging me."

She scoffs. "Who am I to judge anyone?"

32

 August 1942, The Duchess of Richmond

When I arrive at the ship's hospital, Adah's reading lamp is on and she's sitting up in bed, her reading glasses perched on the edge of her nose. The book falls to her lap as she sees me walking over. The black leather shows signs of wear and the gold cross on the front of the bible remains unspoiled. With a soft smile, I sit on the edge of her bed. "You're looking better."

She nods, rubbing at her temple. "I've still got the shakes and my head hurts like I've been listening to Morag singing, but the fever has quietened."

"You gave us all a scare."

She pulls at the sheet, tucking it into her sides. "I scared myself."

At night, the ward becomes a quiet place, interrupted by the soft rustle of fabric, the tread of rubber soles, and snores. Our voices remain low, so as not to disturb anyone.

"John's a good man," I say, looking at her medical chart; it makes for happier reading.

Adah's lips stretch into a smile, her eyes sparkle, and her face glows in the low lighting. "He is. Effie said he's been coming every night to check on me. I must have been a dreadful sight."

"Matron's been on the warpath, so he's had to keep a low profile. Plus he didn't want to clutter up the place."

She chuckles. "He's well trained, my John."

Effie walks over, and I stand. "Sorry, I didn't know you were coming. I'd have got you one too."

She lifts the teacups and I wave off her apology. "Don't worry, it's just a quick visit. They brought Alick in earlier today, and I promised him a song."

Adah takes the tea. "A bit of music wouldn't go amiss. It can get rather glum in here."

"It's good to see you're back on form," I say, laughter in my voice as I walk over to Alick's bed, checking on the other patients as I pass.

My smile fades and my insides turn to mush. His medical chart records a suitable response to treatment, though his fever remains unbroken. It's a step in the right direction, but not enough to dampen my fear. Heat pushes up against my skin as I touch him. My hand trails along his face, and his eyelids flutter as he blinks. There is no hint of recognition in his fevered gaze. His eyelids close and I sigh. We stay like this for a while, me watching him as his eyes move under closed lids. When they open again, a smile tugs at his lips. It doesn't take form, more of a flicker.

"Noo then, Nightingale."

"Alick."

"Ye look awful, what's worryin' ye?"

What's worrying me? I lean closer. "I'll let you into a secret. No matter how a lady looks, you shouldn't tell her she looks awful."

"Aye. That's probably hoo come mah wife hates me. Ah'm nae one for dancin' around the truth. Better tae say it than lie."

A ten-ton weight pushes down on my heart at the mention of his wife. I'm not sure if it's the fever that's making his speech less guarded, or his confession that he's married making the subject less taboo. Either way, the mention of his wife stabs at my insides.

His fingers reach for mine. "Ye promised me a song, Nightingale."

His eyes close as my lungs inflate. I sing one of the few Scottish songs I know, *Loch Lomond*—it's not the right song, given the circumstances, but it's the best I've got. The lyrics transport me back in time, to the song I sang another Scottish soldier. I hope this time the ending will be a happier one.

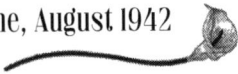

Dear Jane Anne,

I am a woman flitting between crises. While Adah responds well to treatment and we wait for the doctor to release her, another catastrophe comes hurtling towards me. Alick has malaria. There has been some improvement since his arrival on the hospital ward, which I am grateful for, but he's a long way to go until he's out of the woods. In my last letter, I wished for a glimpse of the future. Now, I worry what I would see and am thankful my wish hasn't been granted. Life is dealing blow after blow, and I am no longer sure if I am on foot or horseback. Morag is concerned over my rapid weight loss. My uniform hangs from me, and she is forever bringing sweet treats from the kitchen. Food tastes stale when mixed with anxiety. I nibble on her sticky treats; it's easier than upsetting her, so Pearl says. She's right, of course. I shall have to eat a proper meal; my excuses are wearing thin.

Alick is talking openly about his wife. Frankly, I hate the name Mary. Or rather, I do now. Not that Alick says anything complimentary about her. Small references are the only mention she gets. Her name still pierces my heart each time he says it. I am becoming an awful person. It's not jealousy his wife brings out in me, but the hurt and betrayal she caused Alick. Maybe there is a bit of jealousy.

Not that I have the right to such emotions. After all, Alick is married and I'm with Joe. Can a heart be black? That's how I envision Mary's. To force a man into marriage is despicable. Perhaps what I am doing is just as hateful. With Alick, I no longer see clearly.

Joe is being a darling of understanding, which makes me feel worse. We spend little time together. Stolen moments on deck. Between my shifts, Alick, Joe, and commitment to providing entertainment, life is unbalanced. Malaria is affecting everything. It is important to keep morale up. The requirement to reschedule acts because of a decline in available artistic bodies has increased my singing rota. I dread where my head will take me when things slow, and I'm forced to reflect on other matters. Given this, I shall become a tennis player. That way, when disaster strikes, I can bat it off. Somewhere far, far, far away from the *Duchess of Richmond*.

Lillian Elizabeth

33

 August 1942, The Duchess of Richmond

*M*orag walks into our cabin, a telegram clasped between her trembling fingers. Pearl slides off the bed and I walk over, stopping at her side.

"Will ye read it, Pearl, ah dinnae think ah kin."

Pearl opens the telegram, and we watch the colour drain from her face.

"Pearl?" I say, pulling Morag to me.

She stares at the telegram, clears her throat, and reads the contents.

```
ROBBIE AND JAMIE DIED – (STOP) – 1ST OF
AUGUST 1942 – (STOP) – ROBBIE DROVE THE
TRACTOR INTO A LAKE – (STOP) – JAMIE
WAS ON BOARD – (STOP) – BOTH UNCON-
SCIOUS AND INEBRIATED – (STOP) – SORRY
TO BRING YOU SUCH HEART-BREAKING
NEWS – (STOP) – LOVE MA
```

Morag's legs give out and we crash to the floor. Pearl falls to her knees, at our side. We hold Morag as she sobs, our tears and anguish over our friend's pain stabbing at our hearts. There are no words to dampen the grief.

"Ah'm goin' tae miss them … Whoo am ah goin' tae argue with?"

"There's still Fergus," I remind her.

"Aye …" She nods.

"You've got me, Morag. We disagree a lot, more than you did with your brothers. See, Jamie might have been your Ma's favourite, but you're mine."

"Och, Pearl …"

I kiss the top of Morag's head. "You've always got us, no matter what happens."

Pearl places the sheet over the soldier's face. The time of death is 8 p.m. Her hand lingers on his chest. A soft breath of air releases from her parted lips. No words can change the situation, so I stand at her side as we grieve in silence. With no family member present, it is up to us to mark his death with the respect he deserves. At twenty-eight, Simon Gunn is dead. His rank is of no consequence. What is of consequence is that he won't be around to watch his four-year-old son grow up. We've all seen the photographs of his boy more times than we have fingers or toes to count. Pride and love flowed from Simon's being as he produced the pictures. When they appeared, we smiled like it was the first time we had seen them—I hope his son grows up remembering how much his daddy loves him. I'm a firm believer that love is not an emotion to be placed in the past tense. Trevor Henry is dead, yet my father's love lives inside me; such emotions don't fade when the body dies.

The privacy screen that wraps around his bed hides the soldier from the other patients. It affords us a few precious minutes to say goodbye. We should feel each death, otherwise it becomes lost in the masses. A forgotten soul that becomes a number—no one should die a number. James Andrews, Robert Williams, David Jackson, Bruce Jaimeson, and Simon Gunn—five men have died since the first case of malaria was diagnosed on the 24th of July. Five men who will never see their family again. Five men that will never grow old. It would be easy to blame the infected mosquito, but the real blame is Hitler and those that support his madness.

We have been at war for nearly three years and there is no end in sight. The world is changing. Back home food is in short supply. Women have joined the fight, becoming spies, building weapons, tending the land, and taking up jobs normally undertaken by men. Children are growing up never knowing their fathers or uncles, mothers, sisters. London is under attack and children leave their homes to live with people they don't know, to locations deemed safer for them. And for what? Over one man's dream of a super race. To rule the world and dictate how we live, and who dies. If Hitler thinks he can suck the life out of us and our freedom, he is delusional.

As the death toll mounts, a wave of anger towards this senseless destruction festers inside me. The world isn't the only thing changing; I am. A shiver runs down my spine, and I let it pull me from my darkening thoughts back to where Simon Gunn lies.

"At least Alick is going to make it," Pearl whispers.

I nod, staring at Simon Gunn's sheet-clad body, guilt sweeping over me. Rather him than Alick. "Yes, he is."

"You can mourn Simon's passing and be thankful Alick will live. It doesn't make you a bad person. Just human."

"No, it doesn't. What does is Joe and Alick. One I can't have. The other deserves better."

"Life isn't all roses, Lilly. Yes, you've some tough decisions to make. You'll get hurt, and so will Joe and Alick. Love is messy. In the end, we all end up alone."

I grab her hand, squeezing. "I love you, Pearl. Don't think that no one cares about you because they do."

Tears sit within her eyes.

If Joe and Alick could morph into one, there would be my perfect man. Reliable, fun, caring, supportive, wild, and free to marry. Perhaps it is not the morphing that is the problem, but Mary McNavis. I'm aware I can't have my cake and eat it as they say, however nice that would be. There it is, all sewn together—I have fallen for both men, one more than the other, and I don't want to choose. Ostriches hide when faced with a predator's attack. It's where the saying 'Burying your head in the sand' comes from. If ignorance is good enough for an ostrich, then I shall adopt its stance with Alick and Joe. My stomach churns. I'm sure the ostrich's stomach doesn't respond this way when hiding behind a bush from a predator. Stupid stomach.

"You're frowning," Pearl whispers.

I grimace, wishing my face wasn't so transparent. "Sorry."

"What were you thinking?"

My lips twist. "You don't want to know."

"That's where you're wrong. I want to know more now than I did. Your face is a picture of emotion."

"I want to become an ostrich."

Pearl stares. "Why would you want to be an ostrich?"

"Joe. Alick … If I was an ostrich, I could bury my head and remain ignorant."

I let go of her hand, turn, and walk from behind the privacy screen. Pearl follows. Ahead, Alick sits up in bed, a book in his hand. If Matron allowed him, he'd be out of bed, sitting with the other patients. She has pinched his ear and guided him back to his bed several times. The last occurrence carried the threat of cleaning out the used bed-pans; a duty no one enjoys. Alick knows when to concede defeat and remains in bed.

"I still don't understand why becoming a flightless bird is going to help," Pearl murmurs.

My stomach gurgles and I scowl down at it. As we inhabit the same body, it should be on my side. With a shrug, I come to a stop at the bed nearest Alick. "At least an ostrich gets to ignore the situation."

Pearl snorts, looking over at Alick. "Good luck with that one."

Joe walks onto the ward, Adah at his side. Pearl gestures her head in their direction. "And that one."

Like a bull, my nostrils flare in frustration and Pearl laughs.

Adah is back at work. Matron has placed her on a reduced shift pattern, for recuperation. "There is no point in overtaxing yourself," Matron said. Translated, this means Adah needs to be fighting fit for when we get to wherever it is we are going.

"I'll go take care of Simon Gunn," Pearl says. "I'll catch up with you later. Just don't go flying off." She smiles. "Oh, wait you can't, your wings haven't the strength."

"Smarty-pants," I say, and her smile grows.

The time for keeping myself distanced from Alick has long passed. His presence on the ward strengthens our bond. Sickness breaks down barriers. As does fear. Days spent at Alick's side, a few conversations when the fever quietened, and bang … with no warning, here I am, spinning a web of emotions so tight they remove any pretence of sanctuary. What I realise is, if I couldn't let Alick go before, it is now impossible.

Tommie Brian Dalton smiles up at me. With his leg in plaster and three bruised ribs, I'd say he has nothing to smile about. He fell off whatever part of the ship he was using as a stage to show off the legendary Highland dance. Rumours confirm Brian's dancing wasn't the only thing to make an appearance that night. With his kilt around his waist, he's lucky he only broke his right leg and bruised his ribs.

A Scot's ego is hard to break, and Brian remains proud of his skills as a dancer and lover. As he's currently incapacitated, I believe it doesn't say much about his fancy footwork, or love-making skills. The location of the incident is under dispute. Brian either refuses to say or he can't remember. My view is that he's not telling. He wasn't on his own when the incident occurred, but soldiers stick together, and it appears they are all suffering from the same memory loss.

"Now then, Brian, how are you today?" I ask, picking up his medical chart.

"Better when ah kin get a good night's kip. This bed creaks tae much."

A round of groans meet Brian's comment. He snores, and as we cannot turn him onto his side, we have no choice but to accept it—I'm glad I don't sleep on the ward.

"A better night's kip?" Alick gasps. "Yer like a foghorn, Brian. We'll all be glad when ye kin leave 'n' we kin all have a better night's kip."

A round of nodding heads backup Alick's remark, along with a chorus of 'Aye'.

"I wouldn't worry, Alick, you'll be out of here long before Brian," I say, tapping my pen on the metal folder containing Brian's medical information.

Alick smiles at me, his book resting on his legs. "Ah'm nae thinkin' o' me." He waves a hand at the surrounding beds. "Tis the rest o' this unfortunate lot ah'm thinkin' aboot."

Brian's cheeks turn crimson. "Och, Alick, ye just like complainin'. Mah snorin' isnae that bad. The wife never complains."

Alick rolls his eyes. "Yer wife is deaf."

"Aye, well, she kin feel vibrations 'n' if ah was that bad, she'd say somethin'."

"Vibrations ... Have ye ever heard somethin' so daft? She's in a bed, nae on a dance floor with a brass band. Yer snore like a hog, Brian."

"'Oink, oink ... 'ere piggy, piggy," someone calls from behind me.

This gets the others laughing and I try not to smile.

"Don't listen to them, Brian. Think of your snoring as setting the base for our songs."

Brian's hand flies in my direction. "See, hoo come ye lot cannae be nice? Ah might snore a bit, boot tis got rhythm."

There is a mix of groans, snorts, and laughter.

Joe walks over and the banter stops. "Was it something I said?"

"It's the white coat of authority, it scares them," I say.

"I see. Better a white coat than a peep show, eh, Brian?" Joe winks at me.

I shake my head. "I'd hate to think what Matron would say if she caught sight of Brian in full exposure, kilt around his waist, and caterpillar on display."

"Not on my ward, deary ... Now be a pet and swing by my office," someone shouts across from Alick, his voice high-pitched.

I put down Brian's medical chart, shaking my head, trying not to laugh. "On that note, I think I'll leave you to it."

"A caterpillar!" Brian exclaims as I leave.

Oh dear — poor choice of word. I make it off the ward, tears welling, my face trembling from the pressure of trying not to laugh. It takes a while to compose myself before I can return.

Two hours after starting my shift, I complete my first round of checks. Pearl sits writing to Simon Gunn's family. With a smile, I scan the sleeping forms of our patients. There are three fresh malaria cases, which are responding well to treatment. Given Simon Gunn's departure from this world, it's good to update their medical records with positive news. My training covers sanitation, mental health, and administering anaesthetic. It doesn't prepare me for the emotional toll of losing a patient. Doubt often niggles, questioning if we've made the right decision when administering medical care on the back of split-second decisions. The medical decisions I make here are more challenging from those I made at Cheyne Children's Hospital. Speedy decisions are often of the essence. They can save or end a wounded soldier's life; like a light switch, with one click, we know if the decision we made was the right one.

Pearl comes over, her cheeks flushed, and in her hand is a note. "Look …"

I stare at the crumpled paper and my mouth waters. English scones, with jam and cream await our attention, Morag's distinctive writing informs us. Our Scottish wildcat is doing well after the news of her brothers' deaths. I wish I was as strong as her. Morag, bless her, has paid a visit to the ship's chef, asking him to whip us up a batch of scones, to cheer us up after the earlier loss of Simon Gunn. The note informs us they are stowed away in the cupboard near reception. Like school children with a big secret, we sneak from the ward. Adah watches us, her eyebrows arching in question. Pearl waves her to follow, passing her Morag's note as she reaches us. She nods in understanding, joining our merry band. Within a few paces, we stand at the cupboard, glancing over our shoulders. The hinges creak softly, doors gaping open, as collectively we gasp.

"What …"

Ants congregate over our scones, nibbling away at Morag's surprise.

"How?" I ask.

We watch the creatures, transfixed on their activity.

The soft tread of shoes behind makes us jump. Joe looks puzzled. "What's going on?"

I point at the shelf. "The ants are eating our scones."

Pearl scowls, throwing the crumpled piece of paper on the desk. "Blast it! How did they find them so fast?"

Joe reaches for the note, unfolding it. His lips twitch.

"What's so funny?" Adah asks, hands on her hips.

Joe points at the piece of paper. "It's the note."

"What?" we say, exchanging confused expressions.

"See… 'scones in the cupboard near administration, yum, yum'. That's how the ants found them. They read Morag's note."

"Well, I hope they choke on them. Bloody stowaways," Pearl says, making us laugh, even as our stomachs groan.

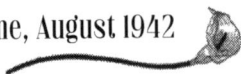

Dear Jane Anne,

Gone are the days when my brothers argued over who was the tallest, or how a few months made a tremendous difference in the line of authority. John Edward always used his eldest child status against us. If there was one biscuit left, it was his. If the yard needed sweeping, the eldest supervised. Arthur James would grumble, passing the work down the line until it reached me. As the only girl, I got landed with all the unpleasant jobs. I complained under my breath about the lot of them. Now, I would give anything to be sweeping the yard. Trevor Henry would be alive. Charles Jason would be whole. And Hitler would be a nobody. If it were possible to turn the hands on a clock back, I would.

My friendship with Morag, Pearl, Adah, and Effie helps to balance the pain that losing a patient brings. Whatever the future holds, we will always have each other. It's like I told Pearl when Simon Gunn passed from malaria, we are never truly alone. Not when we have each other. Love may not conquer all, but it helps to heal and guide us, giving us strength and courage. And while it breeds conflict and sadness, above all it provides us with a foundation. When the ground beneath our feet shakes, our love will steady us.

My heart fills with guilt over Alick and Joe. Sometimes, when I'm talking on the ward with Alick, I see Joe gazing over at us; not that I am anything but professional when on duty. Still, I wonder what he's thinking.

Does he suspect anything between me and Alick? About my feelings for him. I keep telling myself, there is no me and Alick, but whatever door opened inside me, won't close. My fear of being alone is consuming. What if Joe finds out and leaves me? Oh, what to do …

Lillian Elizabeth

34

August 1942, The Duchess of Richmond

A few days after Morag's telegram and the scone incident, the on-duty doctor releases Alick. His eyes search for me as he leaves. With my arms filled with dirty sheets, I follow him from the hospital, making my way to the laundry room. "Be careful, Alick, I can't withstand another shock like that for at least fifty years."

He reaches out, brushing his hand against mine. "Aye, ah'll see what ah kin do. Though the view is as bonnie as ever."

I snort.

Alick stops as we reach the laundry room. His hands resting on my shoulders, I turn to face him, my back against the door. The narrow corridor isn't the right place to loiter like a couple of lovesick fools. "Perhaps I'll see you on deck, while I'm singing."

There's a sadness about him. I'm not sure what it means, but it's not good. "Aye, mibbie."

My brows raise in confusion. "Alick?"

"Ah'm sorry, Nightingale, ah've nae been fair tae ye." His fingers trail along the side of my face. "We cannae keep meetin' up. Tis wrong o' me, ah ken that noo."

His lips touch my forehead, and I want to cry. To throw down the stained bedding and yell until every ounce of fear and frustration seeps from my body. I want to tell him not to do this, time is running out, and we need to spend what we have together. There's nothing wrong with talking and singing, storing away these memories. Soon Alick will be on the frontline, and I will patch up the injured or hold them as they die. I stand silent, the dirty laundry pressing against my chest as my heart squeezes into a tight ball, and tears threaten.

"Ah love ye, Nightingale."

The world around me crumbles as I watch him walk away. Realisation comes too late. I don't just love Alick; he is my everything. My heart stumbles, like it's trying to adjust to beating of its own accord. How do I learn to live when part of me walks away? I am a shadow, disappearing within the light, emerging in an altered state, but never the same. Time will reinvent me, but never will I be whole. My time with Alick has ended and so too is the person I was.

"I love you, Alick," I whisper, tears rolling down my cheeks.

The laundry room is quiet and on a sob I drop the linen. In this tiny room, alone, I break down, my back sliding against the door, my arms around my knees as I bury my head. Charles Jason is right. Alick is braver than both of us. He has done what I couldn't; chosen Joe over him.

When I'm not working nights, the increase in humidity and heat forces me, along with the other QAs, to move our sleeping accommodation to deck with the soldiers. QAs huddle together, away from the men, enjoying the light breeze that evening offers. It also creates an awareness. Somewhere on deck, Alick sleeps, as does Joe.

The day after my world collapsed, the winds pick up and soon the darkening sky brings the threat of high winds. Our stomachs roll as the storm gathers momentum, whipping down hallways, screaming through small gaps. The ship rises and dips over the high waves, rocking from side to side. Regardless of the rising nausea and sliding equipment, we continue to look after the sick. A book falls from a bedside table, sliding along the floor into Pearl's path. Her right foot hits the cover and together they slide towards Brian's bed. He catches her as she loses her balance. She falls on top of him and his arms lock around her waist as she grips the bedframe, preventing her full weight from pressing against his bruised ribs.

"Noo then, ah dinnae ken what mah wife is goin' tae say aboot this. Boot ah'm sure glad o' the company." Brian's hands glide over her bottom.

Pearl pushes herself off the bed, straightening her uniform. "Keep dreaming, Brian, you have this ghastly storm to thank for our brief interlude, not choice."

"Noo that's na way tae speak tae yer rescuer, 'n' an injured one at that."

"You're right, Brian, but those hands of yours got a little friskier than they had a right to. We both know what your wife would do to those hands if she found out."

He smiles, his hands stretched out in front of him as he wiggles his fingers. "Bad hands, what was ye thinkin'. Noo consider yeselves told off."

Pearl's lips twitch. "You're incorrigible, Brian."

"So mah wife says."

By the end of our shift, the winds have died down and we fall onto our makeshift beds on deck in relief.

The next day, when we wake, we arrive in Aden. Rocky cliffs, that contain no vegetation and a sprinkling of trees, greet us. My nose wrinkles as I sneeze. It's hot—boiling—and I flop back down on my bed, grabbing a book hidden beneath my pillow, and fan myself. Half-measures don't exist, we sail within the eye of a storm or bake from the inside out.

Pearl groans. "Waft the book in this direction."

"If it means moving, you'll have to get your own," I say, turning my head to gaze over at her.

Pearl tuts. "Call yourself a sister."

"That's medical sister."

She rolls onto her stomach, her hand dangling at her side. "You've been around Morag too long."

Her eyelids drop, and she falls back to sleep.

Our stay in Aden lasts for a few days. With a grand salute and cheers of good wishes from *HMS Frobisher*, a Royal

Navy cruiser, our ship leaves. With no battleships or smaller boats flanking our sides, we move along the Suez Canal, a lonesome liner embarking on its next chapter. With my back against Joe's chest, we sit on deck, watching the scenery slip away. To the west, the sun sets, in a kaleidoscope of colours. From the southeast, the moon shines down. Camels plod, making their way along the side of the canal in silence. There is nothing but desert, miles and miles of sand. Bizarre posts, where British Tommies hold fort, sporadically appear. Their frantic waving and fingers making victory Vs cause us to laugh.

Joe looks at his watch and sighs, laying a light kiss on my cheek. "I'd best make a move."

"Have fun," I call as he leaves.

The entertainment has finished for the evening and people are finding their sleeping spots. Men and women part, voices becoming whispers. During our travels, we have become a large family. An intense spirit of camaraderie wraps us within its protective shield. It's hard not to think about Alick, and I often wonder what he's up to. On a whim, I visit our hiding hole. Two Tommies sit smoking, the smoke billowing around them. With a smile, I walk past. Alick was never mine to lose, I understand that. But this feeling won't go away. The door to my home appears to have closed, taking a vital part of me with it, and I'm unsure if it will ever open again.

On the 11th of August, we pack for disembarkation. The next day we wake to find we have arrived at Port Suez.

In the corridor, feet beat against the floor and voices flutter into our cabin.

Morag throws her kit bag over her shoulder. "'Ere we go again."

Pearl glances up from where she's sitting on the bed. "Or as Shakespeare once wrote, 'Cowards die many times before their deaths; The valiant never taste of death but once.' Let that be a warning to Hitler and his allies."

My heart hammers in my chest. With everyone preparing to leave, there is no time to find Alick. To wish him well, stay safe and don't be a hero.

"Lilly?"

Morag's voice snaps, gaining my attention. There's a scuffling down the corridor, followed by numerous indignant huffs, and Alick rushes in, filling the doorway with his bulky frame. His kilt swings about his legs.

"Nightingale."

Pearl pulls Morag out of the cabin, as he steps inside.

He opens his arms, and I run into them, tears falling down my cheeks.

"I thought … I …"

His lips brush my hair. "Sh …sh … ah'm sorry, Nightingale, sh …"

"Oh, Alick." I bury my head between his neck and shoulder.

"Ah cannae leave withoot seein' ye, ah'm sorry."

"Don't. Never be sorry."

Outside, preparation for disembarking is underway.

"Don't be a hero, Alick. You might think you've nothing to live for, but you do. Live for me."

His lips find mine, and I pull him to me, moulding myself into him, wanting this moment to last. "Aye, Nightingale, for ye." He stops as he reaches the door. "We will be taegether, Nightingale, ah promise ye. Nae in this world, mibbie, but haime is haime, 'n' our souls will find each other. Between the light 'n' dark, I'll find ye."

He disappears.

I stare at the space, my heart racing. Tears slide down my face, and I'm unable to move. Pearl runs back in, Morag at her side. They wrap me in their arms, and we cry together.

"I'm sorry, Lilly," Pearl whispers into my ear.

I sniff. "I-it was a-always going to be this w-way."

"I'm still sorry."

Our arrival at Suez signals the end of our company with the women's services. At 10 a.m., the officers and men leave the ship. The hairs on my arms stand to attention as I search for Alick. A lump of sadness lodges in my stomach. "Look after him, God," I pray. The *Duchess of Richmond* is fast becoming a ghost ship. I'm sure it took less time for the captain and crew to abandon the *Mary Celeste*, and the insurance company to charge the unscrupulous captain with fraud, than it is taking those aboard the *Duchess of Richmond* to desert her.

How many of us will return? Only time and the end of the war know the answer. It may be selfish, but I hope my losses aren't too many. I've already lost Trevor Henry and Uncle Anthony Kevin Broadman; I don't want to lose anyone else. But what we want, and what we get, are two different things. With the ship emptying fast, the sight is sombre. Joe comes to stand at my side, his hand sliding into mine. Guilt rises, and my cheeks warm in response. If Joe asks about my high colour, I'm blaming my sudden flush on the heat.

Morag comes running up to us, Pearl in tow. "Orders are in, we leave in an hour."

"Half four then," I say, looking at my watch.

"Bet it's more like ten, nothing round here runs to time," Pearl grumbles.

Joe bends, kissing my cheek. "See you on the other side."

"Be careful, Joe."

He smiles. "Don't worry."

It seems all I do is worry.

"He'll be fine," Pearl says.

"Hmm …"

In the distance, bagpipes play.

Pearl looks over the deck as the Highlanders prepare to disembark. "They'll both be fine."

"I hope so."

Morag taps her foot in time to the music. "We've made some good friends. Tis strange seein' them go."

I rub my arms, warding off the chill slithering through my body, despite the heat. "We'll meet again. After all, soldiers need nurses."

Pearl nods. "It's good to hear you sounding so cheerful, Lilly."

"Och, ye make her sound like a right misery."

I hold up my hand, stopping Pearl from responding. "Don't ..."

On my left, Effie squeezes between those of us left on deck, grimacing.

Pearl points. "I wonder what's wrong with her?"

Morag turns, lowering her hand from her forehead. "For someone not due to leave for a bit, she's in an awful hurry."

Her arms flapping at her sides, Effie stops in front of us. "Are you lot coming or are you waiting until this war is over? Matron wants us lined up and ready to leave."

Morag's eyes raise skyward, and Pearl huffs, but we don't comment. Where Matron is concerned, everything has ears. Instead, we pick up our kit bags, slinging them over our shoulders.

"Come on, troops," I call, following Effie over to our waiting sisters.

35

August 1942, The Birds Nest

*A*t 4:30 p.m., we leave the ship to sit in a lighter until 6:30 p.m. The flat-bottomed barge is used to transfer goods and passengers to and from the moored ships. Given we've been ready to leave for hours, it's a long wait until the lorry arrives, taking us to a place called Aviary—which the troops refer to as Birds Nest. Birds Nest sits six miles, in the desert, outside of Suez. A constant hum of activity floats around the huge campsite.

WRNS and families, evacuated from Alexandra, settle into their temporary homes. Close by, a Young Women's Christian Association (YWCA) offers cheap accommodation. Morag, Pearl, Effie, and I share a tent, and Adah shares with three other QAs. Pearl remains unusually tight-lipped as she stares at the narrow camp beds, which take up most of the room. With no modern conveniences, we press our uniforms on top of a tin truck with a flatiron. A Beatrice oil stove heats the iron. Water arrives by tanker, with no set pattern or schedule. Given this, water rationing is in place—two pints per person, collected from the Mess in camp kettles. One pint we save for drinking, the other for washing our faces and strip washing our bodies in two halves, the best we can. When this is done, we boil the used water on the Beatrice stove to wash our uniforms. Sand blows from sunrise to sun-down. Bugs, mosquitoes, flies, scorpions, and rats roam the camp and surrounding area, forming the apparatus of our daily assault course.

"Blast it," Pearl swears as she tugs at a knot in her hair. "I hate sand."

Morag lifts two long clumps of hair. "At least yer's is nae matted taegether like mine."

Pearl presses her lips together, nodding. "Yep, you win, again, in the hair department."

The flap to the tent lifts and Effie walks in. "We're on the move, you need to pack."

"You mean we're leaving this hell hole? Thank the Lord for that," Pearl says. "I've always hated the seaside. This is my punishment, isn't it?"

Smiling, I throw my arm over Pearl's shoulders. "She's not been the same since we visited Suez."

Morag's face twists. "Ugh … what a squalid place that was."

"It was the goats roaming round, pooing and urinating wherever they pleased, that got to me. You never knew what you were about to stand in." Pearl pouts.

Effie slaps her neck, removing a dead fly from her skin. "They had some decent shops."

I clap my hands. "My favourite trip was when we went to Ismailia on that lorry. Travelling by the side of the Suez Canal, taking in the scenery, maize, sugar cane, peaches, dates, pears, grapes—"

"Me too. The views were delightful," Pearl sighs, cutting me off mid-sentence.

Morag snorts. "Whoo ye tryin' tae kid? Views mah bottom, Pearl. Mare like when we were aboard that hospital ship at Ismailia, meetin' those American Officers. Ye were all flutterin' eyelashes 'n' poutin' lips, as ah recall."

Pearl smiles, jabbing Morag with her elbow. "They were darlings, weren't they?"

"Their accent was dreamy," I say.

Pearl places a hand over one side of her mouth. "Don't let Morag hear you say that. The whole Alick thing was bad enough."

Effie's brow wrinkles. "Wasn't Alick the one who saved your brother?"

I nod.

"Ostrich," Pearl coughs into her hand.

Morag's hand's flap about her. "Ah was very understandin', ah'll have ye ken."

Effie frowns. "Why did you need to be understanding?"

Morag ignores Effie's questions. "Lilly and Joe are like beavers. They're made for each other." She raises her hands, forming a heart.

Effie looks shocked. "You haven't, Lilly … have you? You know, with Joe?"

My cheeks are on fire, I swear they are. "No, of course not."

In a fit of giggles, Morag and Pearl fall onto the narrow bed behind them.

Colour lights up Effie's face. "I'm sorry ... I didn't mean ..."

"It's alright," I say, waving a hand at her. "We'd best pack or we'll all be in trouble."

Letter Home, August 1942

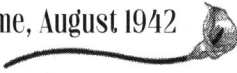

Dear Jane Anne,

We travel through the desert from one British General Hospital to another. The conditions are basic, and sand gets everywhere. My hair is like straw, and my skin is dry. Insects bite us wherever we go, using us as a tasty snack, while scorpions scuttle towards us, their tails aimed. For small creatures, they are formidable, even the flies leave them in peace. Unlike British rats, Egyptian rats are brazen creatures, with an unhealthy appetite for plaster of Paris. They sit on patients, gnawing at plastered limbs, not one bit afraid of us, noise, or light. We spend our days beating them off with a broom or stick. Whatever happened to rats disliking daylight?

Presently, we aren't seeing much action and the hospital remains at half capacity. A quarter of patients are locals. Given the language barrier, we use hand gestures to communicate. Alick's regiment left the *Duchess of Richmond* long before us. I can still hear the bagpipes as they disembarked; though a cheerful tune, it was poignant. Perhaps because of what it represented — the end of Alick and I. Emotions and situations tangle, wrapping round me like a vine. The time and place always clash and it's never the right time, or place, not for me and Alick. Though I remain true to Joe, my heart and soul left with Alick. I don't want to sound theatrical, but loving Joe is not the same. My love for him is softer, it doesn't consume or make me whole, it just is.

Alick says we will be together, not in this lifetime but another. Do you think there is a place where souls reunite? I hope so, because as things stand, that is where I will meet Alick. War may bring uncertainties, but I am determined to do right by Joe. Alick is my soulmate, but here on earth Joe will have my heart—not that I want to sound like an Emily Brontë novel. Over the last few weeks, I have done little but dwell on my relationship with Alick and Joe, and have stopped feeling guilty over emotions I can't control. So long as I love Joe and he loves me, and I remain true to him, there is nothing to be guilty about.

I pray you are all remaining safe in London and that my brothers are well. It has been so long since I laid eyes on them, and I wonder if I will recognise them when war is over. And them, me. Family is important and I miss you all.

Lillian Elizabeth

36

*M*uch to Morag and her stomach's delight, we arrive at No. 1 BGH, stationed at EL Qantara, at 12:30 p.m. EL Qantara is near the ancient Egyptian city of Selē. Halfway between Port Said and Ismailia, on the Egyptian side of the canal. During the Great War, EL Qantara, or Kantara, as the Allied troops call it, was Headquarters No 3 section, Canal Defence, and Headquarters Eastern Force.

Hitler's actions reinstate the town's importance as a hospital centre.

"Ah cannae help it if travellin' makes me hungry."

"Everything makes you hungry," Pearl says, swiping at the bugs as they zoom in for the attack. "I hate these loathsome creatures."

Morag scratches at her head. "Ugh … ah swear they're nestin' in mah hair."

Pearl peers at the top of her head. "I can see why. It makes the perfect nest."

Effie and I wave our hands in front of us, warding off the hungry insects. They must see this as a challenge because they double their efforts. Bugs, unfortunately, remain a problem, along with scorpions and rats. Our tent, we discover, is an upgrade from the last one. The hard floor sends us squealing in delight, and we jump, dance, and walk over it. The surface doesn't stick to our shoes or move. Compared to the Birds Nest, this is pure heaven.

I grab Morag and Pearl. "Let's check out the washing area. Do you suppose we'll have toilets? Proper toilets."

We stand transfixed in awe.

"These are … super," I say.

Pearl sniffs. "Better than at the Birds Nest."

I groan. "Anything is better than the Birds Nest."

"Did ye notice there's a sittin' 'n' dinin' room, 'n' a bar in the Sisters' Mess? We've hit paradise," Morag sighs.

I nod in agreement. "EL Qantara is an oasis."

"Birds Nest had its challenges, and has made us appreciate the finer things, like hard floors, and pit toilets. Anywhere is better," Pearl says.

My hair falls over my face, and I tuck it behind my ear. It needs cutting. "Still, we had a fun time."

Morag smiles, nudging Pearl. "Some o' us mare than others, eh?"

Pearl scowls. "Stop elbowing me. I don't know what you mean."

"Aye, o' course … doll."

Pearl giggles. "When I first heard that American Officer use the word doll, I thought he meant a toy doll. Why do they call women dolls?"

"'Cause we're so bonnie o' course." Morag laughs.

"Well, I prefer darling or sweetheart," I say, walking back to our quarters.

"Is that what Joe calls ye?" Morag asks, catching me up.

"Or Nightingale," Pearl adds.

"A lady," I say, ignoring Pearl's comment, "doesn't discuss such matters."

"You're wicked, Lilly." Morag gasps.

"I know, isn't it terrible."

Birds Nest may have lowered our expectations, but EL Qantara has lifted our spirits.

With duties and rotas allocated, we settle into life at EL Qantara. Rats run across the floor, no matter the time of day. Sticks are scattered around the hospital, ready to beat them off the patients. As the hateful creatures have made it their mission to make life difficult, the sticks quickly become our best friends. We go nowhere without them, including the latrines.

The trench toilet pits are around four feet by five feet deep. I try not to contemplate what goes down them and concentrate instead on not falling in. Sanitary personnel keep the latrines in good condition. The officers hand this duty out as punishment when soldiers break regulations. It isn't deterrent enough to stop them from being disobedient. The three Tommies on sanitary duties relive their latest exploits, unaware of our presence. Morag, Pearl, and I, stifle our laughter as we sneak out the latrines to the hospital. The three Tommies huddle together, cigarettes dangling between their lips, their backs to the toilets.

"Did you see Matron's face when she saw your sketch?" one soldier asks.

"How was I to know she didn't like rats."

It wasn't the rats that had got them into trouble, but the excessive size of Matron's bosom that the rats were bouncing on. Her sketched finger pointing towards the hospital doors. A stern expression etched on her face, the soldier had written under the cartoon; "You loathsome creature. I'll have no rats in my hospital!" The rat on her right breast held a striking resemblance to Adolf Hitler.

Rats often build their nests in the short, concrete walls at the base of the tent sides. Not in Morag's hair, despite Pearl's overwhelming assurance that's where they are breeding. They scurry up the mosquito netting, running over patients' heads to nibble at plastered limbs, forcing immobilised patients to beat them off with a stick. Life at the No. 1 BGH is interesting. Morag scowls at a rat as it scurries along the hospital floor under a patient's bed. As bold as they come, it climbs onto the bed, sniffing at the bedsheet before stopping and looking at Morag. It leans closer to her, taking a fancy to the nurse as she glares at it. It's dreadful how the bugs and rats have taken an instant liking to her. Though, it's also entertaining.

A squeak erupts from the rat as it moves onto the bedframe. Its tail swinging it sits on its hind legs. Nose twitching, it stares at Morag. With the rat taking an unnatural interest, Morag puts down the patient's medical file, her gaze locking on the stick propped by the side of the patient's bed. Pearl and I watch from across the hospital as she reaches for the stick. The rat sniffs at the space between them. Its jaws are covered in white powder from the plaster of Paris.

"Go, shoo." Morag waves the stick at the rat.

In fascination, the rat stretches towards the stick, inching closer to Morag. Its constant squeaking grabs the attention of the other rats.

Pearl leans into me. "I believe the rat thinks Morag has asked it out for dinner."

No sooner does Pearl say this than the rat launches itself at Morag. She screams, dropping the stick. Pearl and I gasp as it chases her around the hospital ward. The other rats must think it's a party and join in. Her face draining of colour, Morag leaps off the floor onto the nearest bed. Our hands covering our mouths, we stand mesmerised at Morag's crazed form. It's as well Matron isn't around. The soldier occupying the bed looks more than happy to help Morag out. From the width of his smile, I'd say he's enjoying her company more than he should. His arms tighten around her, pulling Morag closer. With the rats still running for her, Pearl and I grab the sticks sitting redundant at the patients' bedsides and beat them down on the creatures. They squeak and dash over the floor, leaving for less threatening pickings.

Morag sags in relief. "Ye could have done that afore they attacked me."

"What, and miss the show?" Pearl says, trying not to smile.

Hands on Morag's waist, the soldier steadies her against him, placing her squarely on his lap. Unaware of the effect her squirming is having on him, Morag wiggles about, looking for rats.

"I'd stop doing that if I was you. It's been a long time since a pretty girl sat on my lap."

With her face the same colour as her hair, Morag stills, her mouth forming an 'O' shape. By the time we reach her, her face is turning so red I'm sure she is going to explode like an overripe tomato.

"Excuse us," I say, pulling Morag off the soldier.

His arms fall onto the mattress, unhappiness clouding his face. The Tommie next to him chuckles. Joe walks onto the ward, laughter dancing in his eyes as he stops next to the soldier's bed. Picking up the medical file, he scans the notes. "If you aren't careful, soldier, it will be more than a stray bullet we'll be treating you for. Now let's see if we can get your blood pressure down."

Nurses dip their heads to hide their smiles, while the surrounding patients jeer. Rats and bugs are the worst things about the desert; if we aren't battling with one, it's the other. I think they are working together. Bugs fly inside a patient's plaster, causing irritation, and forcing us to remove it, applying a fresh one. Rats sit in wait, ready to pounce on the discarded plaster before we get rid of it, in a two-pronged fly-and-rat attack.

The beds on the ward sit inside paraffin tins to prevent ground bugs from climbing up into the mattresses. Even though we disinfect the ward, cleaning down the equipment, and floors, within minutes the bugs are back. If bugs and rats side with Hitler, we're doomed. The nights, though, are beautiful. In these moments, it's possible to forgive Egypt for its infestation. Palm trees sway in the breeze, their silhouettes dancing against the night sky, while their leaves rustle, creating a beat to a song. Nomadic Arab tribes, known as the Bedouin Guards, call to each other at intervals, the noise echoing across the desert.

37

 August 1942, No. 1 BGH, El Qantara, Egypt

*M*ost patients entering the hospital are here because of erratic sniping at the frontiers or suffering from prevalent diseases associated with the Middle East.

With fresh dysentery cases diagnosed daily, the new drug, sulphaguanidine, used to treat intestinal infections, and prevent infections before and after surgery, is in short supply, and surgeon Commander Davidson refuses to use it.

His control over sulphaguanidine is so intense that he keeps it on him, in small packets, forcing us to treat the patients using old-fashioned methods—salts and castor oil.

Recovery is a slow process.

Sand-fly fever, scrub typhus—spread by the bites of infected larval mites—malaria and typhoid are claiming too many lives.

Most of the time, we are unaware of the infection until they collapse. With the body's heat-regulation mechanism thrown out of gear, they stop sweating. The only way to reduce their temperature is to strip them naked and cover them with a thin sheet. An electric fan generates a cooling airflow. With ice packs under the groin, armpits, and spine, we douse them down with cold water. Cold enemata, intravenous transfusion of saline, and glucose is used to reduce internal heat. Once a response to this treatment occurs, we slowly warm the body, monitoring the patient.

Outbreaks of poliomyelitis (polio), and diphtheria are also prevalent.

At the start of each day, Matron and Regimental Sergeant-Major, in his position as Wardmaster, discuss patients on the Dangerously Ill list. When their rounds are complete, the nursing staff on duty receive an update. Beneath lowered lashes, Morag and I watch Matron and Wardmaster walk past us to Corporal Stevens' bed as we tend to a malaria patient. A privacy screen partially shields the corporal's bed. Matron and Wardmaster step behind the screen, and Morag and I exchange nervous glances.

Diagnosed with diphtheria, Stevens has been on the ward for two days. Diphtheria spreads from person to person through respiratory droplets, (coughing and sneezing). Joe inserted a tracheostomy tube during the night to ease his laboured breathing. With ice packs in place and a thin sheet covering the patient, Morag and I walk closer to the screen, sneaking a glance between the small gaps. Wardmaster's face is grim as he looks down at Stevens, the soldier's medical chart balanced in his hands. Morag nudges me; the outcome doesn't appear good for him.

Wardmaster turns, dismissing the patient. "He won't make it."

Matron's eyebrows raise, and her lips draw into a tight line. When she doesn't follow him, he turns, looking at her from over his shoulder. "The tracheotomy is helping his breathing."

"That may be, Matron, but he's no better off."

Without a word, Wardmaster continues along the ward. Matron takes a last look at Stevens and joins Wardmaster as they finish their round.

Morag and I stare at each other, moving away from the screen.

The list of who dies and who lives is unkind but practical. Too many times, we are forced to remind ourselves that we can't save everyone.

From behind the screen, Corporal Stevens becomes agitated, his breathing laboured. From the opposite bed, Pearl rushes over to him. Morag and I follow. Pearl picks up the catheter, using it to suck out the mucus from the tracheotomy. Morag grabs my hand, and we watch in horror as Pearl places her life in extreme danger to save Stevens.

The soldier takes a breath and Pearl places a gentle hand on his forehead. "Better."

His eyes flutter open, and a ghost of a smile graces his lips.

Matron watches as she walks the ward. Her face remains impartial. If she is concerned about Pearl's actions, she doesn't show it. Morag's fingers grip mine like a vice, and we follow Pearl, catching up with her as she passes reception. Morag releases my hand and together we each grab Pearl's arms, steering her towards the storage area where our conversation won't carry to the patients or Matron.

Worry lines crease Morag's brow as she turns on Pearl. "What were ye thinkin'?"

Pearl looks at me for allegiance and I shake my head. "Sorry, I'm on Morag's side, that was a stupid thing to do."

"You both would have done the same thing."

My arms fold over my chest as I stare at Pearl. "That's different."

"Aye."

Pearl lifts an eyebrow at us. "How come?"

"'Cause tis me at risk 'n' nae ye." Morag sticks her finger into Pearl's chest.

I nod. "Same here."

Morag jabs at Pearl's chest as she tries to bat it away. "Ouch … stop that."

"Then stop bein' reckless."

Fear heightens my emotions, losing Pearl too imaginable to comprehend. "We could lose you, Pearl. What then? What are we supposed to do without you?"

"You're being dramatic, Lilly, I'll be fine."

Morag circles the small room. "Matron won't have ye on the ward, nae with the threat o' cross-contamination."

"You'll need to be quarantined, Pearl. Somewhere we can monitor you," I say, scratching at my head, trying to think of where we can put her.

"But I'm not infectious."

"Not at the moment you're not," I say.

"It will be bed pan cleanin' duty for ye. Until we kin be sure."

Pearl pales at Morag's comment.

She smirks. "Aye, ye never thought o' that, did ye?"

"Poor Pearl," I say, rubbing her arm.

"Ah'm monitorin' ye over the next few days." Like a tiger scared of losing her cub, Morag's pacing intensifies. Her hands flapping around her, she stops. "Any signs 'n' ah'll have yer bottom in hospital."

Pearl's eyes widen at the wildcat in front of her.

"Nae matter what Commander Davidson says, ah'm gettin' the sulphaguanidine."

Pearl kisses Morag's cheek. "I love it when you talk dirty to me."

"Bugger off, Pearl," Morag says, wiping at her cheek.

I sit outside the Sisters' Mess, water rotating around the glass as I spin it. It's been three days since Pearl used the catheter, removing the buildup of mucus from Corporal Stevens' tracheotomy. She's shown no symptoms and Stevens is improving. It is a mystery how Pearl didn't contract diphtheria. But this is what we do daily, place our lives on the line. Easy to say when the threat has subsided, I know. Pearl's recklessness reminds me of Alick. Hope and prayers aren't helping me feel better about him out on the frontline, where danger is everyday life. Old habits are hard to break, and he's spent too long putting others first.

Joe walks over. "A penny for them."

"I was thinking how lucky we've been with Pearl."

The water licks the side of the glass. He sits next to me, swatting at the flies as they do their crazy dance around us.

"Joe ..." A fly lands in my glass and I fish it out. It sticks to my fingertip, a lifeless black speck. "I haven't worked everything out yet, but I wanted you to know, in case something happens, I love you."

This needs to be said. There are no guarantees, and life is precarious. The future no longer exists. It's about now, and I don't want something to happen to either of us, but if it does, at least Joe will know how I feel.

He kisses the top of my head. "I love you too."

"You will be careful, won't you? It's difficult putting ourselves before others. It's our job to tend to the sick. But promise you won't be reckless. Before doing something like Pearl did, you'll take a second to weigh the odds. If you still choose to do it, that's fine, but you'll make that decision with a clear head."

"And what about you, Lilly? Will you do the same?"

"I'll promise if you will."

"Then I promise to think first, act later."

My hand grazes his cheek, and I place a light kiss on his lips. "Thank you."

In the middle of September, new orders require us to move to the 64th BGH at Alexandra. An outbreak of smallpox places our relocation on hold. It's extraordinary how quickly the disease spreads, even with all the precautions we implement, and we lose a sister and doctor to the disease. Not to sound uncaring, but it is no one close to me, and it's a relief that my little family remains safe. The original smallpox patient continues to be nursed in a tent one mile from the hospital, under strict barrier conditions. A Royal Army Medical Corps (RAMC) Sergeant and State Registered Nurse (SRN) administer the patient's treatment. While this should stop the spread, it doesn't.

When patients within the perimeter ward contract smallpox, the Commanding Officer visits the Isolation Tent.

If we can't contain the outbreak, it will spread through here as deadly as gunfire. An earlier investigation failed to find the root cause. As a precaution, they moved the Isolation Tent further away from the hospital. Our hopes of gaining control over the infection rest with the Commanding Officer. Can he achieve what has been impossible in the past? With Effie, Adah, and Pearl at my side, we stand staring over at the Isolation Tent.

Morag walks over to us, shielding her eyes from the sun. "Did ye 'ear?"

"As I've heard lots of things, you're going to have to explain yourself," Pearl says. "Is the lack of sentence construction a Scottish or a Morag thing?"

I smile. "It's a Morag thing."

Morag ignores us. "Well, accordin' tae Matron, who was speakin' with Wardmaster, the Commanding Officer suspects ants for the spread of smallpox."

"Ants?" Pearl and I say together.

"Aye, he saw a trail o' ants crossin' the tent floor."

"But … ants?" I say, bemused.

Effie surveys the area. "Ants have been here since, well, forever."

Adah nods. "I can see why the Commanding Officer blames them."

"Really?" Pearl asks, her eyebrows raising.

"Ah wish ye'd let me finish." Morag huffs. "The ants have carried the crusts off the patient's skin from the Isolation Tent tae the hospital, causin' the outbreak."

"Oh, right, that makes sense," Pearl says, her chin wrinkling, as her bottom lip scrunches up.

With a shudder, I look at the floor. Ants run, going about their business. "I've never liked ants, and with good reason it seems."

Effie wrinkles her nose. "Me neither."

"That explains why they moved the Isolation Tent a further five miles from the hospital this morning," Adah says.

Morag pushes her hair back, placing her fingertips on her ears. "See, it pays tae have big lugs."

"So it seems," I agree.

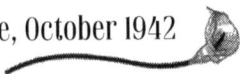

Dear Jane Anne,

With so much happening here, it's good to revel in memories of bygone times. To allow the past to remove the pain for a spell.

Winter in England is a miserable time. My brothers and I moaned when it was bedtime. With the fires remaining unlit upstairs, we never wanted to leave the warmth of the backroom. Money was tight, and unpopular decisions needed making. As children, my brothers and I never understood this. In secret, we called you both Scrooge. Now, I long for a reprieve from the hot, uncomfortable climate of Egypt. Here, temperatures reach a heady thirty-nine Celsius in summer. In winter, the temperature is more palatable at twenty-eight Celsius. I spend my days wiping away sweat and pulling at my clothes to create a draft. Can you imagine a winter with no snow?

The heat here is intense, wiping away the hardship of our terrible weather in England. Do you recall the horrific weather in October 1938, when severe gales ripped through England and Wales? The damage was considerable, with some losing their lives to the gales. Christmas that year produced around a foot of snow. Oh, how I grumbled my way to Cheyne Children's Hospital, slipping on the ice, my feet frozen inside my wellington boots. The weather disrupted the transport system, forcing me to use the cramped buses as the rail network ground to a halt. From the 18th until the 26th of December, snow fell.

But Christmas was beautiful with snow's white blanket. Trevor Henry roasted chestnuts on the fire, and my brothers and I sat on the carpet at the feet of your chairs, singing carols and playing Snap. It was magic. As November approaches, and with Christmas imminent, it feels strange to spend it with the sun high in the sky and sand covering the ground. Even far from home, I am sure when Christmas arrives, I will join the festivities, singing carols and rejoicing in the wonder of the festive season.

These memories make me smile. You and Trevor Henry have given me such a wonderful gift. It's strange how I never realised it before.

Lillian Elizabeth

38

 November 1942, 64ᵗʰ BGH, Alexandra, Egypt

On the 21ˢᵗ of November, almost two months after receiving our orders, we leave the No. 1 BGH, heading for the 64ᵗʰ at Alexandra. Joe left ahead of us, heading for the Advanced Dressing Station (ADS). One minute he is standing at my side, the next, gone. With a light kiss on my cheek and a smile on his lips, he leaves me standing, waving as his transport sends out a cloud of dust. The Highlanders' bagpipes play in my head, and I remember with too much clarity Alick's departure from the *Duchess of Richmond*. In a vacuum of loneliness and worry, I'm left to pick up my kit bag and tend to the injured.

With the ADS stationed four hundred yards behind the Regimental Aid Post, Joe travels closer to the danger. The purpose of the ADS is to treat the sick and wounded, returning them to the frontline. Injuries requiring prolonged treatment go to the Main Dressing Stations (MDS). One mile back from the ADS, the MDS is for immediate lifesaving operations. It's not equipped to deal with a high influx of casualties. Patients deemed not requiring immediate medical treatment, go to the nearest Casualty Clearing Station (CCS). Unfortunately, many entering the CCS will not survive the next twenty-four hours.

We are losing our grip in North Africa. This knowledge intensifies my concerns for Alick and Joe, though it's not clear how bad the situation is. While the number of casualties would confirm a graveness to the situation, I maintain the hope that things will soon change.

General Claude Auchinleck being relieved of his duties as Commander-in-Chief, Middle East Command, dashes my optimism. Lieutenant-General William Gott replaces him, and I look for the fading glimmer of hope.

Rumour places Auchinleck's dismissal at Churchill's door, after refusing to counterattack German troops. While I'm unsure how factual this is, I listen with morbid fascination and fear, colour draining from my face.

It seems our enemy hasn't finished toying with us, and on his way to replace Auchinleck, they shoot down Lieutenant-General William Gott's plane. Within a beat, they appoint Lieutenant-General Bernard Montgomery as Commander-in-Chief, Middle East Command. I wish him better luck and longer service than Lieutenant-General William Gott.

A lot is happening and the information we receive is often out-of-date. The wireless is no better. I'm convinced the government heavily influences the broadcasts. It makes sense; we won't be the only ones listening.

Under the rat-a-tat-tat of MG 42 machine guns, and the high-pitched whizzing of rocket launchers, we arrive at the 64th BGH. It has been a frightful and long journey. Ambulances, driven by RAMC men, wait in line to unload the casualties coming in from the CCS. Each arriving casualty carries Joe's face—I must stop staring at them. There is no end to the convoy. They stop, unload, and drive off, one after the other.

A hand touches my shoulder. "Try not to worry about Joe," Effie says.

"Easier said than done, I'm afraid."

Adah nods at the ambulances. "Work is the best remedy for worry."

"You've not heard anything from John, I take it?" Pearl asks Adah, her kit bag slung over her shoulder.

"No, nothing since he left the *Duchess of Richmond*."

We don't tell her everything is going to be fine; with the casualties pouring into the hospital, reassurances mean little.

Morag's kit bag hits the sand. "Ye never ken, Joe might be back for Christmas."

"I hope you're right," I say, my face pinching as I continue to stare at the wounded being unloaded.

"Come on, troops, let's get rid of these and roll our sleeves up, there's work to do." Pearl strides to the nurse's accommodation.

Within minutes of arriving, we are categorising the patients, providing those not requiring immediate surgery with a hot meal. We send those who can walk for a bath, washing away the sweat, blood, and sand that sticks to their skin. With no sign of Alick, I pray he remains healthy and safe, and that he doesn't do something stupid. My brothers too, though God has his hands full with them. Stupidness sticks to my brothers like a stain on fabric.

War has separated and changed us, scattering us across the world, with no knowledge if our siblings are alive or remain in one piece, excluding Charles Jason. Though it shows good foresight on the military's part, that they stationed my brothers in different regiments. Perhaps the military thought it best for their sanity to split them up. Jane Anne was always receiving complaints from our neighbours over my brothers' exploits.

Miss Higgins, three doors down from us, was their much-loved target. They often sniggered—out of Jane Anne's earshot—over the gifts they posted through Miss Higgins' letterbox. She once came stomping round with her doormat. Stuck to the thick fibres were gooseberry jam sandwiches. Gooseberries are evil, with their sharp sour taste that even sugar can't hide—it is the one thing my brothers and I agree on. The ants were more appreciative than Miss Higgins. The spinster was the headmistress at our local primary school—I think that's why my brothers targeted her. She was stern and unfair when issuing punishment, the cane too readily used. When my brothers left for secondary school, it was time to gain their revenge.

The current number of patients at the 64th BGH is one thousand eight hundred and eighty. By the time my shift ends, that number will swell, along with the death count. Our shift patterns become erratic, with many of us working doubles. At the end of our shift, we trundle to the Sisters' Mess for a bite to eat, before making our way to the nurses' accommodation. Row upon row of beds, each separated by a bedside cabinet, make up our sleeping quarters. Around me, my sisters ready for their shift. With mine just finished, I lounge on the bed, my pillow against the bedframe, supporting my back.

To my left, Susan Pendle points at a sister laying in her bed five rows down. "She's the one I was talking about," she says in a hushed voice to Patricia Smith, who occupies the bed next to her.

I glance over at the sister huddled on her bed; a thin sheet covers her from head to toe, and my curiosity mounts.

"How far gone is she?" Patricia asks.

"Three months."

A sour expression falls over Patricia's wrinkled face. "Such shameful behaviour."

Susan Pendle and Patricia Smith are spinsters in their mid-forties. If you ask me, they were born old busybodies who have never known what it is like to love. Though I don't know the sister they are gossiping about, I instantly feel sorry for her.

Patricia's lips curl with indignation, her arms hoisting up her ample bosom. "What is Matron doing about it? She can't stay here."

"She's sending her away with the other one."

"Goodness, there's more?" Patricia exclaims, her eyebrows nipping together.

If I listen to them much longer, I'll say something, not that I expect either of them to understand the meaning of empathy. I turn onto my side, my arm under my head, gazing over at Morag and Pearl as they get ready for their shift. Morag is on convoy duty tonight. One nurse and doctor from each hospital is given convoy duty. It's their job to receive the new casualties and medical supplies. The rota is one night in three. Tonight, Morag will work alongside dreamy Doctor Daniel Jessop—these are Morag's words. Daniel Jessop is a Scot with the same untameable red hair as Morag, broad shoulders, freckles, and is as tall as Ben Nevis.

"What do ye think?" Morag asks, her hands brushing down the length of her uniform.

"You look … nice?" I say, grappling for a better response.

Morag glances down. "Nice? Is that all ye've got?"

Pearl finishes pinning back her hair, an irritable expression on her face. "Morag, you're wearing your uniform, what more can you expect?"

"Ah dinnae want tae look like every other QA. Nae taenight, with Danny."

"Oh, Morag, you've got it bad," I say, pushing up onto my elbow and resting my head on my hand.

"Ah cannae help it. Ye've seen Danny, he's …"

I place my hand on my chest and flutter my eyelashes. "Dreamy."

Pearl shakes her head. "Don't encourage her. It's the babies they'll make I worry about."

My head snaps up. "What babies?"

"Morag and Daniel Jessop's, of course."

Amused, I stare at Pearl. "But Morag and Daniel aren't married. They aren't even stepping out."

"Me 'n' Danny are just friends," Morag protests.

Pearl sighs. "We need to prepare ourselves, Lilly, for when they marry, and the babies arrive. Those pour bairns don't stand a chance, what with Daniel and Morag having flaming bushes on their heads."

Morag pats down her hair. "Leave mah locks oot o' it, 'n' that o' Danny's. Our babies will be gorgeous."

"They will, will they?" Pearl's smile broadens.

Morag whacks her on the arm, laughing under her breath. "Ye crafty bugger."

"What's this about Morag and Doctor Jessop getting married? I wasn't aware they were courting," Effie asks, walking over.

I try not to laugh. "They aren't getting married or courting. Not yet."

"Huh? I don't …" She lets out a frustrated sigh. "You three are awful. Most of the time, I'm not sure if I'm on foot or horseback with you."

"Come on, best get to the ward. Matron will have our guts for garters if we're late," Adah says, waving at Effie, Morag, and Pearl.

Morag winks. "As much as ah would love tae stay 'n' chat, Adah's right, ah need tae get goin'. Cannae keep the doctor waitin'."

"I blame you for this." Pearl jabs a finger at Effie.

"Me! What did I do?"

"It's all that romantic notion you keep filling her head with."

"She's just messing with you, Effie, pay her no attention," I say. "Deep, deep inside, I'm sure Pearl has a romantic side."

Pearl shivers, pulling a face. "Ugh ... You've gone bonkers, Lilly."

I turn onto my back, my head falling to the right as they leave. The girl Susan Pendle and Patricia Smith were gossiping about remains cocooned within her sheet. With the room empty of those going on day shift and most of night shift asleep, I climb out of bed, tiptoeing over to her. Cross-legged on the floor at her bedside, I play with the hem of my pyjama bottoms.

"I'm sorry about what those two spinsters said. They're opinionated fuddy-duddies who don't understand what it's like to fall in love."

A sniff emits from under the sheet.

"When I'm sad I sing. Sometimes, if that doesn't work, I read. My favourite book is *Winnie the Pooh*. He's a wise bear. Anyway, I don't know if it helps, but one of my favourite sayings from Pooh is 'You're braver than you believe, stronger than you seem ...' Those words have helped me over the years, I hope they do the same for you."

The girl moves under the sheet, and her head pokes out. Her black hair falls about her face, and her hazel eyes fill with tears. She blinks, wiping the edge of the sheet over her cheeks. "They're going to take my baby. I don't understand why I can't keep it. I've already lost Percy; he died the day before we were to get married. Unwed girls make bad mothers, they said ... Why do they say that? I love my baby."

I hand her my handkerchief. "People in authority always think they know what's best, that's how they justify

367

their actions. It doesn't mean they're right. And it doesn't make the pain go away."

"I hate Matron."

"Yeah …"

"And I hate those two old crows … Mostly, I hate myself for letting them take Percy's baby."

"Don't, it's not like you can stop them."

"That's what makes it worse."

She pulls the sheet over her head, and I sit, listening to her sobs.

When I wake, the girl is gone. On the bedside cabinet, under my *Winnie the Pooh* book, is a note with the scribbled words, 'Thank You'.

39

November 1942, 64th BGH, Alexandra, Egypt

*A*week after arriving at the 64th, John Benson enters on a stretcher with a further hundred casualties. Shrapnel has torn holes in his face and upper torso. He has a hairline fracture (fissure fracture) on his second metatarsal bone (below the knuckles of the second toe). The likely cause of the fracture comes from running long distances and jumping into trenches. John has also suffered a proximal humerus fracture (a break in the upper part of the arm). His arm is swelling, and he has decreased movement in his right shoulder.

His injuries aren't life-threatening, and he lies on the cot washed, dressed, and waiting to be taken down to theatre for the removal of the embedded shrapnel. Adah is amazing. Whatever torment churns and nibbles at her insides remains hidden as she tends to his wounds. With the plaster of Paris ready, I help her apply it to John's arm, securing it in place with a sling. John returns from theatre as our shift ends. Adah stays, watching his chest rise and fall as he sleeps. I take the medical chart from the bedside table, updating it.

He stirs, his eyes fluttering open, his hand catching Adah's. "I ..."

"It's alright. You're safe, that's all that matters," Adah says, her fingers wrapping round his.

Effie walks over with a cup of tea in one hand and a bully sandwich in the other. "Here." She hands Adah the plate, setting the cup on the bedside table. "Make sure you drink this while it's hot."

Adah nods.

With a quick look over her shoulder, Effie removes a couple of biscuits from her pocket. "For later," she says, winking at John, placing the biscuits in the folds of his sling. John smiles. Effie turns to her sister. "Don't forget to rest."

"I won't."

"Promise."

"Promise."

Adah gives John's hand a last squeeze. "I'll get rid of these,"—she points at the soiled sheets—"and be right back. Watch him for me, Lilly."

I nod, taking her seat.

Tears well as she turns to follow Effie, shooing her sister off with a shake of her head as she reaches out to console her.

"In all the years I've known her, Adah's been a rock. I don't know how she holds it all together," John says, his gaze lingering on his sweetheart.

I smile. "We wouldn't want her any other way."

"No, she's grand the way she is."

"She is that."

John scratches at his beard. "Take care of her, won't you. I know she thinks she doesn't need looking after, but she does."

"Don't worry, we've got her. Now get some rest and don't forget to eat the biscuits before Matron notices. You'll get us hung drawn and quartered if she finds out."

"Yes, nurse," John says, saluting me.

Adah returns. Her cheeks are flushed, but her armour is back in place. Satisfied, she nods her thanks and walks over to collect a pile of spent sheets.

"Let me help with that," I say.

"Thanks." Her voice cracks as she bends to gather the laundry.

Orderlies normally undertake the collection of the soiled sheets, but with time being of the essence, and beds needing making, we muck in.

"How are you doing?" I ask as we leave the ward.

Her lips twist. "It's hard to say. I've mixed feelings about it all. John's condition isn't life-threatening, and he'll be fit and sent home before I know it." Her eyes fill with tears. "That's the hard part. Now I worry about what he'll do when he gets home, and if he'll make it. At least his injuries mean he won't be placed on active duty." Her voice fades.

"It's more important than ever that we spend time with those we love. I think we're all feeling the strain. While I agree to a certain professionalism, that shouldn't mean we are duty-bound to care less for those we love. Look at what I was like with Charles Jason. Enjoy your time with John, Adah, you've sacrificed enough already, you deserve this."

I grab her sheets and walk towards the laundry room, turning to glance over my shoulder. "You don't have to worry about Matron, I've got you, just like you supported me at Stanmore."

"Bless you, Lilly."

Hours of writing reports cause my fingers to cramp, and I stretch them out, releasing aching muscles. The pen rolls off the table and I bend to pick it up. Effie's feet appear in the space between the table legs, her footsteps brisk. My unease growing, I track her progress.

It's times like these, when emotional discord peaks, that I rely on the professional etiquette drilled into us at nursing school.

1. You never run except in case of a fire.
2. Always stand when a senior member of staff enters the room.
3. Always open the door for the doctors.
4. Never overtake a senior member of staff on the stairs.
5. Hair should not reach your collar …

At the mix of emotions fluttering across Effie's face, my anxiety heightens. A nurse does not leave her post, I remind myself as my stomach rolls, and my heart thumps. Despite her haste, it takes an eternity for Effie to reach the table where my fingers drum with impatience. My eyebrows raise when, without a word, she moves the privacy screen sitting redundant behind me, shielding us from the sleeping patients.

"What's wrong? Nothing's happened to Joe, has it?" Effie shakes her head. "What about Morag? Pearl? Adah? John?" With my rapid heartbeat blocking my ears, the whispered panic in my voice fades to nothing.

Confusion pulls at Effie's brows. "It's nothing like that."

In war, the mind concentrates on the worse scenarios. "Then what's got you fired up?"

Effie giggles into her hands.

Not being able to raise my voice makes it hard to get her to focus. "Effie …"

"Sorry, I'm just bursting with news."

My heart slows down. She doesn't appear sad. That's good.

"Morag and Pearl are going to be cross, but as I can't find Pearl and with Morag on convoy …"

"Effie, please …" I grind out.

She draws a breath, her hands sweeping down her body in a soothing motion. "Be calm," she says, giggling again.

My foot taps and I fold my arms. I understand now why Pearl gets grumpy with us. "I can't spend the night behind this screen."

"John asked Adah to marry him, and she said yes … They're getting married!" she squeaks.

My agitation dissolves, and I smile. "That's fabulous. You had me going there."

Her forehead wrinkles. "Oh … sorry … But isn't it wonderful? My big sister is getting married …"

I tap my pen on the desk. "We should do something after our shift, before Adah starts hers. Pearl has a bottle of whisky stashed; we can have a glass to celebrate. Of course, I'd suggest the Ritz, but transport is an issue given the war. So, our tent at eight a.m. it is."

"It's a bit early for drinking, isn't it?"

"It's teatime for me. Besides, a little sip won't hurt."

"I'll round Adah up," Effie says, placing a hand on the screen ready to push it back. "On our next day off, we should go to Port Sid and see if we can get them something nice as a wedding gift."

"Have they set a date?"

"Oh … sorry … the wedding's set for next week."

My jaw drops in shock. "Next week! Blimey, that's fast."

"War waits for no one," Effie says, her expression solemn.

I stop tapping the pen. "You're right. We'll talk about going to Port Sid later, over whisky."

Effie peeks from behind the screen, searching the ward. "Where's Pearl?"

"She went to bathe a new admission."

"I hope he doesn't fall asleep on her like the last one. She was very cranky about it."

"It wasn't the soldier falling asleep that riled her, but Morag's insinuation."

"Ye're losing yer touch, Pearl, there's goin' tae be nothin' risin' 'ere …" Effie says, mimicking Morag.

My hand covering my mouth, I laugh. "Your accent is terrible."

"What's so funny?"

Effie and I jump at the sound of Pearl's voice.

"I'll leave you to break your news, it's time I started my morning round."

"Deserter," Effie whispers, pushing back the screen.

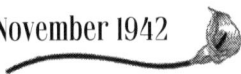

Dear Jane Anne,

What a dreadful time some of us are having at the 64th British General Hospital. As nurses, we see death every day; it is wrong to expect this not to change us. Fear creeps into our daily lives. A sense of urgency whips around the 64th. It's very different from France, and with no end in sight, instinct and fear are all we have guiding us.

Each day we sit at the bedside of soldiers and civilians, holding their hands while they die. This impacts us, and some of us take risks in our personal lives we'd normally never contemplate doing. War lowers inhibitions and two of our fellow, unmarried, sisters find themselves with child. Matron is uncompromising in her approach, as are the older, stuffier nurses. Unwed mothers may not keep their babies. How awful for the child growing in your belly who will never call you mother. That you will never hold your baby or gaze upon their face. Though I don't socialise with the sisters involved, I have heard their cries. It is the most desolate sound.

When war casts doubt over tomorrow, you grab at life before a bullet snatches it from you. I understand this too well. Look at how I am with Alick and Joe. There is no fairness in my love for Alick. He is my everything. It doesn't mean I don't love Joe, just that I love him differently. But I will love him the best I can and make him happy.

Fear strengthens emotions. The need to feel love when the sound of battle echoes all around you is stronger. No, there is no judgement here for my pregnant sister. Instead, my heart constricts in pain with what they force her to go through. I cannot help wondering how it can be best for these mothers not to keep their babies. Are these poor women not hurting enough?

While I write, the casualties flood into the 64th and tonight some will die, without family or loved ones at their side. A nurse will be with them to care for their emotional and medical needs; I wish I could hold on to that nurse and tell her I care. When our comrades become our greatest enemy, what do we have left but despair?

Lillian Elizabeth

40

We walk down the pier to De Lesseps statue, which stands at the entrance to the Suez Canal. Ferdinand de Lesseps was a French diplomat in the 1800s. He developed the Suez Canal, joining the Mediterranean and Red Seas, reducing the sailing distance and time between Europe and East Asia. Our journey here took long enough. To think it would have taken even longer pre-1800s is unbearable.

Adah drops her shopping bags on the pier and sits, dangling her legs over the side. The sun glistens down on the blue water, and tiny crystals dance in lazy contentment. Times like these are precious. Before the war, I never appreciated how beautiful nature is, and the pleasure of being surrounded by friends. Since Chamberlain made his announcement on the 3rd of September 1939, so many have died, and I wonder how many more will join them. I sit staring at the water, contemplating how, on the 30th of September 1938, on his return from Munich,

Neville Chamberlain could ever have declared, 'Peace for Our Time.'

Like so many that day, I joined the thousands of people waiting at London's Heston Aerodrome for Chamberlain's return. None of us cared about the rain that seeped through our clothing, as we waited for a glimpse of our Prime Minister. And when the door to his aeroplane opened, our cheers were so loud that my ears rang for days after. Londoners responded in a wave of celebration, relief washing away our fears, like a prisoner freed from a death sentence. Chamberlain's words now resonate with bitter disillusionment. 'I recommend you to go home and sleep quietly in your beds.' And while we slept, the German army marched to Czechoslovakia. By March 1939, Hitler occupied the whole of Czechoslovakia. With no one to stop them, the Nazis crossed into Poland. And all within eight months of Chamberlain providing us with the illusion of 'Peace for Our Time.'

People like Adah, who lived through the Great War, tell me that this one is different. It's more unpredictable, destructive, and volatile. Weaponry is developing and with it the death count. The army sends us to hostile environments, never knowing where our orders will send us next. Many of us have little military experience. Few of us have been abroad, and most of us were still living within the safe environment of our parental homes. Before this war, the army didn't place female nurses close to the frontline. The shift in medical policy is profound. Our inclusion in frontline duty is at last acknowledged. When a bomb lands close to our quarters and fear creeps in, I remind myself of this, that our role against Hitler is vital.

Effie sits nestled in the middle of Adah and Pearl. On Pearl's right is Morag.

"Where is it …?" Morag says, digging around in her shopping bag. "Ah, 'ere it is." She pulls out a bag of fresh fruit, popping a piece in her mouth.

"You're going to share those, aren't you?" Pearl asks, watching the rapid depletion of fruit.

"Ah wasnae plannin' on it." Pearl reaches for the fruit and Morag nudges her arm away with her elbow, moving the fruit further from Pearl's grasp. "Go get ye own."

Effie passes Pearl a bag of fruit. "Here, you can have mine, I'm not hungry."

"Thanks, Effie, you're such a good friend. Dependable, not at all pig-like."

Morag snorts, stuffing another piece of fruit into her mouth.

"Oink oink, little piggy," Pearl says. "Try not to choke, I'm not giving you the kiss of life."

Morag smiles. "Aye, ye will, 'cause ye looove me."

"You keep believing that if it makes you happy. Right now, I prefer Effie."

I look out across the water, listening to their bickering.

Our shopping trip has been productive. Adah has her wedding dress. It's a long, emerald-green gown with gold metallic thread. Tiny buttons run down the back and the bias cut is flattering on her. She was apprehensive, loving the dress but feeling too old to wear something so fashionable. We stayed clear of traditional white, as Adah was against it. "White is for young brides, not someone approaching mid-life." Pearl was the one who found the lamé Buddha print dress. The colour matches Adah's eyes, and we took it as a sign, that it was the perfect dress.

Morag, Pearl, Effie, and I clubbed together, buying Adah a matching chiffon silk shawl. The thin thread of soft blue around the edges was our something blue. For something borrowed, I am lending her a crystal and pearl comb to put in her hair, which Granny Nutman left me in her will. At the time I questioned my decision to bring it, but now I'm glad I did. With success eating at our feet, we grabbed our fruit and came to the pier.

Under English folklore, we have everything required for Adah to marry John: something old, something new, something borrowed, something blue, and a sixpence in your shoe.

The sixpence in the shoe sounds uncomfortable, but then the silver coin is a symbol of prosperity, warding against the evil of frustrated suitors. Better not ignore it, it's a crazy world out there.

I gaze out at the Mediterranean Sea. Somewhere out there is Doctor Joseph Lawrence and Sergeant Alick McNavis. "Do you believe in fate?" I ask, Adah, keeping my voice low so it doesn't carry to Morag, Pearl, and Effie as they sit chattering about Adah's coming wedding.

Adah nods. "John and I are proof of it. When my parents died, my role changed. I was no longer just a sister to Effie, but a mother and father too. How could I place that level of responsibility onto John? We were both so young. He needed to spread his wings and enjoy being young. Not a man weighed down with the responsibility of looking after me and my sister. So, I broke off our engagement. Of course, looking back, I should have given John the choice, but I was too busy stepping into shoes that didn't fit. I was the one making all the decisions—I knew best, and no one else had a say. Fate has a way of dealing blows you don't see coming. But then fate reunited me and John."

I look at her in surprise. "John doesn't appear to be a man who easily gives up. Didn't he try and win you over?"

"He tried, but I was too stubborn to listen. He deserved better than a ready-made family, that's all that mattered." A ghost of a smile flutters over her lips. "I wasn't just stubborn, but silly as well. My mind was set, and my pride was too big. John loved me then and he loves me now. So many wasted years but come tomorrow we'll be husband and wife."

Adah lays a hand on mine. "It's hard to trust in fate sometimes. Fighting it will bring torture. Stop worrying about Joe; I'm sure everything will work out."

Tears threaten and I turn away, focusing on the rolling waves. Sometimes emotions are too complex to place only one sentiment against them. I will probably never see Alick again. But I shall spend a lifetime thinking about him, that I know. Destiny has no plans to reunite us, not on earth, Alick has already told me that. In the distance, a camel plods along the water's edge. No matter how we feel, life around us carries on.

41

 November 1942, 64th BGH, Alexandra, Egypt

The day before Adah and John's wedding a sandstorm hits the 64th BGH. Sand gets everywhere, in our hair, mouths, eyes, eating at our skin. Insects aren't the only thing I now hate. As a child, I loved the beach. With Trevor Henry working so hard, taking on extra work where he could, we didn't go to Ruislip Lido as often as I wanted. With seven hundred acres of woodland and a natural lake and sandy beach, it was my favourite place to visit. Jane Anne would make a picnic and my brothers would help carry it. We'd kick off our shoes and socks, and run into the lake, water tickling our toes, our feet sinking into the soft sand. Family outings may have been rare, but they still hold the magic to make me smile. I've eaten too much sand to think of ever visiting Ruislip Lido again. Besides, with Trevor Henry gone it wouldn't be the same.

Sometimes I see the Tommies scooping up the sand, placing it into small bags. I'm not sure of the importance of the sand, though I suspect it is more about collecting the memory than the sand itself. Sandstorms last around a couple of hours. Adah's wedding tomorrow morning will go ahead as planned. Had we been in England we would send up prayers for sunshine. The Egyptian weather guarantees the sun, and we certainly don't have to worry about rain; Egypt's rainy season is in January. Still, it is nothing like England where it rains most of the time.

At the Sisters' Mess, we gather for a pre-drink, water all round, to keep our heads clear for tomorrow. Adah sits nursing her glass, wiping away at the droplets of condensation forming on the outside.

"A penny for them?" Effie asks.

Her eyes glaze over, her mind floating elsewhere. She blinks, lifting her head. A soft smile touches her lips. "Sorry, I was thinking about our parents."

Effie reaches across the table, resting her hand on her sister's arm. "They'd be so proud of you, and happy."

"I haven't missed them in years, but somehow, marrying John makes me wish they were here. When a woman gets married, it's expected that their father walks them down the aisle. I'm too old for such nonsense, but …"

"Nothing can replace your parents, but we'll be there."

"Thanks, Lilly."

"I'll walk you down the aisle," Effie says, her eyes like saucers, in silent pleading.

"I'd like that."

Morag and Pearl walk into the Sisters' Mess, their heads almost touching as they talk in low voices.

"Ah dinnae ken what the problem is. The stuffy doctor thinks he kens better than General Montgomery. What with his whingin' aboot nurses gettin' underfoot," Morag says, pulling out a chair and sitting next to me.

Pearl's hands hit the table at the same time her bottom hits the chair. "Cooperman's ancient, with his bushy eyebrows and saggy skin."

"He's sixty," Adah says, "that doesn't make him ancient."

"Well, Brigadier Cooperman's views are ancient," Pearl huffs. "I've had to listen to his derogatory comments about women throughout the day, and how he disagrees with Montgomery." Her eyes narrow as her annoyance grows. "The old coot needs his eyebrows trimming, then he'll see how important nurses are in boosting men's morale."

"Aye, ah agree with Pearl, give me a pair o' scissors 'n' let's get them trimmed."

"Morag!"

"Dinnae look so shocked, Effie."

"What happened?" I ask.

"Ancient-Bushy-Eyebrow-Cooperman was overheard complaining to Wardmaster about us."

I stare at her. "What did he say?"

"Women are too delicate to be placed close to the danger of the frontline, their fragile disposition will cause too much conflict," Pearl says. "Fragile disposition, indeed. I can't stand the man."

"Neither kin ah," Morag huffs.

"Fragile disposition!" Pearl spits. Her lips twitch. "I'll show him delicate when my shoe connects—"

"Don't get vulgar, Pearl," Adah says.

"Why would he say such a thing?" I ask.

Pearl rests her head on her hand. "Because he's a thousand-and-two-year-old turnip head, that's why."

Effie's hand covers her mouth, hiding her smile. "You'll get us shot."

"More like an ear-bashing from Matron, less blood that way," I say, smiling.

Adah shakes her head. "You've got yourself all worked up over nothing. It's what General Montgomery believes that's important, and he's an advocate of British nurses. He knows how our presence has a beneficial effect on men's morale. That's why he's allowing us closer to the frontline. Soldiers sacrifice so much—some even their lives. If our presence provides a boost to morale, it's nothing compared to what they do for us. That's what is important. Not Brigadier Cooperman."

I raise my glass of water. "Well said, Adah."

Effie raises hers, and we clink them together.

Like a ball of fire, the sun glows in the sky, tanning our skin and making us sweat, eating away at our energy. The heat makes sleep difficult and even though I've just come off night shift and should catch a quick nap before Adah and John's wedding, I find a shady spot to sit, closing my eyes and tilting back my head, my mind drifting. There is no focus on its wandering, and my limbs become heavy as the evening shift washes from my mind, finding peace in the soft tickle of the breeze. Even by Egypt's standards, it is unseasonably warm for November. A shadow blocks the sunlight from behind my closed eyelids. With my hand forming a canopy, I peel my eyes open. A loud, frustrated groan falls from Pearl's lips as she plonks herself on the sand next to me.

"This heat is killing me."

"You can't sleep either?"

"Sleep, what's that?" Pearl says, her elbows resting on her knees, her hands propping up her head.

"When I find out, I'll let you know."

Pearl nods at the ambulances lining up outside the hospital tents. "No matter what we do, it's not enough. They stretchered Jack Teanby in today. He's got third-degree burns."

She runs a hand over her face, wiping at the sweat and tiredness. "It doesn't seem that long ago he was twirling me round the deck on the *Duchess of Richmond*, standing on my toes with that daft grin on his face." She glances over at me. "Through charred skin, he looks at me, eyes like liquid blue saucers, and asks me to hold his hand. He says, 'Don't let go, Nurse Pearl. I don't want to be alone. It's so cold today.' But it's not cold, is it, Lilly? No, it's bloomin' sweltering, that's what it is. Sweat's dripping off me, and Jack's shaking like we're in the middle of a snowstorm. Do you know what I said? 'Don't worry, Jack, I'll get you an extra blanket.' Like he needs a blanket. He grips my hand, blistered fingers wrapping round mine, no sign of pain … a bad sign, right? His fingers grip so tight, and he wants me to sing to him. I'm no songbird, Lilly, and if I was, I'd be a crow. But I sing because he needs me to. He closes his eyes, and there's no Jack. Just a body, needing moving because we need the space." She nibbles at her bottom lip. "But it's not just a body. It's Jack, and I feel so guilty for telling him to go find his right foot because his two left ones are killing my feet."

Tears run down her face, and I take her into my arms. Emotions run deeper when you're tired. When someone you know dies, it's harder than looking at the face of a stranger. It cuts deeper. You see their face as it crinkles with laughter. And you miss every one of those wrinkles when death comes.

Jack Teanby was twenty-one and from Leeds. He had four brothers, all older than him, and a sister three years younger. His father died during Dunkirk, and his eldest brother, Jacob, lost his right arm due to lack of treatment on his escape to the UK from France. No longer suitable for active duty, they sent him home. Jack was the sparkle which made you laugh when there was nothing to laugh about. As Pearl cries, I hold myself together; two blubbering women won't make a difference. Pearl needs a shoulder to cry on, not someone to cry with her.

Adah and John's wedding breathes life back into our camp. We are a hive of bees, busy making plans and giddy with excitement. Matron has granted Adah a day's leave and the army has delayed John's transport back to the United Kingdom. They plan to stay at Port Sid.

As soon as Morag returns from her shift, Pearl whips out her brush and hair pins. "Lilly, pass me the pins when I'm ready, will you?"

I pick up the grips, saluting her. "Ready and reporting for duty, Hairdresser-Pearl. It looks like it might be a tough mission we've got ourselves here."

"One we're going to win. We shall not weaken or tire, Pin-Passer-Lilly."

Morag scowls at us. "Mah locks are nae that bad."

She covers her head, shielding her hair from the hairbrush. Pearl taps at Morag's fingers with the flat side of the brush. "Off."

"Ouch, Pearl, do ye have tae be so rough."

"Be patient, I'm almost there."

"Ah'll nae have any locks left at this rate."

"Yes, you will, you've thick hair," Pearl says, securing a strand in place.

Finished, we stand back in wonder. We've achieved the impossible. A million pins hold Morag's hair captive. A blue lotus flower, Nymphaea Caerulea, sits behind her ear. The vivid blue petals and bright yellow and purple centre, look stunning against the vibrancy of her red hair.

"Just *wow*, Pearl," I say in utter disbelief at the vision she has created.

Pearl smiles. "I know."

"Let me see." Morag races over, picking up her mirror. With delicate fingers, she touches her hair. "Is this mah locks? It looks bonnie."

Pearl bounces the hairbrush against her palm. "See, all that fuss, and for what? You look gorgeous, Morag. Now come on, no time to waste."

Handkerchiefs dabbing at our faces, we watch Adah as she walks towards John, who stands with the aid of crutches. Her left arm hooks through Effie's, and in her right hand she carries a small bunch of Egyptian flowers. The gold thread in her dress shimmers as she glides along the makeshift aisle. Her curls cascade like a waterfall, secured by Granny Nutman's pearl comb. A huge smile wipes the nerves from John's face as he watches his bride stroll towards him. In a world of chaos, it is comforting to see love shining through.

The wireless in the corner plays Johann Sebastian Bach, *Prelude No. 1 in C*. The flow of the piano music, rising from broken chords, hypnotises us. It is the most beautiful sound, carrying the bride to her love. Given Pearl's aversion to anything romantic, I keep these thoughts to myself. A small buffet of sandwiches and local fruit sits on a table in the dining area. At 7 p.m. I sneak out of the Sisters' Mess with Pearl and Morag, to get ready for our shift. When we enter the 64th to release the day shift, there is a flurry of activity. They finish what they're doing, leaving to get ready and join the wedding celebrations.

Letter Home, November 1942

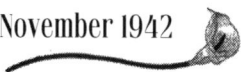

Dear Jane Anne,

How do I remove the images from my mind of the bodies that pile up, waiting to be buried? The large pit that consumes them is a temporary measure--or at least, I hope. They deserve a better resting place. The destruction never stops and won't until this war ends. My worry for Joe and Alick increases. Joe remains at the Advanced Dressing Station. I miss him terribly. Sometimes I lie in bed and wish for nothing more than to be back onboard the *Duchess of Richmond*, my back pressing against his chest as we watch the flying fish. And what of Alick? Deep inside, I know he is still alive. I can sense him within the fabric of my being. I sound daft, but not saying it and feeling it doesn't make it less so. We can never be more than what we were on the ship. Not friends, or lovers, but something I have no words to describe. Is it wrong to love a man, yet long for another? When the pain becomes too much and all there seems is death, that is when I reach for Alick.

The local Jewish Berber and Arab communities are full of stories about the German and Italian forces. We sit gasping at the terrible atrocities they commit. When these stories reach Lieutenant Bridgemore, they fuel his dislike towards the Italians. He's so fired up that I'm keeping a low profile, hoping it's enough to keep from gaining his attention. He can be such a bore, all stuffy and opinion-ated. Isn't this why we are at war, because one man wants to stamp his opinion on another? Not that I'm suggesting Lieutenant Bridgemore is anything like Hitler, but he has a moustache. It's a walrus, thick bristles covering his top lip in the most unhygienic fashion. The other day I swear I saw bits of bread sticking to the tips, yuck. You would think a doctor would know better than to allow the un-sanitary growth of facial hair.

Lillian Elizabeth

42

 November 1942, 64th BGH, Alexandra, Egypt

They stretcher Marion Cartwright into the 64th with malaria at the end of my shift. This leaves the orthopaedic surgeon, Brigadier Jones, minus a theatre nurse. At the sight of Marion's fevered body, Matron signals me and Jessica Emmerson to her. Jessica is in her late fifties, with snowy hair that looks like a dog has urinated on it. The bright lights of the ward and Egyptian sun take delight in highlighting its patchy yellow tones. Her sallow, crape skin, and eyes the colour of wet clay, give way to a morose personality. Jessica is friends with Susan Pendle and Patricia Smith. Like them, she can be cruel in her opinions of us younger nurses. With Jessica's reluctance to undertake a double shift, I offer my services in theatre.

With the volume of casualties high, and only ten percent of those operated on surviving, Brigadier Jones operates on those he believes he can save. War is a brutal world. Brigadier Jones is a giant of a man, with long bony fingers and a muscular frame. He has little hair and what there is disappears within the harsh light of the operating theatre. He walks to the table and, with a curt nod my way, looks down at the patient. Peter Taylor has extensive soft tissue damage to his lower extremities, right thigh, and buttock, a fractured pelvis and damaged rectum. He sustained the injuries from a WIA artillery shell.

Prior to Brigadier Jones entering the operating room, I packed Taylor's wounds with sulfa and Vaseline gauze. The wounds are now ready for the Brigadier to apply a bilateral hip spica, a cast incorporating the lower torso and limbs. Once this has set, we move along Peter's body, cutting away part of the left abdomen of the spica. The surgeon then performs a simple sigmoid colostomy through a McBurney incision. Taylor is in a poor state, but he has lasted this long, and as Brigadier Jones agreed to operate, he must feel the patient's chances are within his survival spectrum.

Life in the theatre is exhilarating. The buzz it generates keeps tiredness at bay and even as one casualty replaces another, there is a sense of achievement. Ten hours later, as they wheel the last patient from theatre, I follow Brigadier Jones outside where the full force of the early afternoon sun hits us. My hand on my forehead to reduce the sun's glare, I take a deep breath, acknowledging that I am spent and ready for a few hours of sleep. Beside me, beads of sweat appear along Brigadier Jones' brow, and he wipes it away with his handkerchief. Lines deepening at the corners of his eyes, he squints against the glaring sun. He produces a pack of cigarettes, tapping one into his hand.

At nearly six-feet-eleven, standing next to Brigadier Jones is like standing next to Big Ben. It seems no one ever told him it was time to stop growing. His excessive height makes my slight stature resemble that of a garden gnome. He takes a long drag on the white nicotine stick and a plume of smoke engulfs me. I bat it away with my hand. I've never been one to indulge in smoking; there is something about it I find unappealing. A strange noise emits from Brigadier Jones. His hands clutch at his chest, and he falls at my feet. With his face frozen in pain, his mouth gaping open, the cigarette falls as the last of the smoke clears his airways. I drop to my knees at his side.

"Harrold!" I shout, trying to gain the orderly's attention.

Harold races over, sand flying behind him, as I loosen the Brigadier's clothes and perform CPR. A thin layer of sand coats the Brigadier's clothes, and the imprint of shoes surround him as we gather to save his life. Regardless of medical equipment and training, there is no saving him. Nor is there a chance in hell I'm ever taking up smoking, not after today. Within five minutes of lighting his cigarette and taking his first drag, the Brigadier is dead.

In silence, I watch them place his body onto a stretcher. Covered by a Union Jack flag, they stretcher him into the hospital. On a hum of whispers, news of the surgeon's death travels round the 64th. Without a word, I follow the stretcher, carried by four soldiers, through the surgical lines. The Brigadier's patients watch open-mouthed as his body passes. Those who can stand salute in stunned, respectful silence. With little time to grieve, or to make sense of what has happened, Brigadier Jones comes to his resting place. I stand with the Chaplain, singing Brigadier Jones' favourite hymn, *Jerusalem*, a poem written by William Blake.

The Chaplain hugs his closed bible to his chest, his head bent as I sing. Even though field burials are commonplace, death has a way of puncturing the heart. Emotions crash down on me like heavy rain, and I tell myself to remain strong as I continue to sing.

Tears running down my face, I sing the last verse. It is a fitting tribute to a man who has saved many lives; we are all truly grateful to him.

43

 December 1942, 21st CCS, Mersa Matruh, Egypt

*O*n the 1st of December, Morag, Pearl, and I, along with several other QAs, receive new orders. At 10:30 a.m., on the 7th of December, we climb into the back of an ambulance, assigned to take us to the 21st CCS near Mersa Matruh—leaving Effie and Adah behind at the 64th. The ambulance's cramped conditions, and the nearness of our bodies, add to the heat. We are hot, uncomfortable, and our bottoms have gone numb from the ambulance's constant bouncing on the sand.

A hundred miles into our journey, a loud bang echoes through the metal walls. The vehicle lurches forward at a dog-leg angle, dipping at the front. We cling onto each other, screaming, our backs hitting metal as we tumble around the interior. Air flies from our lungs, and on the tendrils of fear, adrenalin floods our system. A thin line of sweat trickles down my back, and I grit my teeth as the ambulance comes to an abrupt stop. The doors fly open, and our breath sticks in our throats as, with wide eyes, we stare at our driver.

"Sorry about that, ladies, the right front tyre burst. Are you all alright?" the driver asks.

Unable to speak, we nod.

Sand covers his uniform, and his feet sink into it. Sweat dampens his hair and soils the armpits of his shirt. "I'll have the tyre changed in a jiffy. Why don't you come out and stretch your legs?"

On shaking limbs, we exit the ambulance. Outside, sand billows around us as we huddle together and watch the driver loosen the nuts on the wheel. A screw jack suspends the ambulance in the air at an odd angle. There is nothing we can do to help—we're nurses, not mechanics. Broken bones we can fix, replacing tyres is a completely different matter.

"Ah thought we were goners," Morag says, her arm looping through mine.

My mouth is dry, and my fingers still tremble. "Me too."

Pearl stares at the damaged tyre. "It was a tyre." She laughs. "It sounded like gunfire."

A shudder goes through me. "Don't say that. It's tempting fate."

Morag squirms, pulling on my arm. "Och ..." She looks around her. "Ah'm needin' tae pee."

"It's your nerves. Don't think about it, and it'll go away," Pearl says.

"It's nae goin' tae work. Ah really need tae pee."

I grab Pearl's arm, pulling her to my side. "We'll form a cover for you while you squat."

"Ah cannae pee while …" Morag waves her hand at the driver's back.

Pearl huffs. "No one's looking at you. He's too busy replacing the tyre."

"I'm afraid you've got two choices, Morag. Pee or hold it in," I say.

Morag's lips twist and she looks unhappy. "Why kin there nae be a bush or somethin'."

Pearl shakes her head. "Because we're in the middle of a desert, that's why."

"Ah'm goin' tae have tae pee."

Two other QAs move closer, adding to our human shield. "That better?" I ask.

"Nae tae sound ungrateful, boot na."

Pearl faces Morag. "Stop your complaining and get on with it, otherwise the tyre will be on, and he'll be heading this way."

"Ye're all heart 'n' understandin'."

We stand the best we can, screening off Morag. There is a sigh of relief, a ruffling of fabric, and a gush of water. The driver walks over, and we tighten our shield, blocking out as many of the gaps between our bodies as we can.

"We're ready for the off."

Behind us, Morag squeaks.

I smile at our driver. "Sorry, the burst tyre has made her jumpy. She thought it was gunfire."

"Sorry about that," he says, wiping his brow and walking back to the ambulance.

Pearl leans into me. "Thanks, Lilly, now we look like a bunch of frightened ninnies."

"It sounded better than, 'give a lady some privacy, can't you see Morag's urinating?'"

Pearl rolls her eyes. "Humph."

I laugh. "That's what I thought."

"Ah cannae see what's so funny aboot me needin' tae pee," Morag says, joining us, indignation lacing her words.

I pat her shoulder as we climb back into the ambulance. "It's just the relief of it being a blown tyre."

The ambulance doors close behind us, and we're back to bouncing over the sand. Twenty-five minutes later, the left front tyre bursts.

BANG …

"Why us!" Pearl throws her hands in the air as the back door opens and we climb back out.

After the two blowouts, we arrive at the 21st CCS late evening.

"*Wow*!" Morag stares at the activity. They're like ants, scurrying about the place, each on a mission.

Pearl steps out of the ambulance and stands next to her. "What happened to Mersa Matruh?"

Once a coastal port, east of the wire, halfway between Cyrencia and El Alameri, Mersa Matruh is now a shell, with only a few walls remaining. The buildings have no roofs, and the only presence is the Army, Air Force and Navy. No civilians.

With the 21st stationed behind the front line, just outside the range of artillery, the whiz and boom of bombs greet us. Whenever practical, CCSs are located close to transport facilities, a railhead or river. This allows for the efficient dispatch of casualties for further treatment.

Our primary job at the CCS is to assess the casualties, carry out emergency treatment, and evacuate them to the general hospital.

"Come on, let's get rid of our luggage," I say, following the other QAs to our sleeping quarters.

Pearl tucks her mother's poetry book under her pillow, giving it a soft pat. It's the only item, that I'm aware of, she possesses of the woman who gave her life. With her strong distaste towards romance, it is ironic that her mother's prized possession is a poetry book. Inlaid with a daisy design along the brown leather-bound book, the tiny flowers form a love heart. Along the top, in gold lettering, it reads *Poems 1908–1914*. I've never seen Pearl read the book, and I've never asked about it. If she wanted to talk about its importance, she would.

"Best get movin'," Morag says, straightening her cap, and we leave our accommodation to take up our duties.

Under a barrage of gunfire, we run for the safety of the CCS.

"Blimey," Pearl says as we enter.

Some of the QAs who came with us from the 64th have never attended a CCS and the colour drains from their faces, their fingers shaking at their sides.

"Ye'll get used tae it," Morag says.

They stare, and with blank features prepare themselves for what lies ahead. Never, ever show fear when on duty. It is a code that makes our anxieties easier to control. Within a few hours of the sound of gunfire and landing bombs, casualties pour in at a heavy rate. With reception inundated, Morag, Pearl, and I ready the injured for treatment. Their wounds vary from light to horrific; some die before we can reach them. War is not pretty.

As boys, my brothers had a set of toy soldiers, which they shared. By the time my brothers grew out of playing with them, the paint had worn off, disfiguring their faces and uniforms. Those tin soldiers are in better shape than their human counterparts entering the CCS. Their clothes in shreds, wounds leaking, blood flows from their bodies. Some sit, incapable of making a sound. Shrapnel removes jaws, shattering bone and teeth, severing the tongue. One soldier lies on a stretcher, his right leg blown off. Sometimes it's simpler to ignore the horror. To protect the mind until all that remains is treating the casualties and keeping them alive.

The Military Chaplain walks from casualty to casualty offering spiritual support and moral guidance. Some of them he will bury. With most of the casualties taken care of, Pearl, Morag, and I wrap the dead in blankets. Sadness creeps in, tearing at my insides, filling me with an overwhelming sense of utter desolation. With the blanket covering the face of a young soldier, I say a silent prayer. Once wrapped, the dead are taken for burial.

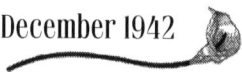

Dear Jane Anne,

This letter finds me at the 21st Casualty Clearing Station in Mersa Matruh. The 21st is the primary CCS and things are hectic here. It is a long time since I have been close to the frontline, and I've forgotten how loud and fearsome the sound of battle is. The whizzing of bombs and rat-a-tat-tat of gunfire booms through the air, pulling me from sleep with a heart-thumping jump.

Many of the soldiers entering the unit haven't eaten for over forty-eight hours and their clothes hang from their shoulders. Dirt lines their skin, and their hair matts with sand, blood, and flesh. Where possible we provide them with a meal; it's nothing flash, a slice of bread and butter. For those returning to the frontline, we give them food and water before they leave. Goodness knows when they will get to eat again. The most terrible part of patching up a soldier and sending him back to fight is when they return. They declared George Hargreaves fit for battle; within twenty-four hours of being stretchered back on the ward, shrapnel had removed his jaw and tore into his chest. An hour later, George died from his injuries.

We work as quickly as we can, treating their wounds and readying them for transportation to the nearest British

General Hospital. Some we lose before we can treat them. These men prey on my mind the most. Even in a busy place, you can feel alone. It's why I like to hold them, so they know we've not deserted them.

With the CCS located so close to the battle line, none of us are safe. Yesterday we lost a sister to a stray bullet. I'm told her name was Janet Collins, she was twenty-two. We live to serve our brave soldiers and die while saving them; it is how things are here. Quieter days will come, and we shall move on to the next medical unit.

Lillian Elizabeth

44

 December 1942, 21ˢᵗ CCS, Mersa Matruh, Egypt

*N*ew orders send me to the 63rd BGH. Malaria is taking its toll at the hospital, reducing staffing numbers, and my experience in the operating theatre is required. I leave with two other QAs, assigned to the 63rd until further notice. Pearl and Morag are remaining at the 21ˢᵗ CCS, and for the first time since joining the war, I am alone, without my friends. My insides are like jelly as I stand outside the waiting ambulance, my kit bag at my feet. "Stay out the way of gunfire," I say, my mind centring on Janet Collins' recent death.

Morag looks crestfallen as she pulls back from my embrace. "Dinnae worry aboot us, just make sure ye come back in one piece."

"Stop it. I won't have any talk about coming back, gunfire, and pieces. Stop being glum, the pair of you. No one is losing anyone, Lilly is going on an excursion, like a holiday."

"Some holiday ye goin' on, Lilly."

"Morag!" The warning shoots from Pearl.

She always acts tough, but she's not. Worry seeps into her eyes, and the muscle in her cheek pulsates.

"You're right, Pearl," I say, hugging her. "It's just a holiday."

The ambulance driver signals, and I climb inside with Lizzy Harrison and Elsie Temple for the 63rd BGH at Helmieh. Morag and Pearl wave as the ambulance doors close and I'm left with two strangers, and my old anxieties over making new friends. Excitement and apprehension clash in a mix of emotions as we arrive at the 63rd BGH, and the doors of the ambulance open to organised mayhem. Outside, trucks arrive with overloaded ambulances. The trucks collect sterile supplies, and the ambulances drop off the casualties. The 63rd BGH is the central depot for sterile supplies and is the first of its kind. It's busy, busier than I've ever seen a hospital or CCS. Before establishing the central depot, each medical unit handled its own dressings, theatre linen, and gloves. With few facilities, it wasn't a simple task. The 63rd changed that and performs a crucial medical base.

"G'day, nurse."

I turn to see an Australian soldier being stretchered in. His right leg is in shreds. The grin on his face never falters. He is like the Cheshire Cat from *Alice's Adventure in Wonderland*. 'We're all mad here,' the quote pops into my head. It's right to be there. If we are to survive, we all need to be a little bit bonkers.

"You'd be best to watch them. They're a wild lot, the Australians. He's from the Australian 9th Division at El Alamein. Given my experiences with this cunning lot, it's as well they nurse the New Zealand and South African casualties at their own hospitals. I'm not sure we would cope. They have a strange sense of humour. One that lands them in more trouble than I've ever seen a soldier get into."

I jump at the sound of her voice. The British VAD laughs as she steps from behind me. "Sorry, I shouldn't laugh, but the look on your face ..." She sticks out her hand. "I'm Alice Smith."

Alice—irony is shining down on me today.

Her grip is firm as we shake hands. "You're the three new ones from the 21st. Matron said to greet you. Let's get your things dropped off and take you to meet her."

Alice Smith towers over me like a weeping willow. Her stoop is probably an unconscious attempt to lessen our height difference. It makes her appear awkward within her own body. She is an animated talker, her hands flying about her. Her blonde curls bounce around her cap, and her blue eyes sparkle with mischief.

"Last week, while Sister Jane Brook was walking the ward, she saw one of the Australian soldiers was dripping with sweat, his teeth gritting against the pain. She stopped and asked if he needed anything. He smiled, saying, 'I'm as good as a box o' birds.' What a box of birds has in common with how you feel is curious, don't you think? Anyway, Sister Jane wasn't buying his 'box o' birds', so she gave him an injection to relieve his pain. He then apologised for being a nuisance. When he was back on his feet, Sister Jane said he was a right devil." Alice giggles.

"Goodness," Lizzy says, looking shocked.

Lizzy and Elsie are both seasoned nurses, missing out on serving in the Great War by a couple of years.

Alice shakes her head, smiling. "The Australians are undisciplined. Why, the other night, two of the patients got out and left the hospital." Alice opens a door, signalling us inside, showing us to our beds. "Right, now we've got your stuff sorted, best take you to Matron."

My kit bag under the bed, I walk over to Alice, waiting for Elsie and Lizzy. "Where did the soldiers go?"

Alice points to her left. "To Helmieh and got drunk. The guard challenged them on their return, and they punched him, right on the nose." She places a finger against her nose.

My jaw drops. I've never heard anything so outrageous. "What happened to them?"

"Matron gave them a stern talking to. They were very apologetic. But Matron still sent them to the Commanding Officer to explain why they left the hospital."

Lizzy's steps falter as we walk back down the corridor. "Were they court-martialled?"

Alice shrugs. "No, but they didn't leave the hospital again."

"How does a patient leave a hospital to get drunk?" I ask, puzzled.

Alice snorts, wiggling a finger. "A cast on a leg won't stop this lot from drinking. Why, they're like whippets, the drink being the rabbit in their case."

"They sound like a rebellious lot," Elsie says, her voice carrying a hint of uncertainty.

"I know." Alice places a guiding hand on Elsie's back, moving her forward. "But for all their devilment, they aren't a bad lot. Sister Jane says they're excellent soldiers. They ended up here because they walked straight into a minefield, clearing a path, sticking to their guns until they fired the last mine. Men like that are worth their salt, as my aunt would say."

We continue down the corridor, stopping when Alice sees Matron. She nods, turning to us. "I'll leave you here."

With that, Alice disappears down the corridor, leaving Elsie, Lizzy, and I to receive our shift patterns. Matron reminds me of Queen Victoria in later life. Her white hair parts in the middle, secured in a knot at the back of her neck, her cheeks are puffy, and her eyes are tiny dots in an overly round face.

"Lizzy Harrison and Elsie Temple, you will work night shift, and Lillian Nutman, you're on days. When you're not required in theatre, you'll attend the ward. Right, let's get you settled."

In silence, we follow Matron to the ward.

The last patient on my shift for theatre is Patrick Green. He has yet to gain consciousness. Shrapnel has chewed up his right leg, and there is nothing left to save. With no other choice, the surgeon amputates, sending Corporal Patrick Green back to the ward minus his right leg. It's unsettling when a soldier arrives at theatre unconscious, unaware of what is happening. Leaving theatre, I enter the ward, stopping by Corporal Patrick Green's bed. His eyelids flutter, he blinks, scratches, closes his eyes, then opens them again. This time, he is conscious enough to take in his surroundings. The painkillers he's on cause him to become disorientated, so I ready myself to calm him.

His hands trail over his body, his eyes flickering as they dart around the area without seeing. In silence, I wait for him to make sense of where he is.

"You're at the 63rd."

I don't understand why I'm drawn to Patrick. Apart from being similar in age to Charles Jason, there is little resemblance, but whatever draws me to him keeps me at his side.

Patrick's nails rake along his right upper thigh, his fingers unable to reach further. "Did you save it?"

"I'm sorry, Patrick, we couldn't."

His face turns several colours from white to red in a beat. "You took it then. Well, that's bloody great. Bet you didn't even try to save my leg. Took the easy route, did you? Thought you'd got a sleeper and could chop off his leg just like that." Patrick raises his right hand, snapping his fingers.

He grinds his teeth, anger burning within the brightness of his eyes. His hostility surprises me. Most are grateful to be alive, though amputation is difficult to come to terms with. Patrick Green holds no gratitude.

He inclines his head. "Get lost. I'd rather be dead than lose my leg. You rotten thief."

My face warming, tears sting my eyes—I will not cry. I'm tired and want nothing more than to place my hands over my ears and tell him to stop being ungrateful and shut up. Instead, I straighten, gazing down at him. "I'm sorry you feel that way. You're a young man with a lot of life left in him. A man capable of achieving many wonderful things. I wonder, if asked, if your family would rather have a son with one leg or a dead one. You're being quite selfish, and I'm putting it down to shock. It's not your leg that people care about, it's you. Perhaps next time you want to die to keep a rotten leg, you think about all those soldiers that won't get that option."

In the neighbouring bed, a man stares at the ceiling. He lost his right arm to the same bomb that left his jaw hanging by a thread. With dark brown eyes, he looks from me to Patrick Green, his head shaking. He turns away from Patrick.

Without a backward glance, I walk away. Even though I'm trembling inside, my hands are steady. I shouldn't have spoken to Patrick that way, but things needed to be said and I'm so cross. I don't care if I was out of line. With no Morag or Pearl to talk to, isolation beckons. Sleep is elusive, and my head sends me into a vortex of unhealthy emotions. Charles Jason's image keeps floating through my head, replaced by Joe then Alick. In the morning, my head aches as if I have sipped on one too many of Pearl's whiskies.

Back in surgery, I try to put Patrick Green from my mind. Fortunately, surgery doesn't allow the mind to linger on unresolved issues. Blinking, I focus on the soldier in front of us. Shot through the face, x-rays have revealed pieces of shrapnel embedded in his cheek and the roof of his mouth. The bullet went through his left cheek, below the jawbone, exiting through the right cheek, and taking his upper teeth, gums, and most of the lower teeth.

45

 December 1942, 21st CCS, Mersa Matruh, Egypt

*O*n the 20th of December, Lizzy, Elsie, and I are told to pack ready for transportation back to the 21st CCS.

Patrick Green remains angry over the loss of his leg and is taking it out on the nursing staff. It's hard to inject reasoning when a missing limb becomes the be-all-and-end-all. Alice has decided I'm the nurse to tackle him over his attitude. Her assumption of me is a surprise. I'm not a forthright person, and my earlier run-in with Patrick did neither of us any good. If Alice wants forthrightness, she needs Morag or Pearl, not Lillian Elizabeth. But Alice remains steadfast in her belief in me. My aversion to confrontation also makes me a glutton for punishment, and I allow myself to be pressured into speaking with Patrick Green.

The soldier raises his head as I walk towards him. His teeth scraping together, he folds his arms over his chest, monitoring my approach.

"Patrick." I nod at him, a smile in place. "How are you today?"

"Minus a leg."

Inside, I stifle a moan. His medical chart shows he is responding well to treatment and should be ready to travel shortly. Good news for all at the 63rd.

"What you doing here, anyway? Come for the other one? Or have you come to gloat?" His lips roll back as he speaks.

I sit down on the edge of the bed, my hands resting in my lap. My lips stiffen, muscles straining under the pressure of maintaining a neutral expression. "Neither."

Hostile eyes stare at me. "Then why don't you bugger off."

My dislike for the man festers, and I take a breath, summoning tolerance.

"Well … what you waiting for?" Patrick's voice has my back stiffening.

Face passive, I regard the soldier. "My brother, Charles Jason, lost his leg during Dunkirk. You'll have heard the stories from surviving soldiers. But this is Charles Jason's story, and I'm hoping it will make you understand how lucky you are."

I take a breath. "They reached the beach, with no food or water, nowhere to hide, nowhere to go, and nothing to defend themselves with. For forty-eight hours, they sat on that beach, waiting for the order to be given. The day before Charles Jason got there, a German opened fire, shooting him in the leg. Sergeant Alick McNavis used his last bullet to save my brother's life, dragging him to the beach. They possessed nothing but each other. As they sat on the sand, they watched the Germans bomb the ships coming to save them.

"With the signal given to board, Alick hauled Charles Jason off the sand, wading into the water to the waiting ship. By the time my brother arrived in England to receive medical treatment, his leg was gangrenous and had to be amputated. I was there when they brought him to the hospital. Despite everything he went through, he was never rude to the doctors and nurses treating him and blamed no one for losing his leg. All he asked was for me to find his Sergeant and thank him for saving his life.

"It might appear strange, but I've never been so happy to see my brother as I was at Stanmore Orthopaedic Hospital. Two legs or one, I didn't care. What mattered was that he was alive, and I could hug him and tell him I loved him. Bravery, I now understand, isn't about how many bullets you take, or how hard you fight. It's having the courage to face life no matter what it throws at you. To be grateful that you're still able to be with those you love, no matter how scared you are. You can make a difference, Patrick. One leg or two, you are special, because you're more than a limb. Don't make people miserable because you're feeling sorry for yourself. Show them you're still you, and that you're a man who won't let Hitler define him. Be the man who expresses himself by the people who love him."

I stand up. "Now, if you will excuse me, the ambulance is due to take me back to the 21st Casualty Clearing Station. Have a good life, Patrick Green."

The muscle in his cheek twitches and his eyelids lower. Without another word, I exit the hospital. There's nothing more I can say. It's now up to Corporal Patrick Green.

Letter Home, December 1942

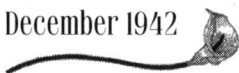

Dear Jane Anne,

Even though my visit to the 63rd General British Hospital was fleeting, it has left its mark. While I've seen many horrors to flesh and mind, never have I experienced such hate and anger. Through all the bravery, the comradery, and the sterling efforts of the surgeons and QAs, Patrick Green entered my life. Whatever ails him is not the loss of his leg, but something much deeper. His anger towards anyone who has helped him is unforgivable, and his hatred leaves me feeling wretched. While we work tirelessly to put these brave men together, stitches can't always seal the holes war and life make. What underlining problems make this soldier so volatile? We've our mother/daughter issues, yet we can both be kind and thoughtful. So why can't Corporal Patrick Green?

I have asked Alice to keep me posted on Patrick's recovery while he is at the 63rd. This soldier affects me like no other. He makes me sad and frustrated. Why can't he see past his amputated leg and embrace life? How rude of me for writing this, but Patrick Green is a misery guts. Each night since meeting him, I pray, asking God to send Patrick the courage he needs to accept the loss of his leg and live a beautiful life. One I hope provides him with treasured memories, like those I have of Trevor Henry.

A deep tiredness grips me, and for the first time I fall asleep in the ambulance on my return to the 21st Casualty Clearing Station. I wake when the rocking stills and Lizzy nudges me. The tiredness has not abated. Maybe when I am back with Morag and Pearl, my sadness will resolve itself. Let us hope.

Lillian Elizabeth

46

*M*orag and Pearl are in high spirits when I return to the 21ˢᵗ CCS. Adah and Effie have arrived, and our little group is back together.

"Lilly, pay attention." Pearl nudges my leg with her foot as we laze on Morag's bed. "We've accepted invitations from the Coastal Battery Officers Mess for the twenty-sixth of December, followed by dinner at the New Zealand Officers Mess on the twenty-seventh."

"Aye, 'n' she's arranged for us tae go tae the South African Officers Mess for the thirtieth."

"Morag, don't interrupt. Where was I ... yes ... and the East African Officers Mess is welcoming in the new year with a dance."

I pull a face. With Joe still based at the ADS and no word of Alick, I'm not in the partying mood. Casualties pour into the CCS like a tropical storm, with five hundred being admitted by day shift the day I arrived back from the 63rd. Since then, we are receiving an average of between three hundred and five hundred casualties daily.

I push off the bed, tidying my hair, avoiding Pearl's stare. "I'm not sure I feel up to partying."

"You're kidding."

"Dinnae start, Pearl, Lilly's been tellin' ye this for the last three days."

"But it's Christmas Eve and we're supposed to be going over to the RAF. It'll be fun."

With hair grips in my mouth, it's hard to talk and I send her a lopsided smile as I secure my hair at the nape of my neck. With the last grip in place, I turn to Pearl. "Sorry to be a pooper, but I'm just not in the mood for dancing. I know I'm being a spoilsport, but Joe's still at the ADS and God knows where Alick is."

Pearl pulls a face. "It's Christmas, Lilly. Joe and Alick wouldn't want you missing out on the festivities because they're sitting in a trench or looking at x-rays."

"We'll have time to have our party later, just the five of us. Besides, I've already signed on to do the extra shifts. You, Morag, and Effie party for me and you can fill me in with the gossip when you get back. I'm not the only one not going. Adah's spending Christmas Eve with John."

Further delays in the troop ships returning the injured to the United Kingdom are to blame for John's continued presence. On good terms with the Commanding Officer at the 21st CCS, he's been transferred here until after the festive season.

Pearl looks glum. "It won't be the same without you."

I hug her. "Will it make it any better if I go with you to the dance on the first of January?"

A look of horror falls over Pearl's face. "Aren't you going to any of the Christmas festivities?"

"Ah told ye it would nae go down well," Morag says, flopping back on the bed.

"I'll be at the Officers Mess on the twenty-fifth for dinner. Matron has agreed for me to have the night off, given the extra shifts."

Pearl pouts. "If I was thinner-skinned, I'd feel bad about you doing the extra shifts while I party, but as I'm shallow, I don't. It's nice to have time to be young. That said, we'll miss you, won't we, Morag?"

"Aye."

"You're anything but shallow, Pearl," I say.

She shrugs. "That's not what the whisperers say."

"Let them talk. They don't know you as we do. Besides, when did you pay any attention to what the stuffy QAs say?"

"I always listen, Lilly, I just choose not to let it bother me."

"Good. I'd hate to think that their vicious tongue-wagging upsets you. You're a beautiful person, Miss Jones. Gossipers are mean people, jealous of others." I grab Pearl's hands, pulling her off the bed and spinning her round. "Go make yourself look glamorous. You don't want to disappoint the officers."

Pearl laughs. "Like that could ever happen."

"It will if you don't start getting yourself changed. You don't have that long to get ready, and Morag needs her hair pinning."

Pearl lets out a dramatic sigh. "Don't remind me".

Morag throws her pillow at me. "Ah have ye ken that men like a woman with wild locks. It shows character."

Pearl sputters in disbelief.

I walk over and kiss Morag's cheek as I leave the tent. "You're one in a million. You and your hair."

A scattering of stars light my way as I walk over to the CCS. We are getting around eleven hours of daylight, with dawn breaking through at 6:20 a.m. and dusk at 5:30 p.m. Evenings have always been my favourite time. Clouds allowing, the stars add a wistfulness and serenity to the evening. I'm no astrologer or stargazer and can't point out a constellation, but I do like to see them. A small local child is being administered as I enter the ward. Tears run down his face and he's screaming in pain. His mother holds him by his shoulders, too scared to press him against her body for fear of hurting him. Burns cover his chest and arms, and his t-shirt sticks to his scorched flesh. The medical notes don't mention how mother and child got here and with the language barrier as it is, I don't probe.

"I'll take him," I say to the nurse on duty. She sends me a tired smile. The boy stops screaming as I kneel in front of him. "My name is Lilly and I'm here to help make you better," I say, using my hands to help him understand.

Watery, large brown eyes so dark they're almost black, stare at me as he backs into his mother. Her hair falls over her face as she presses her lips to his ear, pointing at me. "She helps you."

Still unsure, the boy watches, his lips trembling, tears dripping down his cheeks. "Come on," I say, holding out my hand.

He faces his mother, she nods, and he takes my hand, his little fingers curling around my palm. We arrive at an empty cot, and I carefully lift him onto the bed, laying him on his back. A basin of saline appears, delivered by an orderly, and I use swabs to soak away the remains of the boy's t-shirt. Progress is slow and I try to be as gentle as I can. His mother sits on the floor at his side, her arm wrapped over the top of his head. She kisses his cheek. It takes three hours to finish treating the burns, by which time the boy, exhausted, falls asleep. After coating his skin in Vaseline, I leave mother and son to rest.

"Thank you," I say, as an orderly takes the spent basin of saline and Vaseline away, and I start my rounds.

Four rows in, a soldier lies with a bandage covering his eyes. Given his age, I'd say this isn't his first war. "W-where am I?" he asks, an undercurrent of fear in his voice.

Unable to get his bearings, he sits up, shaking. Unsteady hands grip at his bandage as he tries to remove it. I rest my hands on his shoulders, pressing him down on the bed and removing his fingers from the dressing. "Shh, it's alright, you're at the Casualty Clearing Station at Mersa Matruh."

He raises his hands, touching the fabric of my dress. "A-a-are you a-a Nightingale?"

His words catch me off guard, and I immediately think of Alick. "Yes, I'm a Nightingale."

"Mah da always said, find a Nightingale and you'll know you're safe … I'm safe … I'm safe … Bless you, Nightingale … bless you … Da … I'm safe …"

What horror fills his mind I don't know, but whatever it is, the one thing I know is that this soldier's da gave him hope. And that hope has arrived as a Nightingale. I hold him to me. His chest rises and falls against mine as he comes to terms with the fact he is no longer on the battle-field—that he is safe. He quietens, falling back into un-consciousness, and I tuck the blanket in at his sides; shock has a way of making the body cold even in this tropical climate. The medical file by his bed confirms that shrap-nel has eaten away at the soft orbital tissue. He will never see again.

I walk the ward, checking on patients, updating their medical records. With my reports finished, I ready myself for the end of my shift. Despite the long hours, time moves at an extraordinary pace when on duty. If it wasn't for the tiredness pulling at stiff muscles, I'd find it hard to believe it has been over twelve hours since I started. With three hours of sleep before the next shift starts, I make my way to the nurses' sleeping quarters. Morag and Pearl have arrived back from the RAF party and are sleeping off the festivities. Not bothering to change, I collapse on top of my cot, closing my eyes.

On Christmas morning, I prepare to start my shift before spending the rest of the day with Morag, Pearl, Effie, and

Adah. It's a short shift and I'm looking forward to getting it over with and spending time with friends. Lieutenant Bridgemore signals me over. Three hours of sleep is not enough to ready myself for him. Internally, I groan, ensuring my face remains neutral as I walk over.

"You're assigned to me. We need to locate the German Casualty Clearing Station. Look for any wounded."

Without hesitation, I follow him outside into the waiting vehicle. Lieutenant Bridgemore is an orthopaedic surgeon at the 21st CCS who takes his job too far. It's not healthy for a surgeon to go looking for enemy clearing stations. The Lieutenant and I are the same height; for a man, that places him on the short side. Pearl says his height isn't the only thing small about him, that's why he barks at people. What he lacks in size he makes up for with poor etiquette and manners. He has a mop of brown curly hair, a stout frame, and thick stubby fingers. Before I'd met Lieutenant Bridgemore, I always thought a surgeon's hands should be like those of a pianist, long and slender.

Not one for idle chatter, we make our way over the sand in awkward silence. In front is our driver and a soldier, his gun braced, ready for use. We bounce in our seats like jelly, quivering at the slightest movement. Owing to Lieutenant Bridgemore's size, the backseat is snug, and I grip the side of the vehicle to prevent bumping against him. I can understand why the Egyptians use camels; the ride is probably much smoother.

Evidence of a tank battle, with twenty-five abandoned Jerry tanks, appear on my right. Shot up, with some burned out, the tanks scatter the area. Evidence of shell damage echoes over the site. We travel further, looking for the German CCS. A mile up the road, we come across a pile of abandoned Italian guns and boxes of ammunition, and Bridgemore signals the driver to stop, climbing out the vehicle. The sight makes me nervous, and I scan the area, looking for snipers. With no time to squander, the enemy retreated from their posts. What they couldn't carry, they left. To the far left is a machine gun nest; bodies spew over the gun, their fingers still poised on the trigger. Left to rot in the sun, they provide a meal for the Egyptian vultures, (Neophron percnopterus).

Lieutenant Bridgemore's lips disappear at the sight of the bodies.

"Bloody Italians," he mutters coolly under his breath as he climbs back into the vehicle.

Several miles down the road, we meet up with some Poles in lorries. Our driver pulls up alongside them and Lieutenant Bridgemore gets out, signalling for me to stay where I am. A moment later, he returns, shaking his head. His large jowls wobble, reminding me of an Old English Bulldog. The flabby jowls are where the similarity ends— the bulldog having more appeal. The Lieutenant is neither cute nor approachable.

"Well, that was a jolly lucky escape," Lieutenant Bridgemore says. "They found seventy Italians, unsupported and still fighting. If it wasn't for the Poles, we'd have driven straight into them."

My mouth goes dry as I stare at the lorries. Clear-ups are supposed to stop this from happening.

"Cowardly things, Italians," Lieutenant Bridgemore says, interrupting my thoughts.

Unsure if his comment is conversational, or for reference, I don't speak. His behaviour is peculiar at the best of times, with a reputation for being outspoken over his dislike towards the Italians and his hate of the sand. We all hate sand—we just don't tell everyone how much we hate it.

"Well, nurse, what do you think about the Italians?"

"I'm not sure what to think, sir," I say, opting for a diplomatic approach.

"That's very un-British of you. You must have an opinion. Even women should have a view of the Italians. Never mind, this might help to give you one."

He lights a cigarette, taking a long drag, smoke shooting from his nostrils as he runs a finger over his moustache.

"They sent those Poles to clear up an old Italian strongpoint the other week. When they arrived, the few Italians left surrendered, waving a white flag, as you'd expect. When the Poles stepped out of their vehicles to take them prisoner, the Italians opened fire on them, the white flag still flying, killing all but three of the Poles. Those three Poles that crawled away met up with their pals in Bren carriers. They drove straight back, right over the Italians, squashing the lot of them. Serves them right."

The Lieutenant turns in his seat, cigarette smoking between his fingers. "How many Italians do you think we've provided medical treatment for, nurse? Hundreds, I'd say. Most of them drop from exhaustion and require a bit of patching up. It's as well we didn't show them the same courtesy. Cowards, that's what they are, complaining about pain and grumbling over conditions. The same conditions we're all in. Shameful."

I sit listening to Lieutenant Bridgemore's tirade, hoping we find the German CCS soon or turn back. The thought of being squashed by a Bren gun carrier isn't appealing, even if deserved. They are for transporting personnel and equipment, such as support weapons and machine gun platforms. Not for squashing Italians. We've been travelling for over two hours, and there is no sign of the station. Silence falls once more, and this time I soak it up. The sun lowers and we head back to the 21st CCS, our mission unaccomplished. Next time Lieutenant Bridgemore wants to go on one of his excursions, I'm hoping I'm not around to accompany him. Back at the 21st, I try hard not to look over at the Italians.

On the evening of Christmas Day we hold a carol concert, lifting everyone's spirits. A spark of Christmas magic buzzes around the CCS. I've always loved Christmas. It seems even war can't dampen the cheer it brings. Morag and Pearl are full of stories from the RAF party as we enter the Officers' Mess.

"Mah feet still hurt from all the dancin'. Ye should have come, Lilly. '"T'would have done ye good," Morag says, linking her arm through mine.

"Never mind, I'm here now."

Someone squeezes my shoulder, and I yelp in surprise. Morag's arm falls away, her smile widening.

Spinning round, I stare at the man standing in front of me. "Joe!" I scream, throwing my arms around him. Christmas has just got better. "When did you arrive?"

"Last night."

I grip his arms, leaning back, checking him over. His hair tickles the collar of his uniform, and his clothes are looser than I remember. Dark circles sit under his eyes, and there is the beginning of tiny lines at their corners, which crinkle as he smiles. But my Joe is here and that's all that matters. "I can't believe it. This is going to be the best Christmas ever."

Joe laughs, hugging me, kissing my cheek. "I've missed you."

"Me too … I mean … I've missed you … not me."

My head is foggy with happiness. He's here, my Joe is here. No more sleepless nights wondering if he's alright. That a stray bullet hasn't pierced the canvas fabric of the tent at the ADS. Joe is safe. Adah walks in with John and I'm conscious we're blocking the entrance. We shuffle over to the right, exchanging greetings. The men shake hands in the silly way they do, stating each other's names.

"Joe."

"John."

Adah and I hug.

"Isn't it great?" I say.

She smiles at me, her eyes sparkling.

I clap my hands, jumping. "Oh, I love Christmas."

Morag pats my shoulder. "Are ye comin'? Foods up, 'n' ah'm famished."

"You're always hungry, Morag," Pearl grumbles. "Whatever happened to good manners? Poor Joe, there's not so much as a hello, Happy Christmas, up your bottom, or anything. No, it's all about your belly."

Morag turns to Joe. "Happy Christmas … hello … 'tis crackin' tae see ye … up yer bottom … noo kin we eat?"

Her arms flying in the air, Pearl shakes her head, trying to keep the smile off her face. "Morag! The up your bottom was a reference to you not being polite. You weren't to say it to Joe."

"Hoo was ah tae ken that? Ah thought 'twas some weird English thin'."

"No, it's a weird Scottish thing."

"Huh?"

"You're hungry, remember. Come, let's get settled at a table ready for the food." Pearl looks over her shoulder as she drags Morag over to a vacant table. "You lot coming?"

We follow behind, laughing at them.

The food is gorgeous, and our stomachs are stretched, but comfortable as we relax, ready for the music and the dancing to begin.

Joe takes my hand. "Let's go for a walk."

Outside, the music carries through the canvas and the odd gunfire echoes. We wander from the Officers' Mess to a small clearing. As we walk, I circle my arm around Joe's waist, hugging him to me. "Have they said how long you're back for?" I ask.

"At the moment, I'm stationed at the 21st until further orders."

I wrap my arms around Joe's neck, our lips almost touching. "In that case, we had better enjoy this moment while we can."

His lips meet mine.

"I love you, Joseph Lawrence."

His forehead against mine, he lets out a breath of air. "I should go away more often."

I give him a playful push. "You're awful."

We fall onto the sand, holding each other tight, looking up at the stars. Joe's hand strokes my neck as I snuggle into his shoulder.

"There aren't enough stars to spell out how much I love you, Lilly. I know it sounds corny, but that's how I feel."

"It sounds wonderful, Joe."

After such an eventful year, I never dreamed that 1942 would end so perfectly. Not everything in war is about death and gloom. Adah has found John, and I've got Joe. Though 1942 has had its moments, we're all together, alive, and well.

47

 January 1943, 21ˢᵗ CCS, Mersa Matruh, Egypt

We end January 1943 with an outbreak of jaundice, placing further strain on the CCS. Rats and fleas within the trenches are the most probable cause. Personal hygiene is non-existent for soldiers trapped in the dugouts. This facilitates the spread of gut-borne infections. Some doctors say that a portion of the jaundice cases result from cross-infection during the rollout of the yellow fever vaccination. This also fuels the rumours linking the treatment of wounds and shock by intravenous blood, serum, or plasma. These treatments expose the soldiers to several blood-borne pathogens, including hepatitis. True or not, we have a hundred fresh cases of jaundice entering the 21st.

Their skin and whites of their eyes (mucous membranes), hold a yellow tinge, because of high levels of bilirubin. We no longer send soldiers suffering from jaundice back to the battlefield when the acute phase subsides, but to the BGH, as many relapse. Progress in medicine allows us to treat the jaundice cases more effectively, prescribing a high-protein diet and strict bed rest. With a strong link between movement and early ambulation, we need to reduce hospitalisation time. So much for 1943 treating us better than 1942.

With my rounds almost complete, I check on the new admissions. Flight Lieutenant Jeremy Sinclair, an RAF pilot, lies on his cot. Sister May leans over, trying to cut away his tunic that sticks to his wounds. Jeremy Sinclair bats off her attempts with his bandaged hands. They fly about him as if swatting off a bothersome fly. May sends me a silent plea for help.

"Now then, what seems to be the problem?" I ask, reaching for Jeremy's file.

"I need my wings, don't let them take my wings."

"I'm not trying to take your wings," Sister May scoffs.

"We need to get your tunic off, Jeremy, so we can see to your wounds," I say, closing the medical file. "Why don't I cut them off and place your wings in a bag and pin them into your pyjama pocket, for safekeeping."

Suspicion clouds his features as he places his bandaged hands on either side of his head. "Confounded bandage, you'll need to remove it so I can watch you place them in the bag."

Sister May and I exchange glances.

I cover his hands with mine, stilling them. "Jeremy, there are no bandages on your head."

"What are you talking about, of course there is."

Poor Jeremy.

"When your plane went down, Jeremy, during the crash ... your head suffered trauma, damaging the optic nerve. I'm sorry, but there is no reversing the damage."

"No, you're wrong. I passed out ..." He tilts his head. "Come to think of it, I can't remember going down."

"It's common not to remember the crash. It's often better that way," I say.

"But my vision ... You sure it won't come back ... ever?"

"There is no treatment for traumatic optic neuropathy."

Jeremy stills, a series of emotions flashing over his face. Tongue darting out, he lifts his head, focusing on where I sit at his side. "You'll put my wings in my pyjama pocket, won't you?"

"I will, Jeremy, as soon as we get you sorted, I promise. You'll be able to feel them in the bag."

"Right," he says, nodding, "best get on with it."

Sister May removes Jeremy Sinclair's tunic. The movement of fabric cause his injuries to re-open and blood trickles over his chest. Morphine removes the pain as we treat the wounds and apply the dressing. His pyjamas on, Sister May bundles up Jeremy Sinclair's clothes and takes them away. With his wings pinned inside the pyjama pocket, I take Jeremy's hand, laying his exposed wrist against the fabric so he can feel the bag.

"Your wings are here. They're quite secure, and I've placed a note inside so that they know your wings are there when you get to the base hospital."

His bandaged hands hold mine in place. "Nurse."

Tears fall down his face, and I hold him as he cries. "Is there anyone you want me to write to, to let them know?"

"M-m-my wife. Hazel and I married the year b-b-before I signed up. She's a good woman, but I'm afraid I'll be more of a burden than either of us thought."

"Not a burden, Jeremy, you will both adapt, I'm sure. When you get to the hospital, they'll help you. You'll be able to do lots of things you did before. Your other senses will adjust to compensate."

"But I'll never see my baby, Gladys. One photograph isn't enough."

"You will see Gladys, Jeremy." I grab his wrists. "When your hands have healed, they will become your eyes and you'll see your baby girl."

He frowns. "Perhaps."

"Give it time, there's a lot of healing that needs to be done first."

He lays back on the bed, falling into silence. I sit with him until his breathing becomes shallow and he falls asleep, my hands resting on his arm, so he knows I'm there. Helplessness always descends when the surgeon makes his rounds, deciding who will make it through the anaesthetic and surgery, and who will die. It is not a decision I would like to make. Lieutenant Jeremy Sinclair may not know it, but he is one of the fortunate ones.

When my rounds are complete, I sit down and write to Hazel Sinclair. My letter is one of bravery. I tell her how Jeremy survived after his plane received a direct hit from a Jerry. It takes a lot of skill to land a smoking plane. That her husband has lost his sight because of a head injury and is coping with the loss remarkably well. There are many ways Hazel can help her husband readjust when he gets home. Life will change, but it would have changed even if Jeremy still had his sight.

In early February, Pearl and I receive orders to attend the ADS, leaving Joe, Effie, Morag, and Adah behind. The 21st remains busy, and they can spare only two nurses. There is no picking or choosing how close we get to the battlefield. Orders are always orders and we are happy, if somewhat reluctant, to leave friends behind and assist in whatever way we can.

Morag sits on her bed, watching Pearl and I pack our kit bags. "Tis goin' tae be quiet withoot ye. Whoo's goin' tae complain aboot mah locks or pinch mah thin's when ye're gone?"

With her hands on hips, Pearl glances over. "Honest, Morag, you amaze me. All you do is complain about me borrowing your stuff. Now you're complaining about me *not* borrowing them."

"Promise ye'll take care o' ye selves while ye're there. Stray bullets are forever flyin' through the tents 'n' bombs dinnae always land where they're supposed tae."

"We'll be back within a blink, stop worrying."

Morag twists round, ignoring Pearl. "Make sure she keeps focused, won't ye, Lilly? Dinnae let her do anythin' stupid like she did in France."

"I'll watch her, Morag."

"Aye, 'n' while ye're at it, take care o' yerself. Ye're always lookin' after others, ye need tae watch oot for yerself tae. Yer ken? Ah'll miss ye both like crazy."

Pearl tucks a stray lock behind her ear. "Stop fussing, you're making me nervous."

I've never seen Morag like this. Nerves eat at her, and her eyebrows draw into a solum arch. "Yer the sensible one, Lilly, oot o' the three o' us. Joe will fret while ye're at the ADS. So, ye have tae take care."

Unease settles over me, it's like Morag has had a premonition. "I will, please try not to worry."

"Tis wrong, ye goin' like this … just … take care …"

"For goodness sake, Morag, you've got to stop this. We've been through a lot worse. Keep this up and your red hair will be white by the time Lilly and I get back."

I hug Morag. "I'll look after her."

"Aye … remember ah love ye."

"We love you too," I say, my throat constricting.

Joe steps out from the CCS as Pearl and I prepare to climb into the ambulance. He's had his hair cut and it now sticks up like a hedgehog. It makes me smile.

"I'm glad I caught you before you left."

Pearl huffs. "Don't you start with the fretting. We've just spent half an hour with Morag telling us to be careful like we're a group of novices."

Joe frowns. "Wouldn't dream of it, Pearl. I wanted to say goodbye, that's all."

Pearl takes my kit bag and I turn and hug Joe. "It's not so easy, is it, saying goodbye?"

He runs a finger along my jaw. "It's getting harder."

"I'll be careful."

"Watch for stray bullets, won't you."

I nod. "Morag's already told us."

Joe kisses me lightly on the lips. "I'll be waiting."

"Take care of yourself while I'm gone. Not too many double shifts, you're still tired from your stint at the ADS."

Pearl leans out from inside the ambulance. "Sorry to break the goodbyes up, but it's time to go."

Letter Home, February 1943

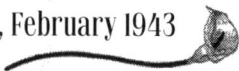

Dear Jane Anne,

Pearl and I are leaving the 21st Casualty Clearing Station, for the Advanced Dressing Station. This move brings us close to the battlefield. Poor Morag is in pieces about our new orders, and some of her trepidation is manifesting in me. I'm remaining strong and not allowing my nerves to show; Pearl will be cross if she knew. Adah and Effie's ears are going to be raw from Morag's constant fussing during our absence, and though I've yet to leave the 21st, I can't wait to be back. Isn't it ironic that with Joe's safe return, I'm the one now leaving? Still, we had Christmas together, and it was amazing. It is wonderful to have him so close again. Not even war can remove the smile from my face.

I have received a letter from Corporal Patrick Green. The letter comes as a surprise, the contents even more. Rather than jabber on about it here, I've included it. If I ever send these letters, you will read his letter for yourself. And if I don't, at least they are all together in my diary, and everything will make sense should I ever decide to read them, years from now.

Lillian Elizabeth

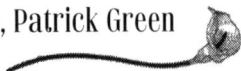

Dear Nurse Nutman,

You said the number of limbs does not define a man, it is the man inside. That may be true, but it does not excuse the surgeon from taking my leg without consent. I am a farmer's son, and one day I will take over the running of the family farm. How does a man with one leg feed and tend to his livestock? We shoot lame animals. This is the brutal world I live in. It's why I chose death over losing my leg.

There is no loving wife waiting for me back home, and my mother and father's love dried up the day they lost their only daughter, some twenty years ago. Life is cruel and vengeful. It has never shown me a second of kindness. Until you entered the hospital. A man who receives no kindness shies away from it, yet, despite my unpleasant-ness, you didn't give up on me. Thank you.

You've woken something inside me I thought long dead—Hope. Though tragic, many will recount your brother's story before this war ends. Your love for your brother shone from you like a lantern. And I find I want someone to love me with the same unconditional love you hold for him. I've never experienced such tender emotion, but then, I've never given it either. The bitterness I've carried for so long has not served me well. Before I took up my duty to serve king and country, I was to marry a young girl from the neighbouring farm. I saw our union as my responsibility, orders from my parents, nothing more. I hadn't thought how the girl would feel marrying a man void of kindness.

Christina Applegate is a shy woman, with pale blonde hair and freckles. As a farmer's daughter, like a farmer's son, she knows the weight of duty. While I've seen the thirst for love in her eyes, I've ignored it. Love is a fanciful emotion that fills a young girl's head and heart with un-realistic longing. That was my opinion until I met you. Now I understand the importance of love, and a yearning to have someone love me drives me to be a better fiancée and husband. Christina Applegate deserves a man that will love and respect her. I see that now. What surprises me is my determination to be that man.

The man that left for war is not the same one returning. I've you to thank for that.

Patrick Green

48

 February 1943, ADS, Egypt

The hissing and boom of bombs, follow the rat-a-tat-tat of gunfire through the walls of the ambulance as we approach the ADS. Aircraft fly above, the drumming of their engines causes a lump to form in my throat, and it refuses to move, no matter how much I swallow. Next to me, Pearl twists a stray lock around her fingers. We don't talk about the nerves nesting in our stomachs, it's better not to voice them—that way, they don't seem as real. With a sudden lurch, the ambulance swings left, then right. We grip onto the empty litter, our fingers slipping through the crisscross straps. Colour drains from our faces, our skin stretching in fear as we exchange glances. The ambulance bounces over the sand as the whizzing noise of a bomb gets closer and closer.

"We'll be there soon," I say, my voice sounding hollow.

Pearl unlocks her jaw. "My ears are ringing. How close do you think the bomb was?"

"I'm not sure, but it sounded close."

"I'll be deaf before I reach thirty at this rate."

BANG …

BOOM …

My hold on the litter increases.

The ambulance draws to a stop, and the normal feeling of relief on reaching our destination doesn't materialise. Apprehension grows as we prepare to climb out. Sunlight shines into our eyes. With a grin, the RAMC driver stands at the rear of the ambulance. "Sorry about the ride, a Jerry dropped a bomb. Good job they're a poor shot."

Pearl steps out. "Hmm …"

He laughs. "With the practice they get, you'd think they'd have better aim."

I reach for my kit bag, my knuckles whitening over the handle. "Let's pray they never get the chance to improve."

"Amen to that, sister."

The RAMC is a non-combatant unit, with the men issued with weapons for self-defence purposes only. It's disturbing how little combat training they receive, given how close they come to danger each day. In front of us, rows of tents line the sand. We are now within four hundred yards of the battlefield. The noise is intense, and I swear someone has miscalculated what four hundred yards look like—it feels more like a hundred. Like most things, the army has produced a list of desirable features when selecting the location of an ADS. Top of their list is protecting it from enemy fire and remaining a convenient distance to stretcher the wounded in for medical treatment. While the military lay out their requirements, they make it known that there are no definite rules. The general rule of thumb is that an ADS is within three hundred to eight hundred yards of the rear of the frontline. War has a suck-it-and-see mentality.

The reception area is where we record the casualty's name, rank, division, injuries, and treatment. With this information taken, they move to the examination area where they're sorted. Those made fit for duty return to the frontline. Those classified unfit we take to the re-dressing area for evacuation to the CCS. We administer the soldiers sedatives and prophylactic medication, such as aspirin, before loading them into the ambulance. Soldiers treated for shock and exhaustion receive hot food and water before being sent back to the battlefield. The ADS is a patch-it-and-move-on facility, with the x-ray and operating rooms used for life-and-death situations.

Life here is fast, much faster than at the CCS. It is like a sandstorm, only the storm never passes, and we're forever caught within its eye. With no delegation of duties, Pearl and I work where needed. Most casualties coming through suffer from burns or shrapnel. For some, their fight ends here. These soldiers will move to the CCS and then to the BGH, before being transported on the hospital ships back to the United Kingdom.

I stand next to a Tommie laying on the table, waiting for the results of his x-rays. He's been flitting in and out of consciousness since arriving. Before the surgeon can operate, he needs to know where the bullet is. Everything happens at hyper-speed here, and within minutes of the x-ray being taken, Brigadier Clarkson walks into the tent, x-rays in hand. "The bullet is lodged in your pelvis, old chap."

The orthopaedic surgeon is in his mid-fifties. Cigarettes have discoloured his dense beard and moustache to a murky yellow. Thick, round glasses perch on the end of his nose. Unlike the lower part of his face, Brigadier Clarkson's head is as bald as a newborn rabbit. At five-six, he is as tall as he is wide, and it is like working alongside a steep hill. For a large man, Brigadier Clarkson is light on his feet and performs surgery like a maestro conducts an orchestra. What he doesn't mention is that gunshot wounds to the pelvis can cause injuries to various organ systems.

The soldier smiles. "Best get it out, sir, so I can be back at those Jerries."

Brigadier Clarkson's moustache twitches, revealing tobacco-stained teeth. "That's the spirit, old chap. Nurse."

I scurry over, working alongside Brigadier Clarkson as he stabilises the fracture and prepares to remove the bullet.

With the risk of infection high and casualties waiting for surgery, we battle between prevention and speed. Pelvic injuries have a high morbidity and mortality rate. To avoid further fractures and penetration of abdominal vicus, the Brigadier works with extreme caution. With the sacrum above the tailbone, below the lumbar spine, and responsible for supporting the entire weight of the body, one wrong move and the Tommie will live out life in a wheelchair.

Brigadier Clarkson works methodically to prevent the bullet from moving while he extracts it. Sweat lines his bald head, bleeding through his cap. Dampness causes the hair at the back of my neck to stick to my skin. It is a long and torturously slow procedure. On Brigadier Clarkson's signal, the soldier is littered towards the waiting ambulance. Without a chance to catch my breath, the next soldier arrives for surgery.

A month at the ADS comes and goes in a blur and in mid-March, Pearl and I are on standby for further orders. After two weeks of standby, in early April we stand, our kit bags at our feet, waiting for the injured to be loaded onto the ambulance. Impatience nibbles as I wait. I long to be back at the 21st CCS with Morag, Adah, and Effie. Pearl stands tight-lipped at my side as we watch them stretcher the casualties into the ambulance.

Amongst them is Alick. I honestly don't know if I'm relieved to see him, frightened he's injured, or overcome with the need to hug him. A bandage wraps around his right leg, and blood and dirt taint his uniform. Fighting back the overwhelming need to grab him and run like a crazy woman, I take a deep, stabilising breath. With the ambulance loaded, I step inside, using my kit bag as a stool to sit by Alick's litter, Pearl next to me.

"Now then, soldier, what brings you to a place like this?"

At the sound of my voice, Alick rolls his head in my direction, opening his eyes. "Nightingale?"

"In the flesh."

"Ah'm nae dreamin, am ah?"

"If you are, your dreams are weird."

He laughs. "Aye."

"What's happened to your leg?" I ask, pointing at the bandage.

"Shrapnel. Tore at mah knee like a spoon through porridge."

Alick's skin is slick with sweat, the fever confirming infection. The whizzing noise of aircraft infiltrates the roof of the ambulance as a bomb hisses nearby. John Turner, our RAMC driver, diverts the ambulance. With a sharp right, he counteracts the angle, correcting our course. Foot off the accelerator, he slows down, allowing for the safe change of direction. When I was a child and the road snaked sharp right and left, Trevor Henry would say, "There's squashed worms ahead." Funny, the things that fly through your head. Speed increasing, the ambulance makes its way across the sand as the noise of approaching planes falls over us.

On the litter near Pearl, a soldier screams, his terrorised yelps echoing back at us. Pearl lays a hand on him. "Sh ... I'm here."

"Ray! Ray!" he cries over and over. "No ... Ray ... Get off him ... get ... off ..."

The soldier weeps in Pearl's arms as she holds him tight. "Sh ..." she murmurs.

A muffled shriek comes from the RAMC driver as overhead the whistling noise of an approaching bomb forces him to change course. Sand hits the ambulance and we rock. I hold tighter onto Alick. Kooouuuueeee ... BOOM ... Another bomb lands. The ambulance swerves sharply. Sand flies in all directions, kicking up from the tyres and landing bombs, hitting us like a storm. My jaw locks as I wait for another incoming bomb to land. Kooouuuueeee … BOOM …

"Hold on tight! It's going to get bumpy," John Turner shouts.

Pearl sprawls over the soldier, gripping the litter, her feet wrapping through the straps, pinning the soldier, and herself, to the stretcher. At John's words, the soldiers sitting on Pearl's kit bag grab onto whatever they can. Alick looks at me, concern shining in his eyes. Another bomb hits the sand, and the ambulance slides. I fling myself over him, grabbing at the litter, twisting my feet through the straps, securing us in place.

The RAMC driver screams, losing control of the ambulance, and we tumble over the sand. Metal creaks. Soldiers shout out in a mix of fear and pain. My knuckles turn white, straining to keep hold. THUD … THUD … THUD … Injured soldiers fly, screaming, shouting, and groaning around the ambulance as it rolls. Tighter and tighter I grip the metal, sweat threatening to loosen my hold. Alick throws an arm around my waist, holding me against him. With his other hand, he clasps the metal poles. My head pressing against Alick's shoulder, I breathe into the fabric of the litter.

There is nothing we can do but wait for the ambulance to stop, and pray we make it out of here alive. The sound of glass cracking echoes as the vehicle settles onto its side, sliding over the sand. Bodies stop their tumbling. Their silence chills my blood. John Turner screams. The screeching of glass and metal follows. Then nothing. With my heart hammering in my ears, blood rushing my system, I listen to every breath, groan, and bump. Silence flows, louder than any bomb, making its presence felt within my core. Death always follows silence.

"Pearl!" I shout.

"Here," she says, her voice straining as she grips onto the litter, securing her and the soldier in place.

I close my eyes—thank you, God.

"Hold on and I'll give you a hand."

The ambulance lies on its right side. Pearl's stretcher is now on the ceiling.

"You ready?" I ask Alick, preparing to let go.

He nods.

My muscles protest as I try to move my fingers. With Alick's arms still gripping my waist, we roll onto the side of the ambulance. A groan flies from his lips as his injured leg strikes steel, and he lands on top of me. Air leaves my lungs at his weight.

The pain clears from his face, and he smiles, white teeth against a dirt-stained face. "Noo, Nightingale, 'ere's a position ah never thought tae be in."

My head hits the ambulance and I laugh. "You're daft, you know that, don't you." I cup his face, kissing him.

Alick rolls off me. "Ye ken how tae dampen a man's ego."

"Aye," I say, mimicking his accent as I get up to help Pearl.

Alick chuckles as he pushes himself up to sitting, rubbing at his injured leg.

Pearl grips the litter rails, her legs spread wide, feet hooked under the railing, her hair fanning out behind her.

Beneath her, the soldier trembles, his face frozen in fear. Alick limps over, his legs unsteady as he uses the stretcher to support himself. "Noo then, soldier, the nurse 'ere next tae me is goin' to move the lassie away from ye. Ah've got ye, so dinnae worry."

I tap Pearl's leg. "There's no easy way to do this, just release your grip and prepare to fall."

Pearl unhooks her legs, fingers unfolding, and together nurse and soldier falls.

Alick cushions the soldier's descent as Pearl and I collide, sprawling spread-eagled onto the base of the ambulance.

She hugs me, spreading out her hands, releasing the tension in the muscle. "Is he alright?" She nods at the soldier.

"Aye, he's fine, aren't ye, laddie? A wee shaken is all."

Bodies spill about the ambulance, blood dripping like a slow stream over the walls, ceiling, and floor.

Pearl reaches for my hand. "We should check to see if there are any survivors."

I nod, and together we turn over the bodies, checking for a pulse.

They are all dead.

Walking over to Alick, Pearl crouches at the soldier's side. "What's your name, soldier?"

"Archie Lambert, sister."

"Well, Archie Lambert, I'm going to look at your injuries, see if everything is as it should be."

I move over, looking over Pearl's shoulder. "How is he?"

"His injuries are under control. A bullet wound to the left shoulder and burns to his right leg, arm, and chest," Pearl says, as she continues her inspection.

"The burns?"

"Clean and all dressings in place."

"Good," I say, nodding.

"Archie, Alick here is going to take care of you while me and Nurse Lilly"—Pearl points at me—"put our heads together and do a bit of thinking." She stands up. "Alick, you alright with Archie?"

"Aye, me 'n' the laddie is fine, aren't we, Archie?" The soldier nods silently.

"What now?" Pearl asks as she reaches me.

Visions of my time with Lieutenant Bridgemore flash through my mind, and I'm listening to him recounting the Poles' story about the Italians.

"With snipers in the area, and no way of knowing when, or if, someone will come for us, we've no option but to make our way to the CCS."

"How?" Pearl points at the buckled ambulance doors. "It doesn't look like they're going to open."

"You're probably right, but it's worth a try. Then we know for sure."

Stepping over corpses, I reach for the handle. It won't budge.

"We can try kicking them. See if we can force them open."

I nod. "On three." We step back to gain traction and strength. "One ... two ... three."

We kick at the misshapen doors. Metal rattles and groans. I place my hands on my knees, panting. Pearl steadies herself, taking a deep breath.

"Let me try," Alick says, pushing himself up.

I glance over my shoulder. "Stay where you are, Alick. They aren't budging."

Pearl straightens. "What now?"

I point over to the front of the ambulance. "We'll have to crawl through the internal door at the front."

She watches as I make my way over. The small door leads into the driver's cabin. Stepping over the dead, I reach across and pull on the door handle; it creaks, but doesn't move. Frustration gnawing at me, I grab the handle with both hands, utilising my full body weight, yanking it. The door flies open and I lose my footing, falling backwards, tripping over the dead. BANG … my head strikes metal. The door bounces against the ambulance. BOOM … BOOM … BOOM …

Archie begins to whimper and Alick pulls him to his side. "Noo then, laddie, ye're safe, nothin' bad is goin' tae happen. It's just a door."

Pearl races over. "You alright?"

My teeth grate as I grab her outstretched hands, and she hoists me to my feet. "Just wounded pride," I say, rubbing at the back of my head. "Sorry about the noise, Archie."

"Nightingale …" Alick calls, still holding Archie against him.

"I'm fine … I'm fine …"

The internal door rests against the ambulance, and I walk over, wiping the sweat from my palms down my uniform.

Pearl looks at the small opening. "You sure about this?"

I shrug. "No, but it's the only way out. I'll crawl through and make sure it's clear. Stay inside until I get back."

"Be careful, Lilly."

I nod at Pearl, then glance at Alick. "No heroics. Your leg has already taken a battering."

"Aye, Nightingale, dinnae worry aboot me."

Blood coats the windscreen and seats. John Turner's body slumps over the dashboard, his head and shoulders protruding through the windscreen. A thin film of sand coats everything and, if not for the blood and wreckage of the cabin, he looks to be sleeping. Heat pours in and sunlight bounces off the glass shards. I turn away from the RAMC driver and grab hold of the door, releasing the lock and climbing out.

With the ambulance on its side, the drop-down is steep. I jump, my feet sinking into the sand, and small particles of grit fill my shoes. Outside there is nothing but sand and sun. With my hand casting a shadow over my eyes, I gaze out at the bland landscape. In the distance, dust flies over the sand at a great height. A sandstorm is approaching. April to May is the prime season for sandstorms in Egypt. The Egyptians call the storms khamsin. They blow at intervals of around fifty days, occurring once a week. Khamsin can last for several hours at a time. With time against us and night due to fall in a few hours, we're going nowhere. I turn and climb back inside as the storm sweeps our way like a fever, ravishing everything in its path.

Alick pulls me in and I turn, shutting the door.

"What's wrong?" Pearl asks.

"Sandstorm."

Her arms flap at her sides. "Great, can this day get any worse?"

I grimace. "Don't ask."

Alick sits next to me as we bunker down to wait out the storm. The few medical supplies we have aren't enough to tend to his and Archie's wounds properly. Blood seeps through the bandage. We need to get Alick to the CCS before the infection spreads and we're forced to amputate. Hopelessness cascades over me like a fly in a spider's web. Restless, I get up and start looking for more supplies. Once the storm is over, we need to get moving. Next to me, Pearl covers the dead with blankets.

49

 February 1943, ADS, Egypt

*T*houghts of Morag and her unease over our orders seep into my sleep, making it elusive. I question my decision to leave the ambulance, contemplating our other options. At some point, someone will find us, and there is nothing to suggest it will be our allies. The ambulance offers safety from the heat, but nothing else; I've already shooed an Egyptian spiny-tailed lizard away. Daylight leaks in, and it's time to get moving. Before we leave, I give Archie and Alick a painkiller from the supplies I've stashed in the canvas first aid bag.

Alick stirs as I move, his hand falling on my shoulder. "Be careful, Nightingale."

"You worry too much."

"Na, ah only worry aboot ye."

I get to my feet, turn, and place a kiss on his forehead before walking over to the internal door. Sand falls into the ambulance as the door creaks open. Pearl comes to my side, and I crawl through. Sand covers John Turner's body, spilling over the driver's cabin. With my feet braced, I turn my arms out in front of me. "Ready, when you are."

Alick's head appears through the gap, his head and shoulders emerging. I hook my arms under his shoulders, pulling him through the small doorway. His features harden in pain and sweat drips down his face, his injured leg taking most of his body weight.

"Do you want to rest?" I ask.

"Na, let's get this over with."

The sound of grinding teeth follow his words, and I pull his bulky frame, none too gently, through the narrow gap. He glances at the open door on his left and stumbles forward, grabbing hold of the frame. Together we stand on the body of the ambulance; the sandstorm has created a ridge in the sand, decreasing our descent. We sink into the small grains, Alick's right leg dragging behind him as we make our way over to the front of the ambulance, the front wheel hovers above our heads.

Hand against the chassis, Alick waves me off. "Go get Archie, ah'm fine 'ere."

I make my way over to the ambulance, lowering myself back inside. Archie's head pokes through the internal door. His thin frame makes it easier to pull him through, but skin pulls along the burns and his flesh tears where the shrapnel's entered. His screams blast into my ears, eating at my eardrums, but we don't stop. Blood seeps through the bandages and still I force Archie out of the ambulance. I hate what I'm putting him through, that I can't remove his pain, and that I'm adding to it.

"We're almost there," I say, encouraging him forward.

As I move Archie from the internal door, Pearl steps out, and together we get him out of the ambulance, onto the sand, making our way over to Alick.

"Noo then, laddie, come rest next tae me for a bit, 'n' enjoy the sunshine," Alick says as Archie flops, his skin slick with sweat.

Pearl stands looking over the desert, her hand hovering above her eyes. I walk over to her, my back to the ambulance. Unsure how far we've rolled from the road, or how close we were to the CCS before the air attack, uncertainty ignites in the pit of my belly.

"Any idea which way to the Clearing Station?" I ask.

Pearl gazes across the sand. "None."

In the distance, the noise of war echoes. We turn at the sound of movement.

Alick limps over. "Ah'd say we're aboot half a mile from the road, 'n' around a mile or so from the Clearing Station. We need tae head northwest, keepin' away from the road. It'll be safer."

I steel myself for the gruelling journey ahead. "Right, we'll fix yours and Archie's dressings and get moving."

Without giving him chance to protest, I walk back to the ambulance for the medical supplies. It takes a while to locate the canvas bag containing the extra supplies, as they've slipped under a litter. Pearl and I used most of the supplies yesterday to re-dress their wounds. With the bag secure across my body, along with the canvas water carrier, I leave, grabbing John Turner's gun before I go. The dark metal looks wrong in my hands. Though I've seen plenty of guns, I've never touched one. Better safe than sorry, I tell myself, shoving it inside the canvas medical bag, and making my way back to the others. One gun isn't much in the way of protection, but it's better than nothing.

"Ready," I say, securing Alick's bandage.

Pearl nods as she finishes re-dressing Archie. With her arm round his waist, she moves forward. Alick's arm rests on my shoulder and I grab his hand, wrapping my arm around his waist. Careful not to slip, we make our way over the sand, leaving the bodies behind to be collected later. The sand makes walking difficult, and our feet slide in all directions. Flies gather, buzzing around our heads, landing on our skin. A scorpion moves with ease over the sand. We stop, allowing it to continue unchallenged, legs scuttling, tail curled over its body.

The sun beats down and our clothing sticks to our skin. Archie screams, losing his balance and taking Pearl with him as they crash into the sand, sliding down the edge of the dune. She yelps, disappearing with Archie. The BANG ... BANG ... of gunfire sounds, and Pearl's screams fill the air. Leaving Alick, I run over to the sand dune, the canvas bag banging against my hip. As I reach the top, air leaves my lungs. Blood pours from Pearl's chest, her mouth falling open in disbelief. In front of her, a German soldier stands, his gun smoking. Sand shoots up as Archie kicks out, and the soldier turns and aims ... BOOM ... A hole appears in Archie's forehead, blood spilling over his uniform.

Alick grabs me and we hit the ground as the German turns and fires. I pull John Turner's gun from the bag, raising to my knees as Alick holds me. I squeeze the trigger … BANG … The recoil sends me tumbling back. The German smiles, his lips twisting as he raises his gun. Alick pulls himself up, launching at the Jerry. Before the Jerry can react, I rush over and, at point-blank range, I shoot again—and again—and again … BANG … BANG … BANG … until there are no bullets left in the chamber.

Tears run down my face as I run over to Pearl, flinging the gun to the ground. Blood trickles from her mouth, and her breathing is unsteady. The light in her eyes dims and my heart squeezes in pain.

"Please, Pearl …"

She smiles. "Don't cry, Lilly, I always knew this day was coming. I've had a good life, enjoyed it. Don't cry."

"No, Pearl, no, you can't give up …" My fingers dig into her flesh. "Please, Pearl … don't give up … you've got to fight it …"

My pleas make no difference. Blood leaks from the holes in her chest, coating my hands and clothes. With shaking fingers, I brush her hair from her face, turning it red. I drop a kiss onto her forehead, my tears falling onto her skin. "I love you, Pearl."

Her lips move, forming a slight smile. "I know, I love you too, Lilly. Don't blame yourself for what's happened here. It's destiny, that's all. That's why I never contracted diphtheria. Destiny had a plan for me."

My lips tremble, tears clouding my vision. Even as Pearl's words sink into my head, I blame myself. I had the gun. If I'd got it out of the bag sooner. Maybe kept it in my pocket. Or if we'd stayed in the ambulance and waited for someone to come get us, this wouldn't have happened.

"Pearl …"

Her eyes close, and her chest stops rising. Archie Lambert lies next to her, his blood soaking into the sand. At his side, Alick shakes his head. My sobs won't stop. Air can't get through the snot blocking my nose. I rock. "P-p-poor Morag, w-w-what am I going to tell her? … I-I've let you down … I-I've let both of you down … Pearl … don't leave me … please …"

Stupid pleas that will never get answered fill the space between us.

Pearl is dead.

Alick folds his arms around me. "Ah'm sorry, Nightingale."

"W-why, Alick? … Why Pearl?"

Tiny lines sit at the corners of his eyes, sadness replacing their vibrant colour. "War, Nightingale, that's why."

Blood covers the bandage on his leg.

Blood — everywhere I look, there's blood.

"Nightingale, we need to get movin'. There could be more out there."

From behind my tears, I stare at Alick. "I-I can't leave h-her here, Alick, not alone."

"Ye're goin' tae have tae, Nightingale." He sits next to me, his hands covering mine. "Ye need tae let go."

But I don't want to let go.

This is Pearl.

"Nightingale … let go …"

Where there is one German soldier, there are bound to be more. There is no measuring the time it takes for

Alick to prise my fingers from Pearl. Hand against my cheek, he kisses me as my fingers release their hold on Pearl's body. On hands and knees, I sink my fingers into the sand, digging a shallow grave. The sun beats down, heating my skin. But there is no warmth in it. There is nothing but the coldness of losing Pearl. Together, Alick and I take her body, folding her arms over her chest. We turn and get Archie, laying him next to her. If I don't look at the hole in her chest, she looks like she's resting. They both do.

"Ah'll make sure they come for them, ah promise," Alick says.

My throat constricts, and I nod. I run my arm under my nose, wiping away the snot. "At least you're not making the journey on your own, Pearl."

We stand, gazing at the slight mound in the sand. It all feels unreal.

I draw the sign of a cross over my body. "Take care of Pearl, Lord. Tell her mum I'm sorry."

Kneeling, I remove the red cross from my arm, laying it on the sand, holding it in place with the German's gun, its nozzle sticking into the sand, marking their grave.

"I love you, Pearl."

The sky is turning dark, and soon we will lose the light altogether. Arm under Alick's shoulder, we walk away. Abandonment niggles at me. That's how it feels, leaving Pearl behind. There are no words for us to say. Pearl is dead and nothing will bring her back. Night closes in on us and we stop where the sand dips, forming a small valley, bedding down. Each time I close my eyes, the German soldier leaps into view, his gun firing. There's a scream and Pearl dies. Alick holds me as I wake from sleep, screaming her name. Pearl's face burns the back of my eyelids as his lips touch my forehead.

"Ah'm sorry, Nightingale."

There is a hole inside me that will forever remain empty. Later, perhaps, I'll be able to quell it. Learn to live with the emptiness Pearl's death has carved.

"Nightingale?"

I gaze up at Alick, my right hand on his chest as I lay next to him. His lips graze mine, and the soft touch ignites the pit of emptiness. Life has shown me how fragile it is. I'm not prepared to leave this world without loving Alick as I've longed to since meeting him. Right or wrong, I need Alick's love.

"Alick …"

"Aye, Nightingale, ah feel it tae."

My lips touch his, and I drink him in.

Careful not to hurt his leg, I straddle him. He takes my face between his hands. "Ye ken what we're doin', Nightingale? What's goin' tae happen 'ere?"

I stare at him. "I need you, Alick. Let me love you."

He nods, and I lean down, kissing him, my fingertips trailing along his body. A peacefulness descends over me as we make love. There is nothing but the two of us. All the horror, the pain, melts until love is all that surrounds us.

Spent, we lay on the sand, and I pray God forgives me for loving Alick and betraying Joe.

50

The morning sun fixes its gaze on my closed eyelids, and light sears through the thin skin. All I want is to snuggle deeper into Alick's side and forget about losing Pearl. Pain. Death. This war ... But I can't. It's time to face reality. Next to me, Alick sleeps, his jaw slack. My hand moves with the soft rise and fall of his chest. A dark stubble lines his jaw, and dirt and blood cover his skin. To me, he looks perfect. There is no waking to regret. Alick was my first. The love we shared last night; it was amazing. But it was more than the act of making love. Part of Alick is still here, in every fibre that makes and defines me—right where it belongs. It's not love, not that I don't love him, it's stronger than that. A soul knows when it has found its mate, and in Alick, that is what my soul has found.

Alick's arm tightens around my waist, and he pulls me to him, laying a soft kiss against my forehead. "Good mornin', Nightingale."

I trail a finger over his chest. "We need to get moving."

"Aye, that we do …"

We stay wrapped in each others arms.

"Wouldn't it be lovely if we could stay like this forever?" My voice is wistful.

He rolls onto his side; sand sprinkles onto me. "One day, we'll have eternity together. When the body dies, the soul remains. That's when we'll find each other. Between the light 'n' the dark."

I gaze at him, searching for something to hang onto, to believe in, and give me strength. "Promise."

"All ye have tae do is find me. Ah'll be waitin'."

His lips touch mine, and my heart pounds as I give in to the need to love Alick for one last time. Until my soul floats between the light and dark and we will be together again. I've always known there is no me and Alick—not on earth. Mary isn't going away, more's the pity. Alick won't leave her, and I wouldn't want or ask him to. All I have left is the belief in the space between the light and dark. We stand, and on a lingering kiss, we shake off the sand, rearranging our clothes. Pain filters over Alick's face. His features contort then turn into a smile. He thinks he's got away with it, that I didn't notice. I let him think he did as I reach for the canvas medical bag, pulling the water canister with it.

"Here," I say, handing him the water and the last of the painkillers.

He nods, taking both. His fever is under control, his body fighting off the infection. If it's remaining that way,

I need to keep the wound sanitary. "Hold still, let me clean this up."

Alick swallows down the water and pills as I remove the bandage, washing his wound and re-dressing it. The patella bone, protecting the knee joint and soft tissue, is in terrible shape. It's likely his fighting days are over.

"Ready," I say.

"Aye."

We walk in silence, my arm round his waist, hand holding his as it drapes over my shoulder. There is nothing I can do about the patellofemoral pain Alick is experiencing, apart from dosing him with a mild painkiller. I can't administer morphine—I need him mobile and alert. His steps are slow, favouring his good leg, as we walk away from the place where our souls collided, and I knew love for the first time. Funny, but I don't hate the sand anymore.

Every step we take feels like twenty. It's like one of those dreams where you're running but get nowhere. The more effort I put in, the less progress we make. Our lips crack with the heat and lack of water. The water ran out a while back. It's hard to place a time on it. All I know is that when the sun moved higher, the water was gone. We keep ploughing on, across the sand, stumbling, falling, getting back on our feet, and repeating the process. With nothing but desert in front of us, and the sun as our guide, we continue. Depression sets in, its voice consuming. *You're never going to make it. Give up. Wrap your arms around Alick and surrender*, its constant chatter says, and I try not to listen. But as we cross the sand ridge to the next, all that greets us is the dessert, and it's getting harder to keep going. I'm not bothered about me, but there is no way I'll let this war take Alick. My jaw locking with determination, I keep moving, ignoring the voices in my head. At my side, Alick tires. My arm tightens around his torso, spurring him forward. Exhaustion makes me clumsy, and I fall, taking Alick with me. Our arms fly about us as we slide along the sand, and as my body stops, I reach for him.

"Alick." I point at the white tents. The red cross flies high above the canvas.

Giddiness erupts, and I laugh. Alick smiles, his white teeth gleaming in the sun.

"We've made it, Nightingale."

The CCS marks the end of our journey and our time together.

Panic rises. "Alick."

He brings my hand to his lips. "Between the light 'n' the dark, Nightingale. Never forget."

Unable to speak, I press my lips to his, drinking him in for the last time before clambering to our feet. We move closer and closer to our separation. Someone shouts, their raised voice reaching our ears, an incoherent noise, carried on a gentle breeze. The only thing gaining my attention is the wild red hair racing over the sand like a fevered storm.

On a cloud of dust, steps never faltering, her arms flapping, the storm comes crashing to us. "Lilly! Lilly!"

Worry, relief, and love clouds Morag's face. Her head turning, she barks out orders. "Get two litters over 'ere, noo."

Alick stumbles, and I hold on to him. My legs buckling, we go down. There's no point in getting up. We sit, waiting, clinging onto each other. The first litter arrives, and they remove Alick from my side. He extends his arm, and I take his hand, holding it tight against my chest.

"Goodbye, Nightingale."

My tears fall. "Between the light and the dark, I'll find you, Alick."

He smiles. "Aye."

They take him away and I sink further into the sand. Morag holds me, drawing me to her. Over her shoulder I watch Alick disappear. Worry replaces Morag's relief, and I watch her frantic stare as she waits for Pearl to materialise. Confusion. Uncertainty. Dread. Pain. Anguish … It all crashes into her.

"Lilly, where's Pearl?"

Tears spilling down my face, I prepare to break Morag's heart. "Pearl's dead."

Her breath leaves her lungs, and she shakes her head. "Na …"

Hurt is everywhere, eating its way along my body, sinking deeper into the blackhole of nothingness that Pearl's death created. Another litter is heading our way, at its side is Joe. He sprints over to me. My legs won't work, and I remain wrapped in Morag's arms. Her sobs penetrate deep into my heart.

Joe falls onto the sand.

Morag lifts her head. "Pearl's dead …"

Shock shadows his face as his hands rub our backs in consolation. I turn my head, looking up at him. "Oh, Joe …"

His lips touch my face.

"It's alright, Lilly, it's alright."

He doesn't understand. It won't be alright, ever again. Pearl is dead. I shot and killed a man, and I slept with Alick. I love Joe, but it isn't the same eternal love I feel for Alick. Joe doesn't know that his world has shifted, and nothing can make it right again. My lips split, blood trickles down my chin, and I give into the darkness that has been with me since Pearl died.

"Lilly ..." Morag says, her fingers pressing deeper into my arm. "Stay with us."

"Someone get that litter here ..."

Joe's voice carries me into oblivion.

51

*H*ow long?" I ask.

Morag sits at my bedside. Next to her a saline drip replenishes the fluids I lost. "Two days."

"Alick?"

"They saved his knee, and the infection is under control. He's going tae be alright."

"That's good."

"Aye, he leaves for the base hospital today."

I stare at the canvas ceiling, trying not to let the pain show. "I see."

Morag touches my arm. "Lilly, ah thought ye'd want tae ken, they found the ambulance, 'n' Pearl."

Her voice trails off as my eyelids close. Grief is a knife, its sharp point pressing against my chest, piercing, driving deeper.

"Lilly …"

I open my eyes.

"Dinnae blame yerself."

"How do I do that, Morag?"

"Give it time, ye'll learn." She gets up.

"Morag."

"Aye?"

"I'm sorry."

"Dinnae be sorry, just get better. Ah'm nae prepared tae lose ye as well."

"Thank you." I close my eyes, allowing the darkness to take me to a place of nothingness.

The next time I peel my eyelids open, Adah and Effie stand at my side.

"Don't look so sad," my voice rasps.

Adah pats my arm. "Not sad, deep in thought."

"It's going to be alright, Lilly," Effie says.

I wish people would stop saying that. How can it be alright? There's no bringing Pearl back. No Alick. And no way to stop the pain when Joe finds out. Alright … no, it's never going to be alright.

With effort, I force my lips into a tight smile. "Yes, Effie, it's going to be alright."

Adah removes her hand. "Rest, Lilly, someone will be here when you wake. You're not alone, we're here for you."

"Thanks."

It's all I can muster.

A week after my return to the CCS, I'm back on duty. The shifts blend into each other and I'm conscious of going through the motions. My head is a mess, and I can't stop wondering about Alick and how hurt Joe will be when I summon the courage to tell him. Pearl's death still hurts, and there's no way to make the pain go away. I'm not even sure if I want the hurt to leave—it keeps her close. Since returning to the nurses' quarters, Morag and I have cried the Nile's water content in tears. They haven't helped a bit. But we have each other, and that is my primary focus, other than Joe and Alick. As our shift ends, Morag and I walk in silence back to the nurses' quarters. We stay clear of the Sisters' Mess for food—our appetites diminished since losing Pearl. Retrieved from the ambulance, Pearl's kit bag sits next to mine, under my bed. It's a sombre sight, but I won't let Morag move it.

"Talk tae me, Lilly," Morag says as we lie on my bed, her arm slung over my side, her chin on my shoulder.

Around us, nurses get ready for their shift, while others try to sleep, wrapping a pillow round their heads to dull the noise. I feel Morag move as I play with the sheet. I'm not sure what to say or where to start. She lifts herself, laying a soft kiss on my arm, before standing, her hand dangling in front of me. I stare blankly at her legs.

"C'mon, let's take a walk 'n' find a quiet spot tae talk."

Her words raise a smile, and I let her pull me off the bed. We head over to the Sisters' Mess but don't go inside. Instead, we loop round back, sitting on the sand, within the tent's shadow.

"Ye ken what mah ma says aboot a problem shared," Morag says as we tuck our legs beneath us.

I rub the tiredness from my eyes, buying myself a bit of time. She sits watching me, an expectant expression on her face.

"I slept with Alick."

There's an intake of breath and my eyelashes flutter up. Her jaw hangs open and guilt, like a bomb, booms inside me. Not about sleeping with Alick, but about the happy dreams Morag had for me and Joe.

"Was it any good?"

Morag's question catches me off guard, and I laugh. "Yes, it was very good, and so was Alick."

"What ye goin' tae do aboot Joe?"

I chew on the inside of my mouth. "Tell him."

"Aye."

"It's going to break his heart."

"Aye."

"I just need to find the right time."

"Aye."

"You're going to have to stop saying 'Aye', it's getting irritating."

"Sorry."

"That's not much better."

"Right."

"Morag …" I tap her knee.

"Alright, so let me get this right. Ye 'n' Alick is over. He's nae plannin' tae go haime 'n' divorce his wife so he kin marry ye."

"Pretty much."

"Then why do ye have tae tell Joe? Do ye still love him?"

"Of course I love Joe. Not the way I love Alick, but yes, I love Joe."

"Then dinnae tell him. Ye ken what they say aboot what the eyes dinnae see, the heart dinnae grieve over."

Shocked, I stare at her. "That sounds awful … How can I do that to him? It's not right."

"Life isnae fair, Lilly. Ah see na harm, so long as ye nae goin' tae see Alick again. Why break Joe's heart?"

I fidget with the hem of my uniform. "It feels wrong, like I'm deceiving him."

"How many women do ye think go tae their marriage beds virgins nooadays? This war is changin' all that. Bet Joe has been with a woman, so why nae ye with a man?"

"The world isn't changing that much. Besides, it's different for men than women."

Morag shrugs. "It should nae be."

"But it is."

"Just say ye'll think aboot it afore ye go tellin' Joe."

I nod.

Both Morag and I have changed since Pearl died. Morag's hair no longer seems as bright or wild, and she isn't as chatty as she was. The blame is mine. It appears I'm not as sensible or reliable as she gives me credit for. My job was simple, keep Pearl alive and stop her from being rash. The idea to leave the ambulance was mine, and even though I had the means to shoot the German soldier, I didn't, until it was too late. It doesn't matter that I didn't see him until the bullet left its chamber and Pearl screamed as it embedded itself into her chest. I should have been more focused. There is no way of time readjusting itself. And I need to learn to live with what I allowed to happen. Even if there was, would I be willing to? If time went back, Alick and I would never have made love and I wouldn't want to give that moment up. Poor Joe, he doesn't deserve any of this. But we all have choices, and when we've made them, we must live with them. Blame lodges inside me with an iron grip. Work, at least, allows a reprieve from the torture.

"Ye comin'?" Morag asks.

An overused smile on my lips, I walk over, stepping into the 21st. When we enter, day shift is admitting the last of the burn cases and I try very hard not to think about Archie Lambert as Morag and I take over. Severe burns take ages to dress. One soldier is so badly burned that charred skin covers his legs, feet, and torso. His uniform has melted into his wounds. He had been driving a tank when a bomb hit his vehicle. Morag and I work together removing his tunic, with large basins of saline, using the swabs to soak the uniform, freeing the cloth from his flesh. Once this is done, we use forceps to pick away particles of dirt and foreign matter.

I've administered a painkiller, codeine, but we've had to top him up with morphine. To prevent septicaemia, we grind four sulphonamide tablets into a fine powder, sprinkling it onto the burns. When we've finished dressing the wounds with Vaseline gauze, the soldier is unconscious. Most shifts are the same, and I try not to ponder how we are doing in this war, concentrating on fixing the injured and providing comfort. A nurse's job isn't just about the wounds, it's about listening and preparing them for what is coming the best we can.

The sun is high in the sky when our shift ends. Today I don't even notice the bugs that crawl and buzz about the place, making life unbearable. Even the rats go unnoticed. There is no hiding what is coming. It is time to talk to Joe about me and Alick. Morag is wrong, he deserves the truth. Sometimes emotions are evil things and are far more exhausting than working at the CCS.

As I walk from the 21st, Joe stands at the entrance, a strange look on his face. For a second my heart constricts and my breath leaves my lungs. Courage and I need to have a conversation if I am to tell Joe about me and Alick. The distance between us Joe has put down to my recovery and losing Pearl. There are a lot of understanding nods, noises, and gestures from him to support this.

"Have you heard?" Joe asks as I stand next to him.

"Heard about what?"

"About the trials conducted at the 98th hospital, in Scouse, east of Tunisia?"

I shake my head. Joe likes to keep himself abreast of any progress made in medicine.

"There's a new drug called penicillin. During the trials, the 98th used it on a patient suffering from gas gangrene. The patient had the telltale bubbles beneath the tissue and was listed as beyond help."

Bacteria called Clostridium perfringens cause gas gangrene. The bacteria gathers in the injury, producing toxins which release gas, causing tissue death. Anaerobic bacteria (Clostridia) does not require oxygen or air to survive. With no known cure for gas gangrene, this new drug, if it works, sounds like a miracle.

"What happened?"

"They administered penicillin and the patient made a full recovery."

"He survived?" I ask, astonished.

Joe nods. "Since the initial trial in April, other reports show an amazing success rate in medical conditions where the death rate is high."

"Wow." I'm still trying to take this information in.

"We'll save so many more lives."

"That's great. When will we receive this drug, penicillin?"

Joe smiles. "It's being reserved for frontline troops in the Mediterranean. Our first batch of this miracle drug is on its way."

"Do you suppose there'll be a time this drug is more readily available?"

Joe sucks in his breath. "The production costs are high, but I'm sure, given time, with our allies onboard, the cost will decrease, increasing production. For now, we'll have to make do with current restrictions."

With Joe in a buoyant mood over the wonder drug, penicillin, I don't mention Alick.

52

April 1943, 21ˢᵗ CCS, Mersa Matruh, Egypt

*W*ithin hours of penicillin arriving at the 21st, medical officers gather to decide who is to be administered the wonder drug. Scepticism is high amongst the older officers, and because of this, when they name the first patient, he's seen more as a lab rat than human. With the penicillin administered we hold our breath, casting glances in the patient's direction. A few days later, the infection recedes, and our jaws drop in disbelief. With the patient responding well, Joe contacts the 98th BGH to find out more about it. He's always been one for the details. There is no mistaking the importance of this new drug, and the advantage it presents. No longer do we stand to lose soldiers because of infection.

Joe sits next to me as we take our break. "Lilly, I tell you, this drug is incredible. I've been speaking with No. 2 BGH. Professor Frost selected a patient with severe wounds to the buttock. With serious tissue damage, exposed bone, he was certain to die. Yet, with the use of penicillin, he survived."

His enthusiasm makes me smile.

"It's hard to believe that such an unassuming yellow powder, with its distasteful, musty smell, can perform such miracles," I say.

His head bobs, reminding me of a donkey.

"This drug will transform the way we treat the wounded, Lilly, and help us win this war."

For weeks we talk about nothing but the marvel of penicillin.

Not long after we receive one miracle, another comes along.

Morag sits next to me, frown lines marring her forehead. "Ye sure?"

"Yes, I'm positive."

"What are ye goin' tae do?"

"I've no choice. They're not taking my baby, Morag, I'm going to leave the 21st and disappear."

"Yer what!" Morag screeches.

Nurses in the Mess turn in their seats, glancing our way. "Sh ... Morag, keep the volume down."

Her cheeks turn red. "Boot ye cannae just disappear, Lilly."

"I can, and I will. They're not taking my baby."

"Boot ..."

"What other alternative do I have? I've done nothing but think about this since I found out. It's the only plan I've got."

"Hoo?"

The skin on my face tightens. "I haven't worked that out yet."

"Well, yer goin' tae have tae do some quick thinkin'."

Tears well. "Yes, I'm aware. Morag … I'm terrified."

"Come 'ere," she says, opening her arms.

From over her shoulder, I watch Effie and Adah make their way over.

"What's wrong?" Effie asks, taking the chair nearest Morag.

I move out of Morag's embrace, drawing a hand under my lowered lashes, wiping away my tears. "Nothing that a decent night's sleep won't cure."

Adah takes the chair next to her sister. "If you ever need to talk about your lack of sleep, I'm here for you."

Not wanting to get into conversation, I send a small smile Adah's way, stretching my arms above my head. "Talking of sleep, I'm going to see if I can catch forty winks."

"You still need to eat," Adah says, pointing at the plate of sandwiches on the table.

The food makes my stomach lurch. "I'm too tired." Like a rat chasing shadows, I walk from the Mess, bumping into Joe. "Ah …"

His arm snakes around my waist. "Sorry, I didn't see you."

"It's my fault. I wasn't looking where I was going."

He kisses the top of my head. "Since we're both here and unable to sleep, let's take a walk. We've spent little time together lately."

In silence, we walk a short distance from the Sisters' Mess. The position of the CCS doesn't lend itself to privacy, but we find ourselves a spot where a shadow falls and the air is cooler.

"You look tired, more than usual," Joe says, his fingers lacing mine. "What's wrong? You've been sad ever since the incident at the dressing station. Where did my songbird go?"

There is no escaping this conversation. I can't leave the 21st without him knowing the truth before the whispers start. Ignorance is not blissful at all.

His fingers tug on mine. "Do you want to talk?"

"Not really, but I need to."

Before us the white tents line up, the red cross burning bright in the sun. A symbol of hope for those who enter. With so many casualties needing medical attention, it's hard to think my work here will be over. I nervously lick my lips as my insides battle with the uncertainty that lies ahead. Joe sits silently at my side, waiting for me to find the courage to shatter his world—I am not the woman he thinks I am. How to do it? Bluntness is the only answer.

"I'm pregnant, Joe," I say, forcing myself to look at him as I reveal the truth about his tainted songbird.

The light dims in his eyes. He looks away into the distance. When his gaze shifts back my way, the pain in them steals my breath. "Alick." His voice holds a hard edge.

His fingers disconnect from mine. Not knowing what to do with them, I pick up the fabric of my dress, winding material around them. He's more perceptive than I thought.

"Yes."

"I see."

He doesn't, not really, but I'm hoping I can make him understand. "It happened after Pearl died, while we were making our way here."

The muscle along his cheek pulsates, annoyance flaring. "He took advantage of you."

"No, I mean, that's when Alick and I ..."

With difficulty, I force my fingers to still their erratic twisting. Every part of me wants to fidget, to be busy doing something. Joe's face clouds, telling me he doesn't understand, but he's going to hear me out. This is dependable, soft-hearted, beautiful Joe.

"When's the wedding?"

His question catches me off guard. "Wedding? Joe ... Alick ... he's married."

He jumps to his feet. "What!"

The word shoots from his mouth like a bullet. It may not tear at flesh the same way, but the pain is the same.

"Alick is married."

"The scoundrel." Joe paces.

I remain sitting.

His hand rakes his hair, and he kicks the sand. "Could he not leave you alone? Get on with his own life ... wife ... Why toy with yours ... ours?"

"Things are rarely that simple."

His feet grind to a stop. "Don't tell me you knew?"

The accusation stabs at my heart. I get to my feet, standing in front of him. "Yes, I've known for a long time."

I reach across to touch his arm. Joe flinches, and I drop my hand before making contact.

"I'm aware this sounds rather stupid, but I love you, Joe. Alick is different, he's … I don't know how to say it … other than he's different. Alick's relationship with his wife doesn't matter, he's married and that's that."

Pain, disbelief, and anger merge on his face.

"I've hurt you and I'm sorry, I didn't intend to … but I love you, Joe. I love you very much. This is all such a terrible mess, and I can't make things right. Pearl is dead. I killed a German soldier, and now Alick is gone, and I've hurt you."

He continues to stare at a point above my head, his jaw flexing, his fingers curling, and uncurling at his side.

"I'm leaving the 21st, Joe."

He turns, surprise showing in his eyes, but the hardness in his features remains.

"I haven't worked the details out yet, but I'm sure I'll find someone to help me disappear. If not, well, I'll do it myself. Matron and those that like to tattle about such things will view me as a disgrace. I'm not, I'm a woman who let herself fall in love. They might view what Alick and I did as sordid; I've heard them talk about the other QAs in my position. A nurse cares for others, she shouldn't have such basic needs. But none of that matters. They aren't taking my baby, and that's that." His teeth grind, and I turn to leave. "I've hurt you, Joe, and I'm sorry."

"Why, Lilly?" he grinds out.

"The only way I can describe it is that Alick is my resting place, my home. There's nothing on earth for us, other than the time we shared, and I will not allow myself to feel guilty about what we did. I've always loved you with my heart. I'm not sure if that makes any sense, but I believe there is a difference between love and a soulmate."

He stares at me without seeing.

"When Pearl died a hole opened and I didn't want to leave this world without loving Alick. It didn't mend the hole, nothing will, but somehow our time together made everything more bearable. For once, I cared only for what I needed. Nothing else mattered. This baby" —I lay a hand on my stomach—"gives me hope. I can see a future again. Pearl isn't coming back, and while I can accept that, I can't accept what I did, or didn't do. That day plays around my head. I see the German raise his gun and fire. Blood covers the sand, Archie, and Pearl. And each time it's the same, I've let them down. Now I've let you down and I'm so terribly sorry. Please, Joe, believe me when I say I am sorry."

His hand pulls at his hair. It's grown long again and could do with cutting. "You can't just leave here, Lilly. Where would you go? Snipers operate in the area. They could kill you. You're safer here."

"I have no choice. I'd rather die than have my baby taken away from me."

"If your baby means so much, why risk it? If you die, so does the baby."

"And if I let them take my baby, what says they will love him or her like their own? I can't take that chance.

Nor will I spend my life wondering what happened to my child."

"We'll find another way."

"Don't, Joe, this is my mess, not yours, you don't need to fix it."

Morag exits the tent and glances over before going back inside. Unlike Joe, Morag has held me tight while I've cried, kissing my head and brushing the hair from my face. Even though she's been grieving for Pearl, she never let go of me. Silence falls, and I walk away. My legs are heavy, and I feel so tired. Tears hover but don't fall. Behind me, Joe let's out a tortured groan. The sound causes my back to stiffen and the weight I carry becomes heavier.

Boots beat against the sand and Joe grabs my arm, spinning me towards him. I lose my balance, crashing into him. He pulls me close, burying his head between my shoulder and neck, sobbing. Tears fall down my face. Why can't life be simple? Is heaven laughing at me? Fate has sent two men to me, and I can't have either of them. One man holds my soul and heart, the other my love. There must have been a point in my life when I did something terrible, that I deserve to suffer. What that something is is a mystery. My hands flat against Joe, I push back. He lifts his head, his eyes filled with pain, longing, and love. Tears falling, I rest my hand on the side of his face. My bottom lip trembles as I lay a soft kiss against his. "Sh … Joe, please."

His eyes are dark, their colour disappearing within the blackness of his pupil. "I won't lose you, Lilly, I won't."

"You'll find someone else, Joe, you will. You just need a bit of time."

"I won't. It's always been you, ever since I saw you at Leeds during our training."

"Joe, please. Do you want to be with someone who is going to have another man's child? It's not fair to ask that of you."

Anger pulls at the hard edges of his face, and his gaze hardens. "Isn't it up to me to decide what I want? What gives you the right to make that choice for me?"

"You're right. But you don't deserve to be trapped like this. Nothing will change the fact I slept with Alick, that I'm carrying his child. When Matron finds out, she's going to arrange for my baby to be taken. I won't let that happen, Joe, I can't."

"It doesn't matter about you and Alick, don't you see … it doesn't matter …"

I shake my head, confused, unsure what his words mean.

His fingers sink deeper into my arms. "Every day we face death. Men come in their hundreds, waiting to be patched up and saved. Many of them die waiting to be seen, and some are unsavable. There is no pretending I understand what happened between you and Alick. I'm aware you've struggled around him, and sometimes I've melted into the background." His hands drop to his sides. "You say you and Alick can never be together. But is there hope for us, Lilly?"

Agony slices through my chest. I place my palm against the side of his face. "Hope? I don't want to leave you. Not like this. But this isn't about me and what I want. I'm doing what's right. What's best."

"And who gets to decide what's best, or what the right thing is? Ignorant minds with shallow lives. Is that it? What about what we want? When do we stand up for what's best and do the right thing for us?"

"Oh, Joe, I wish it was that easy."

He crushes me to him, his lips pressing against my mine. "It is that easy, Lilly. Marry me. Don't tell Matron about the baby. It's only been about six weeks since you and Alick … since … well … just a few weeks. We can get married and tell Matron a month later. No one will gossip. Who's to say the baby isn't mine? It will be our secret. You can keep your baby."

"Morag knows, Joe. It will never just be our secret."

"I don't care about Morag. She won't tell anyone."

A spark of hope lights inside me. "Are you sure, Joe? Is this really what you want?"

"Yes."

"Think about what you're saying …"

His lips come down on mine, stealing my breath. "We'll get married on Saturday, in case new orders come in and we're sent in opposite directions."

"On Saturday! But that's just days away."

"There are rumours the war is ending here. I don't want new orders coming in before we have a chance to wed."

I feel myself relenting.

God forgive me.

"If you're sure," I say, knowing that I'm being unfair.

He nods. "I am."

Perhaps I did nothing wrong, maybe this is how it was to end for me, Alick, and Joe. My hand rests on my stomach, and Joe's cover mine, his eyes so full of love. How can he still love me after I've betrayed him? This child will never know Joe isn't their father, and the weight of the secret sits heavy inside me. For roots to form and provide good foundations, a child needs to understand where they come from. Today, I have removed part of those roots from my unborn baby. I hope no damage is done.

Between the light and dark, when Alick and I meet again, will he want me, knowing I betrayed him, removing him from his child's life? Will my soul ever rest with his?

Between the light and dark ...

53

"Ye're gettin' married!" Morag screams when I tell her. "On Saturday."

"Saturday!"

"Morag, please, you sound like a parrot. I've told Matron. She's not happy, obviously, but, well, there's no stopping the wedding. It's what Joe wants."

"Ah take it Joe kens aboot the bairn."

I flop down on the bed. It rocks, and I end up on the floor.

"Of course I told him. What kind of person do you think I am?" I snap. Morag opens her mouth and I wave a hand at her. "No, don't apologise, I'm being sensitive about the whole thing. I'm sorry for snapping."

"Hoo did Joe take the news?"

"Not good, but better than I thought he would. He didn't seem surprised. Well, he was, but he seemed to know it was Alick's before I told him."

"That dinnae surprise me, seein' ye two taegether, ye were like the other half o' a penny."

I turn, resting my arms on the bed, my head meeting them. "We're going to tell everybody that the child is his. No one can know about me and Alick."

"Aye, ah ken why," she says, with a sharp nod.

"It's such an awful mess, Morag. No matter how much I love Joe, I still went with Alick. What does that say about me?" I hold up my hand again. "No, don't answer that … I'm a horrible person. I'm marrying Joe, and he's going to raise another man's child. I should have told him no and left like I was going to."

Morag sits on the floor next to me, pulling her legs to her chest. "Joe loves ye. He wants tae marry ye. Stop torturin' yerself, ye should be happy."

"I am happy. Guilty and happy if that makes sense."

"Aye, it does."

I drop my head onto her shoulder. "Thanks, Morag. What would I do without you?"

"Dinnae be daft," she says, patting my knee. "C'mon, cheer up, we have a weddin' tae sort oot for Saturday. Best start thinkin' aboot what ye goin' tae wear. We also need tae tell Effie 'n' Adah before it becomes common knowledge. Ye ken hoo word spreads around 'ere."

"I'll tell them tonight before going on shift. As for something to wear, I was going to use my uniform, maybe borrow something of Pearl's. She would like that."

Morag hugs me. "Ah'm sure she will. Let's see what she's got that's suitable for somethin' borrowed."

I watch as Morag slides Pearl's kit bag towards us. She catches me staring. "We cannae avoid openin' the bag forever."

Though I nod, it feels wrong opening Pearl's bag without asking her. She was very particular about her things.

Morag rummages inside. "What's this?"

"What's what?" I ask, leaning over.

"This." Morag pulls out a white dress from the bottom. A photo drops to the floor as she shakes it out. "Why do ye suppose she carried this around with her? Tis nae like she would ever wear it." Morag sniffs the fabric. "It could do with a wash."

The dress is sleeveless with a dropped waist and tiered skirt—very 1920s. Reaching over, I pick up the photo. A three-year-old Pearl stands next to a young woman. "It was her mum's dress."

I hold out the photograph. Her eyebrows nipping together, Morag passes the dress to me. "Oh."

My fingers run over the delicate material. "It probably wasn't about Pearl wearing the dress as much as keeping something of her mum's close to her, like the poetry book."

"Aye, ah suppose. When tis washed, it'll be bonnie 'n' so will ye. Ah'm sure Pearl would like ye tae wear it."

Tears sting. I've become a blubbering wreck these last few weeks. "Yes, I'm sure she will."

"Try it on 'n' see if it fits."

The dress fits beautifully. "What do you think?" I ask as I spin.

"Ye're bonnie, Lilly."

In a flourish, I flop next to Morag, smiling. "I can't believe, I'm getting married."

She holds out her hand. "Take it off' 'n' give it 'ere, ah'll get it washed afore it kin get any mare wrinkled 'n' dirty."

"There isn't enough water for such luxuries," I say, picking at the skirt of the dress, where tiny speaks of dirt line the edges.

"Ah'm sure we kin find a way tae get it cleaned, even if it means usin' up our allowance. Ye're nae gettin' married in a crumpled, dirty dress, 'n' that's that. Na arguin'. Think what Pearl would say."

The following days pass in a blur. Morag runs about the place, overseeing everything, like a wild hen whose chick is about to leave the coop. On Friday evening, I start my shift. Once we've taken care of the new admissions and I've undertaken my reports, I help with writing the letters to the families of dying soldiers. These letters are hard to write, but their families deserve to know what has happened to their loved ones. The man at my side, who I now write for, is one of the many unconscious soldiers that will not make it through the night. It is up to me to tell their families he didn't die in pain.

Flight Lieutenant Douglas Driscoll arrived during day shift. A pilot shot down in his plane. He is unaware of how his body fights to stay alive. With so many wounded admitted, the doctors have deemed this soldier untreatable. Burns cover most of his flesh. Broken bones and a severe head wound have left his brain incapable of functioning properly. This will not go in the letter. Instead, I tell his family of his bravery, that Douglas Driscoll died peacefully. In some respects, he is one of the lucky ones. There is a lot to be said for unconsciousness. That blessed place where there is no pain.

The return of day shift signals the end of my work. As I finish my letter, the soldier's fight ends. He has received his last rites, and now there is no place left here on earth for him. Hopefully heaven will treat him better.

Morag waits outside the 21st as I leave. In two hours, I will marry Joe and become Mrs Lawrence. Lillian Elizabeth Nutman will no longer exist, and my baby will never know its biological father. It is time, like Jane Anne, to grow up. Soon I will be a wife and mother, there is no room for romantic longing. I meant what I said to Joe about Alick, there is no place on earth for us to be together.

Morag's smile widens with excitement as I approach her.

"Stop looking so glum, tis yer wedding day. Ye've na time tae be sad, nae taeday." She threads her arm through mine. "C'mon, we need tae get ye dressed. Effie 'n' Adah are waitin' for us."

Morag pulls me in the opposite direction to the nurses' quarters. "Aren't I getting changed?"

"Aye, but first we need tae collect yer flowers for yer locks. Adah asked Janice tae collect some. Ye ken Janice, she kin find a needle in a hay bale, so Adah says, 'n' she's come up trumps."

Janice stands waiting at the entrance of the Sisters' Mess; cupped in her hands is an Egyptian lotus flower. The heart of the lotus is golden yellow against pure white petals that curve up towards the centre.

She smiles, handing over the flower, and I hold it in the centre of my hands, breathing in the delicate fragrance. "It's gorgeous, Janice, thanks."

"It was no bother." She smiles. "All the best, Lilly."

Before I can respond, Morag pulls me over toward our tent.

"Careful, Morag." I yelp, as I stumble in the sand, almost losing the lotus flower.

"Sorry, we're in a wee bit o' a rush. Ye cannae be late."

She has a point, and I quicken my pace. We enter the tent to find Effie and Adah already dressed and waiting for us.

"I've cleaned Pearl's dress. It's come up a treat. Just like new," Adah says, waving at the dress on the bed.

Effie claps, giggling. "I'm going to do your hair."

Within half an hour, I stand in front of Adah, Effie, and Morag as they run a critical eye over me. 'Well?" I ask, nerves spiking.

Morag steps forward her smile as big as her hair. "Joe is a Jammy-Jimmy."

Effie's nose wrinkles. "A what?"

"Jammy-Jimmy," Morag repeats.

"She means lucky man," I explain.

Effie giggles. "You have some funny sayings, Morag."

"Never mind that now. We need to make a move," Adah says, taking charge. "Let's get you to Joe."

The sun shines down on us as we walk over to where a small group of our friends wait. Joe stands in dress uniform near the chaplain. Any feelings of tiredness after working the night shift melt when I see him. Love radiates from him. Joe wants to marry me—not because he feels sorry for me, but because he loves me. Morag is wrong, Joe isn't the Jammy-Jimmy, I am.

My hand resting in his, we say our vows. On my ring finger sits an Egyptian gold lotus engraved band; how Joe got it, I'm not sure, but it's beautiful. We kiss to the sound of wolf whistles and gunfire. A small distance from the main group of tents is a smaller one, offering isolation. There is no honeymoon. Just one night. At 8 p.m., the following day, I will be back on shift.

As we get close to the tent, Joe sweeps me into his arms, ducking under the canopy. A scattering of cushions and blankets lay on the floor. It makes me blush when I see them. His hand trails along the side of my face as he leans in and kisses me. Any nerves I have fade.

Lips against my ear, Joe whispers, "I love you, Mrs Lawrence."

A small shiver runs down my spine. "I love you too, Mr Lawrence."

As I lay in Joe's arms, I wonder what is to happen next. When Matron learns of my pregnancy, will she send me back to England, or a medical hospital far away from the fighting and Joe?

On the 17th of May, war in North Africa ends and we prepare to leave, returning to Alexandra to staff the 64th BGH. The officers, including Joe, and soldiers head to the Red Sea to practice landing with equipment on their backs. Morag at my side, we climb into the waiting ambulance which is to take us back to Alexandra—Joe has already left. The doors close and I try not to recall the last time I was sitting in the back of an ambulance.

Letter Home, May 1943

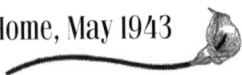

Dear Jane Anne,

So many times, I have picked up my pen to write, but the words get trapped inside and I can't find the right ones. My world is becoming smaller. Those I love are dying, and somehow, I'm supposed to find the strength to present to those under my care an exterior so impenetrable nothing can shake it. Anger, hurt, guilt, and accusations are everywhere, whispering inside my head. They are my effervescent tormentor.

I often see Pearl's face. I know she isn't here anymore, but it doesn't prevent her from being present. Even though the war in North Africa is over and they assign us to the 64th British General Hospital in Alexandra, she remains with me. Her kit bag sits at my feet. Morag says I'm using it as a talisman, urging me to never give up. She's probably right.

As the ambulance moves over the sand, the miles melt away from Mersa Matruh, where Pearl rests. Part of me remains with her. As our time in this war went by, and we remained together, I believed it would always be so. What a delusional fool I was. When I close my eyes, sometimes I see that German soldier. Smoke coming from his gun, and I want to keep shooting and shooting, ploughing bullets into him until his flesh is nothing more than con-fetti, and Pearl lives. Does this make me a terrible person? I'm not sure I know who I am anymore.

During my darker moments, I fear I am nothing more than a failure. I have failed my friends. Pearl's death has dampened the light within Morag; she doesn't glow the same, and is less vocal, more choosing in her approach. I watch, a silent bystander, as she pulls away from Danny. She refuses to talk about it, other than to shrug and say "Tis nae meant tae be." I think she fears losing someone else, allowing herself to love. In failing to protect Pearl, I have killed any romantic notions Morag had.

The ambulance is slowing down. It's time for me to stop writing.

Lillian Elizabeth

54

 June 1943, Cairo, Egypt

*W*e're assigned leave en route to the 64th BGH. Morag, Adah, Effie, and I decide to take our leave in Cairo, as it provides us with the opportunity to shop and do some sightseeing. Matron remains unaware I'm pregnant. My belly has yet to show any signs of the baby and with no bouts of sickness, I'm putting off informing her until July or August. While becoming an ostrich has not worked in the past, ever the optimist, I'm hoping it will help this time.

Cairo is a welcome break, further prolonging the need for action and decision-making. Femina Cinema is a well-known hangout for British troops, offering free programmes to all ranks and services. The current listings are *The Ghost Breakers* starring Paulette Goddard and Bob Hope, and *The Big Store*, starring the Marx Brothers. Not into horror or in the mood for an American comedy, we walk over to the Metro Cinema. The Metro opened its doors in 1940 with the Egyptian premier of *Gone With The*

Wind; three years later, the film is back, and we take our seats.

"I can't believe Scarlett O-Hara preferred Ashley Wilkes to Rhett Butler," Effie says as we walk from the cinema.

Morag links her arm through Effie's. "Neither kin ah. Rhett Butler is such a dashin' rogue compared tae soppy Ashley Wilkes."

"You know they aren't real, don't you?" I ask, following them out with Adah.

"The characters might nae be real, boot Clark Gable is 'n' ah'd say aye tae marryin' him over Leslie Howard any day."

Effie giggles. "Me too."

"You're terrible, the pair of you," Adah says, smiling at them.

Effie pulls her arm from Morag's, looking over at her sister. "I know, isn't it grand?"

Adah groans, shaking her head.

"C'mon, whoo's up for shoppin'?" Morag calls over her shoulder, dragging Effie down Soliman Pasha Street.

On the 7th of June, the military recall us, placing us on standby. Almost a month later, on the 4th of July, we embark the troop ship, leaving Alexandra. A light breeze cools our skin as we sit on deck. Our shopping trip in Cairo is fruitful. I purchase an Art nouveau scarab beetle and lotus flower hair clip, inset with crystals and freshwater pearls for Jane Anne, and an Egyptian blue opal scarab beetle pendant for Aunt Sarah Rebeca. For Charles Jason I bought a leather wallet embossed with images of Egyptian pharaohs. I tuck them away in my kit bag, along with the scarves I bought in Cape Town and never posted. There is no point in sending them; the chances of remaining with Morag, Adah, and Effie once I've confirmed my pregnancy to Matron are remote.

BANG ... The troop ship rocks, sending us tippling into each other. We grapple for something to hold on to as water sprays up, and the engines shudder to a stop.

Someone screams from the other end of the deck, "Torpedo!"

A terrible silence meets the word.

There's a loud screech, and the ship turns onto its side. For the first time since finding out I was pregnant, I think I'm going to be sick. I stare at Morag, grabbing her arm. In my other hand, I hold on to mine and Pearl's kit bag. Objects rain down on us as they slide, diving towards the side of the ship. The ship tips further and we lose our footing. Like a vice, I hang onto Morag's arm as we slide in a mass of limbs and screams. Our feet kick out, connecting with flesh, arms reaching, looking for something to grab onto. There is no way to stop our descent, and nothing to prevent us from tipping into the water. My throat constricts. Next to me, Morag loses all colour. Fear steals our voices, our gaze fastening onto the sea, aware we can't swim. With a sudden groan, the ship rights itself and pools of seawater wash over us.

Effie's head comes sailing our way, eyes like saucers.

"W-what's h-happening?" I ask, my voice quivering.

Adah clings onto Effie. "The ship is righting itself, it does that before it goes down."

"Ah'm nae goin' tae drown. If ah'm goin' tae die, ah'm wantin' it tae be on land. Nae like this …"

If we can choose the way to die, I'm positive we'd all choose a kinder, calmer way, but there is no controlling death.

"This way, ladies, to the boats," a Dutch engineer shouts.

We scramble to our feet, kit bags in hand, and make our way towards the engineer, where the crew lower the lifeboats. We form a single file, waiting our turn. As we get closer to the front, Morag comes to an abrupt stop.

"What's wrong?" I ask, bumping into her.

"There's a hoole in the boat."

I glance down. I swear, every woodlouse known on earth has chomped its way through the wood.

Adah taps me on the shoulder. "There's a boat just launched on the other side."

"Come on, before we end up sinking with the ship," Effie says, heading over to the launched boat.

The nearer we get, the more terror strikes. We stare down—it's a long way to jump.

"Come on, sisters, no time to lose," an English Naval Officer says from behind us.

"Lilly …"

"Don't worry, Morag, we jump together."

She stares at me for a second, then nods. "Aye … taegether."

"Ready?"

Morag nods.

Tightly gripping onto each other, we follow Adah and Effie, jumping over the side of the ship into the waiting boat. The small vessel sways on the water's surface. Around seventy of us crowd together within the boat. My stomach rolls, sickness threatening, and I take a deep breath, concentrating on the movement of air as it fills and empties my lungs. Oars dip in and out of the water as the WRNS row our small boat away from the sinking ship. Night falls and everything becomes shrouded in darkness.

Kit bags on my knees, I lower my head on top, praying we make it. For six hours, we row, taking it in turns. There is no sight of land or allied ships, just water, and our wet clothing sticking to our skin. We shiver, huddling together against the evening cold. Morag's head falls onto my shoulder, her arms draping over my back.

"Ah'll nae lose ye, Lilly," she whispers.

"No one is dying, not today or tomorrow, Morag. We've lost enough." My words sound hollow, but I mean every one of them.

Adah sits in front of me, her back against my legs, Effie at her side. Around us, silence falls until the only noise is the water lapping at the boat and oars as they eat into the darkened depth of the sea. In the distance, the sun rises, a soft glow of orange and yellow, lighting the sky. Adah taps my legs, pointing to her left. Ahead is the Royal Navy *HMHS Talamba*. I nudge Morag. She lifts her head, her gaze following my raised arm, and smiles. Hugging each other, we bask in the wonderful sight of *HMHS Talamba*. A member of the crew throws a scramble net over the side and, steadying ourselves, we prepare to climb onboard. Kit bags in one hand, we reach across for the net. Morag and I are the last to leave the small vessel. The boat dips as Morag steps onto the scramble net, her foot going through it, and she hits the side of the ship. With her other leg still on the boat, it moves away from the ship, taking her leg with her.

"Ah'm nae made tae do the splits ..." she yelps, clinging onto the netting.

With my hand covering my mouth, I try not to laugh as she drags her foot off the boat onto the net, pulling her other foot back through the gap. With slow, awkward progress, she climbs to the waiting hands of the crew. Trepidation slithering down my spine, I follow her onto the netting, leaving the little boat to bob on the surface of the water. The two kit bags bang against the side of the ship. It would be easier to leave Pearl's on the small boat, but I can't; if I lose her kit bag, I lose Pearl. It takes twice as long for me to reach the waiting hands. My hair heavy with sweat, my breathing laboured, and my muscles trembling, I push myself up into the waiting arms of the crew. On wobbling legs, I hit the deck, collapsing in a heap next to Morag, her wild red curls frizzing about her face and shoulders.

"Tis as well Matron cannae see us," Morag says, pulling at her dirt-stained uniform and smoothing back her hair.

I smile. "I'm sure, on this occasion, she would be relieved to have her nurses alive, whatever their dishevelled state."

Effie digs her elbow into my side. "So long as it never happens again."

We laugh, more from relief than Effie's joke.

Our journey along the Mediterranean on *HMHS Talamba* is slow, but we are safe, fed, and that's all that matters. It takes over four days before we see land, and when we do, the captain hangs back.

Adah walks over after speaking with several WRNS her face set in hard, worried lines.

"Why aren't we moving?" Effie asks as she reaches us.

"There are dozens of invasion barges and troop-carrying crafts sailing out of Tripoli."

"Oh," Morag and I say as we peer around Adah, not that there is anything to see.

"Are they ours?"

Adah stares at Effie. "No."

"Oh!" Morag and I gasp again, colour draining from our faces.

With little to do, we sit on deck and wait for the all-clear. At 8:30 p.m., we receive the order to disembark. Leaving the *HMHS Talamba* in Tripoli, we travel via road to No. 2 BGH, winding our clocks back an hour. A telegram waits for me when I reach the hospital. It's from Jane Anne.

```
RECEIVED TELEGRAM – STOP – JOHN ED-
WARD DIED IN ACTION – STOP – JANE
ANNE ELLIS NUTMAN
```

The telegram is two months old.

Tears smart. Questions leap into my head. How? Where? When? Does it matter? Answers won't bring John Edward back. Matron wouldn't understand my personal need to address my grief, we deal with death all the time. It's just another emotion that needs burying—that's when the pain hits. With trembling limbs and quivering lips, I walk blindly out the tent. An olive tree sits to the left of the hospital and I quicken my steps, hiding behind it. My back against the tree, I slide to the ground, resting my forehead on my knees, and cry. There are no loud, gasping sobs, just the quiet need to release the emotions inside.

John Edward's face shimmers as I cry. Even with everything I have seen, I can't believe I will never see him again. He now joins Trevor Henry, Uncle Anthony Broadman, and Pearl. Along with all the soldiers that have died under my care. Their numbers are stacking up. A rustling sounds and Morag walks over. In her hand is a crumpled piece of paper. The paper falls, she bends, picks it up. Unravelling it, she reads its contents. She shakes her head, screws the paper up and glances over. With flying feet, she hurtles to me.

"'Tis Fergus ..." She flops down next to me, opening her hands and gazing at the paper. "Why, Lilly?"

Tears line her cheeks, and I throw my arms around her. "I'm sorry ..." I breathe into her neck.

"Do ye think 'twill ever stop?"

"I don't know."

With our handkerchiefs crushed within our fists, we sit until our tears dry and there is nothing but a darkening sky.

Five days after arriving at No. 2 BGH, we are told to ready ourselves for travel. With no destination provided, we pack our kit bags. When *HMHS Talamba* arrives to collect us, it's loaded with patients, and we spend our time caring for them as we travel. None of the patients aboard will return for active duty. Their injuries vary; a large percentage have lost limbs, sight, or are so badly burned they are now classified unfit.

Time moves at a crazy rate, and July brings some interesting developments. Rumours circulate, and on the 10th of July, we learn of Sicily's invasion. This news brings with it the likelihood of our next destination. Confirmation comes on the 18th of July, and the following day we disembark, swapping *HMHS Talamba* for the Royal Navy Hospital Ship *HMHS Tairia*. Delays are commonplace and *Tairia* sits waiting for further instruction. Four days after we board, we're informed the delay is because things 'Aren't going too well.' It is hard to gauge what this means in extent of the wider the war.

Rumours are rife. Some have our troops experiencing resistance. Others say that the Germans and their allies are gaining ground. Are we losing the battle in Sicily? Rumours are always flying about; sometimes they prove resourceful, other times they're nothing more than a red herring. Most of the time, I block them out, then second guess everything. The only thing that matters is the job we are here to do. Tittle-tattle will not assist us when a patient needs their injuries tending to.

Unsure where Joe is, I pray for his safety, and that Alick is back in Scotland. If not, somewhere close to his native land—aboard the troop ship in the English

Channel—out of danger. I also send a plea to God, for those of my brothers that are alive, Arthur James, Brian Wayne, George Peter, and Charles Jason. There is no mention of my disappointment in him over the death of John Edward; I don't want to antagonise God, but the thought is there.

A few days after the rumours start, we set sail, and on the 22nd of July, at 2 p.m., we arrive off Syracuse. The ship hovers outside the harbour, unable to proceed as enemy aircraft whiz about the sky, dropping their bombs. There's a loud BANG … as the first bomb hits the harbour, sending plumes of smoke into the sky. Horrified, we watch the bombing, each BOOM … making us jump. For three hours, our enemy snares us within their nightmare. Powerless, we watch the destruction. The sky clears, and the whirring of enemy aircraft disappears, the engines of the ship rumble to life.

Adah, her arms crossed over her chest, frown lines deepening, talks with an officer, Effie at her side. Morag and I watch with interest as Effie's hand shoots to her mouth, her face whitening.

"Ah wonder what that's aboot," Morag says.

A member of the crew strides over. The officer turns, nods, and walks off. Effie and Adah stay chatting before heading over to where Morag and I sit on deck.

I grab Morag's arm. "Brace yourself, we're about to find out, and from appearances it's not good news."

"Well?" Morag asks as Adah approaches.

"Well what?"

Morag's tongue clicks against the roof of her mouth. "What was the officer sayin'? Ye dinnae look happy."

Adah smiles. "Oh that." She bats a hand, dismissing our concerns. "He was telling me and Effie about how they apprehended twenty-five Italians, taking them prisoner."

"Twenty-five?" I squeak.

Effie giggles. "The shock on your face, Lilly, it's so funny."

"He didn't capture them single-handed," Adah says.

Effie shakes her head as Morag and I gape at them.

"His unit stumbled onto the Italians while finding a suitable cave to treat their wounded." Our faces must be a picture because Adah laughs at us, before continuing, "The Italian soldiers were using the cave as a hideaway."

"He's very proud of the discovery," Effie adds. "It is rather shocking, though. Had the Italians been more prepared, it could have been a different story."

I relax back against the side of the ship. "From your reaction, Effie, I thought it was bad news."

Adah smiles. "It was bad news if you were one of the twenty-five Italian soldiers."

At 5 p.m., we disembark, climbing inside the waiting vehicle to make our way to the nearest Canadian CCS. The sun goes down and rises as we travel. When our transport stops and the doors open, there is a collective groan of relief, and at 7 a.m., on stiff legs, we step from the vehicle.

A group of Canadian sisters wait for us, taking us to our accommodation. "Matron has arranged for breakfast to be served at the Sisters' Mess," one of them says, leaving us to dump our bags and walk over to the Mess.

Five days later, on the 30th of July, we leave the Canadian CCS, with Colonel Johnson leading the way. As we pass through Avola, our driver points out the beaches where the invasion started. Behind us, looking down from its rocky foundation, is the town of Noto. Pearl would have liked Syracuse, with its almond trees and grape vines around terraces of lava. It is nice to see something other than sand. A few hours later, we arrive at a field and, under Matron's careful eye, we erect the tents for the Field Dressing Station, beneath the canopy of olive trees.

"Blimey, he's not wasting time," Effie says, as Colonel Johnson gets in his vehicle and drives back to HQ.

Adah looks up, tent post in hand. "He has to report back and confirm our safe delivery."

With only a few tents erected, the casualties arrive, and we split into two groups. Group one erects the tents, with group two treating the wounded. Morag and I treat the patients, while Effie and Adah continue with the tents. The sun is ferocious and many of the casualties suffer heatstroke before we can get them admitted. If we stop to acknowledge the enormity of our task, it will have us dropping to our knees in defeat, and with no alternative, we carry on. As I move amongst the wounded, I notice a soldier propped beneath an olive tree, his face turned away. At the sound of my footsteps, he stiffens. When I get closer, I understand why. Shrapnel has eaten away most of his face.

My expression never changing, I sit down next to him. "I see you've got yourself a shady spot."

The soldier nods.

It's always difficult remaining unchanged by the horror war brings to our brave soldiers. But it's imperative not to show any distaste for the disfigurement that ravishes and destroys their flesh. While on the outside I never let him see how his wounds affect me, inside I want to cry from the unfairness of it. The smoothness of his hands and the few freckles on his face that are intact tell me he is around his late teens, early twenties. "I can understand why you wouldn't want to give up such a fabulous spot, but I need to get you prepped for surgery."

He tilts his head, and the sun highlights his torn flesh. His hands shake as they hover over his disfigured jaw. Tears sit in his eyes. "They've made me into a monster."

"A monster never shows its true face to the world, it hides behind a normal facade and inspiring speeches. Hitler is the monster, not you."

His tears fall. "Look at me."

"That's exactly what I'm doing, and I see nothing but a brave and good man."

Spit flies from his mouth as he speaks. "No, you don't, you see a hideous beast from a fairy tale."

"No, I see a scared soldier in a lot of pain. I also know that there are surgeons, specialists in their field, that will do everything to rebuild your face. And I know this because I've worked with them. You need to trust them and believe in yourself. A good man doesn't become a monster because of his disfigurement. He remains a good man."

Skin hangs at his jaw, teeth glisten, bone juts out, and his blue eyes stare with self-loathing. "When I go to sleep, all I see is horror painted across the faces of everyone I love, and strangers walking down the street. I'm terrified of the names they'll call me. Of being alone."

"If you weren't, I'd be worried."

He wheezes, his breath whistling through his remaining teeth.

I shuffle closer. "There isn't a day when I'm not afraid. I use it to fuel me. To remind myself that if I ever give up, give into the darkness, that it isn't me I will let down, but those like you, who need me. That's how I find the courage to keep going. You give me that. War has taken a lot from me, my father, brother, uncle, and friends. I'm not prepared to let it take me, or a good man that fears for a future that isn't yet written. There are going to be times when you feel like all the demons in hell are after you, but you never let them have you. You keep fighting because the world needs you and you need it. That's what I keep telling myself, and that's what I need you to do."

The soldier stares into the distance. Around us men moan in pain, and the ambulances keep coming, unloading casualties. QAs work through the injured, the tents standing tall against the backdrop of olive trees. I feel no rush to leave this soldier. His life is as important as those littering the field.

"Will they be able to rebuild my jaw?"

"I've seen it done."

"What about … w-what about my face?"

"That too. Let the surgeons worry about your injuries, you need to think about the man inside. I reckon he needs you more than he needs a handsome face."

He makes a snorting noise. "I never was the good-looking sort."

"Women want ruggedness, not perfection."

"You think?"

"The last time I checked I was a woman, so I guess I'd know."

A gush of air leaves his lungs, and I think he's laughing.

"You ready to get prepped for surgery?"

"As I'm going to be."

The soldier moves, legs shaking under the strain, and I place my shoulder beneath his, arm circling his waist, supporting him. The action reminds me of Alick and our time in the desert. I let the memory wash over me, giving me strength.

"Shall we?" I say, and we walk in silence to the tents.

I signal for a stretcher, and he grabs my hand. "W-will …"

"Have faith, soldier."

His hand drops and they rush him into theatre to stabilise his wounds. Reconstruction will take place at the general hospital. For now, it's a case of patching him up and sending him on his way.

The next day, I arrive on duty to find we've received one hundred casualties during day shift. Beds are hastily being made for the new arrivals. At the far end of the tent, a soldier lies on the narrow cot, staring up at the ceiling. The surgeon has placed him on the Dangerously Ill list. There is nothing medically to be done, other than making him comfortable.

Smile, I remind myself, forcing my lips to curve up as I walk to his cot. His head turns and he watches me make my way.

"Is there anything I can get you, Ernest?" I ask, looking over his medical file.

"No. See to the others. I'm dying, better to spend your time looking after those you can save."

I lay a hand on his forehead, brushing away the hair falling over his face. "I've nothing but time, so why don't I stay a while. The others will still be there later."

Ernest Herman tilts his head at the canvas roof. Wherever his thoughts take him, he is a long way from where his body rests. Disjointed conversations often take place when a soldier is dying; their jumbled thoughts toss around their heads in no particular order. It's tricky stitching them together and making sense of them, but we try. Messages for loved ones entwine within these tumbling thoughts.

"When I first signed up, my grandpa took me to the station. I remember seeing these grown, strange women, all wearing the same clothes. For someone who has never been ill enough to require medical attention, they were a bizarre sight." Phlegm rattles in his throat as he coughs. "So many women, standing around in matching dresses, like school children. Grandpa catches me staring. I'll never forget what he said … 'They're Nightingales, son. When you see a Nightingale, you know you're in safe hands.'" Ernest pauses, catching his breath.

Silence builds and I wait as he struggles to continue. "Grandpa fought during the Great War. It left him with only one leg, but he said it was worth the price to be treated by such tender hands. Without the Nightingales, he would never have survived … I'm the one dying … not losing a leg … and I've no choice but to find me a bench and wait for my grandpa to join me."

Ernest turns his head, his gaze lingering on mine. "When he gets to my bench, I can tell him he was right … I died in safe hands."

His eyelids flutter, and his breathing labours. The noise of passing aircraft overhead makes him shake. His eyes widen, darting about the tent. I move, lying next to him, holding him in my arms, a pillow over his ears to block out the sound. His trembling subsides as the aircraft moves on.

"Thank you …" Ernest catches his breath. "It's good that the last thing I shall remember is the feel of a Nightingale's arms holding me tight." He rattles out a laugh. "Grandpa will be jealous when I tell him, he likes the ladies … Of course, with Grandma around that's all he dares do. She would have the other leg, and then some."

My throat is tight, and I'm incapable of speaking as I take this last journey with him.

"I'm wondering if I might trouble you for a song. I've always loved music. Before the war, I had visions of becoming a pianist, not that I was ever that good, but we all need dreams."

"Do you have a song in mind?"

"*Somewhere Over the Rainbow*. It will be good to have my dreams come true. Maybe I'll be a brilliant pianist when I get to heaven."

Since losing Pearl and Alick leaving, I haven't been able to sing. The magic in a song has gone. There seems little point in singing when there is no enchantment to transport me to another time and place. As I hold this soldier to me, the wonder returns. "Then that is what I shall sing."

When I reach the end of the song, Ernest is limp in my arms. It is time to write to his grandpa and let him know what a courageous grandson he has. Ernest Herman, the soldier with the dream of becoming a brilliant pianist, is dead. His soul leaving the clouds far behind him has gone to a place where his troubles melt like lemon drops. I can understand why he loved *Somewhere Over the Rainbow*; the words are truly poetic.

55

 August 1943, 33rd BGH, Syracuse

*O*n the 20th of August, more QAs arrive at the Field Hospital. Their arrival signals an end to our work here, and we're transported to the 33rd BGH in Syracuse.

"What on earth ..." I exclaim, unprepared to see such a desolate sight.

The 33rd BGH is in disarray. Patients lay on stretchers outside the hospital, waiting to be transported back to the United Kingdom. Ambulances line up, dropping more patients off. Frail bodies, unable to do anything else, lie, waiting to be processed. A Medical Officer, along with a sergeant, walks from the hospital; in the sergeant's hand is a file.

"What do ye suppose they're goin' tae do?" Morag asks.

They walk towards the patients, and the doctor points at each one as the sergeant consults his list.

"They're grading their medical requirements. The list he's got must contain the spare beds on the ward, see." I point to the sergeant. Someone chalks a number onto the stretcher, and the sergeant nods, updating his list. Two orderlies arrive, carrying off the patient for treatment.

Next to me, Adah sucks in her breath. "No point in standing here, we'd best get to the ward."

Inside the hospital, they record the stretchered soldiers' details and, once their records are up to date, they're removed to the ward. Morag and I help the orderlies undress the patients, wash them down, dressing them in clean pyjamas. We provide a cup of tea to those not requiring immediate attention. Those that can speak say thank you, others nod. Once this is done, we leave them to sleep. As we work, the reason for the buildup of patients becomes clear. The hospital ships aren't arriving to take them back to the United Kingdom, so they pile up outside.

I gaze down at my swelling ankles as I move to the next patient. With my uniform getting tighter, I'm at the stage where I won't be able to hide my pregnancy much longer. Last month, encouraged by Morag, I ditched my old uniform for Pearl's, but even that is getting tight around my swelling abdomen. Out of options, it is time to face Matron's wrath.

"Why do women feel the need to have babies?" Matron asks, sitting at her desk.

Matron Margaret Stewart is a spinster in her fifties. Hair scraped back from her square face in a tight bun, the silvery strands heighten her hawk-like features. Her pen falls onto the table and her heavy-set glasses slide to the end of her nose, which wrinkles in disapproval. Even though I'm standing and a good foot taller, Matron glares down at me, back iron-rod straight, her lips compressing with annoyance. I stand at the other side of her desk, wondering if it is a rhetorical question or if she's waiting for an answer. It's not like I wanted a baby during wartime, more of one thing leading to another—and, well, there is now no wanting anything, other than a healthy baby.

"My husband and I didn't plan—"

"That's obvious," she grinds out, cutting me off. "We are in the middle of a war, Sister Lawrence. Nurses are in short supply, and you took it upon yourself to get pregnant."

The sigh I'm longing to expel stays trapped within my trachea. Alick and I, we didn't think—and that, as they say, is the problem.

"Men have only one thing on their minds, Sister Lawrence. It is up to the woman to prevent such distractions."

Have I now failed as a woman?

When Alick and I made love, it wasn't just him with one thing on his mind, mine was there along with his.

"Look out the window, sister, what do you see?" She doesn't wait for an answer. "Ninety soldiers all waiting to go home. Your pregnancy only adds to that number. With the German U-boats sinking the hospital ships in the Mediterranean, our ships aren't getting through."

What Matron is saying makes little sense. The Geneva Convention protects the work of the Red Cross. Unable to utter a word and interrupt her mid-flow, I blink. I must have heard her wrong—German U-boats sinking the hospital ships … it's too diabolical to consider. Since becoming pregnant, my brain gets foggy, that is what it is, I've misheard.

"The allocation for the next hospital ship is twenty. That's if we are lucky and it reaches us. With the number of incapacitated soldiers growing daily, you're adding to the burden," she spits out, her hand dropping to the table. "You can't stay here. Soldiers don't need to be tended by or see a pregnant woman. They've already suffered enough."

Incapable of understanding how my pregnancy will cause suffering to the soldiers, I remain mute.

"When the next hospital ship arrives, you will leave with it. Don't be expecting a free, lazy journey back to the United Kingdom. You're expected to continue with your duties here and onboard the hospital ship until demobilised. Do I make myself clear?"

"Yes, Matron."

"Change your uniform, you're busting out at the seams. I won't have untidiness at my hospital, sister. See if one of the other sisters can lend you one of their spares."

"Yes, Matron," I say, nervously rotating my wedding ring.

Her lips suck in, and with a displeased expression, she picks up her pen. "Don't expect any special treatment. You attend your shift, appropriately dressed, on time, and carrying out your normal duties. If you are required to work over, you work over."

"Yes, Matron."

Her head lowers, and it appears I am dismissed.

The door clicks behind me, and I breathe, leaning against it, my head resting on the wood. Morag stands in the hall, pacing. She turns as the latch clicks.

"Let's get somethin' tae eat, worry makes me hungry," she says.

My hand resting on my stomach, we head over to the Sisters' Mess.

"All things considered, it went reasonably well," I say.

In the Mess, Adah sits in the corner with Effie. I flop down on the seat next to her.

"You look like you've lost a shilling," Adah says.

"I've just told Matron I'm pregnant."

Effie spins in her chair. "You're what?"

"Lilly said she's pregnant, Effie, now keep your voice down. I'm sure she doesn't need everyone knowing."

Effie's cheeks redden at her sister's rebuff. "Sorry."

"Don't worry," I say with a shrug.

Hands on the table, Effie leans closer, keeping her voice low. "You were only with Joe one night before we left."

"Effie! Don't be rude." Adah sends her a hard stare.

"I meant nothing by it."

My arms folding over my chest, I try not to slide down in my seat, appearing sulky. It's not as if I'm not expecting this question. "Don't worry, I'm sure others will say the same thing. But once is all it takes."

"How did Matron take the news?" Adah asks.

"Like a malnourished tiger sensing its next meal," I sigh. "I'm letting everyone down, selfish, and why did I want a baby when there's a war on." I use my fingers to tick off Matron's list. "There will be no special treatment, I'm not allowed to be anything but immaculate. I need a larger uniform because of the strain on the seams of mine. Oh … and she's sending me home on the next hospital ship." I shrug. "Other than that, I've still got my head."

Effie's jaw drops in horror. "Wasn't she the least bit pleased for you?"

"Matron's too inconvenienced to be pleased."

Adah rests a hand on my arm. "We're happy for you, Lilly."

"We can be aunties." Effie waves her hand at everyone. "I'll be Auntie Ef, Auntie Adah, and Auntie Mo … Where is Morag?" Effie turns in her chair, looking over the Mess.

"She's getting some food … here she comes," I say.

Effie points at the entrance. "There's no food, and she doesn't seem happy."

Morag walks into the Sisters' Mess, her face void of colour. She sits next to me, staring ahead. Her continued silence causes my skin to pinch. Effie has lost her colouring, and Adah's hands lay still on the table.

"Morag?" I say, my voice tentative.

"The Germans have sunk the *Talamba*," Morag exclaims. "It went down off Sicily. She was loadin' patients, there are na survivors."

Adah gasps. "Goodness, how awful."

My hand covers my mouth, and my lungs deflate.

Effie shakes her head. "I don't understand, the *Talamba* was brightly lit, clearly marked with the Red Cross, identifying her as a hospital ship—she's under protection." Fear clouds her features and she takes a steadying breath.

"What's happening out there?"

We sit in silence as Adah's question floats about the space between us.

"Have the Germans taken it upon themselves to operate outside the Geneva Convention? Oh dear …" Fingers flying about her, Adah makes the sign of the cross. "May God rest their souls."

Dumfounded, I stare at Morag. "Matron was saying something about German U-boats sinking hospital ships. With my head the way it is, I thought I'd misheard her. Or that she meant the ships were being sunk in crossfire. It never occurred that German U-boats were targeting our hospital ships."

"That explains why patients are lining up outside," Effie says, more to herself than for general comment.

"Well, there's nothing we can do about the situation."

We all stare at Adah.

"Let's concentrate on Lilly's good news. What about baby names?" Adah asks.

"N-names?"

"You can't go around calling it Baby," Effie says.

"No. I don't suppose I can." I tilt my head, mulling over names. "If it's a girl, I'd like to call her Pearl."

Morag beams. "That's a crackin' idea. Ah'm sure Joe will like it."

"What happens if it's a boy?" Effie asks.

"I can't think of a boy's name, so that's it, I'm having a girl."

Morag smiles in sympathy. "It dinnae work like that, Lilly."

"No matter, I'll cross that bridge when I get there, but for now, my baby is called Pearl."

"If it's a boy and you name him Pearl, he's going to be a tough bugger. I hate to think of the fights he'll get into." Adah holds out her hand. "Hello, my name's Pearl …" Her voice is deep.

"Maybe you could call him Peter. It sounds a bit like Pearl."

We stare at Effie and burst out laughing.

My stomach jiggles like a bowl of blancmange. A loud hiccup escapes, and I place my hand against my lips. Morag snorts, snot colliding with her tears, which has me laughing even more. Effie giggles, holding onto her sides, while Adah smiles at us. Nurses turn in their chairs, staring, and our laughter increases.

Several weeks later, new orders send Morag, Adah, and Effie to the 66th BGH. Even though we knew this would happen, it leaves us miserable. I sit on my bed, watching Morag pack her things, loneliness engulfing me. Clad in her battledress khaki trousers and jacket, her red hair tied at her neck, she sniffs.

"Ye're goin' tae be alright withoot me, aren't ye?"

I nod. We don't have a choice.

"Dinnae do anythin' silly, 'n' remember tae take care of yerself 'n' Pearl." Her hand taps my swelling belly. She flops down next to me on the bed. "Ah cannae believe ah'm leavin' ye. It feels wrong, Lilly. Matron is bein' mean sendin' ye haime."

Trying to appear brave, I smile at her. "Don't mind me and Pearl, we'll be fine. Just take care of you and make sure you come back all in one piece."

"Ah dinnae like it."

"Neither do I, but orders …"

"Are orders," she finishes.

We hug, tears rolling down our faces.

I pull her away. "I love you, Morag. You're more than a friend, we are sisters."

Morag throws her arms around me. "Oh, Lilly."

We don't mention Pearl's name, but I know we're both thinking about her.

"Morag!" Adah hisses, walking into the tent. "We need to get off."

"Here." I hand Morag my handkerchief. "You'd best tidy yourself up and get going."

Morag kisses my cheek, taking the handkerchief.

When she's gone, I sit on the cot, alone, wondering how life got so dishevelled.

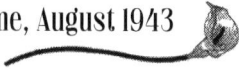

Dear Jane Anne,

I received your telegram, two months after you sent it. This war is taking so much, it sometimes seems there is nothing ahead but sorrow. It's difficult to think of John Edward as dead; he was always full of mischief and cunning plans. I wish we could share our grief and help each other heal. When the tears come, I remember John Edward as he was when I was nine, and how he teased me about the book Father Christmas gave me, *Winnie The Pooh*. John Edward said I was too old for reading such stories and believing in something as stupid as a teddy bear. I was very cross at him and ate my Christmas pudding, even though I hate it, just because he wanted it. He called me a piggy and hoped the big bad wolf would eat me up. On Boxing Day, my book went missing. I searched the house and couldn't find it. Later that day, I caught him sprawled over the bed reading *Winnie The Pooh*! He said he wanted to know what all the fuss was about. *Winnie The Pooh* had woven his magic over John Edward, and I smiled in triumph, asking him to read it to me. Despite his protests and groans, he turned the page and began reading. That was so like John Edward. Too scared to admit he had a vulnerable side.

Life is hard at the 33rd General British Hospital. Morag, Effie, and Adah have left, and I am alone. The only thing left is memories. Matron is a hag; she has an aversion to pregnant women and wants me gone. Until then she treats me unkindly. Her viciousness washes away, my head is full, and I have no space for her harsh words. Let her tell me to "Tidy myself up", that "I'm slow and need to pull my socks up and work", and that "I'm so fat I can't fit between the beds". They're words, nothing more. Memories take me to happier places where even the most venomous words can't touch me.

When the cracks appear, I hear Alick calling "Nightingale", and I'm swept back to the desert, where time stops and only love exists. I miss him so much. It will be this way until I die.

Lillian Elizabeth

56

 September 1943, 33ᴿᴰ BGH, Syracuse

*H*ow to sum up what has been happening and why I am being sent home in a few short sentences? The crumpled paper in my hand does just that; my telegram to Jane Anne is direct and brief. If only it were possible to sum up feelings as abruptly. Despite my assurances to Morag when she left with Effie and Adah and the other QAs to the 66th BGH, I am not doing so well, nor do I want to be shipped off home. But as the saying goes, what you want and what you get are two different things. I unravel the paper and read it one more time. It will have to suffice—I've sent it, therefore there is no changing it.

ARRIVING HOME – STOP – POSSIBLE END
OF OCTOBER – STOP – MARRIED AND PREG-
NANT – STOP – LILLIAN ELIZABETH LAW-
RENCE

What more is there to say? Married. Pregnant. Sent home.

It is my turn to leave the 33rd BGH, and the venomous tongue of Matron and her cronies, who gather round her like an Egyptian vulture. Some Egyptians call the vulture the white scavenger or pharaoh's chicken—both are apt when describing Matron and her leeches. On the 11th of September, I receive word from Joe. His letter is cheery, containing nothing about the war or his location; instead, he focuses on our life together when the war ends. His grandfather died in late January 1939, leaving him a cottage called Seagull's Rest in Stonehaven, Scotland. I'm not altogether sure how I feel about moving to Scotland, but then I appear to have little choice. Let us hope life at Seagull's Rest will prove better than it has been over the last few years.

For the first time since Joe and I parted, I write, letting him know I am to sail back to the United Kingdom on the next hospital ship, *HMHS St David*. I tried to keep my letter buoyant, even though I'm missing Morag, Adah, and Effie. Despite my apprehension over Joe's notion of moving to Scotland, my letter remains positive on the subject. He deserves that. Pregnant with another man's child leaves little room for pickiness. Women's roles may evolve, but we are a long way off being viewed as equals. I won't lie and pretend I haven't considered that a move to Scotland will bring me closer to Alick. Scotland is sizeable, and it's not to say Stonehaven is anywhere near Alick, but the thought has crossed my mind, making the move more comforting.

At my feet rests mine and Pearl's kit bags. I'm not leaving it behind for someone to rummage through, take what they want, and discard. Morag can't lug it about with her, and it will be safer on the hospital ship, German U-boats allowing. When I walk outside, patients wait to embark. Few stand, most lay on a litter.

A sister walks over, a well-practised smile on her face. She does not comment on my condition, and her eyes don't linger on my expanding waist. "Good, you're here. Come with me and we'll get you settled, and you can assist with the patients."

It is the first time I have met a stranger, where, with one glance, they know they have the right person. My hand rests on Pearl, knowing she is the one the nurse recognised, not me. With my two kit bags banging against my legs, I board *HMHS St David*. With the patients boarding, there is no time to unpack, and I leave them sitting on the cot in my room as I make my way to the hospital. Patient beds contain a hard base with a mattress covering. There are cages at each side, unlike those on the *Duchess of Richmond*, which were hammock style and steel rods at either side of the bed. The cages prevent patients from falling out during high seas. The thought of the ship dipping and rocking over rough waves makes me queasy, sea sickness threatening before we set sail. A deep breath refocuses my mind on the patients, settling my stomach. Six hours after boarding, we set sail for the United Kingdom; whereabouts that will be remains to be seen. The United Kingdom may be an island, and compared to some countries, small, but when travelling around it, it is vast.

When I was a child, the journey home was longer than on the way there. Whether this is because of excitement being replaced with boredom on the way home, I can't say. What I know is that this journey is already taking forever, and it's been less than twenty-four hours since boarding.

On the 13th of September, the day after leaving the 33rd BGH, Matron informs us that the Italians have bombed *HMHS Newfoundland*, which was bound for Salerno. One hundred American nurses were on board. She stands with her arms behind her back, a staunch expression on her face. "Carriers *Leinster* and *St Andrew* came to *HMHS Newfoundland*'s rescue. Sixty patients made it onboard *Leinster*, with most of the American nurses. Matron, five of her sisters, eight orderlies, and nineteen crew members died. Let us remember them in our prayers."

Maud's hand sticks in the air, her olive skin waving at Matron. "Was it a direct attack by the Italians, Matron?"

With a soured expression, Matron's lips purse as she stares at Maud. Maud Heslop is twenty and comes from Spanish grandparents. Her mother is Spanish and her father British. She has a head of long black hair that waves about her shoulders when not on duty, and dark brown eyes. At five-four, we are the same height.

"When the American nurses boarded *Newfoundland*, they were carrying spades and picks. It is possible that a passing enemy scout saw them with their equipment. Dressed in khakis, they mistook their spades for rifles," Matron says, her voice clipped, signalling her displeasure at being interrupted.

Maud huffs out her disagreement at my side.

Unaware of Maud's disbelief, Matron surveys the sisters under her command. "It is possible that the Italians believed the hospital ship's position under the Geneva Convention was being abused."

A chill of apprehension slithers down my spine.

"That she was transporting troops, which is why they attacked."

As Matron finishes, we stare at her. The absurdity of what she said has us reeling in anger.

Shocked whispers lace the air. A sister from behind gasps. "How dare they insinuate such terrible things. They are the cowards, not us and our allies. I received a letter from my Bobby telling me how the Germans were using ambulances to gun down our troops."

A series of deep inhales and gasps follow this shocking news.

"That's enough!" Matron's sharp tone cuts through the throng, demanding silence. We obey. "We don't know if the attack was intentional. Let's stick to the facts and be vigilant. As is often the case, our patients will learn of what has happened. We must reassure them, and above all keep them calm and safe."

I rub my belly silently, telling Pearl not to worry, Mummy is going to look after her. Unsure how to guarantee our safety, the burden of motherhood hits. Let us hope there are no enemy U-boats or aircraft out there looking for an excuse to exterminate another hospital ship. I don't want to let Pearl down before she's born.

Matron's news makes sleep elusive. My body aches in places it has no business hurting. Not designed for pregnant women, the narrow beds offer little comfort. Nor are pregnant women designed for speed. Our first air raid warning comes a week into our voyage. With tin hats and gas masks, we run to the meeting point. My run is more of a waddle. Matron doesn't comment; she doesn't have to. Her lips roll back in disapproval, and she resembles the Big Bad Wolf. If she had fangs, saliva would drip from them. Two hours later, the all-clear comes and it's back to our posts.

As we leave the warmer climates behind, we also experience harsher weather. The waves lash at the ship. Where before they were a gentle kiss, now they batter us. *HMHS St David* dips and rises as it rides the high waves. For weeks the sea thrashes the ship. Objects move of their own accord, and most of our time we spend searching for equipment that has no right moving. Our stomachs flip, and appetites diminish. Seasickness is a relentless beast, leaving many incapacitated and in retching misery.

We also live in fear of discovery. Matron Margaret Stewart at the 33rd BGH is a pussycat compared to Matron Violet Juliet Franklin. Authority has gone to her head. In her mid-forties, with jet black hair, chiselled features, and a wiry frame, she patrols the ship hospital, corridors, wards, and deck like a scorpion, tail poised for the offensive. Despite the ship's pitching, Matron's shoes stick to the floor like suction pads. Not even the wind ruffles her hair. I'd love to see her vomit, just once, so I knew she was human. Her skin colour doesn't change and there's no retching noise coming from her cabin. It's positively ghastly for her to remain in such good health. Around us sisters move, their hands covering their mouths, relieving the contents of their stomachs, unaware of Matron patrolling deck.

I tug Maud's shoulder as she leans over the railing, her hair flying about her cap. She groans as another wave of sickness hits. "Maud, it's Matron," I whisper as loud as I dare.

Trapped within her wretchedness, Maud ignores my warning. Her head tipped, staring at the frothing waves. My stomach lurches as the ship rises and falls. Two meters separate Maud from Matron. With no other choice, I try to swallow down the bile.

Matron stops at Maud's side, arching a bushy black eyebrow at me—I stare mutely back. Silence my only form of defence.

"Sister Maud?"

At the sound of Matron's clipped tone, Maud stiffens under my fingertips. In slow motion, she straightens, drawing an unsteady hand across her mouth, wiping away the bile.

"Nurses do not vomit, Sister Maud. They remain focused, poised, and ready for action." Matron's gaze travels over her. She sniffs, her lips pursing in disgust. "Get cleaned up, and remember the next time you want to vomit, you do not do so until you are on UK soil, and behind closed doors."

Tears swim in Maud's eyes, and her cheeks puff. For an awful second, I'm convinced she's going to throw up over Matron. It is a horrifying and amusing thought— poor Maud. My lips twitch and Matron glances my way. I dip my head, and Pearl moves beneath my hand—I swear she's laughing for me.

Matron's angled chin sweeps Maud's way. "Is there any reason you're still here?"

The green tinge leaves Maud's face, taking with it all colour. "No, Matron. Sorry, Matron." Maud scampers, her gait lengthening, her legs moving rapidly along the deck.

"Sister Lillian, do you not have somewhere you need to be, other than cluttering up the deck?"

Wordless, I nod, stepping away. Even though I'm off duty and allowed to litter the deck, I don't bring this to Matron's attention.

There is no resemblance between my maiden voyage from Liverpool in 1942 and now. With no entertainment committee, or evenings spent dancing and singing, time passes at a sluggish and monotonous pace. The closer to the United Kingdom we get, the colder and wetter it becomes. "Hand in hand we come ..." I say to Pearl.

It's the opening line in *Winnie the Pooh*.

Perhaps not hand in hand, but still together, Pearl and I approach England.

Kit bags at my side, I wait to disembark. "Well, Pearl, here we go. Let's wish ourselves luck."

Overcrowded, the train to London offers little comfort. I find a seat in a carriage with five other passengers. Crammed like sardines in a can, they give a lengthy sigh when they see me approach. Pressed against the blackout window, my kit bags in the overhead compartment, I face a woman in her mid-fifties. She frowns at me before continuing her knitting, the needles clicking together as the yarn spins in her bag. Pearl hiccups and my stomach wobbles. She sends me a sharp look, her eyes lingering on my stomach as she pushes her glasses onto the bridge of her nose, omitting a drawn-out sniff. It is the first time I have ever been so heavily criticised by a snivel. The man next to her moves the paper to one side. He stares, his gaze taking in my brown brogue shoes and the khaki trousers of my battledress. Head shaking, he buries it back behind the paper.

A boy looks up at his mum, pointing. "How come she's so fat with rationing in place?"

His mother sends him a sharp glance. "It's rude to point, Humphrey."

"But …"

"Humphrey!"

At the sharpness of his mother's tone, the boy becomes sullen, clamping his mouth shut and folding his arms over his chest with a huff. His sister stares, her eyes glued onto my belly.

I twiddle my wedding band, trying not to let their attitudes bother me.

The train trundles along, the rocking motion making my eyelids droop. I wake yawning, stretching out my back. Pushing the sleeve of my jacket to look at my watch, I'm amazed to find I've slept for over two hours. Soon after waking, the train pulls into Waterloo Station, London.

Letter Home, September 1943

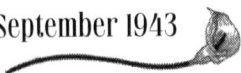

Dear Jane Anne,

This is the last letter I will write. It's like saying goodbye to an old friend. These letters are an extension of myself and my diary. They are not just letters to you, but letters to me. A chance for me to sieve through the niggles swirling around my head, like a bothersome fly. Over the last few years, I've learnt a lot about myself. I shall miss the innocent woman who started this journey to nurse our soldiers, not realising that in the process she would become obsolete.

I never joined the Territorial Army Nursing Services to fall in love. Love is such a strange emotion. It has brought me happiness and sorrow. And made me realise that the heart can love people differently. My life is no longer mine to control. What I do now, I do for Pearl. It is a life of many sacrifices, but I shall hold on to the belief that what I sacrifice now, I shall gain back in death. For Alick and I will reunite. The circumstances of our union and the wait doesn't bother me, it's enough to know we will be together. I've experienced death many times, and for some it has come as a release. I would like to think that, when I die, it is with the same contentment in which Ernest Herman passed. To fly over the rainbow to a new and beautiful beginning. My main concern is whether, when we meet again, Alick can forgive me for not telling him about Pearl. I shall wait and see.

The problem with change is uncertainty. While Joe looks forward to life at Seagull's Rest, in Scotland, the notion sits like a solid and uncomfortable weight in my stomach. Life in Scotland will remind me of Alick. Joe has my heart. He is the dearest man I have ever met. You will love him as much as I when you meet him. Wherever Joe and I live, we will be happy. I won't let Scotland change that.

The journey back home has been tough. I thought I would make this trip with Pearl and Morag. But Pearl is dead. I tell myself this constantly. It still feels unreal, no matter the time that passes. What I take from this war is the knowledge I made a difference to so many brave men. Florence Nightingale helped to change how we treat the wounded, modernising nursing forever. While war has taken us closer to the battlefield, we have upheld what Florence Nightingale taught us. This fills me with immense pride. The satisfaction of helping those that fight so valiantly brings some peace against the horrors I have seen.

I fear I'm getting nostalgic, so I shall leave it there, and bid you farewell.

Lillian Elizabeth

57

 October 1943, London, England

*I*n no rush to see Jane Anne, I leave the train station, catching the bus. Re-equating myself with London, I walk the streets, kit bag in each hand. I'm a solitary figure reattaching itself to the place I once called home, and I gaze at London with fresh eyes. A man sits on rubble, a cigarette pressed between his lips. Dirt covers his black suit, the knees on his trousers are threadbare, and his flat cap sits at an odd angle on his head. In his left hand he holds a photograph, in the other a bunch of wilted flowers. Tears roll down his cheeks. Mixed within the rubble, an overturned chair, its legs protruding, sticking up in the air. Curtains cling to poles, and a Singer sewing machine pokes from tumbled bricks, the large wheel at the back of the machine jutting out. The man raises his head. In one sweeping glance, he takes in the khaki cloth of my battledress, and the white band containing the red cross on the arm of my jacket. He tips his hat, and I walk on, leaving him to his thoughts. When a bomb lands it doesn't just take earth, vehicles, and buildings with it, it takes life, crushing the heart. The stain of the Luftwaffe remains, even though their presence over London dwindled in 1941.

Large cranes line the docklands. Along the side of a building, the ground slopes, wood, tins, and concrete scattering into newly formed crevices. Outside, workers stand talking, black aprons tied around their waist. They puff at their cigarettes, smoke shooting out from their nose. A gust of laughter makes me jump. It sounds wrong against the backdrop of destruction. Devastation is everywhere. It's hard not to feel the loss and misery caused by the bombings. Being posted abroad has shielded me from London's pain. It is one thing to hear of the bombing, another to see it. I'm surprised to find the picture I carry of this wondrous city, until now, remained unspoiled, despite the bombing on the 23rd of August 1940. Here, there is no protection from the damage the German planes wrought. My eyes are forever open.

Houses stand without fencing, the metal melted and reformed into weaponry to use against the Nazis and their allies. The sound of children playing is sparse, and the quietness of the streets eerie. On the 7th of September 1940, German planes flew over London and for two hours they bombed the city, turning the sky black with the smoke of burning buildings. The photographs printed in the newspapers do little to portray the terror Londoners faced. They are a snapshot in time—a small representation of what happened. Like life on the battlefield, photographs will never tell the full story. It will present a token of the horror that the soldiers face each day.

I have seen enough bodies to know we can't stitch everything back together. Under the scars, hidden from view, is a vortex of emotions that cannot be suppressed. They come without warning when the mind snaps and, once again, memories take them back to that horrifying moment in time. I have held many soldiers as these memories flood their minds, leaving the safety they found when they saw my uniform.

How many of my sisters will relive the terrors they have seen? A face that no longer looks human, a body badly torn apart, bone protruding from flesh, limbs so horribly infected the only option is to amputate. Still, it is nothing compared to what a soldier faces when they look in the mirror. Clouds darken to grey, thunder sounds and lightning shoots across the sky. Like tiny needles, rain falls, bouncing off the pavement, soaking through my clothes. I have dallied long enough. It is time to make my way home—to face Jane Anne.

The street leading to my family home remains the same, with no sign of bombing. It is the first time I can recall walking down the street where I can hear my shoes beat against the pavement. Even on a rainy day, people wandered with purpose. Today, the street is barren. Since leaving to take up my duty as a war nurse, the uncomfortable question of whether to knock or walk inside Jane Anne's house has risen. Today, pondering my actions, I knock. Charles Jason opens the door, leaning on his crutch, his shirt sleeves rolled to his elbows.

At seeing me, he lifts his eyebrows in surprise. "Blimey, Lillian Elizabeth, you've put some weight on."

My lips twitch. "One too many bully sandwiches, I'm afraid. They should put a health warning on them."

"I didn't think it was possible to put that much weight on from eating corned beef."

"It's not the corned beef that's the problem, Charles Jason, it's the bread. It bloats you." My cheeks puff out.

"Really?"

"No, you idiot, I'm pregnant."

Footsteps sound behind him and Jane Anne peers over his shoulder. Her hair is shorter, in the style of Princess Elizabeth. A red scarf pulls it away from her face. "Move out the way and let your sister inside."

Charles Jason grins. "It's good to have you home."

Jane Anne taps the back of his head. "Manners, young man, you lost your leg, not your ability to think."

He rubs his head. "Ow."

"Stop complaining, I didn't tap that napper of yours that hard. I wouldn't want to damage that brain of yours. Not that it does much thinking."

The air of friendly banter takes me by surprise.

Charles Jason smiles. "She's mellowing."

"So I see."

"Be a gentleman, Charles Jason, and get your sister's bags."

"That's ok, I can manage."

"You'll do no such thing, not when there's a man around to do the heavy lifting. Women need to take care of themselves, especially when they're in your condition." Jane Anne shakes her head as she looks at my brother. "I swear his brain was in that leg you removed. Unless he's making furniture, it does little else."

He shrugs. "I keep telling her I'm being conservative. I don't want to wear my brain out before I'm forty."

Jane Anne huffs from the back room. "Her? Who's her? The cat's mother?"

"Sorry … Jane Anne."

She folds her arms over her chest. "That's enough cheek from you. Put the kettle on and let your Aunt Sarah Rebeca know Lillian Elizabeth is home."

The house looks the same. Same table, wallpaper, and chairs, but the occupants have changed.

"Sit down, Lillian Elizabeth, you're making the place appear untidy," Jane Anne says, waving a hand at the table. "Your brother will take your bags upstairs if he ever gets that kettle on."

Aunt Sarah Rebeca comes running through the house, smoothing the skirt of her dress down. "Sorry, you caught me on the loo."

My mother's lips come together in a tight line. "Really, must you be so vulgar?"

"I wasn't being vulgar, it's a natural bodily function."

"Don't argue, remember who's the eldest."

Aunt Sarah Rebeca's shoulders hug her ears as she giggles at her sister.

"Sit," Jane Anne says, pulling out a chair near the back wall.

The cushion slides as I sit down, and my back hits the frame; pregnancy is making me as graceful as a hippopotamus.

My aunt sits next to me, her hand covering mine. "It's lovely to have you home."

I smile. "Thanks."

Jane Anne rocks back in her chair, peering at Charles Jason as he busies about the kitchen. "Don't forget the biscuits. Your sister's had a long journey, she's hungry and tired."

He puts the teapot on the table and runs back into the kitchen, the crutch tapping against the floor, returning with an old tea caddy. On the outside of the caddy, King George VI stares into the distance. I've always wondered what he was deliberating over when they took the picture. Jane Anne picks up the caddy, handing it to me. Inside the tin are six Marie biscuits, the name stamped on each of the round rusks. With rationing still in place and unlikely to be lifted soon, I take a biscuit, placing it on the saucer. It slides towards the cup, ready to be dunked. When everyone has a biscuit, we nibble at the wet edges, savouring each bite.

"So, what are your plans, once you've had the baby?" Charles Jason asks, biscuit rotating round his mouth.

A distasteful look falls over Jane Anne's face. "Swallow your food before talking, young man. If Trevor Henry was here, he'd be taking you into the backyard to teach you some manners."

He swallows the biscuit but doesn't correct her. Unlike a lot of parents, Trevor Henry never believed in using his belt as punishment.

"I'm hoping to resume my nursing."

Jane Anne's teacup clatters against the saucer. "That's all good, Lillian Elizabeth, but what about your baby?" I open my mouth to respond, but her hand is already in the air, cutting me off. "Babies don't look after themselves."

"I'll take care of the baby."

Aunt Sarah Rebeca receives a hard stare from her sister.

"A baby needs its mother, not its aunt. I was at home for all my children, no one can ever say I was off gallivanting here, there and everywhere."

True, but we couldn't say she was always there for us, either.

"Do you have a hospital in mind?" Charles Jason asks.

"I was thinking of trying St Thomas and Guy's hospital, given its central location."

Recognising the stubborn tilt of my jaw, Jane Anne sighs. "The Germans bombed St Thomas, striking it twice. The first bomb hit the hospital on the eighth of September, the second on the ninth. Ten staff died along with two auxiliary firefighters. I appreciate that we've had no air raids since 1942, but it doesn't mean the Germans won't be back to finish the job. Don't go throwing caution to the wind, young lady. You're a mother first, a nurse second."

"Nurses of Lillian Elizabeth's calibre and experience are in short supply," Aunt Sarah Rebeca says. "Why, only the other day, Joyce was saying how her daughter, Lesley, was helping in the operating theatre at St Thomas and Guy's hospital. Lesley finished her training in 1940. Her mother says she's like a fish out of water, the poor thing." Her gaze sliding in her sister's direction, she nervously licks at her lips. "Lesley said they've moved the theatre to the basement, for safety reasons. If the Germans come back, Lilly will be safe in the hospital's basement. It's the same as being inside an air raid shelter."

Teeth locking together at the abbreviation of my name, my mother snorts out her displeasure like a bull.

"It's Lillian Elizabeth … and I'm more than aware of the shortage of nurses. But it doesn't change the fact that recklessness breeds carelessness. This war is far from over, the Germans will strike again. What do we tell a baby who will never know its mother? Sorry? I'm not suggesting Lillian Elizabeth sits at home twiddling her thumbs, there is plenty to be done here."

Charles Jason slaps his hands together, crumbs falling onto the table. "Why don't we wait until the baby's born before we give her a hard time over where she's to work, or what's best for the child?"

Jane Anne pouts, raising the teacup to her lips.

I send him a grateful smile.

"Pearl is due on the tenth of March," I say naturally, adding a month onto the due date; it's not unusual for babies to be born early.

Jane Anne takes a sharp breath. "Pearl? Is that it? It's rather short. What happens if it's a boy, you can't name him Pearl. That's … that's … outrageous. What will people say?"

I shrug. "I have a feeling I'm having a girl. I can't think of a boy's name, and Pearl sounds right. Pearl Alexandra Lawrence."

"Oh, that's so sweet, naming your baby after Queen Alexandra."

If only my aunt knew Alexandra is for her father, Alick, but, as they say, ignorance is bliss.

58

 October 1943, London, England

*T*he house is silent as I lay in bed, staring up at the shadows running over the ceiling. Outside, a bin topples over, its metal carcass rattling along the concrete. A high-pitched meow echoes above the vibration of metal. After so long sleeping in a room full of women, though small, my old bedroom is vast, the silence oppressive. Other than the cat that had the mishap with the bin, there is no other sound. Bombs don't land, gunfire doesn't coat the air with sulphur, and planes don't fly overhead. I never realised how accustomed I'd become to the sound of war; without it, sleep is transient.

I don't remember falling asleep, I only know when I see Alick that I am dreaming. *He's smiling at me, a black dog at his side. Where the dog fits into my dream, I have no clue, but it's there. He holds out his arms and I realise I'm carrying a baby. Though I can't see the baby's face, I think it's Pearl. From behind Alick, a man appears. He lifts his right arm, in his hand is a gun. There's a BANG ... Pearl falls from my arms and I leap forward, grabbing her, and we tumble to the ground. A blanket covers her face and I move it away. Pearl stares at me. She's no longer a baby, but Pearl, my friend.*

"Where were you when I needed you? With Alick, that's where you were, Lilly, making love to Alick."

Blood falls from her mouth. She gurgles. Accusation stares from within a death mask.

"Pearl! Pearl! No, Pearl!" I scream at her.

She doesn't move.

"Pearl, please."

She needs to know it wasn't like that.

Me and Alick, it happened after—I didn't abandon her.

I wish the bullet had hit me.

If I could trade places…

"Pearl. Pearl, if we could swap places, I would … I would…"

Winnie the Pooh sits behind her. He tilts his head, looking up at the sky.

"I wonder how many wishes a star can give," Pooh says, staring at the twinkling stars.

Fingers bite into my shoulders. Darkness pulls me away from Pearl.

"Lillian Elizabeth!"

My eyes snap open. Jane Anne grips my shoulders, pulling me to her. "It's alright, Lillian Elizabeth, you're home. No one's going to hurt you."

I fling my arms around her neck, burying my head into her shoulder. Tears roll down my face, soaking into her thick cotton pyjama top.

"It was just a dream."

A dream … I shake … It was just a dream …

"Come on, let's get you tucked up and keep you nice and warm." She draws the blankets up to my chin.

"Will you stay a while?"

She looks unsure. "Yes, of course."

The bed dips as she sits on the edge, and I move over to give her more room. She picks up the book on the nightstand. My head on her lap, she opens *Winnie The Pooh* and reads. I've waited a long time for my mother to be a mother. For the fictional creature that most children have to love me. To feel the safety and comfort that a mother brings to her children—even when there is no safety, and comfort only lasts until the next nightmare. With a ghost of a smile on my lips, eyelids drooping, I revel in the warmth of my mother's love.

"Good morning, Christopher Robin," he said.

"Good morning, Winnie the Pooh," said you.

Jane Anne's voice follows me to sleep.

59

 February 1944, London, England

*P*ush!" Jane Anne shouts at me.

My teeth grit together, and I flop back on the bed as the contraction fades. My face is flushed and sweat drips from my skin as I grip the bedsheet.

Aunt Sarah Rebeca balances on the edge of my bed at my side, a damp cloth wiping my brow. "You're doing great, Lillian Elizabeth."

Jane Anne grunts. "She needs to push."

Wisdom falls and I choose to ignore my mother's cutting comment. Early labour started at 4 p.m. yesterday. The contractions were mild and occurred every fifteen minutes. Against Jane Anne's advice, I go for a walk. Active labour normally starts around six to twelve hours after early labour, and before the contractions became too bad, I needed to move. My mother insisted on coming with me, with Charles Jason loitering behind in case I needed help. At 3 a.m. I went into active labour. It is now

9 a.m. and Jane Anne's constant demand I push is wearing thin—very thin.

Night has come and gone, and with the blackout blind slipping, I can see the sun trying to peek from behind a dark cloud. Another contraction hits and the midwife, Sally Stevenson, pokes her head up from between my legs. A wide smile graces her lips, and for some terrible reason, I want to throw the wet cloth on my forehead at her. Luckily for Sally Stevenson, I choose to scream, pushing as Jane Anne instructed.

"Is everything alright, do you need me to get the doctor?" Charles Jason shouts from behind the bedroom door.

"If I needed a doctor, I'd have told you to get one," Jane Anne snaps. "What good are doctors when a woman's having a baby? Go put the kettle on and make yourself useful."

"Do you want me to bring the tea up when I've made it?"

"No, I don't. Why, in the name of God, would we be wanting to drink tea? Your sister is having a baby, she's in no position to be drinking tea," Jane Anne barks.

Visions of Charles Jason scratching his head in bewilderment flash in my head. "I …"

"Put the kettle on and make yourself a drink. This is no place for a man." On a large intake of breath, Jane Anne stares down at me. "Now push, or we'll be here all day and that boy will wear out my carpet."

"I was only trying to help."

"Charles Jason, if you don't …" Jane Anne's teeth grind, bones scraping together.

"I'm going … I'm going …" With the thud of his crutch, the stairs creak as my brother leaves his post at my bedroom door.

Jane Anne sighs.

From between my legs, the midwife sniggers. At sixty-five, Sally came out of retirement when war broke out. Arthritis stiffens her movements, but her eyes and ears are as sharp as they ever were. Strands of grey hair stick from the top of her cap, and with her starched apron and dress free of creases—Matron would approve. I, however, am a mess. With everything I've got, I push and push. There's a cry, and from between bloody legs, Pearl takes her first breath.

"It's a girl," Sally announces.

"Let me have her," I say, reaching.

Jane Anne stiffens, a look of horror falling over her features. "Good heavens, let the midwife clean the child up first."

"No, I want to see her."

Sally cuts the cord and, wrapping Pearl in a towel, hands her to me. Little bloody hands poke out from the soft towel, her lips smacking together and her cheeks a soft pink beneath body fluid. She is the most perfect thing I have seen for a long, long time. Tiny fingers wrap around mine, and I've never loved someone as I love my baby. "She's beautiful," I say, tears shimmering in my eyes.

Aunt Sarah Rebeca moves the towel, gazing at her great niece. "Let me give her to Sally, and Jane Anne and I will get you cleaned up. That way you can both get to know each other better."

Within a second of Pearl being taken, Jane Anne swoops in.

Unsure how Joe will feel about Pearl's birth, I finally send a telegraph a week later. Will there be an air of excitement? It's hard to be excited over the birth of another man's child—one you are passing off as your own. Doubt settles and I wonder if I made the right decision marrying Joe. Love aside, was I being fair? Adoption isn't new. As far as I am aware, most adoptive parents love their children. So, maybe Joe will love Pearl as his own. Grr ... emotions ... Life would be easier without them. Like the message I sent Jane Anne when I was coming home, the telegram is short and to the point.

```
YOU HAVE A DAUGHTER - STOP - PEARL
ALEXANDRA LAWRENCE - STOP - BORN
10TH OF FEBRUARY 1944 - STOP - WE ARE
BOTH DOING WELL - STOP - AND WAIT FOR
YOUR SAFE RETURN - STOP - LOVE
LILLIAN ELIZABETH LAWRENCE
```

Once I've sent the telegram to Joe, I send one to Morag.

```
BACK IN LONDON - STOP - PEARL WAS
BORN 10TH OF FEBRUARY 1944 - STOP -
```

KATHLEEN HARRYMAN

JOE WANTS US TO MOVE TO SEAGULL'S REST, STONEHAVEN, SCOTLAND – STOP – LOVE YOU – STOP – STAY SAFE – STOP – LILLY

60

June 1944, London, England

*O*n the 13th of June, 1944, the wireless brings the worst possible news. At 4:25 a.m., Germany sends their pilotless V-1 flying bombs over London. The bombs hit Grove Road, demolishing the railway bridge and nearby houses. Six people lose their lives, leaving thirty injured, and two hundred homeless. News reports fill the papers with stories of this latest weapon. The *Evening Standard* runs with the headline:

```
MORRISON ANNOUNCES NEW GERMAN
          AIR WEAPON
PILOTLESS PLANES RAID BRITIAN
  Countermeasures Are Vigorous
```

As an Air Raid Warden, Jane Anne swings into action, leaving Aunt Sarah Rebeca, Charles Jason, me, and Pearl at home. We huddle around the wireless, listening to the news reports as they pour in. With Pearl asleep in her cot, we sit in silence. The Germans refer to the V-1 flying bombs as Cherry Stone—a rather odd nickname for a weapon that causes destruction. Strange as it might be, but we have adopted our epithets for the V-1: doodlebug or buzz bomb. Within hours of the V-1 bombs landing, locals recount their experiences. "The bomb sounds like a motorbike", or "A steam train, struggling uphill". Those who saw the bomb describe it as "A burning plane, crossing the sky with a sword of flame as a tail." With Grove Road Railway Bridge out of action, the rail company quickly construct a temporary bridge. The Great Eastern Railway service, from Liverpool Street to Essex, continues to run on a reduced service.

In the shadow of Germany's fresh wave of attacks on London, I go to work at St Thomas and Guy's Hospital. Jane Anne, now busy with ARP, doesn't comment. My hours at the hospital are long. Most of the nurses stay in a large room underground. As I have Pearl, I travel to the hospital daily. In my absence, my brother helps care for Pearl, along with Aunt Sarah Rebeca. But with so much destruction comes the need for repair and replacement. Busy in the workshop, Charles Jason rebuilds the pews for the local church.

Now that I'm back home, I form an addiction to newspapers. With no way of knowing where Joe, Morag, Effie, Adah, and my brothers are, or the conditions they face, the newspapers provide a glimmer of information. They also keep me connected to them. Each morning as I travel to the hospital, I pick up a newspaper and, greedily gripping its sides, I drink in the headlines.

With the doodlebugs continuing their assault, the hospital is busy. The conditions we work under, though different from that on the frontline, remain difficult. Primus stoves aid in the sterilisation of equipment, allowing us to continue treatment in the converted basement, and provide hot water to the wards. The unmistakable sound of a doodlebug echoes above, and work on the ward pauses, heads turning up to the ceiling. People swallow down nerves. Nurses Fran Archer and Sandra Dillon stare at each other as they tend to patients. The rasping of the doodlebug's engine gets louder. Fran jumps and the thermometer in her hand falls to the floor. With damages requiring paying for, tears well as she looks down at the broken thermometer. From his bed, PC Payne tracks the noise of the doodlebug. It's not the whirring of the engine that has our attention, but the silence that follows. Doodlebugs become inaudible as they drop to the ground. The engine continues, moving away, its rasping becoming faint.

Clad in pyjamas, PC Hill and PC Wright walk over to Fran, her hands shaking as she crouches to pick up the broken pieces of the thermometer. St Thomas and Guy's Hospital is the nominated hospital for police needing treatment, so we have a few of them on the ward. In the corner bed, I sit, my arms around Davy Steel. Tears fall down his cheeks. He doesn't say a word as his body trembles. With the doodlebug passing, the distant buzzing of its engine brings a collective sigh of relief. The threat over, I lessen my hold on Davy. His tiny hands poke out from the saline-soaked bandages covering his arms. The same dressing shields his legs and upper torso, burnt from when a doodlebug demolished his home.

Davy had been playing in the backyard when it landed. His mum carried him, screaming, into the hospital. Burns melted away the clothing from her back, charring the skin along her legs and arms, the bitter smell of smoke wafting from her. Blood ran down the right side of her face from a head wound, but her only concern was that we treat her son. On relinquishing Davy, she collapsed onto the hospital floor. While the burns were extensive, first we needed to stop the blood flow and treat the damage to her skull. With an orderly's help, I loaded her onto the stretcher and took her down to theatre, working through the night alongside the surgeon. A buildup of fluid on her brain (Hydrocephalus) placed too much pressure on it and the surgeon inserted a shunt tube into the brain. With a flexible tube under the skin, we try to drain away the fluid, directing it into the abdomen to be absorbed by the body. For two days, Mrs Steel lay unconscious, fighting for her life, before she died. Her husband, Mr Steel, died instantly when their home collapsed on top of him. Their deaths leave Davy, at eight years old, an orphan. One of many children struggling to understand why his mum and dad can't be with him.

A young woman enters the ward as Davy slumps, exhausted, against my chest. I kiss the top of his head, brushing his hair. Kitten heels click on the tiled floor as she approaches the bed. Her white-gloved hands grip the handles of her bag. A silk scarf covers her blonde hair, and her coat, though worn, is clean. She takes out a handkerchief and dabs at her eyes, before extending her right hand. "I'm Louise Townend, Delia's sister."

The familiar, soft cockney accent stirs Davy, and he looks at the woman, a frown marring his brow. "Auntie Lou, what ya doin' 'ere?"

"Well, Davy lad, with ya mam and dad dead, I thought ya should know when ya well, ya'll live with me and ya Uncle Ted."

I move off the bed. "Here, why don't you sit with Davy and I'll see about getting you a cup of tea."

Louise nods, perching on the side of Davy's bed. The boy launches at her, and they nearly tumble to the floor. She laughs, dropping her handbag, and kisses the top of his head.

"I'm sorry it took me so long to find ya," she whispers into his hair.

Louise Townend reminds me of Adah.

On the 6th of July, 1944, in the wake of the V-1 attacks, Churchill makes a statement from Parliament.

"Up to six am today, two thousand seven hundred and fifty-two people have been killed by flying bombs, and up to eight thousand have been injured …"

Death and injuries are a small portion of the destruction when measured against the lasting effects of war. While the actual numbers affected by the attack differs from Churchill's, he is right on one thing. "London will never be conquered, and we will never fail."

Hitler is merciless in his attack, launching over nine thousand V-1s on London, all fired from coastal sites in occupied Europe.

Newspapers stampede us with information, whipping their readers into a frenzy of panic. With a range of around two hundred to two hundred and fifty miles, the bombs keep us awake.

Hitler has the power to terrorise Londoners from afar.

Months after the first V-1 flying bomb landed in London, Germany launches their V-2 rockets. The long-range bombardments cause colossal damage to dozens of towns and villages.

The *News Chronicle* declares:

V2: HERE ARE THE ROCKET SECRETS.
Our Experts Now Know All About New Weapon

I drink in the printed information, my heart sinking with each word I digest. As I feast on the print, my fingers black from ink, bricks and mortar fall, people die, and children become homeless orphans. The papers are uncomfortable, addictive reading—I'm hooked. With my heart racing, I scan the *Daily Mail*'s declaration:

V2: THE FULL DRAMATIC STORY.
Germans Planned 500-tons-an-hour bombardment of London.

Even though we are told the Full Story, I'm aware we are not being told the 'Full Story'. I drop the newspaper in my lap. Pearl sleeps at my side, in her cot, and I stare into Jane Anne's small handheld mirror. A woman stares back at me. Sometimes, I'm not sure I recognise her, but one thing we both agree on is we won't be happy until Joe is home, and war is over.

Aunt Sarah Rebeca wanders in from the backyard. "You need to think about getting some rest. You're back at the hospital at eight tomorrow morning."

The clock on the mantle chimes eleven. There's no point in going to bed. I won't sleep.

"That won't help," Aunt Sarah Rebeca says, sitting in Trevor Henry's chair, gazing at the newspaper in my lap.

"No, it won't, but I can't seem to help myself. Being on the frontline is easier than waiting for news. It seems all I do is worry about Joe, Morag, Effie, Adah, and my brothers."

"We're on the right side of this war, Lilly. Allied and Free French forces entered Paris on the twenty-fifth of August, and the French government is being handed over to the Free French troops. Can't you sense it? This war is ending."

"I wish I shared your optimism."

When I close my eyes, I see the soldiers fighting, struggling to get to the beaches. Burns from flamethrowers needing immediate attention. Medics run from injured soldier to injured soldier, administering first aid. All while bombs land, scattering dirt and limbs, and gunfire explodes from rifles and machine guns at alarming rates. A weary smile falls on my lips. "How does Jane Anne do it? Keep going. Not allowing the worry to eat away at her.

There's still no news of Arthur James, Brian Wayne, and George Peter."

"Your mother has always been a funny fish and likes to keep her emotions private. I've heard her praying for your brothers' safe return. She's not as strong as she makes out."

"Are prayers enough?" I ask.

Aunt Sarah Rebeca turns her head. Trevor Henry smiles from behind a black veil on the mantle, along with John Edward. "Prayers are all we have."

61

September 1944, London, England

*T*he telegram sits in the middle of the table. Jane Anne stares at it. There are no tears, just the blank gaze of someone unwilling to recognise she has lost another son.

No. CAS/SEA/HRS/142. **Army Form B.** 104–82B.

(If relying, please quote above No.)

.... The Infantry ... **Record Office,**

.... PERTH. ....

.... 28th July, ...1944.

Dear Madam, ...

It is my painful duty to inform you that a report has been received from the War Office notifying the death of:—

(No.) ...33598 ...... **(Rank)** ... L/Corporal. ......

(Name) .... George Peter Nutman. ....

(Regiment) ...... The Seaforth Highlanders. ...

which occurred ... in North–West Europe. ...

On the .... 30th, July 1944. ....

The report is to the effect that he ......
.... Was Killed in Action. ....

I am to express the sympathy and regret of the Army Council at the soldier's death in his Country's service.

I am,

.... Madam, ...

Your obedient Servant,

Charles Jason, unable to deal with the continued silence, stands in the yard, smoking. I've counted four cigarettes so far. He looks in no hurry to come back inside. Pearl lies quietly in my arms, her little face puckered up as she sleeps. From where I sit on Trevor Henry's chair, I have a clear view of the pacing tiger outside who was once my brother. The front door clicks closed and the sound of Aunt Sarah Rebeca's heels clang against the Victorian tiles. In her gloved hand are two telegrams. Jane Anne flinches as her sister places them in front of her, centimetres from the first one.

"That's it then, my boys won't be coming home."

She reaches for the two telegrams, opening them. The tears come as she places one next to the other. Aunt Sarah Rebeca rests her hand on her sister's shoulder. Like a rabbit leaping from danger, Jane Anne jumps up.

"Don't …"

I place Pearl in her cot as Jane Anne screams. Her body shakes, tears and snot merge, falling onto her jumper. Charles Jason limps into the room. His crutch thumps against the wooden floor. He looks at the table. Bewilderment, anger, fear, and disbelief fall in quick succession over his face.

Aunt Sarah Rebeca holds her sister, trying to force her back into the chair, but she collapses to the floor, and I walk over to Charles Jason.

"They're … It's … I mean … It can't be …" my mother stammers, her sobs coating each word.

Grief hits my brother and I draw him into my arms, kissing his cheek as he crashes onto the chair near where Jane Anne sprawls over the floor. There are no words of comfort I can think to say. Needless loss of life is something I've been dealing with for a long time. The pain never dims. There is no getting used to it. Out of five brothers, only Charlie is left. As a family, we have suffered a tremendous loss.

Pearl cries, and leaving Charles Jason, I walk to the cot to comfort my daughter. Jane Anne, her handkerchief scrunched in her hand, stares at Pearl. Without words, I place Pearl in her arms. She takes her granddaughter, cradling her. Pearl's tiny hands reach out, and Jane Anne places her little finger in front of her. Greedily, Pearl grabs hold of her grandmother's finger, bringing it to her mouth as she smiles. She reminds me so much of Alick. He always had a way of stopping the pain and making you aware of the love that surrounds you. I've never been so proud of my baby. For such a little person, she has given us hope, reminding us that while we have lost so much, we have also gained a lot.

Three days following notification of Arthur James, Brian Wayne, and George Peter's deaths, Jane Anne places an obituary in the newspaper.

On Active Service

Nutman — Killed in action in August 1944, in North—West Europe, Lce./Corpl. Arthur James. Lce./Corpl. Brian Wayne, and Lce/Corpl. George Peter.

Sons of Trevor Henry Nutman, and Jane Anne Nutman (nee Ellis) and loving brother of Charles Jason, and Lillian Elizabeth. Nephew of Sarah Rebeca Broadman (nee Ellis).

"Tenderest memories are all we have left. Of those we all loved and will never forget."

62

 April 1945, London, England

The gate bounces against the wall; I grab it, sliding the bolt in place, pushing the pram to the back door. Pearl sleeps, snuggled within the blankets, as the April sun replaces the earlier rain. With the hood on the pram up and positioned out of the wind, I leave Pearl outside to sleep, walking through the back door.

Aunt Sarah Rebeca hands me her copy of the *Daily Express*. "What do you make of it?"

I place the letter from Morag in my pocket and take the newspaper, staring at the headline:

HITLER BOMBED OUT
5 tonnes right on der Fuhrer's house

Does this mean Joe is coming home? Optimism ignites. But fear mingles with anticipation, and I hand the newspaper back to Aunt Sarah Rebeca. "Better not get our hopes up. Until Germany surrenders, there will never be an end to this war."

Charles Jason sits at the table, his cap hanging off the back of the chair. Wood varnish stains his clothes and skin. If Jane Anne were here, he would have washed before sitting down.

Aunt Sarah Rebeca pats the newspaper. "Let's remain positive."

"I'm not saying they're not. Just to exercise caution," I say.

The newspaper drops to the floor, and I bend, picking it up, placing it on the table.

"At least it's a step in the right direction," my brother says.

A shadow of a smile appears on my lips. "It is, Charlie."

Charles Jason pushes away from the table. "I'd best clean up. Jane Anne will be home soon."

"You go sort out Pearl and I'll start tea." Aunt Sarah Rebeca pushes herself out of the chair.

On Wednesday the 2nd of May, the *Daily Mail* pronounces:

HITLER DEAD
News the world's been praying for broken last night
by German radio.

It appears Adolf Hitler, sensing the enemy drawing closer, killed himself. Grand Admiral Karl Dönitz becomes the new Fuhrer, proclaiming the fight goes on. This is the news we've all been longing for. Everywhere I look, people hug, cheer, and smile. The sun climbs above the rooftops and the scent of spring fills the air. Despite the pleasing news of Hitler's death, anxiety raises its head, taking residence in the pit of my stomach. Until Joe is home, and I know Morag, Adah, and Effie are safe, how can I celebrate?

In the street, people rush out of their houses with whoops of joy. Someone grabs me as I make my way home from work, their lips pressing into my cheek before they're gone, grabbing the next unsuspecting person. I turn onto our street; the front door stands open and the sound of porcelain clinking echoes down the hall. Jam sandwiches sit on the table, and everyone wears huge smiles.

Jane Anne picks up the teapot. "Wash up, it's time to celebrate."

With my cape resting on the back of the chair, I wash my hands, taking a deep inhale. Not prepared to take their victory from them, I return with a smile.

We raise our teacups in a salute.

"To Hitler, may you rot in hell," Jane Anne says.

"HERE! HERE!" Charles Jason shouts, his palm hitting the table.

Aunt Sarah Rebeca laughs. Picking up her teaspoon, she taps it against the porcelain cup.

I wish I could join them in rejoicing in the death of a man that has dominated our lives for so long. Pain, sorrow, and grief do not disappear so quickly. My brain, now a weapon of torture, requires caution. Too many questions demand answers. Hitler's passing is too perfect. Where is the proof? Crucial evidence is missing. Are the Nazis exaggerating the circumstances around his death? Their belief that Hitler is a legend is too intense to die so abruptly. Are the Nazis creating a distraction, aiding Hitler's retreat from the scene? Without a body to view, I can't believe in the miracle that Hitler's demise offers. As Doubting Thomas said (John 20:24-29), 'Unless I see the nail marks in his hands and put my finger where the nails were, and put my hand into his side, I will not believe.'

Over the next few days, we receive more good news, and on the 7th of May, 1945, British Field Marshal Bernard Montgomery accepts the unconditional surrender of German forces. From the hospital windows, I watch people gather in the street. Unwilling to wait for King George VI to address the nation, they begin their Victory in Europe celebrations. Under the cover of darkness, the streets of London become a stage for the biggest party I've ever witnessed. Faces hidden by the darkening sky, their shouts of joy and laughter impregnate the walls of the hospital.

Patients sit up in bed, their hair dishevelled and silly grins lighting their faces. The commotion outside brings comfort. Laughter is infectious and before long it fills the ward with the vivacious sound of muffled cheers. The morning sun shines through the hospital windows, my shift ends, and with my cape covering my shoulders, I enter the streets. Hoots of joy greet me.

"Isn't it marvellous?" a man says, hurrying by.

"At last, the end is here," says someone else.

On cries of jubilation, I make my way home. Charles Jason dances in the street, his crutch moving, his stump swinging. Jane Anne stands clapping in time to the music on the wireless that someone has cranked up from within their house. Aunt Sarah Rebeca sways to the beat, rocking Pearl. It is a sight I will never forget. For the first time since Hitler's death, ecstasy runs through my veins. With my cape flying, and the skirt of my uniform swaying about my knees, I join in the morning celebrations. With Germany surrendering, the newspapers waste little time in publishing their headlines. In big black letters, the *Daily Mail* states:

VE–DAY–IT'S ALL OVER
News we have been longing to hear.

There have been many losses along the way, but finally Victory in Europe is ours.

Charles Jason grabs my arm as I dance. "Come on, we're off to Buckingham Palace."

"There will be plenty of time to sleep later. Now we celebrate," Jane Anne says from behind my brother.

People dance, sing, and make trumpets out of newspapers as we walk. Somewhere, a wireless blurts out Churchill's voice as he addresses the nation, announcing an end to the war. "We may allow ourselves a brief period of rejoicing, but let us not forget for a moment the toils and efforts that lie ahead."

Through the streets of London, we flock to Buckingham Palace, our numbers swelling. With smiles on our faces, we laugh like we're drunk, linking arms, carrying our babies, and holding our children's hands. I've never seen so many people in one place.

"Hurry!" Jane Anne shouts over her shoulder. "Look they're coming out!"

At 3 p.m., Churchill's voice fades from the wireless, and we race to join the crowd gathering outside Buckingham Palace. Cheers fill London as King George VI and his family, along with Churchill, stand on the balcony, waving to their people. Hope ignites, and we stand united, cheering, waving, and hugging each other. The Germans first dropped their bombs on Buckingham Palace on the 13th of September, 1940; the palace suffered eight more attacks, with damages to the chapel and the destruction of the Northern Lodge. Still, she stands proudly in front of us. Like the people of the United Kingdom and beyond, Buckingham Palace has come through this war scathed, but triumphant.

At 9 p.m., we sit in the front room, the wireless turned up as King George VI addresses the nation. "Together, we shall all face the future with stern resolve and prove that our reserves of willpower and vitality are inexhaustible. Today we give thanks to Almighty God for a great deliverance."

A month after VE-Day celebrations, there's a knock at the front door. Aunt Sarah Rebeca glances up from darning one of Charles Jason's socks.

My teacup clatters against the saucer. "Stay there, I'll get it!"

At first, I think I'm hallucinating. I blink, but the vision remains standing in front of me, grinning like the Cheshire cat.

"Joe!" I scream, charging at him.

My arms round his neck, he lifts me to him, swinging me round and round, making me laugh. Giddiness, like a drug, sends my insides quivering. I kiss and kiss him.

"I can't believe you're here. You are, aren't you? I'm not dreaming, am I?"

Joe shakes his head.

"You should have sent a telegram; I would have met you at the station."

"I wanted to surprise you."

"Ooo …" Cupping his cheeks, I kiss him again. "It's the best surprise ever."

Hand in hand, we walk into the house. Jane Anne wanders in from the yard, Pearl in her arms.

"Jane Anne, this is Major Joseph Lawrence, my husband."

"Pleased to meet you."

Pearl wakes up as they shake hands, her green eyes, so like mine, stare at Joe. With flushed cheeks, she blows him a bubble, which she instantly finds funny. Jane Anne passes Pearl to me, and I take my daughter, turning to Joe. "This is your daughter, Pearl Alexandra Lawrence. Pearl, say hello to your daddy."

Joe takes Pearl, holding her high above his head. "What do you say Pearl, shall we go for a spin?"

The room fills with her laughter as he spins her, the sound of a plane motor vibrating from his lips. Joe lowers her down, kissing her button nose, and she giggles. Love and tenderness radiate from him as he looks down at her.

"She's beautiful."

Relief has my head spinning. Doubt and worry make an unhealthy partnership, with fear following in their wake. Would Joe accept Alick's daughter as his own? Now, all my anxieties melt as he holds his daughter. I was not the first QA to become pregnant, but I am one of the fortunate ones. Many didn't know their man was married. The truth came out later. Some hid their pregnancy, which, given we're trained nurses, some midwives, it is quite remarkable how well they kept their secret. Once their babies were born, they whisked them away, putting them up for adoption. The mother never got a say in whether she wanted to keep her child. What Joe has done for me, and Pearl, is the most wonderful miracle ever. It is one I shall treasure and, in return, I will love him as he deserves to be loved. With loyalty and faithfulness until the day I die.

63

 April 1945, London, England

*M*orag's letter sits on the bedside table unopened. Downstairs, Joe's voice carries up as I finish feeding Pearl. It's hard to say why I've never read the letter. Guilt, fear maybe. Joe coming home gives me the strength to read it; I am no longer alone. Other than Morag, Joe is the only one who knows the truth about me and Alick. These are the people who understand me. It feels good to be almost whole.

Dearest Lilly,

Ah cannae tell ye how many times ah've tried tae write this letter. So far, ah've torn each one up. So much has happened since ye left. December 1943 found us in Italy. Ah believe this is the point where thin's went wrong. Ah hate Italy. Bombers reduced Cassino 'n' its monastery tae nothin' more than rubble. Stationed at the harbour, 'n' with the war movin' further up the coast, our guard was down. With Bari na longer defended, 'n' the early warnin' radar oot o' action, we dinnae spot the enemy aircraft until 'twas tae late.

The first German Ju 88 bomber arrived after 7 a.m. Thirty ships were in the harbour. The bomber took us by surprise. It wasnae until 'twas within one hundred and fifty feet o' us we ken we were in trouble. Hell like ye've never seen broke loose. They destroyed seventeen o' the ships. Worse, nae that ah suppose ye're thinkin' it kin get any worse, Adah 'n' Effie's ship suffered a direct hit. Lilly, they're dead.

We worked through the night, treatin' the wounded at Bari. Tis what kept me goin'. Within hours o' the first casualties bein' admitted tae the ward, they started actin' peculiar. Ah kept thinkin' if Adah was 'ere, she'd ken what tae do, what with her experience in the Great War. Boot she wasnae 'ere, 'n' we dinnae have a clue hoo tae treat them. They were so thirsty, which is odd 'cause we'd just given them their supper 'n' as ye ken we give them water with their food. Some wandered around the place searchin' for water, complainin' of intense heat. Afore we ken it, they were strippin' off their clothes, with those patients confined tae bed rippin' at their dressin'. Blisters the size o' balloons, filled with fluid, lined their skin. Ah've seen nothin' like it. Withoot knowin' if we were at risk from cross-infection, we treated the soldiers as best we could. It reminded me o' Pearl 'n' how cross we were with her. Noo 'ere ah am doin' the same thin'. We ran tests, but na one would tell us the results. One of the older nurses, Jenny Cartwright, said she'd seen somethin' similar. She called it mustard gas. But it cannae have been, they ootlawed the use o' mustard gas after the Great War. So why would the Americans have mustard gas on them?

They say bad news likes company, 'n' tis true. Last week ah received word that Ma died at the beginnin' of August 1943. Took a while tae track me down, or so ah'm told. Ma had a fatal heart attack. Ah wasnae aware she had a diseased heart. Ah'm surrounded by sisters 'n' ah've never bin so lonely. Ah've na family left, my friends 'ere have died. Lilly, ah dinnae want tae put a smile on mah face 'n' pretend everythin' is alright, 'cause it's nae. All ah want mare than anythin' is tae come haime. Tae go back tae Leeds when we met up 'n' hold ye all close. With Ma 'n' my brothers, 'n' Pearl, Adah, 'n' Effie dead, ah'm so lost. When this war is over, ah'm hopin' tae join ye in Scotland. Nae at Stonehaven, boot Aberdeen, or Dundee mibbie. Ah cannae take the loss anymare, 'n' all ah have is ye. Mibbie Joe, 'n' baby Pearl. A heart kin only take so much, 'n' mine, it just dinnae want the pain na mare.

One day, Lilly, we shall sit at Seagull's Rest 'n' over a glass o' wine, we'll remember our friends. The stories we'll recount will brin' them back, 'n' twill be as if we never lost them. For noo, ah just want tae curl in a ball 'n' kip withoot the night-mares hauntin' me.

Your friend, forever,

Morag

Plop … plop … My tears fall on Morag's letter. There is no end to the pain.

64

LILIBETH

Seagull's Rest, Stonehaven, Scotland

*O*utside, the wind gathers strength, and rain beats against the window. The isolated position of Seagull's Rest provides no protection against the Scottish weather. It whips around the cottage, searching for gaps to whistle through. My head rests against the windowpane as I sit on the cushions tossed over the window seat. My cheeks are wet, and I stare, lost in thought, watching the droplets fall down the glass. Lillian Elizabeth's diary sits open in my lap and tucked within its page are the letters she wrote my great-grandmother, Jane Anne.

Unopened, a letter sits on top of the open pages of my grandmother's diary, addressed to Alick McNavis. Without focus, I stare as it falls to the floor, floating towards the overstuffed sofa, resting on the tartan rug by the fire.

Wood splinters within the inglenook, and flames dance, but no warmth comes from it—emotion does that to me. It sucks the heat from my flesh. With a trembling hand, I move back my jumper, gazing at my watch; goosebumps run over my skin.

What now? Am I to tell Mum about Alick, and let her know Joe wasn't her father? After all these years, does it matter? Biology doesn't make a man a father. But there is nothing to say Alick wouldn't have made a wonderful dad, given the opportunity.

My love for Grandpa Joe hasn't changed, even with the knowledge that out there, somewhere, my real grandpa lives. Or does he? Perhaps, like Lillian Elizabeth, he is dead, though something tells me that isn't so—Alick is alive, old, but alive. So, do I try and find him, and give him the letter my grandmother wrote, hoping I can give her soul peace? Lillian Elizabeth is right; this is a messy situation. One left to me to sieve through and put right.

Mum's face shimmers in front of me, and my mood darkens. Her auburn hair blows in the wind, a wide smile on her cherry pink lips, and she winks. The image disappears, like so many times in my life. Was it a lack of foundations that had Mum spreading her arms like butterfly wings, leaving me in the care of Lillian Elizabeth? I shake my head at the unspoken question. Lack of foundations didn't make Mum, Pearl Alexandra, drift through life, constantly moving from country to country, like hopping on pebbles, across a stream.

Pearl Alexandra is an enigma, and unreliability's best friend. She doesn't seem to know what she is searching for—but she'll know it when she finds it. That something wasn't me. No, a lack of foundations didn't make Pearl Alexandra a lousy mother, she did that on her own. Marriage didn't change her. It lasted one month before she'd had enough and the need to travel called. David Robert Gibson, my father, died on holiday in India with another woman—I was four. With a skinful of alcohol, he drove his jeep into a tree. His death, ruled an accident, was cheaper than a divorce. It's the only reference my mother makes when speaking about the sperm donor.

Funerals are Mum's forte, she adores them. We all have a strange fascination with something, I guess. Pearl Alexandra's is death. She slithered into the church at Lillian Elizabeth's funeral, dressed in classic black, her dress tight but not sleazy. Sleeves capped at her shoulders allowed the firm muscles of her arms to show, along with the pearl and sapphire bracelet adorning her wrist. With her handkerchief patting beneath her eyes, she wiped away non-existent tears. It doesn't matter how many times I see her; I stop and stare. Elegance, class, and grace ooze from her every pore—once seen, never forgotten. And I am her addict.

She breezes into my life, and like a genie—poof—with no time at all, she's gone. Hate, love, jealousy, loneliness, they leave me gagging for more every time I see her. Pearl Alexandra is an addiction—one taste and there isn't a rehab centre in the world able to ween me off her. In a clash of emotions, I realise my mother isn't a bad person. She is what most long to be—herself. There is no self-awareness of the havoc she causes, no scheming or manipulation. She is soft, beautiful flesh, that lights my days, and leaves me bereft when she's gone.

Once, long ago, I wanted to be like her, before I understood. If I was always seeking something, I would never find satisfaction, contentment, or happiness. So, like my grandmother, I became a nurse. Lillian Elizabeth is right, nursing isn't a job. It's woven within each molecule of my being, providing rich rewards, along with lengthy, unsociable shift patterns, aching feet, and bones.

If rocky foundations are to blame for Pearl Alexandra's flighty ways, it is a miracle I turned out like I did, being a product of them.

On reflection, there is no point telling Mum about Alick. It changes nothing. She is a partial shadow of my grandmother. Lillian Elizabeth did not possess the great beauty and grace of her daughter. And her daughter does not possess the strength or outpouring of human kindness of her mother. I am my grandmother's shadow, not my mother's. We are alike, not just in looks, but in the way we choose to live our lives.

With a snap, I tuck my grandmother's diary under my arm. It's time to visit Aunt Morag; cogitating will not provide a solution. I pick up Alick's letter, tucking it inside the diary. With determination at the helm, I grab my waterproof, the hood covering my auburn hair, and run to the car. Lillian Elizabeth's diary tucked within the inner pocket of my jacket, I leave Seagull's Rest.

The wind drives the rain hard against the windscreen, reducing my vision and sending the automatic wipers crazy. I turn the air conditioning on high, demisting the glass as I drive down the narrow road. Aunt Morag came to Scotland on her return from Naples. On the 1st of September 1945, she flew into RAF Glatton Camp,

Peterborough, now part of Peterborough Airport. De-commissioned, she moved to Aberdeen, finding work at Aberdeen Royal Infirmary until she retired.

Stonehaven is twenty-seven miles from Aberdeen. Given the obscene weather, traffic on the A92 moves with sluggish intent. I tap in time to the music bleating from the radio, singing along. Mum can't join a musical note together; at least in this area, like my grandmother, I excel. The typical Scottish whitewashed bricks of Coven Bay Care Home come into view. From its prominent height, Coven Bay Care Home overlooks the harbour, and the sound of waves hitting the stone wall echoes through the driving rain. My neck clicks as I pull on the handbrake, removing the tension.

Isla looks up from the reception desk as I enter, her strawberry blonde hair sliding away from her jaw. Freckles line her nose and cheeks, emphasising her pale skin. The biscuit-coloured uniform drains her natural rosy colouring. "Yer aunt is in the middle o' a poker game," she says, the soft drawl of her Scottish accent making me smile.

"Is she winning?"

Isla snorts. "When dinnae she? Robbie is down tae four chocolate chip cookies, 'n' tis nae lookin' good for the rest o' them."

"You'd think they'd know better," I say, signing the visitor log.

She shrugs. "Nae fool like an old fool, as the sayin' goes."

"True," I call over my shoulder, entering the communal area and removing Lillian Elizabeth's diary from my pocket.

Each resident at Coven Bay Care Home has a room, fitted out with a bathroom, bedroom, kitchenette, and living area, as well as full use of the social lounge. The communal area is where Aunt Morag spends most of her time, playing bridge, dominoes, painting, and reading. This is not one of those homes where their residents sit staring blankly at flowery wallpaper, waiting for death to release them from their boredom.

Aunt Morag sits at a small round table, playing cards fan out in front of the occupants' faces: Gracie Dougal, Robbie Colson, and Gary Mills. Their gaze remains glued to the cards as they nod at my approach. Withered hands reaching out, Gracie splays out her cards, making for the cookies. Robbie and Gary throw their cards on the table with a grunt.

"Nae so fast, Gracie, ye'll find those cookies are mine," Aunt Morag says, revealing a royal flush.

Gracie stares at the cards, curling the white lace tablecloth into her hands. "Ye got extra cards up those sleeves o' yers, Morag?"

Aunt Morag's tongue bounces off the roof of her mouth, and she shakes her head. "Ye're such a sore loser, Gracie Dougal, accusin' me o' cheatin'. Ah've never nicked so much as a kiss, 'n' ah'm nae aboot tae start takin' cookies ah've nae earned fair 'n' square."

"Na need tae be so grumpy aboot it. Ah was just sayin'."

"Na ye weren't, ye was bein' a sore loser."

Jowls wobbling, Robbie slurps down his tea, smacking his lips together. "That's me oot until mah grandkids come to visit. Ah've na cookies left."

Aunt Morag stands up, pulling the sides of her cardigan together. She grabs the walking frame near her chair, her gaze locked on the cookies as Robbie inches his hand closer to them. "Hands off mah cookies, Robbie, there'll be na dunkin' taeday."

"Aww, c'mon, Morag."

"Na point in whingin', ah cannae hear ye, ah've turned mah hearin' aid off."

Gary scoffs, choking on his tea. "Ye dinnae need a hearin' aid, Morag, ye've got antennas, nae ears."

"Gail! Kin ye come 'n' scoop up mah winnin's afore Light Fingers 'ere takes 'em?" Aunt Morag turns, looking over her shoulder. "Ah'm warnin' ye, Robbie, those are mah cookies."

Robbie's hands slide away from the biscuits. "They'll only go soft."

"Ah happen tae like soft cookies."

Gail runs over, placing the biscuits inside a plastic bag. "Ah'll put them behind reception for ye, Morag."

"Thank ye, Gail."

The walking frame rattles as Aunt Morag moves away from the table, leaving Gracie, Robbie, and Gary complaining.

"C'mon, lassie, we'd better go tae mah room where we kin talk in private," she says, nodding at the book in my hand.

She shuffles forward and I step into line at her side. Her fluffy slippers drag across the carpet as the rubber stopper on the frame thump, thump, thumps. She throws back the door and clicks on the lighting, chasing away the shadows.

"Sit down, lassie." Aunt Morag points to the pair of Queen Anne chairs.

I sit in the green jacquard printed chair, hugging the book against my chest. A thousand questions rattle through my head, and I lose the power of speech. Aunt Morag lowers herself into the neighbouring chair. A groan escapes as she lets go of the frame and her back hits the chair. "So, ah take it that ye've read Lilly's diary."

I nod.

"Ah've never felt it made a difference whoo Pearl's father was. Joe was a good man." She points at the book. "Those lack o' foundations Lilly worried over dinnae make yer mother flighty, tis just the way the girl is. Lilly felt guilty nae tellin' Alick aboot the bairn. She loved yer grandfather, boot Alick, Alick was somethin' different. From the moment Lilly met him, she loved him. Nae that she ken it, boot Pearl did."

With a distant smile, she sighs. "Some days ah'd turn up at Seagull's Rest 'n' see Lilly standin' at the edge o' the cliff, starin' across the water. She'd stand there a lot, her thoughts tumblin' round her head. She said 'twas her thinkin' spot. Ah always wondered if at those times, the distance between her 'n' Alick disappeared, 'n' she'd be talkin' to him like they did onboard the *Duchess of Richmond*. Ah was wrong aboot Lilly 'n' Joe. Joe was never her beaver; she was only ever meant tae be Alick's."

"Do you know what happened to him?"

Aunt Morag reaches over, taking the diary. "Lilly was always scribblin'. She shouldn't have felt so guilty over nae tellin' Alick aboot Pearl, boot guilt's a funny thin'. It nae matters hoo rational ye want tae be, guilt won't let ye. When ye mother was four, Joe asked me tae find Alick' 'n' let him noo aboot Pearl. He said 'twas only right that a man kens he has a bairn. Joe's only condition was that Alick never contact Lilly. Ye grandfather was so scared of losin' her, nae that she'd leave Joe. Lilly always honoured her promises, nae matter hoo they hurt."

Aunt Morag sniffs, her hanky dabbing her cheeks as she stares down at the dairy.

"Alick weren't so hard tae track down." She pats the book with a soft laugh. "Ye should have seen the look on his face when he opened the door 'n' there ah stood. Never seen him speechless afore. The only thin' he said was 'Nightingale'. His eyes were like a torch burnin' through the dark. He kept lookin' over mah shoulder as if will alone would make his Nightingale appear. The man loves her like she was breath itself. Ah often wondered hoo they could go on, waitin' tae die just tae be taegether. 'N' would they? Be taegether? Ah mean whoo kens what happens when ye die. Lilly would laugh 'n' say, 'Between the light 'n' dark, Morag.' What nonsense is that? Boot she wouldnae have it any other way. She said that love's made o' both light 'n' darkness, the in-between, that's where immortal souls go tae be taegether."

On a soft grunt, she grabs the walking frame, pulling herself up and setting down the diary. I sit, moving to the edge of my seat, watching as she walks to the sideboard, her walking frame rattling and her feet lagging on the carpet. She opens the middle draw, takes something out, then turns, limping back to the chair. "Here."

I stare at the photo.

"'Tis Lilly with Alick, onboard the *Duchess o' Richmond*. One o' Pearl's boyfriends took it 'n' had it developed while we were in Cape Town. Pearl gave it tae me, the day ah found oot aboot Alick. 'Morag,' she said, 'If ah believed in love, this is what it would look like.'"

Tears threaten; I've never seen my grandmother look so happy. Her head rests on Alick's shoulder, a smile lighting her face. His arm drapes at her waist as he pulls her to him, kissing the top of her head. Neither are aware that a camera clicks, stealing the moment and permanently impregnating it to ink.

"Ah thought Alick was goin' tae burst on the spot when ah told him aboot Pearl. Ah ken he needed tae see her, even though ah'd taken a photograph with me. So, ah took him tae Seagull's Rest when ah ken Lilly would be down on the beach 'n' Joe nae around. We stood on that cliff for over an hour, watchin' Lilly play with Pearl. Then he just nodded, turned, 'n' left. Tears rollin' down his face, he smiled 'n' said, 'All's nae lost. Joe can love mah Nightingale 'ere on earth, 'cause ah've got her for eternity.' Lilly always said that she 'n' Alick were each other's haime. Ah guess noo she's found herself a bench somewhere tae wait for him."

"Do you know if Alick is still alive?"

Aunt Morag scowls. "Some o' us might be auld, boot we've still plenty o' life left in us."

I cringe. "Sorry, I didn't mean to sound rude."

"Ye weren't bein' rude, young people see auld age differently than auld folk do." I offer her the photo, but she shakes her head. "Ye keep it."

"Thank you, Aunt Morag." I stand up, kissing her cheek.

She smiles, handing me the diary. Liver spots sprinkle across her wrinkled hands, and her fingers curl in on themselves.

"Aunt Morag, should I go see him? It's what she wants." I slip the photo inside the dairy, removing the sealed envelope. "She wants me to give him this."

Aunt Morag stares at the envelope. On a sigh, she stands. "We were so young 'n' desperate tae serve our country 'n' take care o' our wounded. There was a time, afore Pearl died, when we thought we'd always be taegether. War exposed us tae so much danger 'n' horrors, boot it dinnae matter, so long as we had each other. Noo ah'm the only one left."

She walks back over to the sideboard. Her gaze lingering on the photograph of five friends, standing on the *Duchess of Richmond*. Morag, Pearl, Lillian Elizabeth, Adah, and Effie. A chill runs through me as I stare at them. It brings home how World War II changed the world. These women were more than friends, they were sisters.

From the drawer, she takes out a piece of paper. "This is Alick's address. Go see him, Lilibeth. Let him ken his Nightingale is waitin' for him."

I kiss her cheek, taking the paper. "I love you, Aunt Morag."

She pats my cheek. "Ye so like her, Lilibeth, in mare than just looks. Sometimes, when ah look at ye, 'tis hard tae think she's gone."

65

LILIBETH

Broughty Ferry, Dundee, Scotland

For three days I've stood at the edge of the cliff, at Seagull's Rest, where Alick looked down on the daughter he would never know, and a woman he wasn't allowed to love.

The world may have moved on, but love remains unaltered. The enormity of the responsibility placed on me by Lillian Elizabeth is consuming. What happens if I fail? Her panic over losing her baby is understandable. Even if Alick divorced his wife and married my grandmother, Pearl Alexandra would have been taken. Divorce doesn't occur overnight, and Lillian Elizabeth was still an unmarried mother. My grandmother's diary has produced a new respect for my grandfather, Joseph Lawrence. He was, as Aunt Morag said, a good man that loved my grandmother with all her heart.

Love is not always kind. It has many compartments, allowing us to love in differing degrees, differentiating between friends, family, and lovers. While Lillian Elizabeth loved Joe, it was minuscule compared to her love for Alick. How do you live with someone knowing that? Greedily, at twenty-four, I want to love like Alick and Lillian Elizabeth, though I don't want to wait a lifetime to find it. To have such a deep connection must be amazing—almost a fantasy. But to find your soul's home here on earth, the thought has my head spinning.

The morning sun burns across the sky, vivid streaks of red, orange, and yellow, setting the clouds on fire as they shimmer over the sea. There is no time to find the courage needed to face my other grandfather, Alick McNavis. If I procrastinate too long, he will be dead, and I will be an old hag forever kicking myself, knowing I let Lillian Elizabeth down. Without allowing my overthinking brain chance to stop me, I walk over to the car and climb inside. The drive to Dundee is too short, and before I know it, I'm sat outside Alick's house on Montague Street, in Broughty Ferry.

With growing nerves, I run the edges of the letter my grandmother wrote Alick through my fingers. World War II was a long time ago. While Lillian Elizabeth may still have loved Alick, there is nothing to say that he would feel the same. Alick is home—my grandmother's words echo through my brain. But even a home needs maintenance.

No resolution is being gained from staring out a windscreen; it is time for action. Action, however, takes ten minutes to muster, before I leave the car and walk up to the house. A brass highland stag stares, challenging me to use it. Not one to back down from a dare, I grab its protruding nose, my fingers wrapping over the antlers. BANG ... BANG ... BANG ... My teeth lock, and my shoulders hug my ears as I grimace at the intensity of the noise. If metal could bend of its own accord, the stag would smile.

At the sound of footsteps, I grab my auburn hair, throwing the long length over my shoulder, tucking the shorter lengths behind my ears. Nervous, I pull down on my coat and square back my shoulders, ready for battle. On a loud EEK, the door opens, revealing a man of slim build, ash blonde hair cut short, and very tall. My head tilting back, I swallow down my discomfort.

The giant presents a friendly smile. "Ye've come, good," he says, his Scottish accent welcoming.

I stare at him, unsure who he is confusing me for. EEK ... the door widens, revealing a large hall. A dark red patterned runner protects the oak floor, and the staircase hangs back like a majestic beast.

"I'm ... em ... here to see Alick ... Alick McNavis."

The giant steps back. "Aye, ah noo."

"Oh ... I ... er ..." Lost for words, I step into the giant's den.

He laughs as the door clicks. "This way."

Out of habit, I kick off my boots and follow him. Much like Lillian Elizabeth, strangers have a way of putting me on edge, conflicted feelings heightening my irrational mind.

The giant stops by a large oak door, hand on the round brass handle. "Ah'm glad ye came. Ah was afraid ye wouldnae make it in time."

Blankly, I stare back at him.

He drops his hand from the door handle and shoves it at me. "Mah name is Kane. I'm Alick's great nephew."

"Oh." My voice squeaks around the tightness of my throat as his hand engulfs mine

"Alick's nae been well."

"I … I'm sorry. If it's a bad time, I can come back later."

"Na need tae be sorry, Alick is thrilled aboot his failin' health. Mah da 'n' ah are tryin' tae be happy for him. We're failin' miserably." His hand disappears into the pocket of his cardigan, and he produces a crumpled photo. "Ye look just like her."

Lillian Elizabeth smiles back at me, explaining the giant's familiarity.

"Yes, I suppose I do."

"He still loves her. Talks aboot her all the time. O' course we've never met, but it's like ah ken her."

As he talks, the stiffness leaves my body. "Lillian Elizabeth never spoke about Alick. I know from reading her diary how hard it was for her, not being with him."

"Aye, ah kin understand that. Yer Aunt Morag often visits. She'd pass on photographs 'n' tell him aboot Lilly 'n' Pearl 'n' you. In the end, that's what he lived for, the chance tae be part of his Nightingale's life, hooever small."

Tears sting my eyes and I blink to remove them. "What about your Great Aunt Mary? Will she be alright about me being here?"

"Alick's wife, Mary, died in 1944. Accordin' tae mah da, she was a currant away from a whole fruit cake. Threw herself in front o' a train. When Alick was sent haime from Egypt in 1943, mah da was sent tae live with him when his parents died durin' the V-1 attacks. Alick had nae seen his cousin for five years, boot took mah da in withoot a backward glance or grumble. Noo tis our turn tae look after him."

I hand him the photo, and he slips it back into his pocket, patting the fabric. "Alick's a good man, ye dinnae have tae be scared. He's waited his whole life tae see ye."

"Me? Not Pearl."

Kane laughs. "Dinnae matter which one o' ye came, daughter, granddaughter, he'll still be thrilled."

The solid wooden door opens, revealing a large, black cast-iron log burner. Flames lick at the iron-latticed glass window. Two worn leather Chesterfields flank the burner. A man sits, looking into the flames, his thick white hair tickling the collar of his plaid shirt. Soft-soled slippers poke out from a red tartan blanket.

Kane touches the man's shoulder, pulling his attention away from the flames.

"Noo then lad," Alick says.

I step from behind Kane, gripping Lillian Elizabeth's letter. Words form but never make it to my vocal cords.

"Nightingale."

From a frail, worn-out body, strength and longing radiate. Alick's gaze fixes on me. Goosebumps run over my flesh. One word—Nightingale—so much love.

"It's Lilibeth, I'm Lillian Elizabeth's granddaughter," I say, my voice cracking.

Kane places his hand on my back. "Take a seat 'n' ah'll poot the kettle on. Tea or coffee?"

"Coffee, please, one sugar, no milk."

The latch clicks in place as Kane disappears, and silence ping pongs around the room. I run the envelope through my fingertips, trying to compose myself.

"My grandmother wanted me to give you this. She died six weeks ago."

Like it's a hot potato, I hand Alick the letter—it falls onto his lap.

He shakes his head. "Would ye read it? Mah eyes, they dinnae see like they used tae."

With a soft smile, he sits back in the chair, his head resting against the leather. I lean over and take the letter, breaking the seal. There have been many times over the past few days I could have opened it—I never did. The contents weren't meant for me.

"Ah dinnae think it will bite."

Alick's voice makes me jump.

"No, I don't suppose it will."

He chuckles.

My dearest Alick,

As *Winnie the Pooh* once said, "The most important thing is, even when we're apart … I'll

595

always be with you ..." There has never been a day you weren't safely tucked within my heart, where no one can see you, and I was free to love you. When I stand at the edge of the cliff at Seagull's Rest, sometimes, as the wind tickles my face, I know you are close.

A lifetime is a long time to wait, and doubt is niggling at me. I'm wondering if you will come when I stand between the light and dark, my arms open wide. Alick, can you forgive this Nightingale for marrying Joe, and allowing him to be the father you should have been to our daughter, Pearl Alexandra? Your daughter was born on the 10th of February 1944. She is headstrong, wild, and restless. A woman yet to find maturity, something I fear she never will. But, Alick, she is perfect in every way, because she is ours.

With you sent back to the United Kingdom, and finding I was pregnant, my strength slipped away. Concerned about losing our baby, when Joe offered the perfect solution, by marrying me, I took it. His only condition was that I never tell you about the baby. Please forgive me for what I have done, for the family I took from you.

There is no sadness in my death. Unlike so many, I don't fear it. The only fear I carry is that on knowing the truth, you cannot forgive me, and I will be left in death as on earth, with my soul yearning for its mate.

Between the light and dark, Alick, I wait for you.

Forever your,

Nightingale

The letter sits in my hand. Pearl Alexandra may not be the best of mothers, but she is perfect, just the way she is—it is time I accepted that.

Alick stares into the distance a smile on his lips. "Sing for me, Nightingale."

His words echo about the room, and the hairs on my arm stand, skin tightening. From behind me, I swear I can hear Lillian Elizabeth sing.

"Between the light 'n' dark … ah'm comin', Nightingale."

Alick's throat rattles. It's the same sound I heard when my grandmother died; death's rattle they call it. His head slumps to one side, and Alick closes his eyes. I don't need to check for a pulse to know he's dead.

"Kane! Kane!"

Kane comes running into the room. He stops at Alick's body. "She's taken him then … Good." He squeezes Alick's shoulder. "Enjoy eternity."

My throat constricts and I'm finding it difficult to breathe. Tears sting my eyes and my grandmother's letter tumbles to the floor.

"Ah'd best go rin' the authorities."

"Kane, I'm sorry."

He shakes his head. "Ye have tae stop sayin' sorry, Lilibeth. Alick has been waitin' a lifetime for his Nightingale tae take him haime."

Tears saturate my hanky as I sit at the kitchen, waiting for Kane to finish making the calls. Outside, evening closes in and shadows begin to dance as the sun lowers. Birds make their way to their nests, and the trees sway in the light breeze as their branches rustle. The kitchen door opens, flooding it with light as Kane walks in, phone in hand.

"All done, they're comin tae take Alick's body away. It'll probably take a few hours."

Some of the light has left his eyes, and tiny lines form at their corners. I marvel at his strength.

"If ye're in na rush tae go haime, there's a bottle o' whisky ah've been savin' for this very occasion."

Home, Seagull's Rest, shimmers before my eyes. A solitary building in which love and heartache soak the foundation. It is the place where I belong. My flat in Aberdeen has served its purpose.

"Yes, thanks, that would be great."

The whisky tumblers chink as he sets them on the table. The bottle glugs and amber liquid clings to the side of the glass as he pours. In silence, we raise our glasses, clinking them together. The sharp woody sting of whisky drizzles over my tastebuds, warming my throat. Kane looks up, his pale blue eyes as intoxicating as the fifteen-year-old whisky in my tumbler.

Through the sliding glass doors, darkness covers the garden, and the glass becomes a mirror. Kane gets up and walks over. I sit at the table, watching as he raises his glass before throwing back the contents. I set my empty tumbler on the table and walk over. He turns, his eyes bright with tears, and opens his arms. I walk into his embrace, breathing in his soft, woody, soapy scent. Together we allow ourselves to grieve for those we have lost and celebrate the reunion of two souls that have waited a lifetime to be together.

"Ah feel like ah've been waitin' mah whole life for ye tae come. Peculiar, isn't it, hoo a stranger kin also be familiar?"

It could be the whisky, but I know what Kane means.

In each other, we have found our home.

Between the light and dark
I'll find you ...

Acknowledgements

This book is a tribute to the nurses who cared for our soldiers and civilians during WWII. My research opened a door into a world of sacrifice and camaraderie, bringing true meaning to the word 'friendship.' Without these wonderful nurses many more lives would have been lost. Supporting the injured with kindness they boosted flagging spirits while tending to their wounds. These nightingales gave everything they had to treat those in their care. *A Nightingale's Last Song* presents a slither of what the nurses went through during the war effort. The horrors and suffering they experienced while treating the wounded showed extraordinary strength. Many lost their lives in honouring their commitment to our forces. Even today, the remarkable work of these brave souls goes, to some degree, unnoticed. This story stands in recognition and dedication to these wonderful people. For you are brave. Your dedication and strength to care for the sick and injured—and their family, places us forever in your debt. What you do each day is truly appreciated. Thank you.

About the Author

Kathleen Harryman lives in the historically rich city of York, North Yorkshire, England with her husband and two children.

First published in 2015, Kathleen has won several awards for her books. Developing a unique writing style, Kathleen Harryman grips the reader, holding their attention until they become part of the story.

Kathleen Harryman is a skilled author of multiple genres, and pens tales ranging from mystery and psychological thrillers to crime fiction, romantic suspense, historical romance, and paranormal romance.

Connect with Kathleen

Website: https://www.kathleenharryman.com
Twitter: https://twitter.com/KathleenHarrym1
Instagram: https://www.instagram.com/kathleen_author

THE PROMISE

How far would you go to keep a promise?

In the heat of battle, one man's promise to another will be tested.

September 1939 – As Britain is gripped by the fear and uncertainty of war, Tom Armitage stands to gain the one thing that he never thought possible - his freedom. Rosie Elliot sees her future crumbling to dust as Will Aarons leaves Whitby with Jimmy Chappell to fight in the war. As she begins work at The Turnstone Convalescent Home, Rosie finds something she thought she had lost. Friendship. But friendship soon turns to love. Can this new love replace Will?

This is not an ordinary love story. It's a story of love, loss, courage, and honour. Of promises that must be kept or risk losing everything you've ever held dear.

Printed in Great Britain
by Amazon